CLIVE CUSSLER
THE IRON STORM

TITLES BY CLIVE CUSSLER

CLIVE CUSSLER

THE IRON STORM

An Isaac Bell Adventure®

JACK DU BRUL

G. P. PUTNAM'S SONS

NEW YORK

PUTNAM
— EST. 1838 —

An imprint of Penguin Random House LLC
1745 Broadway, New York, NY 10019
penguinrandomhouse.com

ISBN 9780593853566
Ebook ISBN 9780593853573

Printed in the United States of America
1st Printing

The authorized representative in the EU for product safety and compliance is
Penguin Random House Ireland, Morrison Chambers, 32 Nassau Street,
Dublin D02 YH68, Ireland, https://eu-contact.penguin.ie.

CLIVE CUSSLER
THE IRON STORM

In the midst of chaos, there is also opportunity.

—Sun Tzu, *The Art of War*

1

March 1917
The Irish Sea

ENGLAND EMERGED FROM OVER THE MURKY HORIZON, THE line between earth and sky partially hidden by shifting bands of rain. The coast was dark and barren, but so very welcome after a stormy passage across the Atlantic that tested even Isaac Bell's notoriously iron stomach. Technically he hadn't spotted England but rather Anglesey Island, off the north Welsh coast, that helped mark the passage into the Mersey estuary and the port city of Liverpool.

Since the start of the war, the docks of Southampton on England's south coast had become Military Embarkation Port No. 1 and were used exclusively for pouring men and matériel onto freighters and troopships bound for France and the front lines and for seeing the return of the countless wounded. As a result Liverpool had become the principal port for all transatlantic traffic.

Bell had been bound for Liverpool once before, but had never made it, as the *Lusitania* had been torpedoed as she turned northward around the southern tip of Ireland and the sheltered waters of the Irish Sea. He reasoned that even with the Germans once again unleashing their wolf packs in the no-holds-barred doctrine of unrestricted submarine warfare, the odds of him being torpedoed twice in the same region were long enough to leave his mind at ease.

The ship he'd taken from New York was far from the luxurious Cunard liner he'd last sailed to England aboard. The *Duke of Monmouth* was barely five hundred feet in length and had sailed under many different flags by even more different owners in the two decades since her launching. She sported a single funnel amidships and had just four decks for passengers. The first-class accommodations were on the top deck and were rumored to be adequate but dated.

For this mission, Bell was joined by Eddie Tobin, another Van Dorn detective. Like Bell, Tobin sailed on a second-class ticket in keeping with their cover. They presented themselves as the employees of an art dealer who was shipping paintings back to England for a client who'd originally sent them to America for safekeeping at the start of the war. In truth they were escorting five hundred pounds of gold bullion that had been donated by dozens of prominent New York and Boston families to help the Allied war effort. Once the crate landed on the pier in Liverpool their job was done.

Bell looked northward. A single British destroyer was on patrol, looking as lean and lethal as a stiletto. She seemed small and ineffective when compared to the mighty dreadnoughts the Admiralty had on hand to blockade Germany, but her four-inch deck guns and torpedo launchers were more than a match for any lurking U-boat.

A signalman on the warship's bridge was working the handle of an Aldiss lamp, sending a coded signal to the *Duke of Monmouth*. Bell turned to look up toward the liner's bridge and saw the blond woman. Like the other time he'd seen her on deck during the miserable crossing, he was struck by both her beauty and the graceful way she carried herself, even now after enduring what must have been a week of mal de mer. She didn't so much as look down. Bell allowed himself another moment to admire her profile and turned back to the sea once again.

The tides on the Mersey estuary are among the highest in the British Isles and so it wasn't too much later that the ship began to approach the river and the city of Liverpool. A black pall of coal smoke marked the distant city, far darker than the pewter sky that had enshrouded the *Duke of Monmouth* since leaving New York. Ship traffic on the water had noticeably increased as freighters and oilers from the United States awaited their turn to unload at the overtaxed port. More Navy ships were also present, mostly other destroyers or small armed launches that buzzed around the merchant flotilla like watchful sheepdogs attending to their flock.

After taking on a harbor pilot, the *Duke of Monmouth* entered the wide tidal estuary. On the left bank, the docks of Liverpool were total bedlam, with steam-powered cranes hauling pallets of cargo from countless ships' holds and armies of stevedores trouping down gangways loaded with sacks of American grain or Indian rice or casks of Jamaican rum. Small coastal boats ducked in and around the bigger ships bringing supplies, while massive coal barges were kept in constant motion by tugs and towboats to feed the freighters' voracious boilers.

Bell became concerned when his liner's course kept it away from the city and along the river's south shore. He was about to find an officer to get an explanation when the chief purser appeared at his elbow. A few of the crew had been made aware of the Van Dorn detective's mission if not the actual cargo. "Begging your pardon, Mr. Bell," the veteran purser said with a courteous tip of his cap. "Captain Abernathey's compliments."

"What is it, Tony? Why are we here and not over there?" Bell asked, pointing to the busy port they were slowly steaming past.

"A freighter is still in our berth. There was a problem with a crane and it's taking much longer to unload. Rather than have us wait, the harbormaster is diverting us to an open dock upriver a bit, near the Runcorn Gap. That'll put us in the Manchester Ship Canal for some miles."

Bell opened his mouth to ask a question, but the purser had an answer at the ready.

"Arrangements have been made to have your crate met just as if we'd docked in our original slot. You have nothing to worry about."

Eddie Tobin appeared just then. Where Bell was tall and straight, with blond hair and handsome features, Eddie slouched in a poorly fitted suit and his bulging eyes and thick neck gave him the look of a frog. His head was more scalp than thin gray hair, adding to the illusion. He worked out of the Van Dorn New York office, which had been Bell's preferred station for a couple of years now, and specialized in the criminal activity in and around the city's countless docks, piers, shipping terminals, and every other place seafarers and fishermen could be found. Said to have salt water in his veins, he'd had little trouble stomaching the rough Atlantic passage.

"Any sign of foul play?" Eddie asked before Bell could.

"Foul play?" the purser said, cocking his head slightly.

"Sabotage of the crane at our assigned berth," Bell clarified, "to force us to switch last-minute."

The Englishman's entire profession was predicated on keeping people happy and so it was clear by the look on his face that he didn't know the answer to the question and hadn't thought to ask it himself. "I, ah . . ."

"Doesn't really matter, Isaac," Eddie reminded his boss. "Our job's done when the crate's off this tub. What happens to it here is on the local boys, not us."

"Call it a professional courtesy," Bell said.

"We've got some time," Tony the purser said. "I'll have the wireless operator signal the harbormaster again and find out what exactly happened to that crane."

Bell considered the offer and despite having no stake in the crate's fate once on English soil, he agreed and sent the man off to the radio shack.

"You don't ever quit, do you?" Eddie remarked, resting his arthritic hands on the rail.

"I don't have it in me," Bell agreed.

"And that's why you're old man Van Dorn's chief detective and I'm still grubbing around the docks like some greenhorn."

Bell chuckled.

At Eastham, a short distance upriver from Liverpool, the *Duke of Monmouth* entered the Manchester Ship Canal through a tight-fitting set of locks. Such was the state of the tide that they needed to only be lifted a couple of feet before the water in the lock equalized with that of the canal, which, when it first opened in 1894, made the city of Manchester an actual seaport, though it sat some thirty miles from the coast.

More first- and second-class passengers were coming out to the decks to take in the sights now that the ship was no longer tossing them about. Many still looked a little sickly, but most had color returning to their cheeks and obvious relief in their voices as any threat of a submarine attack was well and truly over.

The canal hugged the southern bank of the Mersey River, which remained busy with the tide still up and the sandbars and shoals buried deep under the water. At low tide, much of the estuary was a great mudflat that, in the right conditions, could smell something awful. At points the canal was narrow enough that it seemed they were sailing through earthen fields rather than on water. Bell felt he could lean over the rail and pluck a skeletal branch from a tree growing on the berm separating the canal from the river.

A detective all his adult life, Bell relied as much on instinct as he did on intellect, both of which he honed to a keen edge with every opportunity. He loved what he did and was therefore very good at his job. His instincts were telling him something his intellect said was unlikely, but he listened to his gut all the same. He turned around and looked up to where the first-class passengers were enjoying their superior view of the Lancashire countryside. He caught the blond woman watching him. He smiled as he saw a slight blush against her alabaster skin. Bell tipped his hat and she flustered for only a moment before regaining herself. She turned away with a look that managed to elevate her haughtiness to some form of high hauteur.

That brief exchange quickened his pulse the same as the first time he'd seen her.

Quickly though, reality intruded as a noxious smell enveloped the liner in a cloud that sent multiple passengers back into the salons and reception areas.

"Lord, that's awful," Eddie remarked. This from a man who'd once sorted through several tons of rotten oysters to find a gun used to kill a dockside security guard.

The *Duke of Monmouth* had passed around Weston Point and was approaching the docks at Runcorn. They were about nine miles from the sea. The air was heavy with coal smoke and the other odors of the industrial revolution, but atop it was the farm smell of animal manure, which was somehow much worse, like the noisome discharge of a diseased herd already in the throes of death.

Another ship was tied to the dock that ran parallel to the canal. She flew the Canadian ensign, a predominantly red flag with the Union Jack in one corner and the Great Seal of Canada toward the center. She was an animal transporter about halfway finished unloading hundreds of horses destined for the front and hundreds more sheep destined for the soldiers' mess. The passage had to have been even worse for the animals than it had been for the passengers aboard the *Duke of Monmouth* because the quay was awash in loose dung.

Men with hand-pumped hoses were washing the treacle into the canal, but that did little to alleviate the cloying stench. All the horses Bell could see stood with their heads low, their tails motionless, and their mien listless. The sheep that had already been unloaded and fenced inside temporary corrals bleated miserably, their once-white coats stained down almost to the skin.

The cowboys who'd tended the animals all the way from Halifax, sleeping near their stalls and keeping them fed and watered despite the rough seas, were struggling to keep their charges together. Only a few had mounts well enough to ride, leaving just a handful of the ranchers to coax the seasick animals into a semblance of a line so they could be herded to a nearby railhead. From there they would be transported to farms around the south of England, where they would be acclimated and then trained to become warhorses.

Bell had read somewhere that the British were losing around three hundred horses per day on the front. It was early March. He doubted any of the animals on the pier would see the summer.

The *Monmouth* slid past the livestock transporter and came up against its pier, the harbor pilot working the ship's rudder and engine to ease the liner up against the dock with barely a kiss. Below, workers with scarves tied over their noses and mouths because of the smell prepared to unload the ship.

Bell assumed that whatever cargo and passengers she'd return with to North America would be loaded at her regular slot back in Liverpool. Providing for a nation that was fielding millions of men in a foreign country to fight a war no one really wanted was an exercise in precision timing and industrial might on a scale never seen in all of human history.

One group of men on the pier caught Bell's eye. A couple were obviously dockworkers, but two looked different. They wore plain clothes but had the look of cops, sharp-eyed and situationally aware. They stood around an open back lorry with a canvas cover protecting the driver and passenger compartment. The stevedores smoked cigarettes while the two police guards scanned the ship. They knew he was coming in as a second-class passenger and so ignored the people on the top deck already getting ready to depart the ship via a long switchback set of gangways.

The second- and third-class passengers returning to Europe after working in America wouldn't disembark until the premier passengers had all cleared customs and were on their way to London or wherever they were headed. Just by interpreting their body language, the British police recognized the two Van Dorn men slouched against the *Monmouth*'s railing. While other passengers gawked at the sights of the harbor and the canal traffic still moving past or stared in fascination at the chaotic unloading of the horses, Bell and Eddie Tobin watched the cops.

The older of the two cops pointed in Bell's direction. In turn Bell pulled a slender flashlight that was no bigger than a cigar and used the nonstandard AA batteries from his overcoat pocket and flashed the Morse code of his initials: *Dot, dot. Dash, dot, dot, dot.*

The policeman acknowledged the gesture. Bell swung his gaze toward the *Duke of Monmouth*'s bow. The forward hatch had already been knocked open and an operator was standing by the mast derrick. Near him was the ship's third officer, as previously arranged when the assignment had been discussed with the ship's owner and captain. Bell's cargo would be the first off the ship and the police in charge to receive it would be well on their way before anyone else cleared customs with their luggage.

As the crane hook vanished into the hold, Eddie nudged Bell and pointed at something happening on the dock. "Hey, boss man, what is that thing?" he asked.

Bell wasn't sure. It was a wheeled tower made of metal struts with a ramp that spiraled down from the top all the way to the ground. The floor and outer wall of the helical were made of individual rollers that would spin freely if something were to pass over them or bump against them in the case of the outer wall.

"If I'd have to guess," Bell said as the odd tower was wheeled closer to the ship, "it's some Rube Goldbergian contraption for unloading steamer trunks. A guy on the ship sets a trunk on top and with a little shove it coils down and around the ramp until it reaches the bottom and another stevedore is there ready to heave it onto a waiting truck. If you notice, the struts can be jacked up or down depending on how high up on the ship the trunk storage compartments are."

"Damned clever."

"Necessity is the mother of invention," Bell said. "The Brits are facing a massive labor shortage with all their men off in the trenches, so they need to get creative."

Dockworkers pushed the unloading ramp toward the ship, while the crate Bell and Eddie had been hired to protect rose from the forward hold. It looked like a standard packing crate, maybe with thicker-than-average wood, but unremarkable in all respects. Once the crate was high enough to clear the ship's rail, the boom was swung outward enough for it to lower the package directly onto the waiting truck. The two cops stepped back as the stevedores craned their necks back and reached up with their arms to guide the load into position.

As soon as the crate landed on the truck's open bed, a carefully set trap was sprung.

Transporter bridge across the Mersey

2

THE TWO STEVEDORES TURNED ON THE POLICE OFFICERS, SWING-ing leather cudgels with lead-shot heads, while a third supposed dockworker raced to the scene and leapt onto the truck's bed to slash the knots securing the crate to the crane. Bell gave credit to the operator on board the *Duke of Monmouth*. He was quick on the controls, but when he spooled back the iron hook, the ropes had just parted and the crate remained on the dockside in the bed of the AEC Y-type lorry. The bobbies were laid out on the dock, dark stains around their heads where the coshes had likely cracked bone.

Bell's mission had ended the moment the crate landed in the back of the truck, but that didn't end his personal commitment. He could no more let the crime unfold before him than he could stop the sun rising in the east.

The gangway to unload passengers was two decks up and half the ship away. Out of the question, so Bell took the alternate route off the *Duke of Monmouth*. With a startled grunt from Eddie Tobin, whose shoulder he used to climb onto the rail, Bell moved down the thin wooden rail with the agility of a cat and twice the cunning. As the loading derrick hook swung back around the side of the ship, Bell put on a burst of speed to launch himself at it, not thinking about the thirty-foot drop to the unforgiving concrete below.

He was weightless for only a moment before his hands wrapped around the cold steel hook with a sure grip. Momentum swung the line even farther out, like a penduluming weight at the end of a string. He arced back toward the ship right above the unloading trunk tower. He let go just before he was above the contraption and his body arrowed downward like a dart. He hit where the ramp met the wall, a blow hard enough to knock the air from his lungs in a painful whoosh. But there was no time to find his bearings. The rollers were as finely made as the insides of a Swiss watch and he was soon being flung around the coiling spiral, dropping and accelerating until he reached the bottom and was tossed from the device with all but his dignity.

He rolled once, twice. The third time slowed him enough to get to his feet. The truck carrying off the safe was just pulling off the *Duke of Monmouth*'s relatively calm dockage and into the chaotic scene near the Canadian livestock transporter. Because that was a freighter and not a passenger liner, customs was handled far differently. There were no customs halls or immigration lines. It was all handled quickly and with minimal fuss so that the horses weren't kept waiting unnecessarily. That meant that once the thieves passed the ship, they had an open lane between two brick warehouses and out into the town with nothing to stop them.

Few workers had paid much attention to what had just happened and were thus startled when Bell tumbled off the unloading ramp. No one tried to stop him as he took off running after the truck, his Browning pistol already in hand.

With so many horses being moved from the Canadian ship, not to mention the mounted riders trying to keep them in a loose formation, the truck couldn't make much more than walking speed as it crossed the quay, evoking the occasional curse from a cowboy whose horse they spooked with a blare of the vehicle's horn.

Bell wasn't making much better headway himself. He could dodge and weave around the horses, but there were so many of them milling about that it was like running through a roan-colored maze. Plus he had to be on constant alert because some of the more agitated horses bucked their back legs in explosive kicks powerful enough to stave in a man's rib cage.

He kept losing sight of the truck and finally climbed up on a two-horse wagon loaded with a tightly bound wheel of hay that easily weighed a couple of tons. The thieves were far closer to the exit than he'd expected. With a quick motion he pulled the razor-sharp knife he kept strapped around his ankle and slashed the rope holding the eight-foot-diameter-round hay bale into the bed of the wagon. A snap on the rein jerked the wagon enough for the hay to fall off the back. It hit the dock with a thud and rolled only a couple of feet before its ponderous weight stopped it dead.

Bell snapped the rein again and the two horses hitched on either side of the disselboom put their shoulders into the chase. Unlike the truck or even Bell on foot, the unfettered horses heeded their herd instinct, and while they didn't follow the charging wagon, they got out of its way.

In moments, he found that he'd closed the distance, but saw that they were nearing the narrow alley between the warehouses that led out of the dockland. Once through, the truck would speed away and there was nothing he could do to stop them.

Bell was determined not to let that happen. The moment he'd hurled himself off the *Duke of Monmouth*, his professional reputation, not to mention his own sense of right and wrong, was on the line.

He'd holstered his pistol when he'd leapt onto the hay cart, but checked again that the automatic was secure under his left arm. He cracked the reins again to keep the horses after their target and stepped down off the wagon's driver's seat and onto the yoke pole between the two charging draft horses. The thunder of their hooves grew deafening now that he was standing just eighteen inches above the cobbled pier on a round length of wood no wider than his hand's span.

The horses sensed him in the unfamiliar spot and immediately started sweating, waxy bubbles like sea foam forming under their leather tack. Bell moved like a tightrope walker on a swaying pole, inching himself forward without physically touching the horses because he didn't know how they'd react. If he slipped he'd land under their rear hooves and then get run over by the wagon. Death would be preferable to the paralyzing injuries such a fall would likely produce.

He kept moving forward. The horses had caught up to the truck as it navigated the narrow alley, a darkened passage with just a trace of sunlight reaching down to the roadway. The animals' chests were barely a foot behind the lorry's tailgate. Bell could plainly see the stolen trunk in the bed, and he noted that neither man was looking at the vehicle's side mirrors. They had no idea he was onto them.

Bell reached the end of the disselboom. While he was shimmying out, he'd been able to maintain his balance, but once he stopped he started swaying dangerously. He assumed the left-hand horse was the leader of the pair and so he momentarily steadied himself against the animal's seesawing neck with a light touch.

The horse wasn't the leader of the two. England drove on the opposite side of the road and so it was the horse in the right trace that kept the team working as one. Bell's presence on the cart pole had been troubling enough, but once his hand touched the subordinate horse's neck, its eyes rolled into its head so that only the whites showed, its tongue tried to snake around the bit, and it broke its gait. The lead horse tried to keep up the pace, but it was no use. His partner was in a full panic, and if not for the straps and yokes holding him in place, he would have bolted with every ounce of his considerable strength.

Bell realized his mistake the moment he'd made it, but the damage was done. The fleeting window of opportunity to leap from the wagon onto the truck was lost as the team slowed and the lorry pulled away.

He held on to both horses, cajoling them to slow. "Easy, boys. It's okay," he kept repeating. "No need to bother now."

They emerged from the alley. The thieves were halfway across a mostly empty parking lot. In another thirty seconds they'd reach an unmanned gatehouse and turn onto the road leading away from the Runcorn docks. Bell stepped down off the pole and came around the front of the horses to pet their noses and calm them further.

A cowboy in a fleece-trimmed shearling coat and a Stetson rode up just then, pulling back on the reins hard enough for his mount to rear up for a moment. He dropped the reins across the horse's back, a signal for the animal to freeze, and produced a braided leather whip, which he uncoiled so that its tip fell to the ground.

"You're gonna lose a fair amount of flesh for what you just done," he said in a low growl. "Move away from them horses."

He just started to curl his wrist and raise the whip when Bell drew his 9 millimeter and aimed it dead on the cowboy's beaky nose. "Drop the whip or I drop you."

The cowboy had a big revolver hanging from his hip in a holster fitted with loops for extra bullets. Bell could see the gears turning behind the man's eyes, calculating if he could toss the whip at Bell to foul his aim and draw his own weapon for a kill shot.

"I'm a private detective," Bell said, still unsure if he'd have to shoot the man. "I was chasing thieves who just stole several million dollars in gold."

Just then, a car entered the alley from the far end, its engine keening and its driver squeezing the horn's bulb for everything it was worth. The fast-approaching vehicle was enough of a distraction to defuse the situation. Bell saw the tension run out of the cowboy's shoulders and whip arm.

The car braked almost as hard as the cowboy's horse moments earlier and the beautiful blonde from first class leaned out the window and said to Bell, "Get in. We still have a chance."

Bell gave the cowboy an apologetic look and leapt for the car's running board. The mission was officially over and he was off the clock, as they say, and so he no longer had to pretend his wife hadn't been on the same steamer over from New York as he and Ed Tobin.

Marion Bell eased her foot off the clutch, over-revved the engine a bit, but got them rolling without stalling it. Forced to shift with her left hand in the right-hand-drive Austin 40, Marion had trouble synching the gears, but eventually meshed them with brute force and some unladylike oaths. Bell wrestled open the passenger door and got himself seated as the car began putting on some speed. The truck was too far ahead to see, but for now there was only one way out of the port, so Marion drove with confidence they were going to catch their quarry.

"Where's Eddie and where did you get this car?" Bell asked, unsurprised that she'd come to his rescue.

"Eddie was still trying to find a way up to first class so he could disembark and come after you himself. Remember, you heels in the lower-class cabins don't get off the ship until us toffs are on our way."

Bell cocked a dubious eyebrow. "You've been in England two minutes and you're already using their slang?"

She threw him a cheeky smile. "I do love it here, you know. The car belongs to a Lord something pompous-sounding who was returning to England after meetings with the War Department. He was at the captain's table the first night out and blathered incessantly. Then the weather turned so dreadful. I made it to the dining room a couple of nights, but His Lard Fatness remained in his cabin for the rest of the trip. Oh, and wasn't that just a dreadful crossing?" Marion's delivery was a rapid-fire staccato that was music to Bell's ears.

"It was," he agreed. "The car?"

"Car? Yes, the car. Well, the Earl of Too Many Sandwiches was on the pier arguing with the porters about his luggage and his driver was just standing around. I saw you steal that wagon, so I figured I might as well steal something a bit more practical."

Bell laughed. "You are a marvel."

"And don't you forget it."

All around them were warehouses and small industrial concerns with tall chimneys belching black smoke into the already hazy air. There were countless trucks and horse-drawn wagons and men shouting orders. A heavy booming sound came from a foundry as massive trip-hammers flattened cold-rolled iron. While the thieves could have turned off onto any one of the side roads crisscrossing the commercial area closest to the docks, there was only one major artery out of the maze, and logic dictated that the men would want to put as much distance as possible from the scene of the crime.

The area gave way to some open land and a proper road heading inland. Traffic was light.

"There," Bell shouted, pointing. Up ahead was an open-backed truck moving faster than the rest of the cars on the road, passing where it had barely any room to maneuver.

"Hah!" Marion whooped and tried to sink her foot through the floorboard. The four-cylinder engine responded like a thoroughbred and they quickly started passing the cars that the truck had just rushed by.

As they turned slightly north, back toward the canal and the Mersey River, an odd structure appeared out of the haze. It was a bridge of some sort, but unlike anything Bell had ever seen before. It consisted of two towers nearly two hundred feet tall with a thousand-foot-long steel latticework truss lancing across the river about halfway up. The massive weight of the steel girders was supported by wires like a conventional suspension bridge from the tops of the towers. The span was eighty or so feet above the water, giving clear passage for all but the largest ships. Bell couldn't understand how anything could cross the bridge. There were no ramps up to the truss like those used to access the Brooklyn Bridge back in New York.

Then he noticed a platform big enough for several trucks as well as hundreds of passengers dangling from the truss on a cableway system like an aerial tram. The passenger area was glassed in like a greenhouse, but was as ornate as a decorative birdcage. Above it was a glass-enclosed cupola for the operator. The entire structure had the delicacy and industrial grace of Paris's Eiffel Tower.

The cable car hung just a dozen or so feet above the water, so its trips across had to be timed to avoid ships headed toward Manchester or heading west back to the Irish Sea.

"It's a transporter bridge," Bell said as he suddenly recognized the hybrid structure. "Never seen one before. Not as efficient as a suspension bridge, but a hell of a lot cheaper and easier to build."

"Judging by how slow that platform is moving, if we can't make the same trip across as the thieves, they're as good as gone." Addressing her own concern, Marion flashed past a lorry loaded with bails of barbed wire, doing nearly twice its speed.

"Easy," Bell cautioned. "They don't know they're being followed yet and I don't want to lose that advantage. There's a couple of them and only one me."

"You've got me," Marion said with a defiant lift of her chin.

"I do, but I only have one gun."

"What about the derringer you always carry?"

"Dropped it between two running horses," he admitted.

"Nicely done, Keystone."

The thieves' truck started across the bridge's access pier. Marion's deft driving had managed to get them only a couple of cars back. They would make the crossing together.

"Shouldn't you arrest them now?" Marion asked.

"Too many people," Bell said. A large crowd was gathered next to the road, where they waited their turn to cross the Mersey River on the large cableway platform. "If those guys are armed it could turn into a massacre. Better we confront them in a less-crowded spot."

The transporter reached the loading ramp. A worker was ready to open the safety barrier, while behind him at least fifty people had left the sheltered passenger compartment and waited to rush off the platform. Most were workers from the industrial sprawl on the far side of the river and at least half were boys barely in their teens, while the others were older men nearing retirement. It was a stark reminder that the young men of England were shoulder-deep in muddy trenches across the breadth of France.

The platform came to a stop with a slight slam of metal on metal that caused a few of the passengers to sway. The barrier came down and the throng of people rushed from the transporter, eager to get to their next destination. Then two trucks trundled off the platform followed by a wagon being pulled by a lone pony.

The worker made a hand gesture and the next set of passengers stampeded onto the transport, rushing for the enclosed area to get out of a misting rain that was intensifying. Bell could see ahead that the thieves were ordered onto the platform under the guidance of a worker, who wanted them to park at a specific set of marks.

Next aboard were two Austin sedans a few years older than the one Marion had lent herself. Then came a wagon pulled by a single horse, and finally it was their turn. Mindful that she was driving an unfamiliar car, Marion was easy on the clutch, inching the car onto the platform as if she had all the time in the world.

Without warning, the transporter lurched away from the loading ramp. It took just a second for the platform to pull itself from under their car's front wheels. The bridge worker who directed traffic had a horrified look on his face at the disaster unfolding before his eyes. Marion didn't have time to react. The transport platform slid out from under their Austin and the car's nose fell so that the chassis just behind the engine hit the loading ramp and the vehicle began to teeter over the edge, balanced as if on a knife's edge. The engine stalled and the dying vibration set the car rocking in ever larger arcs.

The sudden drop had slammed Marion into the steering wheel, and had Bell not braced himself at the last instant, he would have likely been launched through the windshield. Their view out the windscreen was of the green waves of the Mersey at ebb tide rushing past at a ferocious speed.

The car continued to rock like a child's teeter-totter. The transport platform was already a few yards away, the worker still standing in shocked awe with a couple of passengers at his shoulder staring in horror at what was about to happen.

Keeping his left arm braced against the dash, Bell used his right hand to grab the back of Marion's coat and pull her back so she was pressed into her seat.

"Don't move. Don't even breathe hard," he cautioned in a whisper. "We're one toot away from toppling into the river."

Bell took a second to study the operator's perch atop the mobile platform. As he'd guessed, there were two men up there now and one looked like he had a knife pointed at the uniformed crewman. The thieves had spotted their tail and forced the operator to try and kill them by pulling away when they were only half aboard.

He cursed, but then set himself the task of saving their lives.

Like a momma cat moving her kittens, Bell kept his right hand clamped onto the scruff of Marion's coat and began lifting her up and over the back of her seat. Had they been in America, and seated on the right, he wouldn't have had the strength, but here he could unleash the full power of his dominant arm. He had little leverage, other than what he could generate by tightening the bands of muscles across his lean belly.

A groan escaped his lips as her backside formed a supple speed bump over the headrest. Finally he managed to deposit her in the back seat. The Austin teetered for a few seconds more and then its rear tires kissed the road once again, though only with a few pounds of pressure. People suddenly swarmed the car, pressing against its back bumper to keep it from going over the edge. They were the workers who'd just gotten off the transporter and must have sensed something was wrong and returned.

The Austin was now firmly planted on the deck. The rear doors were opened, and Marion was pulled to safety. The crowd roared their approval when she emerged from the back seat and Bell was encouraged to climb over into the passenger seats after her.

"Hold it tight," Bell said as he climbed from the car. "It still might—"

No one listened. As soon as he was clear, the men and boys weighing down the back bumper let go as one. The car's rear lifted a few inches, fell back, bounced and lifted again, until it passed a point of no return. The Austin tumbled off the access ramp. It was a fifteen-foot fall into the swiftly flowing river, and by the time Bell reached the edge of the ramp to look down, the sedan was already half sunk and a good twenty yards downstream.

"Think that'll buff out?" Marion quipped.

3

KNOWING MARION WAS NONE THE WORSE FOR THEIR CLOSE call if she could crack a joke, Bell bulled his way through the celebrating throng and raced for the bridge support tower. There was a set of spiral stairs that coiled their way up to the overhead truss within the spindly structure. It was closed off by a padlocked iron gate. Bell had his gun in hand when he reached the gate.

It proved to be a stubborn lock that took two bullets before it fell away. Bell barreled into the gate, crashing it back against its stops before he took the curving steps two at a time. It was an eight-story climb to the level of the suspended box truss that spanned the river and Bell was breathing heavily, but by no means winded. The slow-moving transporter platform was about halfway across, with the fifty-foot-long scaffold dangling just a dozen or so feet above the river.

From this height, it looked smaller than Bell would have thought.

Apart from the great girders that made up the enormous truss, there were two thick cables that pulled the trolley back and forth across the Mersey and a narrow path for maintenance workers to safely traverse the span. Bell took off at a run, mindful that the steel was slick with rainwater and his shoes more befitting of an ocean liner crossing than a high-wire act.

Because of the way the structure was held together, with innumerable cross braces, Bell couldn't see what was happening on the platform below. He imagined the abrupt departure had rattled the passengers, but he didn't know how they would react. He hoped that they stayed together in the enclosed lounge because he was determined not to let the transporter dock at the far side.

He ran at almost twice the speed of the moving platform, but he'd lost so much time in the Austin and then climbing the tower that he had only a few seconds before the thieves would be on the opposite bank. He reached the slowly trundling trolley and its dozens of cables that suspended the platform above the water. There was no easy access because there was no need for anyone to attempt what he was about to do.

Bell double-checked that the Browning pistol was strapped in his shoulder holster as he stripped off his suit jacket. No one down below had spotted him high above the platform, and for that he was grateful. The cables supporting the transporter were as thick around as his wrist and made of countless braided wires. Though the bridge was only a decade old, rust had turned the outer wires scaly, with hundreds of burrs sharp enough to peel the skin from his hands. Bending low to wrap his jacket around the cable, Bell tightened his grip as hard as he could and let himself fall, controlling his descent by yanking at the sleeves of his jacket as though it were a garrote. He plummeted the seventy feet in just a couple of seconds, but slow enough that when he hit the deck and shoulder-rolled away from the cable, he could immediately bounce up onto his feet.

His sudden appearance made the few people standing outside gasp and point in surprise. The thief high above in the operator's cab saw him land as well. He shouted something that was muffled by the glass and he redoubled his threats of violence to the bridge worker. There were two more thieves. One was in the cab of the truck, while the other stood in the back of the lorry guarding their prize.

Bell had always known that guns were hard to come by in England even for seasoned criminals. That was why none had been used in the hijacking back on the dock and why the transporter operator had a knife to his throat rather than a gun to his head. Bell knew he had the advantage when he pulled the 9-millimeter automatic from his shoulder rig and pointed it at the truck.

"Shut off the engine and step down with your hands up," he shouted in his most authoritative voice. It was the type of command he rarely had to give twice.

It didn't have the desired effect.

With a swirl of his waterproof mackintosh, the thief in the back of the truck pulled out a sawed-off shotgun from under his coat. Bell wanted to dive to his right, behind a piece of structural steel that gave the platform rigidity, but it would put the greenhouse-like passenger gondola between him and the shooter. Instead he dove left, finding scant cover behind a high-sprung wagon filled with winter potatoes.

He edged around to the side of the wooden wagon, aware that if the gunman jumped down from his truck he could send a spray of buckshot under the carriage that would tear his legs to shreds.

A female passenger, already on edge because of the odd departure from the canal side of the river, noticed the shotgun and let out a bloodcurdling scream that sent an electric jolt of panic through the rest of the riders. People pushed and shoved in a vague attempt to get away, even though they were all trapped on the platform, which was still several yards from reaching the far bank. Glass shattered as bodies were shoved against the gondola's delicate walls, and soon blood began to flow as people were sliced open by the shards.

Bell understood that the panic would soon morph into a full-blown frenzy, the kind of melee where people were killed for being in the way of someone bigger and stronger than themselves. With little regard for his own safety, he stepped up onto the hub of one of the wagon's wheels. The gunman in the truck had a rough sense of where he was, but needed a second to swing the shotgun a couple of degrees for it to center on his target.

For his part, Bell knew exactly where the shooter was standing and had a bead on him as soon as he emerged over the cart's high side. *Pop, pop.* Two to the chest so tightly grouped it looked like a single hole. The impact drove the man against the truck's bed and he pinwheeled out of the back and over the side of the platform. His corpse hit the water hard enough to sink below the surface and wouldn't pop up again until it was a half mile downriver.

Bell whirled to draw a bead on the knife-wielding thief up in the control cupola, but with the ironwork frames and all the glass windows, it was impossible to take a safe shot that wouldn't hit the operator.

Just then came the painful crack of a Webley revolver firing in Bell's direction. The thieves might have acquired firearms, but they'd had little practice with them. The shot whizzed by several feet wide and overhead. The shooter had been in the cab. He'd taken the shot while standing on the truck's running board and the recoil had lifted his arm, and the heavy top-break revolver, high into the air. So ill-trained in armed combat, the man hadn't bothered to duck back behind the truck's cab.

Bell fired just as the moving platform hit the loading ramp on the far side of the river. The impact threw his aim off and so the round missed. Now the driver ducked back into the cab. The engine had been left running and he wasn't about to wait for his partner up in the cupola to make his way down to the main deck. He gunned the motor as he jammed it into gear.

Knowing he had only one chance, Bell vaulted up to the wagon's seat. The horses must have been used to gunfire because neither of them paused at nibbling from the canvas feed bags the wagoner had tied around their noses. The truck was just starting to move. Bell put a round through the truck's rear window and knew he'd hit the driver when the windshield was suddenly a red dripping curtain. The truck veered slightly, hit a guardrail, and ground to a stop.

Bell swiveled his aim up to the control cupola once again. This time he didn't need to worry about hitting anyone. The third thief had dropped his knife and stood with his hands up. Apparently he believed a few years in prison was better than a lifetime in a casket.

Despite the efforts of the crewman tasked with securing the platform to the ramp, passengers were rushing from the scene en masse. Those waiting on the ramp hadn't been close enough to see exactly what had happened and waited like a flock of nervous sheep.

The wagon's owner, a raw-boned farmer with just a monk's tonsure of white hair, approached, hat in hand. He was clearly more concerned with his animals' welfare than his own safety.

"I'm a private detective," Bell stated, making flicking motions with his Browning's barrel that told the thief to exit the cupola and join him on the main deck. "Those men stole cargo off a ship unloading a ways down the road."

"American?" the man asked.

"Yes."

"Never met one before." He paused, considering something, and then asked, "Why aren't you helping us with this war?"

To Bell it sounded more like an accusation than a question. "For the same reason we didn't get involved the last time the French and Germans had at each other. This is a European problem."

The thief approached, his hands still held aloft. Bell asked the farmer if he had any rope, which the man found after rummaging under the wagon's bench seat. Bell had the thief sit and tied his hands to one of the cable anchors.

"You know this war's different."

Bell did know, but said nothing. The two men regarded each other for a few seconds and then the farmer turned away to lead his team and their load of potatoes off the transporter.

It took twenty minutes for some senior police detectives to arrive and another two hours of interrogations before they were satisfied they had all the details sorted out. The cops and government agents who'd been jumped at the docks had helped smooth the proceedings and had taken possession of the truck for its eventual transport down to London. By then the shotgun-wielding thief had been fished out of the river and the lone survivor had been carted off to a jail cell in Liverpool.

Marion finally joined him on the transporter's first run after its continued operation had been authorized by the police. The few broken glass panes had been replaced with bits of canvas and the shards swept over the side. Buckets of water had sluiced any blood from lacerated passengers into the river.

She pressed herself hard against his body and kissed him long enough for some of the men milling about to turn away in embarrassment. "It's a good thing I don't watch you take foolish chances very often. My heart was pounding the whole time."

"Mine, too," he admitted. "And just so you know, that wasn't a foolish chance, but rather a calculated risk."

"Pish." She dismissed him with a wave and a flash of her Caribbean-blue eyes.

"We've missed our train to London, I'm afraid," he told her.

"No matter. We can spend the night here and head down tomorrow." A sudden thought struck her and her excitement was infectious. "We can get a room at the Adelphi. We always sail out of Southampton, so we've never stayed here in Liverpool. Friends have said the Adelphi is lovely, and everyone is absolutely mad for their turtle soup."

Bell considered the idea for a moment. "Turtle soup it is. I can telegraph the London office from the hotel and tell them we've been delayed a day, as well as notify the Savoy so we don't lose our suite. The police offered me a ride back to the docks now that we're done here and I'm sure the steamship line is holding our baggage."

She threaded an arm through his and said with mock innocence, "If they don't, I won't have a single thing to wear to bed tonight."

4

THE MEETING WAS HELD IN THE WHITE HOUSE, BUT PRESIDENT Wilson didn't attend. He let one of his chief advisers, Colonel Edward House, handle the discussion. House was a Texan who'd made his money in railroads and banking and had transplanted to New York in 1911, where he soon became a close confidant of then New Jersey governor Woodrow Wilson. He was of average build, tending toward leanness with a tall forehead, prominent white mustache, and jug-handled ears.

He sat at the head of a conference table while the secretary of war, Newton Baker, sat at the other end. Between them sat the secretary of the Navy as well as all three men's chief assistants. For Josephus Daniels, the Navy secretary, this was a young, patrician-looking New Yorker named Franklin Delano Roosevelt. He had a long face, stylish wire-framed glasses, and a quick and inquisitive mind.

There was some final rustling of papers and lighting of cigarettes before the meeting got underway.

"Gentlemen, as always, it's good to see you," Colonel House opened. "Thanks for coming across from the SWAN." This was the nickname of the State, War, and Navy Building adjacent to the White House. "I had a meeting with the President last night, and quite frankly he is concerned. As we all know, he anchored his campaign last year on the fact that he kept us out of Europe's war, even after the sinking of the *Lusitania*. The Germans banned unrestricted submarine warfare following intense pressure from our administration, but they have now lifted that ban. I need not tell you that means any and all shipping in the North Atlantic is free game to their wolf packs."

"It's only a matter of time before they sink an American-flagged ship," Newt Baker pointed out unnecessarily. The men seated around the table understood the stakes far more than most.

"When that does," House drawled, "President Wilson is concerned that the American people will demand retribution in kind, and we start going after German U-boats."

Navy Secretary Daniels put into words what House was really saying. "You're talking a declaration of war against the Central Powers."

"Yes."

"And it wouldn't just be the Navy hunting submarines?"

"No," House said bluntly. "We'd send troops to fight in the front lines alongside the British and the French."

The implications of that statement hung over the table in a pall as thick as the cigarette smoke. While everyone in the room was a lawyer by training and had never seen even a moment of combat, including Colonel House, whose title was honorary, they had all read accounts and seen uncensored footage of the carnage and horror of the modern battlefield. Wilson was considering sending American men into such a meat grinder.

House continued. "Newt, your predecessor was quite the war hawk, and for that President Wilson accepted his resignation. You're a more measured man, like the President. We need an honest assessment of what our boys will be facing. Lord knows I've been to Europe and back for two straight years trying to broker a peace deal to no avail, but in all that time I never got within a hundred miles of the front. The President wants a firsthand account of life in the trenches.

"The Brits and the French have made all kinds of assurances, but given the circumstance it would be foolhardy to trust them at their word. It seems a good amount of what they tell us is more sugar-coated than a pastry at a county fair."

"Is this to be an official fact-finding mission?" the war secretary asked.

"No. This is personal for the President. He all but told me that. He needs to know what our men will be marching into before he asks Congress for a declaration of war."

"Hell," said Secretary Baker. "He's sending them to hell. The British have lost about half a million men. The French twice that if you include all the civilians."

"He understands that, Newt. He also understands that every military aide he's spoken with is eager to get into this fight. Tanks, airplanes, submarines. They all want to play with the new toys. England and France are desperate for us to take up the fight. Their diplomats keep saying that if we enter the war, the Germans would capitulate even before our men reach Europe. But if they don't, and they keep on fighting in the face of our mobilized army, he needs an impartial observer to tell him what the situation on the ground actually looks like."

"Isn't he concerned that if we send a military man, that he'd be as eager as the generals to see us in the fight?" Franklin Roosevelt asked.

House nodded. "Very good, lad."

Knowing how he'd react to being called lad, Josephus Daniels moved to put a restraining hand on his undersecretary's arm. He was too late.

"With all due respect, Colonel House," the thirty-five-year-old rising star said icily, "it's Secretary Roosevelt, Mr. Roosevelt, or if you prefer, Franklin."

Unused to such a rebuke, especially from one whose presence here was more of a courtesy to Daniels, House sat open-mouthed for a solid three seconds before saying with overexaggerated politeness, "Mr. Roosevelt, my apologies."

"Think nothing of it, sir," Roosevelt said.

House gave a tight grimace, but then carried on with the meeting. "Mr. Roosevelt hit the crux of the problem. The President is concerned that getting a field report from some West Point graduate itching to see combat for the first time is as counterproductive as listening to the Allies' propaganda."

Newt Baker asked, "What about someone who's retired from the military and has no dog in the hunt, so to speak?"

"That's our thought exactly," House said, pointing a finger across the table at the secretary of war. "We need someone who is seasoned. An officer, of course. A man who won't let himself get carried away and who will understand what he's seeing firsthand. Does anyone come to mind?"

"I'd have to think about it," Baker admitted. "Joe?"

The Navy secretary shook his head. "This will have to be an army veteran who understands the weapons and tactics he's seeing in front of him."

"I have a suggestion," Roosevelt said. If he felt his role in such distinguished company was to be seen and not heard, he gave no indication. "I know someone outside the military, but who is more versed in fighting than anyone I've ever known. The President even met this fellow some months back after he thwarted an attack on the presidential yacht as it was sailing down the Potomac."

"I know who you're talking about," his boss exclaimed. "You told me about him. You knew him when you were both in school."

"Yes, sir. His name is Isaac Bell. He's the lead investigator for the Van Dorn Agency, which should tell you plenty on its face."

That was greeted with several nods. Everyone knew of the fabled Van Dorn Agency. Though not as large as Pinkerton, they had a stellar reputation and lived up to their motto of "Always getting their man. Always." The fact that Roosevelt was suggesting the top man within that organization carried some considerable weight.

The Navy undersecretary continued. "I imagine the President feels some urgency in this matter."

"Yes he does," House replied, any lingering issue over being reprimanded by the brash upstart having evaporated. "Now that the Boche have unleased their submarines, they could sink an American-flagged ship any day now with tremendous loss of life. We could be at war within weeks or even days."

"Isaac Bell has something else going for him. I know for a fact that he is in England right now. If we hire him for this fact-finding mission, we wouldn't have to wait a week or ten days for some retiree to get himself across the Atlantic, provided we can find such a candidate in short order."

"How do you know he's in England?" Joe Daniels asked his subaltern.

"My wife was involved in a charity fundraiser among New York's high society that collected several million dollars' worth of gold to give to the British government for their war effort. Bell's wife was involved as well. Bell got Joseph Van Dorn to offer his company's services to guard the bullion until it reached England. Bell and another agent from their Manhattan office made the voyage. Eleanor and I saw them off."

"And you say he has combat experience?" House asked.

"Not in the trenches like they have in Europe, but over a few dinners we've had this past year, he's told me about some of his tougher cases and the gunfights they invariably end in. He knows his way around violence."

"I don't like it," House said. "I'd rather have a man who's been in uniform."

War Secretary Baker leaned forward in his chair. "I wouldn't be so quick to dismiss Roosevelt's suggestion. I read what Bell did aboard the *Mayflower*. He shot down an airplane that was bombing the yacht with a Hotchkiss gun. That's combat experience in my book. Also, if we send a retiree over as our eyes and ears, he won't have any experience with this type of warfare, either. The days of cavalry charges ended in the fall of 1914 when they started digging trenches from the Alps to the North Sea."

"Colonel House," Roosevelt said respectfully, "Isaac Bell really is an ideal candidate for this mission. He's already only a few hours from the front. But more importantly, he's a trained observer who will sense if his escorts are hiding any truths from him. He'll give the President the accurate assessment he's looking for. I'm sure of it."

"Joe, what do you think?" House asked.

"Franklin is the youngest person to ever hold his position and it's no coincidence that his cousin Teddy once held the same role, so you can imagine his ambition." Roosevelt remained stone-faced, though it was little secret that he had White House aspirations. "That means he holds himself to the highest standards of any man I know. He's been my right hand for four years now and he's never steered me wrong."

"Do you think he would go if we asked?" House asked Roosevelt.

"I wouldn't be surprised if Isaac isn't already talking his way into a visit to the front. But yes. If we do ask on the President's behalf, he would go without hesitation. Especially if he knows that he's helping better prepare our soldiers if we do end up in the war. He's a patriot, Colonel House, who has gone over and above for his nation on many occasions."

House remained quiet for many long seconds, weighing the pros and cons of Roosevelt's suggestion. He finally came to a decision. "President Wilson made it very clear to me that time is of the essence for this mission. That being the case, I authorize you to reach out to Mr. Bell and relay the President's requirements." He slid a set of papers across the table to Roosevelt and an identical one all the way across to Newton Baker. "I drafted this following my meeting with the President this morning. These are the types of things he wants to know. If you or anyone on your staff has anything to add to it, do so today, because I want Bell in France no later than Thursday. We can't get caught flat-footed if Germany takes out one of our freighters or, heaven forbid, an ocean liner."

When Roosevelt and his boss cleared the White House front door on their way back to the adjacent and overly ornamental State, War, and Navy Building, the former New York State senator said, "Thank you for the vote of confidence in there, sir."

"I wasn't just blowing smoke, Franklin," Secretary Daniels replied. "You've done a hell of a job for me, and I know you wouldn't stick your neck out if you thought it might get chopped. If you think Isaac Bell can get the President the intelligence he feels he needs, I have no reason to doubt you."

"It's still reassuring to know I maintain your confidence. Butting heads with Colonel House like I did wasn't the smartest move, but I couldn't let that dig about my age slide."

"I knew you wouldn't. House has been around long enough to know not to let something like that get in the way of the job. That said, I'd avoid him for a while if you can."

"Good advice, sir. Thank you."

"Do you have a way of contacting Bell in England?"

"Van Dorn has an office in London. I'll send a cable to schedule a transatlantic call with him once I familiarize myself with House's briefing packet. If we're lucky, Bell could be headed to France by Wednesday. We are going to need a liaison with the British military. I confess to not having any real contacts in England."

"Don't worry about that. Although the Brits have gone through a handful of Admiralty Lords recently, I've got just the man in mind."

Anarchist strike at the Post Office

5

P EGGY O'SHAUGHNESSY WAITED OUTSIDE THE CONFESSIONALS in her neighborhood church in Brooklyn. In the more than ten years since she and other Irish immigrants were forced out of the Vinegar Hill area when the Manhattan Bridge was built, Peggy wasn't yet comfortable with the little Catholic church nor its French-Canadian priest. She still missed old Father Donner. He was a man who knew how to pour on the guilt and make confession a real soul-cleansing torture, and the acts of penance he meted out could take days if the mood struck him.

The Frenchman, Father Rivard, was too easy on them for their sins in Peggy's opinion. She hadn't had to ice her knees from praying on a hard stone floor since moving here with her sister and husband and their eight children, all but two grown and gone, and making this her parish.

She was by her very nature a judgmental person. She wore her morality on her sleeve, and woe to anyone who didn't adhere to her standards. For that reason her days were filled with unkind thoughts about nearly everyone she met. Just yesterday she admonished a young teen because her ankles were showing. It turned out that the girl was ashamed that she was outgrowing her hand-me-down skirt and that her older sister was now shorter than her.

Peggy vowed she would double whatever penance Father Rivard asked of her for that one.

There was no one else in the church, so it was dead silent, and the light coming through the stained glass windows was weak, which gave the stone chapel a cold, eerie feeling. The glow of candles on the altar looked as distant as the nighttime stars.

She was thinking about other sins she had to confess when she heard a strangled gasp from the priest's side of the confessional. She'd never heard anything in all her years except faint whispers. This was the Catholic confessional, the sacred and secret rite between parishioner and priest. Such a show of emotion from Father Rivard just wouldn't do.

But . . .

Peggy O'Shaughnessy inched forward a couple of steps, knowing if someone opened the church's main doors she'd have time to jump back before anyone saw her. She was fifty-eight and her hearing wasn't what it once was. She heard a man's voice, as sibilant as a snake's hiss, but not individual words. She took another step.

". . . knife . . . belly . . . blood . . ."

Father Rivard gave another little gasp and Peggy stepped back quickly. She turned to look down the length of the church. The doors were still firmly closed. The overcast sky and threat of rain were keeping others away from the confessional this Wednesday evening. Despite herself, or maybe because of it, Peggy O'Shaughnessy crept even closer to the mahogany confessional cabinet to eavesdrop again.

". . . screamed . . . too late . . . remain unborn."

Peggy and her priest both gasped. Knowing she'd gone too far, she rushed back to the pews, sat and bowed her head as if she'd been at prayer since vespers the night before. The confessional door swung open. Peggy kept her head down, her fingers working her rosary like a pianist practicing Rachmaninoff. The stranger paused at the confessional door. She could feel his eyes on her, feel some sort of primal heat washing off him.

She prayed in earnest.

He closed the door and began striding down the aisle, his shoes loud on the flagstone floor. Peggy dared give him just a small glimpse as he passed and then cast her eyes downward again. The church's outer doors creaked open and slammed shut with an echoing finality.

Kindly Father Rivard stepped out from his side of the confessional. His face was flush, his hair unkempt as if he'd been trying to pull it out in tufts, and his eyes had a wild, frightened look to them. Peggy stood and crossed to him. She was a big woman, broad at the hips and busty, while the French clergyman was small in stature. She had little problem guiding him to a step and helping him sit.

"Are you all right, Father? Do you need some water?"

His breathing remained ragged for another minute and so he didn't answer.

Knowing he couldn't tell her anything, her natural curiosity got the best of her and she blurted, "Who was that, Father Rivard?"

He finally pulled his gaze from the distant closed doors and regarded her face. "The devil, Peggy. I believe he was the devil." He paused, contemplating his words. He asked, "What does Satan look like?"

They both turned to study the doors the man had passed through moments before. "The truth, Father? An angel. He looked like a beautiful young angel."

THE ANGEL HAD HAD MANY NAMES IN HIS YOUNG LIFE. HE CURrently went by Balka Rath, a name his brother had given him before he'd emigrated from Europe the year before. His brother, now called Karl Rath, had stayed behind as leader of an anarchist cell that had all but raised Balka. While other children learned fables and fairy tales, Balka had learned political theory and the best way to disrupt a society. He'd killed his first man when he was fourteen, a French tax collector known both for his corruption and for the protection given to him by a particularly powerful superior.

The decision to come to America had been Karl's. Their cell had been in German-occupied Belgium for some time and the fact that Balka was a conscription-aged man not in the military was just too hard to cover up. Karl, a mountain of a man in his forties, already looked like he'd served, given his flame-ravaged cheek and missing eye. But Balka risked being accosted by recruiters and had twice nearly fallen into the hands of a roving press-gang searching for laborers to be sent back to Germany. He could not remain in Europe. Karl had assured him that while their fight was with the aristocracies of the Old World, America would suffer in the upcoming anarchist revolution.

Balka Rath wasn't Catholic. Even before becoming an anarchist he'd had no religious training at all. His family were from the Carpathian Mountains in Eastern Europe. They were itinerant woodcutters who poached trees from royal forests in the summer months and shaped them into lumber during the long winters. Religion had no place in such a nomadic and risky life.

He went to confession before embarking on one of his missions because he felt the need to tell someone else what he was about to do, in the off chance he was killed. It wasn't an unburdening, nor was it bragging. He simply wanted another person to be an unwitting chronicler of the evil he committed. He chose to tell Catholic priests because he knew that in the Church's nearly two thousand years of existence there was not a single incident of a priest breaking the sanctity of the confessional. Not one. No matter what he said inside the tight little cabinet, the priest would never divulge it, not even to another priest.

When he'd started this tradition, he'd considered visiting the same priest over and over just for cruelty's sake, but then he decided to never go to the same church twice. He liked to imagine some New York priests getting together to talk theology and faith and all of them burdened with a secret they could never share.

Tonight's mission wasn't particularly dangerous, but he'd wanted to tell a priest about a woman he had killed who was trying to extort one of the Irish mobsters he did occasional work for, because her body would doubtlessly be discovered soon.

While he'd been waiting in the church for his turn, dusk had become a cool, moonless night. Balka Rath turned up the collar of his wool coat as he took the church's steps down to the sidewalk. He had a Ford parked at the curb. It wasn't his car. It belonged to a local anarchist cell that was run by the son of a wealthy Wall Street broker. In truth, the cell was only financed by him, to be more precise. It was his passive retaliation for his father's aloof distance. Rath considered him a spoiled fool, but welcomed the money.

A quasi-intellectual Columbia dropout named Frederic Fowler was the cell's real brains. He led discussions in the back rooms of bars near various college campuses, expounding on anarchism and the class struggle, and trying to recruit new members.

Rath started the car and headed southeast to meet Fowler and a couple of the other cell members. Karl had cabled him recently and told him to suspend all operations because he had a big role in an important upcoming mission, and it was no longer worth the risk helping the various criminal organizations who used his ruthlessness. That also included the cell he'd joined, but Balka thought tonight's job, while high-profile, was actually low-risk, and was thus worth him defying his older brother.

The city quickly gave way to rural Nassau County. It was always a surprise to go from the world's second-largest city to a pastoral setting of farms and country lanes in just a few miles. Cities in Europe seemed to go on forever before slowly petering out. Twenty miles from the church, Rath pulled the car into the parking lot of a clapboard restaurant that sat on a crossroads alongside a general store with a pair of gas pumps out front and across from an old swaybacked barn that was being dismantled to make room for something newer.

He pulled into the lot next to Fred Fowler's car, a Ford built more than a decade earlier that burned nearly as much oil as gasoline. He killed the engine and stepped out into the chilly air.

The restaurant was cozy, with low ceilings and mismatched chairs and tables, but the smell of the food was enticing. Rath hadn't eaten for a while and the aroma kicked off a series of eager sounds from his belly. Fred and one other man were at a back table, away from the two couples sharing a meal and the lone man who looked like he'd been out on sales calls across Long Island and needed a bite before pushing on to the city.

A waitress caught his eye. He indicated that he was joining the party in the back corner, and she nodded.

Fred poured beer into a glass from a heavy pitcher as Rath approached. Fowler's wire-framed glasses flashed in the light of the dining room's overhead lamps.

Rath slid into a seat and accepted the glass. They never shook hands. "Good to see you, Fred." He spoke with an accent that no one could place because he'd grown up in more than a dozen countries. "You, too, Stan. Where's Marcus?"

"Pneumonia or the flu or something. He couldn't get out of bed."

"Doesn't really matter. Is everything set?"

"The device is in the trunk. Stan's gone over it a dozen times. It's foolproof."

"The timer?"

"You set it yourself a couple of blocks from the target," Stan the bombmaker answered. "Fifteen minutes is enough time for you to get away, but not enough for them to discover it. Here's the thing—"

"Ahem," Fred said softly. The waitress was approaching.

"Sir, your friends are having the roast beef and fried potatoes. Would you like that, too?"

"That'll be fine."

"We have some apple pie for afters. Can I save you a piece?" She smiled at him. Most women did.

He'd used his looks many times in the service of the cause, but the drawback was that people, women especially, tended to notice him, when all he wanted was anonymity. He'd found indifference worked better than rudeness to retain some semblance of privacy. He turned away from her and declined the offer with little more than a grunted "No."

Her smile faded and she returned to the kitchen to add his order.

"What were you about to say about the timer?"

"Once you set it, you can't stop the countdown."

"Why not? What if there's a delay?"

"I did it that way in case a worker discovers it before it goes off. Any kind of tampering, like cutting the visible wires or moving the clock's hands, will set if off immediately."

Balka thought about that for a moment and nodded. It was a good idea. "And how big is it?"

"Not as big as we'd like, but it can't weigh too much or a worker could become suspicious when they roll the bags off the truck. There isn't that much mail coming in from out this way."

"That was the trade-off," Fowler said. "Easy to ambush a truck here in the sticks, but the load is far lighter than one coming in from New Jersey or another part of Manhattan."

"Risk versus reward."

"It won't matter anyway," Fred Fowler said, his eyes glittering again as he moved his head in birdlike bobs. "We don't need to destroy the building. This is a symbolic strike to show that Washington is losing its sacred trust with the people. My God, governments have been in charge of the mail for thousands of years. Postal service is often the first thing they establish. If we can disrupt it, it'll show that the control they have over their subjects isn't as great as they think it is."

Stan added, "If we're successful tonight, other cells in other cities will follow our example. We can collapse the whole system."

Fowler made another gesture and the conversation paused while the waitress, far less friendly than before, doled out their plates of food, asked perfunctorily if there was anything else, and retreated once again.

"The schedule?"

"Marcus timed the truck every night for two weeks. It never varies by more than a couple of minutes and it's always the only vehicle he sees that early in the morning. This one's an easy one, Balka."

No one in the cell knew much of his past, certainly no details of the violence he'd committed, but still they were in awe of his stillness and calm. They recognized that he was dangerous, a coiled spring ready to go off even if they'd never seen such a thing occur. The cell was almost entirely composed of men of words. Stan was a little different. He was a tradesman, good with his hands, who understood the needs of the workingman. But the others were romantic talkers and dreamers who saw the struggle in the abstract. Tonight was the first time the abstract was about to become reality.

Rath suspected the delicate-featured Marcus had faked an illness in order to spare himself having to witness the violence that was forthcoming. Fred was trying to hide that he was a little ill at ease. Only Stan seemed to understand and accept the reality of consequence.

After the meal, they found a secluded lane to wait the several hours before the postal truck carrying mail from eastern Long Island into the city was due. Balka sat alone in his car and dozed. The other two were in Fred's car. Whenever Rath looked over at them, he saw Fowler smoking cigarette after cigarette. Yes, he was definitely nervous.

About fifteen minutes before the earliest mail truck would pass their ambush spot, the men left the lane and made for their intended rendezvous. It was a lonely patch of the main two-lane road that was hemmed in with trees along both verges. They parked their cars so it looked like they had been in a head-on collision that left most of the oiled dirt lane blocked.

Twenty minutes later, the sound of a vehicle approaching from the east cut the silence. Fred crushed a half-smoked cigarette beneath the toe of his shoe. Stan cracked his knuckles. Balka remained impassive.

A few seconds later, as the noise grew, a glow showed from around a bend in the road. It brightened and then turned dazzling as the truck made the turn. The engine beat immediately changed as the driver saw what he thought was an accident. The men began waving down the driver. The six-wheeled truck slowed, its brakes rubbing a little under the sudden deceleration.

He came to a halt five yards short of the "accident" and opened his door as the three "victims" approached.

"You fellas—"

Balka rushed the final couple of steps, twisting his wrist and opening and closing his hand in order to release the blade of his Filipino butterfly knife. The move was oft-practiced and took under a second. He rammed the blade between the driver's ribs all the way to the knife's handles, twisting when he felt it stop against the bone. The damage to the man's heart was instantly fatal and Balka just let him collapse onto the lonely road.

Mostly stoic Stan retched at seeing the amount of blood that had managed to leak from the wound before the driver's heart stopped. Balka's knife was slick with it and his hand was half covered. Fred Fowler went very pale and watched in sickened fascination as Rath bent to clean his weapon and himself against the driver's white shirt. In the glow of the headlights, the stains looked black and as thick as tar.

"This is what the revolution looks like," Balka said as he stood. "Get over it or get the hell out of it."

Fred shuddered and managed to drag his gaze away from the dead postal driver.

"Stan," Balka snapped. "Help me."

Together they dragged the body twenty yards into the woods and covered up their trail by straightening bent branches and ruffling some shrubs they'd knocked flat. For his part, Fred had gathered his wits and retrieved a large box from the trunk of his car and brought it to the mail carrier's cargo truck. He set it on the ground and opened the truck's tailgate. The mail was in large cloth bags fitted inside tubular metal frames that had wheels so they could be rolled around more easily. There were four such hoppers and they were loaded nearly to the very top with letter-sized envelopes and packages.

He emptied one of the hoppers of most of its contents and placed the bomb inside. He opened the container. The clock was attached to thirty pounds of dynamite that they had stolen from a Hudson Valley construction company. Fred then packed loose mail around the device and placed a thin layer of letters over the top.

Balka inspected his handiwork when he and Stan returned from disposing of the hapless driver. Balka now wore the dead man's jacket. The bloodstain was nearly the same color as the dark blue fabric.

They'd worked fast given how exposed they were. Balka tossed his car keys to Stan, climbed up into the truck's seat, and fired up the engine with its electric ignition. He gave his two companions a sardonic wave, eased off the clutch, and pulled away from the ambush.

New York's principal post office was located in lower Manhattan in a five-story Second Empire building on a corner near City Hall Park. It was widely considered to be one of the ugliest buildings in the borough. The lower floors and basement were used by the postal service, while upstairs there were courts and offices for judges and their clerks. The building was only open during regular business hours, but the mail-processing center never stopped receiving and resending mail by the truckloads. The loading docks were in back, visible as an eyesore to the daytime visitors of the adjacent park.

Forty minutes after stealing the truck, Balka Rath guided it off the Brooklyn Bridge and continued on for several blocks. The post office was dead ahead. It was three in the morning and there was no other traffic. Two blocks from his destination, Rath pulled the truck over to the curb and climbed out. He looked up and down the street. Not even an alley cat could be seen. He jumped up onto the tailgate, pushed aside the letters covering the box, and opened its lid.

Stan had instructed him on how the mechanism worked. The hands both pointed to twelve. Using his finger he reset the minute hand back to the nine-o'clock position. Done. He covered the box again and hurried back to the cab. He'd left the engine running, so he hit the clutch, palmed the heavy gear lever into first, and pulled from the curb. It had all taken less than thirty seconds.

The wheels came off his plan when he was about to turn the corner to access the building's multi-bay loading dock. Several trucks identical to his own were parked nose to tail, their drivers still in their seats, many of them with a hand out their window and lit cigarettes held loosely in their fingers.

Unsure of what was happening, Balka pulled up behind the last truck. He set the brake and opened his door, only to have a pugnacious supervisor he hadn't noticed rush up to him before he could step to the pavement.

"What do you think you're doing?" The man had a squint and an unlit stub of a cigar in the corner of his mouth. "You know the rules. You can't leave your truck for any reason."

"What's the holdup?" Rath asked, matching the man's bellicose attitude.

"Loading elevator crapped out. They just got it working, but as you can see, there's a backlog of trucks to unload. You're lucky. Should be twenty or so minutes for you. Some of these schmoes have been here for more than an hour."

The man walked away.

Balka was uncertain, a feeling he despised. He didn't have a watch, but knew the minute hand on the bomb behind him was slowly winding back up to twelve. How much time he had was unknown. Ten minutes? Five?

The truck ahead of him suddenly lurched forward as space was made at the dock. But not enough for him to reach his destination. There were still several trucks ahead of him. He felt trapped and he felt time's relentless march. Once he'd pulled forward a couple of feet, he stopped and opened his door a second time. Just as before the supervisor appeared.

"You deaf or stupid?" the man barked around his relit cigar.

"Listen, I need—"

"Pal, does it look like I care what you need? Sit down, shut up, and wait your turn."

Rath's eyes darted around. The other truckers were in their vehicles facing forward. There were no pedestrians around and they weren't yet in sight of the busy loading dock and the hive of postal workers unloading the mail. The butterfly knife came out of his coat pocket without the supervisor noticing and he had the blade open and secure in a blur too fast to follow.

He stuck the blade into the man's chest with a roundhouse blow that allowed him to step down from the truck, move behind the startled man, and bodily heave him up into the cab in a fluid motion as pretty as any dance. He twisted the blade as he got the supervisor into the seat. The man wasn't very big, but he had a strong heart.

Despite the damage, it kept pumping blood for several seconds, soaking Rath's hand and pooling in the man's lap.

At last, he shuddered in a death rattle and went still.

Just then another truck pulled up behind him. Rath closed his door, crossed between his vehicle and the one ahead of him, and made his way back down the street, keeping low so the driver of the new truck didn't see him. Once clear of the logjam, Rath started running, turning at every block he reached in order to put as much distance as possible between him and the inevitable blast.

He'd been running for four minutes when he heard the blast echoing up the canyons of four-story brick row houses. The acoustics made it sound like the explosion had taken place at more than one location. There were too many intervening structures for him to feel the pressure blast, but he knew it would have blown out windows for several hundred feet.

He slowed to a casual walk. He was far enough from the explosion that no reasonable person would think he was connected to it. It hadn't been the blow against the government he'd hoped for, but the symbolism would still strike a chord with those dissatisfied with their government as well as the people in power whose grip, they had to realize, had just slipped ever so slightly.

6

ISAAC BELL HAD BOUGHT THE NECKLACE BECAUSE ITS FOUR matching gemstones, each the size of an acorn, were the exact shade and depth of blue as Marion's eyes. It always struck admirers when she wore it that nature created the same lustrous hue in both warm living flesh and icy cold stone. Her gown was the same color as the necklace's platinum setting and had a playful little train and winglike sleeves. Her thick blond hair was up and held in place by two diamond-tipped platinum pins he'd bought her in Paris.

She was every inch the vision and more beautiful now than the day they'd met more than a decade ago. He couldn't tear his eyes from her. His direct, appraising gaze made her start to blush self-consciously.

"What?" she asked demurely.

"You look spectacular."

"I have no choice but to believe you, since you are a trained investigator who misses nothing." They were in the living room of their suite at the Savoy. She did a twirling pirouette for him, but then sidled up close so her lips were near his ear. "What you likely did miss, Mr. Detective, is that under my slip I'm wearing nothing at all."

She danced away and was out of range when that sunk in, and Bell tried to grab her around the waist. "You've bewitched me," he said.

"Good. That was my plan all along."

The phone rang. He picked up the speaker and leaned into the microphone. "Isaac Bell."

"Mr. Bell, this is the doorman. Your car is here."

"We will be right down." He held out his elbow for Marion to slip her arm into his. "In town for twenty-four hours and we're already going to a royal party."

"You are many things, Isaac Bell. A procrastinator isn't one of them."

Their trip to England had grown ever stranger since the chase and subsequent capture of the gold shipment thieves. They did get a room at the Adelphi and Marion did relish their famous turtle soup, but they'd also run into the minor royal whose car she'd stolen and subsequently sank in the Mersey River. His anger was an all-consuming pyre that looked about to give him a heart attack as he raged in the hotel's lobby when he first saw Marion come through the door. In the end, he did not accept her apology, which had been rather insincere in truth, but he did accept a guaranteed check for twice the car's value.

A cable was waiting for Isaac when they reached London that the man was a day late in receiving, leaving Bell only a couple of minutes to rush to the small office the Van Dorn Agency maintained in the city. He then had a thirty-minute transatlantic conversation with the secretary of the Navy, Josephus Daniels, and his assistant secretary, Franklin Roosevelt. Bell immediately accepted the opportunity to give the secretary an unvarnished assessment of what American troops could expect on what even the Allies called *die Westfront*, the Western Front.

Daniels and Roosevelt had already set up a liaison meeting with a previous Admiralty Lord, who'd assured them that the whole expedition would take a week at most. To mollify Marion that he was leaving her alone in London while he went to play scout in France, the meeting would be preceded by an invitation to a gala at a Chelsea mansion that very night.

Marion had spent the day with the hotel's stylist while Bell made lists of the things he'd need and was just now seeing what they'd put together for the evening.

"Because of the war, no one is going full-out with all the regalia of a real ball," she explained as they waited for the lift. "That's why you can get away with just a tuxedo rather than white tie and frock coat and I'm in a dinner gown."

"The aristocrats doing their part," Bell said sarcastically.

"Don't be snotty," she said as they crossed the lobby for the hotel's famous forecourt.

The car was a Rolls-Royce with handcrafted coachwork painted in a deep blue with gold accents. It was one of the loveliest cars Bell had ever seen and he had to resist the urge to ask the driver about its mechanical specifications. Instead he sat back with Marion's gloved hand in his and enjoyed the ride across the city to their destination.

Lit up like a movie premiere, the main mansion stood three stories tall and had two newer extensions that took up almost the entire block. The façade was brick with granite accents and a forest of chimneys rose from the slate roof. It offered an impressive view of a tree-studded park across the road and looked like it had well over a hundred rooms. New York society was stratified by new and old money, those who'd gotten wealthy in the industrial age versus those whose wealth had been built generations earlier. This place made Bell realize that the oldest old money in New York was nothing compared to what the Europeans had been amassing since the Renaissance.

A procession of luxury cars was disgorging well-heeled guests in a steady stream. Once it was their turn, a footman in white hose opened the door and held out a hand for Marion. She flowed out of the Rolls in a stream of shimmering silk. Bell followed after and pulled a card from a case that he kept in an inside jacket. The reception hall was an octagonal room so tall that it should echo painfully, but was so well designed that it didn't. The floor was pink marble and the double wings of the staircase in the back of the room were intricately carved mahogany.

They took their spot in a reception line, and when it was time, Bell handed his card to an attendant, who then whispered his and Marion's names to their hosts, Lord and Lady Shirling.

"So nice of you to come all the way from America, Mr. and Mrs. Bell," His Lordship said.

Bell held back a quip and replied, "We are honored by the invitation into your lovely home."

And just like that they were past. Arm in arm, they drifted into an adjoining room, where waiters were carrying platters of champagne and canapés. Marion was enraptured by the elegant clothes and the size of some of the jewels the women wore at their throats or around their wrists and fingers. They had been to some impressive parties back in the States, but this put them all to shame in terms of opulence and decorum. She told him that the beadwork on one of the gowns she pointed out likely took two years to stitch.

The champagne was perfectly chilled and the right balance

between sweet and dry, while each bite of the food was a sensation unto itself. Once someone overheard them talking and asked if they were American, they became the center of attention. Bell gave vague answers about what he did, but one of the ladies in the growing circle recognized Marion's name and had seen several of the films she'd directed.

Gossip was the lifeblood of all levels of society and once she started in on stories of actors whose fame had crossed the Atlantic, Marion became the darling of the affair. Knowing she could hold court for hours, Bell ambled away in search of his contact. While Bell knew the man's name, he wanted to test his detective skills by trying to find his target using just the brief physical description he'd been given.

He needn't have bothered. A moment after leaving Marion's side someone tapped him on the elbow. He turned and knew this was his man. He was a couple of years older than Bell with a pugnaciousness about him that made him seem older still. He was barely five and a half feet tall, but he had the presence of a giant. His eyes were a cutting blue, but also playful.

"Daniels told me to look for a strapping blond fellow with the most beautiful woman at the party on his arm," he said in a cigar-roughed voice. "I'm Winston Churchill."

"Isaac Bell." They shook hands. "The secretary gave me your biography and I admit to being very impressed. Member of Parliament at twenty-six. Admiralty Lord just ten years later."

Churchill made a demurring gesture. "If I'm not engaging in something new, I find myself growing bored. They've just made me minister of munitions. Any chance you can delay your trip to France by a month or so? You can accompany me on my first inspection with my new posting."

"I would have enjoyed that," Bell replied. "Unfortunately, the President wants my report as soon as possible."

"You Americans are going to come in on our side." Churchill said this as a statement, but it was more a question.

Bell took a second to reply. "Wilson's reluctant. His entire campaign last year was based on the fact that we hadn't entered the war. A good part of him is unwilling to turn his back on that legacy. On the other hand, if the Germans kill enough American sailors and ships' passengers, he's going to have no choice but to respond by asking Congress for a declaration of war."

"The Kaiser's no fool," Churchill responded. "He knows that, but he also believes that if his U-boats can strangle our little island for a bit longer, America won't have time to mobilize significant forces before we sue for peace."

"It's a gamble."

"Wars usually are."

They'd found their way to a bar. "Martini, please," Churchill told the barman. "Very light on the vermouth."

"Same," Bell said and turned his attention back to Churchill. "I had drinks with Secretary Daniels's chief confidant a while back. The man practically drowns his martini in vermouth. Good to see you have taste."

"Josephus mentioned him. A relative of your former President, Teddy Roosevelt."

"Franklin Roosevelt is T.R.'s cousin." Bell paused, considered something, and nodded to himself as he came to a quick conclusion. "Franklin is a lot like you, strong-willed and driven to succeed. I think you'd like him."

"I hope to meet him one day." Another gentleman approached. Churchill welcomed him over with a gesture. "Valentine, good to see you, old boy. I thought you were in France. How's Evelyn? Wait, more important, how's your son? Did he get the books I sent over?"

"Winston, hello," the newcomer said. He was a bit younger than Bell, but had gray in his mustache and a receding hairline. "He's almost back to full strength, and yes, he got the books. He especially loved the Kipling one about spies in India."

"*Kim*. One of my favorites. I knew he'd like it," Churchill said. "Val, this is an American envoy I'm helping out, Isaac Bell. Mr. Bell, may I present Major Valentine Fleming, my regiment mate in the Queen's Own Oxfordshire Hussars, as well as a fellow MP."

"Former," Fleming clarified.

"His son, Ian, has been laid up for a month with a pneumonia the doctors feared would become tuberculosis. Glad to hear he's doing better. Stand you for a peg?"

"Scotch," Fleming said and greeted Bell with a handshake. Churchill relayed the order to the barman, who handed over a cut-crystal tumbler of thirty-year-old Balblair single malt.

"Of what or who are you an envoy, Mr. Bell?" Fleming asked after taking an appreciative sip.

"The President of the United States, actually," Bell said, drawing raised eyebrows from the man.

"I just had an idea," Churchill interjected before Bell could add anything further.

He ushered them out of the public spaces and into a room that hadn't yet been converted to electricity. The four wall sconces were all gaslit and glowing at their very lowest settings. Churchill turned up the brass knobs on the two lamps along the right wall. The room was decorated for a more feminine taste, with much lace and embroidered fabrics. The walls above the chair rail were covered in pale pink watered silk.

"Val, I said earlier that I thought you were in France," Churchill said.

"I was. I've only been here for two days, some regimental business. I'm shipping out in the morrow."

Churchill nodded through a wreath of smoke from the cigar he'd just lit, heedless of the fact this was a ladies' drawing room. "Mr. Bell here has been tasked with reporting the frontline situation directly to President Wilson. Their Navy secretary reached out to me to see if I could facilitate his visit. And it looks like I can if you're willing to play tour guide for a couple of days."

Valentine Fleming looked more than a little uncomfortable.

Churchill understood right away. "You're worried about the spring offensive." Hearing this, Fleming's face lost color. "Relax, Val. Everyone knows we've planned a springtime attack. It's not exactly a surprise when the guns start blasting away to soften up the German lines. The Boche will know exactly where and when our lads are going over the top."

Fleming saw the logic even if it went against strict military protocol. "I, well, yes I suppose that's true."

"We need this, old friend," Churchill went on. "We need the Yanks in this fight, or this never-ending conflict is going to make the Seven-Years War look like a skirmish."

"What is it you need to see?" Fleming asked Bell without committing himself.

"My instructions were vague, to be honest. Wilson fears we're going to get into this scrap before long. Unlimited submarine warfare all but guarantees it. I think he wants to understand what exactly our soldiers will face. It won't change his mind, but I think he needs to personally appreciate the risk and sacrifice his decision will have on those he sends to fight. I think my presence here has more to do with his conscience than any tactical or strategic necessity. That said, I would like to get as close to the front line as possible, as well as make an aerial reconnaissance of as much of the battlefront as I can manage."

"Without giving away any military secrets, my regiment isn't going to be in the thick of things even after the balloon goes up, so you can come with me for a couple of days. Have you nose about and I can send you to a British aerodrome about ten miles behind the lines."

"Crabby's outfit?" Churchill asked.

"Yes," Fleming replied and added for Bell's sake, "Captain Geoffrey Crabbe was once in the Queen's Own Oxfordshires with Winston and myself. That is until he swapped his horse for a plane and took to the sky. Made ace in just six weeks. 'Course that was back before the Germans deployed their new Albatross D.IIIs."

"You'll do it, Val," Churchill said with a deep chuckle. Bell could tell that he was a man accustomed to getting his own way.

"I don't know," Fleming prevaricated.

"Sod it, Val. It's an opportunity to single-handedly help shorten the war."

The major thought for a moment longer before nodding. He said, "Once we've rejoined my regiment, I'm turning you over to a subaltern, an enlisted man." His tone made it sound that this was a punishment for making him break the rules.

Bell smiled. "That's even better, Major. I think the President will prefer learning the common soldier's experience of the war."

"Thanks, old friend," Churchill said with a jovial slap on Fleming's back. "There you are, Mr. Bell, your problem solved in under ten minutes. Make sure you tell Secretary Daniels that we more than accommodated his request." The mercurial statesman paused before saying, "Something tells me our two nations are going to be at war very soon. And for the first time in history, not against one another."

"Speaking of wars," Bell said, "I have to find Marion and tell her I'm leaving tomorrow. She was mad enough at me for accepting this assignment and ruining our stay. You see, the last time we were in London we had just missed sailing aboard the *Titanic*. You can imagine the black cloud that threw over our visit. Anyway, she believed it would be a couple of days before I found my way to France and has been planning accordingly. Theater tickets. Opera tickets. A private shopper on Bond Street."

Ever the wit, Churchill said, "Sounds like going to war means you've dodged a bullet."

7

T HE DOCKS AT SOUTHAMPTON WERE AS BUSY AS BELL RECALLED, but with one critical difference. Gone were the elegant express liners with their gleaming black hulls and cloud-white superstructures topped by brightly colored stacks. Gone, too, were the gentlemen in tailored suits and ladies sporting the latest fashions surrounded by dockworkers unloading matching sets of steamer trunks.

What greeted Bell when he arrived in a military staff car alongside Valentine Fleming was an armada of warships in muted gray livery, each bristling with cannons of every caliber from massive naval fourteen-inchers to twenty-millimeter close-in defensive weapons. There were also dozens of freighters and troopships either loading or being unloaded. Many of the cargo ships that had come from America in convoys still sported the now defunct "dazzle camouflage," which consisted of oddly shaped geometric blocks painted in various colors on the hull and superstructure in an attempt to fool

U-boat range finders. The scheme hadn't worked as its early support-
ers, including Winston Churchill, as Admiralty Lord, had hoped.

Gone, too, were eager passengers ready to board their ships or
enjoy their stay in Europe if newly arrived. Bell saw a sea of men in
matching brown uniforms, with flat helmets that reminded him of
armor from Cromwell's reign. They were burdened with heavy
packs and belts and ammo pouches made of webbing material. Most
carried rifles with long bayonets scabbarded at their waists, their
shins covered in puttees as defense against the inevitable mud they
would face in the trenches.

It was a sobering sight, Bell thought as the driver threaded the car
along Southampton's massive quay in search of their assigned ship.
The war's death toll was already horrendous, and by the looks of
things, it was only going to get worse.

He wondered about the United States entering the war. "This is
a European affair" was so often the reason given for American neutrality. But that would no longer be the case now that Germany had
declared war on any ship plying the Atlantic. Bell thought about
Wilson's upcoming decision, which wasn't really a decision at all,
but rather a response to changing circumstances. He thought about
his own reasons for taking the assignment. He decided that what he
had said the night before, about Wilson's conscience, was the answer
to why he was here.

He didn't mind that he would play no role in deciding if the
United States joined the fight, but he was happy enough to serve the
commander in chief if it helped him accept the inevitability of total
world war.

"Ah, there we are," Valentine Fleming said and pointed to their
right. Their ride to France was the HMS *Acasta*, a thousand-ton
destroyer that had been severely damaged the year prior at the Battle

of Jutland. She was returned to service as a Channel escort following extensive repairs.

Compared to the large freighters and heavy cruisers in port, she was a small ship, narrow in the beam and only some two hundred and sixty feet. She was lightly armed with only four cannons and a pair of torpedo tubes, but she was devilishly fast with a top speed better than thirty knots.

Smoke coiled from her single funnel and joined the general pall that settled over the port, the smog a mix of coal soot, harbor stink, and the very real fear of the men boarding the troopships.

At the base of the destroyer's gangway, the staff car squalled to a halt on poorly maintained brakes and Fleming practically leapt from his seat. Bell joined him on the quay. Now that they didn't have the car's engine blatting away, they could hear the sounds of the mighty embarkation around them. Thousands of men and thousands of tons of matériel were going to be poured into the upcoming spring offensive, and so the loading proceeded with an air of urgency. Sergeants blew brass whistles to get their men in order and great overhead cranes struggled to swing pallets of artillery shells into waiting holds. Farther down, Bell caught the whinny of horses being loaded for the front and wondered if any of them were the ones he'd seen in Liverpool.

The corporal who'd driven them wrestled a heavy trunk off the sedan's rear cargo deck and caught the eye of a passing stevedore pushing an empty metal-wheeled dolly. The two men hoisted the trunk onto the handcart and, with Bell and Fleming carrying their own leather bags, the three men made for the HMS *Acasta*.

The ship's first officer greeted them at the head of the gangplank, checked their identification, and welcomed them aboard. Churchill had smoothed out the whole thing. Since the weather for the crossing looked good, Fleming gave permission for the trunk to be lashed in a protected nook just outside the ship's small pilothouse.

"Are you going to tell me what it is you felt you had to lug to France?" Fleming asked.

"You'll see," Bell said, smiling. "I will say it had all the hallmarks of my loving and caring wife."

They were allowed onto the small bridge provided they stayed up against the back wall and that they were to evacuate to the officers' wardroom at the first sign of trouble.

Twenty minutes after boarding, the captain called for the boilers to be run up. Jets of inky smoke boiled from the stack. Up and down the pier, other ships were making ready to cross the channel in a tight convoy. Some of the larger vessels required plucky little tugboats to pull them from the dockside and aim their noses toward the open sea. The *Acasta* soon joined the exodus, and when they reached the Channel she swung out to the south and east of the main body of ships to act as a picket against any U-boats that had somehow made it into these heavily patrolled and defended waters.

The sea was relatively calm, but appeared in an ominous dark gray shade that made Bell think of the slag fields outside a Pittsburgh iron mill. Fleming didn't look like he was enjoying the experience despite the flat waters, and not long after they'd made the channel, he asked if he could make the crossing on a bridge wing. The captain okayed his request and Bell went with him.

Fleming didn't look ill, but apprehensive, and Bell quickly understood why. The major scanned the water from horizon to horizon, his eyes never still, his neck on a swivel. The other ships in the convoy sailed as tightly as possible and seemed to fill the ocean with their bulk. Bell caught an occasional flash of an Aldiss lamp as coded messages were passed from ship to ship.

"I was on the *Lusitania* that fateful morning," Bell said. "I tell you this because the odds of me being torpedoed twice in the same war are staggeringly low."

"If it's all the same, I like to keep an eye out," Fleming said after finally getting a cigarette lit.

A few companionable minutes passed.

"I shouldn't tell you this," Fleming said without looking at Bell. "Lord knows Winston would have my hide if he heard me give an unfavorable opinion about the war to you. The thing is, Mr. Bell—"

"Isaac."

"Isaac. The thing is, the individual no longer matters on the battlefield. Not in this mechanized industrial style of warfare. We stand in the middle of the most dehumanizing event in human history. It matters not how well trained a soldier is or how well equipped. Nothing matters out there but random chance.

"Not to be immodest, but I am a very good horseman. Been riding since before I can remember. At another time and place my skill would mean something. I would be able to ride into battle faster and safer than anyone else because I have an eye for covering terrain and a mastery over my animal.

"But not here. Not in this war. My skills mean nothing against a double line of crisscrossing German machine guns and a tangle of barbed wire. That's not to mention the artillery barrages that have raged without end it seems since the opening salvos back in 'fourteen. To the lads in the trenches, it doesn't matter whether you're a good soldier or not. All he needs to be is lucky. Lucky that a fifteen-centimeter shell full of high explosives from one of the German howitzers lands at any spot other than where he is standing.

"It's the same out here. You were a victim of it. It mattered not that the *Lusitania* was a fast ship in closely watched waters and crewed with plenty of well-trained lookouts. That morning, chance put her abeam of a U-boat that managed the luckiest shot of the war. Twelve hundred perished when she went down for no other reason than they were in the wrong place at the wrong time.

"Not much I can do in the trenches if shells start raining down, but out on the water I can at least keep a weathered eye for a periscope or a torpedo already heading for us. It's my way of trying to stay alive long enough to see an end to this whole wretched business."

Bell understood the randomness of a gunfight. He'd been in far too many to count. He understood what Fleming meant. He practiced shooting every week to keep his skills honed to a razor's edge to give him the advantage of speed and accuracy over an opponent. But what good would that do if your enemy threw up a wall of lead with Maxim guns while at the same time shelling you with a hundred big guns?

"Grim," was his one-word reply.

"Depending on what you see and don't see on your tour, it's something you needed to know."

"Thanks for that."

The channel crossing was without incident. The French port of Le Havre was just as chaotic as Southampton, with strings of ships arriving from all points on the compass—Aussie soldiers fresh from the Outback, troupes of French colonial police pulled from duties in Africa and elsewhere, and freighters hauling goods from all over the world in an all-out effort to defeat the Central Powers.

Dockworkers swarmed like ants, while parallel lines of soldiers disembarking from the troopships made straight for waiting trains that would take them to the front to the north and east of Paris. Bell saw the inevitable strings of horses. No matter how mechanized armies were becoming, the mud and mire of trench warfare meant that equine power and agility still ruled the transportation sector.

With the French countryside ravaged by war, and so many of its men in uniform, the country relied on food imports, and so much of the cargo coming off the freighters was lowered directly onto flat-bottomed barges that would then be towed up the Seine to Paris. Word was that rationing in Paris now required that bakers make only one type of bread. Gone were the beloved baguettes and brioches, replaced by a utilitarian loaf called *pain national.*

To the average Frenchman this was a sacrifice of the highest order.

Bell also saw the rows of ambulances pulling up to a hospital ship from the run across to England. Some men could walk under their own power, their bandages white against their khaki uniforms. They had drawn, gaunt faces and eyes made hollow by pain and the horrors they had witnessed. The blind walked with an arm touching the man ahead. Those coming out of the ambulance on stretchers lay under army blankets, but their silhouettes were off. Limbs were missing, oftentimes more than one, blown off on the battlefield or sawn off by an overworked surgeon just behind the front lines.

It was a sobering sight that made both men grunt in that understated way men have who don't want to show how deeply they were affected.

The *Acasta* had no place to berth as she was not discharging any cargo and would soon return to England. Instead, Bell and Fleming and their bags and mysterious trunk were rowed to a boat ramp down one of the port's artificial channels. The seamen helped unload the baggage and were gone before Bell and Fleming realized they had no transportation off the ramp.

Being of a certain class and having a certain flair, it didn't take long for Valentine Fleming to enlist the help of a pair of dock boys of no more than thirteen to drag the steamer trunk up the ramp and onto the quay. They were further convinced with a few shiny coins to find them a car to take them back to the railhead and the troop trains.

They found no automobile, but rather a wooden wagon pulled by a single donkey with such bad flatulence that Bell and Fleming walked beside the carriage rather than in it.

"*C'est la guerre*," Fleming quipped.

It took an hour to make their way across the sprawling port, but then things accelerated quickly. Fleming was an officer, a major, with travel papers that couldn't be questioned and an air of studied indifference that made all around him want to be at his beck and call. No one bothered to check Bell's hastily drawn-up orders signed almost illegibly by the munitions minister.

The trunk was loaded aboard a railyard flatbed with hundreds of wooden crates of .303-caliber ammunition. Rather than travel in an officer's carriage, Bell wanted to head to the front with some of the regular soldiers. The enlisted soldiers' railcar had no amenities, the seats were roughly hewn wood, and the windows didn't open. The men lucky enough to find a seat sat packed shoulder to shoulder. Others were relegated to a spot on the floor atop the packs that had been dumped as soon as the men boarded.

Bell and Fleming shared a bench that normally would have accommodated three men. A couple of the soldiers who were forced to the floor looked resentful until Bell pulled a bottle of Portuguese port wine from a rucksack. Because the nights were still cold, Marion insisted that port was better than claret because it warmed the blood.

The distance was roughly a hundred and thirty miles, but took the better part of ten hours because they were forced to stop on sidings at random intervals to let other trains pass. The closer they got to the front lines, the more the countryside bore the scars of battle. Whole forests were reduced to blasted stumps and disarticulated branches that looked like the skeletal hands of giants that had been lopped off by the gods. The earth, too, was torn and pounded with topsoil pushed deep under the surface during one barrage, only to be flung high into the air at some later cannon fusillade, so all that remained was pockmarked mud as cratered and desolate as the moon's surface.

As they neared their destination, the young soldiers' boisterous talk, their bragging of feats past and boasts of future glory, slowly petered out until, as the sun's final rays were retreating to the west and the landscape took on a funereal air, they no longer looked each other in the eye. Closer still to the front, when they realized the rolling thunder they heard in the distance was thousands of cannons, howitzers, and mortars firing in a crescendo without end, some began to tremble and a few began to weep.

As seasoned fighters, Bell and Fleming knew this moment was coming for the boyish conscripts and enlistees, and said nothing.

The marshaling area behind the front was as chaotic a scene as Bell had ever experienced. Under the glare of powerful arc lamps that were nearly blinding at a mere glance, tens of thousands of men were being organized into groups according to their units. New replacements stepping off the trains were met with the bellows of sergeants gathering their men, like militarized carnival barkers drawing in a crowd.

Fleming led Bell into the melee, freshly laid gravel along the rail line crunching under their boots. Though miles away, the scent of burnt powder drifted in from the mass of gun emplacements bombarding the German lines. They had made it just a few steps from the carriage when one of the NCOs tapped Fleming on the shoulder.

"Oi. Where da ya think you're 'eading?"

"Queen's Own Oxfordshire Hussars, if you must know," Fleming replied, only half turning to face the cockney sergeant.

"Queer oddities on 'orses, ay?"

Fleming had heard the nickname many times. "Sergeant, before you dig your grave any deeper, look at my insignia," he said with a sting like a hornet.

The man went green. "Begging the major's pardon. I, ah . . . You stepped off an enlisted carriage. I thought you—"

"Truly a comedy of errors. I will gladly forget this incident if you get me two men to carry a rather heavy trunk, another for our bags, and a vehicle to take us south to our sector of the front."

"Right away, Major." The sergeant snapped off a parade ground–quality salute and vanished into the night.

An hour later, the borrowed lorry deposited Bell, Fleming, and their gear at a compound of army tents set up in a clearing amid one of the only surviving copses of trees in this part of France. Nearby were pens for horses, whose breath steamed the quiet night. They were too far away to hear the barrage raging to their north.

"Last thing," Bell said as the driver shut off the engine, "what was it the sergeant said back there? I couldn't follow because of his accent."

"The QOOH is a cavalry outfit, as you know, but there hasn't been a proper cavalry charge since the disastrous early attempts that saw horse and rider cut down by the barrelful. We keep our horses, naturally, and exercise them regularly, but don't use them in battle. Other units have taken to calling us Queer Oddities on Horses, as we do look rather ridiculous practicing maneuvers we will never use in battle."

"War is hell."

"Your General Sherman, I believe. So where do you want your trunk?"

"I suppose wherever your NCOs congregate. I've brought stuff for your men, and it's best the sergeants pass it about."

The NCOs had a ten-person tent they used as an informal club, with some furniture either pilfered from abandoned farms or lugged up from Paris. Their prize position was a sideboard with a couple of liquor bottles that had been pilfered from an antechamber at the Hotel George V. Fleming wrapped a knuckle on a tent pole before entering the space, as was customary for all officers.

"Sergeant Major Everly, permission to enter."

"Major Fleming. Welcome back, sir," said a grizzled veteran with iron-gray hair and a brow as furrowed as a freshly turned farm plot. "By all means."

There were a half dozen other NCOs in various poses of relaxation. The air in the tent was warm from the body heat and cozy with the scent of pipe tobacco. Light came from a pair of kerosene lanterns hanging from two poles.

Two of Fleming's men lugged in the steamer trunk. "Gentlemen," Fleming started, "this is Mr. Isaac Bell. He's an observer from America who is to report directly to their President Wilson about the war. Sergeant Major, he will be your responsibility for his time here."

"Isaac, this is Sergeant Major William Everly."

The command NCO didn't look too happy about this new responsibility, but took Bell's proffered hand.

"Thank you, Major," Bell said. "No one likes to have someone looking over their shoulder and quietly judging, so I promise here and now that I will make all my judgments as loud as possible." That got a few polite chuckles. "I also know that nobody likes a mooch, so I brought along some things for you and your men." He opened the trunk with a theatrical flourish.

The men had gathered round, and when they saw the standard white and blue labels for Tickler's Jam, a regular commodity on the battlefront, a couple groaned aloud. This was no treat.

Bell plucked one of the tins from the trunk, hiding the label a bit with his hands. "I hear that the plum and apple flavor is jolly good." He spun the can so they could all read the label. "But strawberry is much better."

At this the men roared their approval for such a rare delicacy. There were at least thirty such prized cans of jam. Under it were tins of kippers and crackers, a couple of bottles of scotch, bundles of thick wool socks, expensive cigarettes that actually contained more tobacco than filler, stationery to write home, chocolates, several vinyl records in case they had a phonograph, and anything else Marion could think of to give a common soldier a lift.

"I think this'll cover your stay for a few days, Mr. Bell," Sergeant Major Everly said. He'd splashed some whiskey into one of their bar's mismatched glasses and handed it over.

"I was hoping it would." Bell smiled back, noting that one of Everly's eyes was slightly clouded by a cataract and that there was an old scar running down from its lid to his cheek.

Everly usually never talked about it with strangers, but he felt compelled to tell the mysterious American. "German with a trench knife two years back. He thought he'd blinded me when he saw all the blood. He stepped back for an instant. I kneed him in the clackers and whacked the back of his head with a shovel. Earned me a month of convalescence, though I'll be blind in that eye soon enough and away from all this."

That last bit was said with true regret. Bell saw that he was a career soldier who wanted nothing more than to shepherd his boys through the war and see them all returned home in one piece.

8

AFTER TAKING AN EMPTY COT IN A TENT RESERVED FOR SIX sergeants, Bell was awoken before dawn the next morning and got his first good look at the camp. There were two companies bivouacked in the forest clearing and they were far enough behind the lines that all the men got to sleep in tents rather than holes and tunnels dug into the earth. They would face that horror once they rotated up to the lines and another two companies of men were given a week or so to stand down.

Mess was an open-sided tent with a metal chimney poking through the roof, and in the predawn shadows, men were already lining up for a hot meal, something that would also be a rarity at the front. The men ate on the ground, spooning boiled beef, which they called "bully" after the French verb to boil, *bouillir*, from mess tins they carried as part of their personal kit.

This was the last morning of their rotation away from the front, so they looked reasonably rested, their uniforms were cleaned, and any rips or missing buttons repaired. Though they were miles from the fighting, each man had their rifle within easy reach and all looked cleaned and oiled. Bell was able to sense rather than see the apprehension of returning to the battlefield. Their sector was quiet for the time being, but the fear of a German attack never went away. It was a shadow behind their eyes or a tremble in their fingers as they ate or held a cigarette. Month after grinding month was taking its toll and robbing these men of their youth.

Sergeant Major Everly sidled up to Bell. He hadn't realized the night before because the NCO hadn't gotten out of his chair, but the top of Everly's head barely reached Bell's chin. "Figured a civilian like you would still be abed."

"Back in the real word I'm a private investigator. I tend to sleep when I can and wake when I detect others around me are moving about."

"Real Sherlock Holmes type?"

"Minus the seven percent solution," Bell replied, referencing Holmes's famous use of cocaine. "When do we head to the front?"

"Trucks should arrive in about an hour. Get yourself some hot food while you can. I'll find you when it's time to load up." Everly moved away at a brisk clip, but came back an instant later. "Let's have a look at your gear."

He inspected Bell's boots, clothing, and coat and the contents of a leather dispatch bag he had over his shoulder. "Not bad for a civvy, especially the pistol. What is it?"

"Browning automatic in nine millimeter. I prefer the stopping power of the Colt .45, but I am simply a better and faster shot with this."

"You want stopping power, you need one of these." He pointed to the heavy Webley revolver strapped around his waist.

"I hear they use those against rhino in Africa."

"And elephant in India," Everly said in a deadpan. "Listen up, I'll ask Major Fleming's batman to find you a helmet, gas mask, and a pair of puttees for your legs. And you're going to want to muddy up that coat once we're on the line, so you don't stand out."

"Will do. Thank you, Sergeant Major."

"And one last thing. I don't think either of us are used to taking much guff. How about for the duration I'm Evs and you're Bell?"

"Evs?"

"It's what my mates call me."

"Evs it is."

A convoy of trucks arrived at the camp two hours later, muddy and bedraggled soldiers sitting on benches in the rear or leaning over the wood-framed sides of the cargo beds. Some of the men called to one another, comrades who hadn't seen each other in a bit, but for the most part the men coming off the line were quiet, introspective, and ashen.

Bell had heard that their sector of the front hadn't seen much more than a couple of patrols and a few random snipers in months. If this was the toll taken for just defending a quiet section of the front, he couldn't imagine the horror of a proper battlefield, and he was beginning to think he didn't want to, Wilson's conscience be damned.

As with all things in the military, unloading and reloading the trucks took far longer than need be, with time spent simply standing around and awaiting orders that weren't really necessary. It was near enough noon when they were ready to leave and since the mess was opening up for lunch, the men were allowed to disembark and have a final proper meal before their deployment.

They finally arrived at the rear-most battle positions at two in the afternoon. These were fields of artillery embankments, like giant anthills made with sandbags with cannons as big as trucks in their centers. A few were far bigger, monstrous fieldpieces sitting on iron wheels that were fashioned of steel plates and looked like a circle of metal feet. These siege guns had barrels as thick around as beer kegs and could hurl a projectile weighing in the hundreds of pounds.

A short while later they arrived at the first of three trench lines dug into the oft-pummeled earth. The men quickly exited the trucks. Bell stayed close enough to Everly to not get lost, but far enough away to let the man do his job.

The trenchworks were heavily supported with timber balks and boards built into their faces for stability. The floor of the trench, some seven feet deep, was covered in more wood to prevent mud from building up. There were storerooms and barracks built into the sides of the trench and sandbag parapets and bulwarks along the forward rim of the zigzagging trench. Trucks in their convoy had been carrying additional supplies. The soldiers worked tirelessly to unload the vehicles and stow ammunition, food, and crates of military gear.

This was the third line of defense and was the best of the three, having not been overly shelled, and thus was in great repair. A series of connecting trenches ran forward for a thousand yards to the second line. This trench was also laid out in a zigzag pattern to help absorb the explosive forces of a direct shell hit. Staying close to Everly, Bell noted more mud in this trench, some standing water in a few places. Many of the sandbags had been holed by shrapnel and appeared partially deflated.

A farther thousand yards to the west they entered the main trench that faced no-man's-land and the German lines some half-mile distant. It smelled of raw sewage and decay. Clots of mud stuck to Bell's boots even though it hadn't rained in a couple of days. Rats the size of racoons and just as fearless scampered amid the offal. The men barely gave them a second thought. The soldiers tried to keep themselves clean, but in such an environment it was nigh on impossible. Some were so filthy they made Bell think of Appalachian miners coming up from working a coal seam with nothing more than a pick and their bare hands.

It was a thoroughly awful and dehumanizing place, a circle of hell that Dante failed to mention.

"Bell, on me," Everly barked and strode off.

The trench was so narrow in places, especially corners, that the men had to turn sideways and still brushed against each other. Fifteen yards from where they'd entered the main trench, they came to an observation stand, a bench built into the western face of the trench with a dual-lens periscope mounted on an adjustable tripod. Two men were taking turns sweeping the no-man's-land with the device.

Bell followed Everly up the short ladder to the bench. Neither soldier saluted the sergeant major, but there was deference in their stance. Everly took a few moments with his face pressed to the eyepiece as he traversed the periscope from left to right, surveying the disputed territory between the lines.

He stepped back and made a gesture to Bell. "Your first look at no-man's-land."

The trench was paradise on earth compared to the ground laid out when he peered through the eyepiece. Crater holes overlapped each other so that the very large ones might contain the scars from five or six more high-explosive detonations. Skeletal poles for strings of barbed wire rose up from the tortured soil like accusatory fingers. Of the barbed wire itself, there were acres of the stuff, as thick and dense as hedgerow. There was no human way through it, and finding a path around looked impossible. In the far distance, Bell saw brief flashes of movement and it took him a moment to recognize the coal-scuttle helmets worn by the German soldiers. They were working on their own trench, and he caught an occasional head pop up as more sandbags were piled onto the edge of their embankment.

"I see some of their men," Bell said as he stepped away from the apparatus.

"They do that from time to time to dare our snipers into firing at them."

"Why?"

"So their countersnipers can zero in on one of our lads," Everly explained.

"What happens now?"

"We're on the line for a week before rotating to the second trench and then the third trench, while others in the battalion rotate in. Up here, there's no privacy, little sanitation, lousy food, and chronic insomnia. After a week a soldier loses his edge in those conditions, so we keep them on rotation."

"What about during a battle?" Bell asked, thinking of the men amassing to the north for the spring offensive.

"All bets are off. We try to get men off the line, but there's no guarantees. First battle of Ypres, I fought for six straight weeks. Slept in craters in the no-man's-land and pilfered rations off the dead. My ears still ring from all the explosions I somehow dodged."

There was nothing left to say.

The next couple of days went by in a sort of tense boredom. The thought that there were a couple thousand German soldiers eager to kill them less than a thousand yards away was a thought that never left the forefront of anyone's mind, and yet the tedium of the day was a boring routine that seemed to never vary. It was well known that the main offensive was going to happen to their north, so there was no real need to worry about the Germans crossing the no-man's-land, and yet every day, all day, sentries kept watch for movement in the wire, as they called it.

Bell got a true sense of what life would be like for American troops forced to fight in the trenches of Western Europe. Over and above the horrors of battle was the continued misery of living, as one Tommy put it, "like bleeding mole men." One story that stuck with him came from a corporal who'd had a friend vanish wholly when a shell struck their trench, only to have his body discovered a month later when another shell disinterred his corpse.

On his last night before being escorted off the line and eventually to a nearby airfield, Bell handed out the last of his chocolate bars to the dozen or so men hunkered down in a shelter below the rim of the trench. Light came from a heavily veiled hurricane lamp. The dim space smelled of earth and unwashed men. There were three actual chairs, one in which Bell sat at the men's insistence. Everly took one and another sergeant named Moss had the third. The rest of the men sat on their trench coats on the floor. The men passed the bars around, taking a square for themselves until they were all equally divided.

"It's the scorned women who are the most vicious," Bell said. He'd been regaling the men with stories from his fabled career. "I'd rather face down a hired goon or a stone-cold murderer than go up against some of the wives who I've shown that their suspicions were right and their husbands were cheating.

"Early on, I'd bring them on a stakeout so they could see with their own eyes, but that proved to be a disaster. More than one jumped from my car when they saw their dearest one backing out of some floozy's house with her lipstick on his collar. I was too slow the first time and she stabbed him with a steak knife where no man who plans on having kids should ever be stabbed."

That got a collective groan as the men caught his meaning.

"Never seen so much blood in my life," Bell said. "And did he scream like a little girl."

"'Cause he was one," one of the men said to a chorus of guffaws.

At the very edge of his perception, Bell thought he heard a noise under the raucous laughter. He was about to dismiss it and launch into another story about a vengeful wife when he happened to glance at William Everly. His weathered face was creased in concentration as he, too, tried to understand what he'd heard and place it into some sort of context. A moment later the tension left his face as if he were ready to discount the almost-heard noise. That's when he saw Bell looking at him and both men knew they'd heard something important even if they didn't understand what it was.

They leapt to their feet, knocking their chairs into men who were lounging on the floor behind them.

Everly raced for the flap of cloth that covered the dugout's entrance, bellowing, "On me!"

9

BECAUSE OF THE CLOUDS, IT WAS A NEAR-MOONLESS NIGHT, NOT so cold considering it was still March and tranquil for the exhausted men resting against the trench's far wall while a few of their mates manned the observation posts.

Everly's shout shattered the quiet as he erupted from the underground bunker. Men who'd been half asleep roused themselves. They were owl-eyed and blinking as they reached for their nearby weapons.

Bell was right behind the sergeant major, his Browning already out of his haversack. Everly's big Webley was in his hand, a lanyard connecting it to his gun belt. He ignored the soldiers coming awake and ran for the elevated observation platform. Something wasn't right about the men manning their posts. They stood unnaturally with their heads and shoulders resting atop the sandbag parapet.

Everly threw himself up the ladder and grabbed the nearest man's upper arm. There was a little resistance, but the man was sudden dead weight and he toppled lifelessly off the platform. Bell caught a glint of something metallic in the man's hand, but quickly realized it wasn't in his hands but through them. A long knife had been used to pin his hands in place so from a distance it looked as if he were still watching over the no-man's-land.

A moment later the corpse of the second lookout tumbled to the floor of the trench in an untidy heap. He'd been shot with a silenced small-caliber bullet between the eyes.

Everly fired the six bullets in his break-action revolver, aiming generally into the no-man's-land, but not having a specific target in the darkness. The sound was what he wanted. He needed to alert his men to the incoming tide of German soldiers he knew were approaching.

Bell clambered up next to Everly. It was so dark, they dared look over the top of the fortifications rather than limit their vision by using the periscope. There was nothing to see. The landscape appeared black and lifeless, not even a glimmer of starlight flashing off the coils of barbed wire.

A vigilant soldier twenty yards down the line fired a flare pistol into the sky with a whoosh like fireworks. When the shell exploded hundreds of feet into the inky night it lit up with the radiance of a small sun. In the flat light it cast as it drifted downward on a small parachute, Bell and Everly saw a horde of Germans moving across the no-man's-land no more than fifty feet away. Bell had heard the Brits talk about Germans tunneling close to the Allied lines and popping up so close that they achieved near-perfect tactical surprise. He assumed that's what these men had done. They were fully kitted out for battle and had rifles at the ready, their barrels fitted with razor-sharp bayonets.

With the night torn open by the flare, the Germans dropped all pretense of stealth and bellowed in berserker fashion as they broke into a running mob.

Bell gave himself a fraction of a second to let the gut-sliding fear he felt at that moment turn into a surge of adrenaline that gave him clarity of thought and more courage than he realized he possessed. His were the first shots fired at the advancing tidal wave of enemy soldiers. The range was close enough, and the wall of men packed so tightly, that every bullet struck a target, and Germans began to fall.

His first shots unleashed a floodgate of fire from the British line as first riflemen and then machine gunners manning the Lewis and Vickers guns added their overarching thunder to the battle's opening salvo. Sergeant Major Everly tossed a rifle left behind by the dead sentry into Bell's hands. In one smooth motion, Bell swung the buttstock to his shoulder, turned to face east, and loosened the first round at the closest of the approaching Germans.

The bullet snapped the man's head back so viciously that his helmet continued forward for a moment while he collapsed behind it. Bell worked the Lee-Enfield bolt without taking the stock from his shoulder and continued firing until the ten-round magazine was empty, and ten Germans lay dead on the field.

Everly stood next to him, pouring on devastating firepower of his own. He had a belt of ammo pouches slung over his shoulder. Bell pulled two magazines, slapped home a fresh one into his rifle, and took aim at the onrushing swarm. No matter how many they scythed down, two more were ready to fill their place. The range was becoming ridiculously close. It felt as though the muzzle flashes would sear the Germans' greatcoats.

Bell spotted movement out of the corner of his eye in a place where there should be none. It was on the top of the trench to his left, but inside the rows of sandbags placed along its rim. It was a man, lying prone, tucked up against the bags like a spider in its lair. He had a pistol in his hand, tipped with a long silencer, and he was turning his aim to Everly. This was the assassin who'd silently killed the sentries, the tip of the German attack.

With only a second to react, Bell twisted and fired just in front of Everly's face, doubtlessly stippling his skin with red-hot unburnt powder, but saving his life in the process. The .303-caliber bullet shattered the assassin's jaw and punched clear through his neck. He was dead even before he tumbled from his hiding spot and fell to the filthy trench floor.

"Thanks, mate. I think," Everly said, rubbing at his irritated eyes.

The enemy wasn't just taking the brutal onslaught of fire from the British. They were firing back, usually from the hip, as they tried to overwhelm the defenses, so their accuracy wasn't great. Yet so many rounds were screaming past Bell and Everly and all the other brave Tommies who were trying to hold off the attack that lucky hits were inevitable.

Bell felt a round pass through the sleeve of his jacket, and another grazed his thigh like a hot thin wire was laid against his skin. The side of Everly's head was slick with blood from a partially shot-off ear. It didn't slow him at all. They were holding back the Germans in their immediate front, but off to their right, in the light of freshly launched flares, part of the Allied line was collapsing. German soldiers reached the top of the trench and were firing down at the men scrambling below them. One Tommy managed to fire off one of the Lewis gun's pancake magazines like a reaper cutting through wheat, but he was soon struck down as more Germans appeared.

With rifles too long to wield in the tight confines of the trench, the men fought with knives, sharpened edges of small shovels, or with their bare hands. It was a fight of such savagery that these were no longer men, but mindless animals relying on instinct alone to stay alive.

Bell didn't dare shoot into the pack of brawling men for fear of hitting one of the British soldiers. He again focused on the Germans advancing to their left. They would soon overwhelm the British defense on that side as well. It wouldn't be long before the German forces would split around their position and then meet up behind them in the trench, blocking any chance of escape. Everly recognized the fight here was lost.

"Come on," he grunted and leapt off the observation platform, the second sentry's rifle in his left hand while in his right, his reloaded Webley fired at any German foolish enough to challenge him.

Bell jumped down and together they battled their way through the scrum. Bell abandoned his borrowed rifle, knowing there were plenty more to be had judging by the number of dead Englishmen lying on the bottom of the trench. He concentrated on using his Browning pistol, holding it in a double-handed grip and firing only head shots as he twisted and turned his way toward the trench that led back to the second line of defense. His boots sloshed through standing water turned red by blood.

They had just made it clear and into the communications trench when a grenade sailed over his head. He threw himself at Everly's knees as he ran ahead. Both men splashed into the mud and felt the explosive force ripple over their backs. Bell got up a second slow and barely parried a bayonet thrust at his gut by a German who'd followed them. He avoided being run through by swinging the tough leather sack for the gas mask he'd been issued.

He backhanded the unbalanced German and felt the mask's metal canister connect with the man's jaw. Dazed, the soldier almost dropped to his knees, but kept himself upright and started bringing the long knife to bear again. Bell pulled the trigger on the Browning only to realize the slide was racked back against an empty magazine. He was defenseless.

The German forcefully slashed at him as his wits recovered. Everly was still down on the ground, having taken more of the grenade's overpressure, and would be no help. Bell tried to block with the gas mask bag again, but this time the German stabbed right through it in a lightning thrust that nearly impaled Bell in the stomach. The bag ripped apart and the clunky mask, with its full-head hood, long flexible hose, and chemical container at its end, fell free.

In a move even faster than the German's knife thrust, Bell took hold of the hood and whipped the two-pound metal filter around the German's neck. He caught the book-sized tin in his left hand while smashing his foot into the German's right knee. The joint buckled with a slurping pop and the soldier spiraled to that side as he went down. He was now facing away enough so that when Bell tightened the hose around his neck, the vulcanized rubber and canvas crushed in on the man's airway. By the time he tried to stab back at Bell, the veteran detective had placed a knee against the man's spine to better control him and to exert even more force, ratcheting up the tension until the soldier was clutching at his throat with hands that grew weaker and weaker. Bell didn't ease up until the German had gone still for fifteen seconds.

He rolled off the man and lay on the trench floor, panting with exertion and raw emotion. He took only a second for himself before remembering Everly. He scrambled over to the short noncom just as the man groaned and pushed himself off the ground with his hands.

"Are you all right?" Bell asked, loading his last magazine.

Like Bell, Everly needed only a second to recall their dire situation. "Doesn't matter if I'm not."

He lurched to his feet, staggered a few steps until Bell steadied him with an arm. Bell left behind his rifle because he was out of spare clips, and so with pistol in hand, he and Everly shuffled down the trench, following its zigzag course for what seemed an eternity. The air was thick with the sound of constant gunfire and reeked of gunpowder, while overhead dozens of flares burned brilliantly as they drifted under their chutes.

Over the din of battle, Bell heard soldiers running up behind them. Everly heard them, too, and both men turned as an advance patrol of German soldiers appeared around a sharp bend in the trench. The three-man patrol was surprised by the unexpected encounter, but Bell and Everly were ready.

With Bell on the right and Everly to his left, they each fired at the man on their side of the trench, putting them down with a single shot, and then both men fired at the soldier in the middle, blowing him back in a swirl of his greatcoat.

The two men turned and ran on. A few hundred yards later, Everly began shouting "Pomegranate" over and over. Bell realized it was a recognition code to the men stationed at the central defensive line to warn them that friendlies were inbound and not advancing German troops.

Bullets suddenly peppered the sandbag wall over Bell's shoulder, showering him with grit. He dropped flat as the sound of two rifles firing at once crashed against his ears. Everly had just rounded another tight bend and rushed back. Two Germans were above them and were about to jump into the trench. One was in the air when the sergeant major's Webley roared.

The leaping soldier changed direction in midair when the heavy bullet hit him center mass, as though he were a rag doll in a terrier's mouth. He landed in a contorted lump. The second German didn't look like he'd been hit at all, but struck the ground face-first without any attempt to protect himself. He lay completely still, his spine severed by a lucky shot.

"Pomegranate," Everly shouted again as he and Bell continued their race back toward a modicum of safety.

A hundred yards ahead, the earth began to erupt, great clots of mud soaring into the artificially lit sky to be joined by dazzling blooms of rolling fire. The concussion knocked both men off their feet despite the distance and the protection of the trench walls. Seconds later, clouds of dust boiled down the trench's confines, a billowing malevolence that engulfed them in a filthy haze.

"Sapper charges," Everly shouted and coughed at the same time. "They're blowing the trench."

Another pair of blasts shook the night, closer than the first, and then a third and fourth.

"Come on," Everly said and began running back toward the advancing Germans.

Another blast jolted the earth out from under them, the biggest of the night, and once again they were sent sprawling. Bell looked back to the west and saw the connecting ditch had been collapsed by the specifically laid charges in order to prevent German forces from using it as a means of breaching the second line of entrenched fortifications.

"We can't stay here," Everly told him as they got back onto their feet.

"What's happening?" Bell asked. Despite all the action Bell had seen in his life, this was his first time in actual combat and he found the experience wholly bewildering.

"I'm not sure. This is too big of an attack for a simple probe, but not large enough yet to draw forces away from our main offensive in the north." Everly gulped water from a canteen, using some of it to sluice blood off the side of his face from his ruined ear.

"What now?" Bell gulped from his own canteen.

"I need to get you the hell out of here, but to do that we need to get to our lines. Only way there now is on the surface."

Bell immediately grasped the problem. "With Germans shooting at us from the rear and your boys shooting at us from the front."

"You catch on fast. Might make a soldier out of you after all."

There were no ladders to climb out of the trench, so they had to head back toward the British lines again and carefully scale the debris blown into the trench by the explosives. The ground was unstable, and acrid smoke from the blasts coiled up through the loose dirt like brimstone. As they neared ground level, the sound of rifle fire intensified because the Allied soldiers in the middle set of trenches were trying to stop the advancing Germans from reaching their goal.

Bell and Everly had a hundred-plus yards of open ground to cover that wasn't exactly open. Like the no-man's-land to their rear, the Allies had sown the ground between the trenches with barbed wire and other obstacles. Also the land still bore countless crater holes from the years it had been disputed over between the two sides. Some would serve as good cover, others were inescapable pits filled with diseased mud.

Random bullets zipped and pinged near them as they lay on their bellies and tried to acclimate to the surrounding chaos that seemed to draw closer with each passing second. Behind and below them came the sound of men's voices, dozens of them. They were British soldiers making a break from the first trench to the second, running down the connecting dugout, not knowing it had already been blown. It was the headlong rush of panic and it turned out to be something the Germans had anticipated.

A new bloom of light appeared on the battlefield, a directed jet of fire that lanced down into the trench at the pack of running Tommies. They ran into the wall of fire from the German flamethrower and the screams of agony pierced the night. The German carrying the awful weapon raked the stream of flickering death back and forth until the trench was filled with burning men.

The range was too much for his pistol, so Bell took off at a sprint, running hard for the soldier and his flamethrower, heedless of the rest of the battle still raging around him. He needed to take out the shock trooper quickly in case there were more British soldiers trying to make it to their line. With the element of surprise on his side, he could chance getting closer than necessary.

Bell stopped at a hundred feet and raised his pistol. He was so focused on killing the flamethrower bearer he never saw the other one standing on the opposite side of the communications trench.

There was no warning before the roar of jellied oil shot from the flamethrower wand carried by a second team of soldiers. Bell saw the flare out of the corner of his eye, a streaking finger of flame reaching out for him at sickening speed. The merest brush by the wavering jet of fire would turn him into a human pyre.

He hadn't paid attention to the ground around him as he'd charged the first flamethrower team, so he had no idea what was behind him when he launched himself backward. He expected to become entangled on a nest of barbed wire just as the flame reached him and so he closed his eyes and awaited his fate.

Bell didn't hit the ground for a second and a half and he didn't hit the ground at all. He'd thrown himself backward into a crater carved out the previous year by a French battleship cannon mounted on a reinforced railway carriage when this territory had been controlled by the German army.

He splashed into a body of stagnant water a dozen yards wide and sank below its surface just as the jet of flaming oil streaked over the crater like a comet with its tail on fire. Even with his eyes closed, Bell could sense the brightness of the flame overhead and feel its heat boiling the top inches of the fetid pool. He let himself sink a little deeper, dazzled by the light he could see through his closed eyes.

The flaming streak suddenly vanished. Bell swam to the surface and cautiously pulled himself from the water. A sniper from the Allied lines had hit the fuel canister carried on the German's back. He'd vanished along with an assistant carrying a spare tank of fuel in a fiery spire that rose fifty feet.

A moment later another massive gush of fire lit up the night when the sniper found the original flamethrower team with a perfectly placed shot. That fiery blast took out an eight-man German patrol.

Bell dragged himself out of the crater and made his way back to where he'd left Everly.

"Are you mad?" the sergeant major asked.

"As a hatter, according to my wife," Bell said.

"Joke aside, if you were one of my boys, I'd dress you down for half an hour, then put you in for a gong, maybe even the Vic Cross. Damned brave thing just then."

"Futile, too. It wasn't me who took them out, but one of your marksmen."

"Then you can forget all about the VC," Everly said with a gallows chuckle. "Let's haul ourselves out of here. This is far from over."

Attack by night

10

—— ❧ ——

CRAWLING THROUGH THE MUD ON ELBOWS AND HIPS, IT TOOK Everly and Bell twenty minutes to reach the approach to the second set of Allied trenches. Bullets cracked and whizzed over their heads the whole way as the Germans tried to press their advantage and overwhelm the sector. Both men were covered in mud, but at least Everly's inner clothing was relatively dry. Bell was soaked to the skin and the chill night air was slowly freezing up his joints.

"Pomegranate," Everly yelled in a sort of stage whisper when they were closing in on the line. He didn't want the Germans to overhear the code word for a Brit caught in the open, but he also had to be heard over the sounds of war. When he got no answer, he abandoned stealth and bellowed the word at the top of his lungs.

The Tommies firing over them from the top of the second trench paused their murderous fusillade long enough for Everly to shout "Pomegranate" again and flash the silvery side of his canteen as a facsimile of a white flag.

"Oi!" shouted a Brit. "Who's there?"

"Sergeant Major Everly and another man. We were ambushed on the first line."

"Sir. Come through quick like."

Mindful of gunfire still pouring in from the Germans, Bell and the English NCO slithered up to the line of sandbags at the rim of the second trench. When they were close enough, helpful hands reached for them and dragged them over so that they nearly tumbled headlong into the trench. No sooner had they reached safety, the men on the line opened up again with their Enfield rifles.

Bell and Everly were trying to get their breath back when mortar rounds started dropping out of the sky, exploding indiscriminately all around the British lines. Bell had lost his helmet at some point in the night, he didn't remember when, so he took one off a dead soldier lying on the floor of the trench where his friends had propped him up.

The explosions weren't big, but the Germans had dialed in the accuracy, likely from the time they controlled these fortifications. A direct hit in the trench connecting this one to the rearmost line of defense took out several men running up as reinforcements. Another hit an ammo crate left open for convenience that caused rounds to cook off like firecrackers.

"Get out of here," Everly ordered Bell. "Get to the rear. Find Major Fleming. He'll see you stay safe."

Before Bell could reply, a mortar shell hit behind a nearby firing platform where a machine gunner and his mate had been steadily crisscrossing the battlefield with streams of deadly fire. The men took the brunt of the blast on their unprotected backs. Both were propelled forward by the concussive burst and then dropped like fallen sacks into the trench.

Bell ignored Everly's order and rushed for the wounded soldiers. He fell to his knees to check on them. One was clearly dead, his eyes open and fixed. The other man moaned and thrashed and tried to reach for the shrapnel that had riddled his back from waist to neck.

"Easy there," Bell said to the man and restrained his hands so he couldn't do any more damage to his back.

Everly was at his side a moment later, shouting for one of the overworked medics.

One arrived far quicker than expected, his thumb blackened with ink that he smeared in a cross on the wounded soldier's forehead before jabbing him in the arm with a needle.

"What is that?"

"Greek god of sleep," the medic replied, turning the soldier to examine the gashes in his back, some so deep the white of his ribs were visible at their bottom.

Morpheus, Bell recalled, from which the pain-relieving drug morphine's name was derived. He guessed the cross on the soldier's forehead was to prevent him from being overdosed at the next phase of his triage.

"He has a chance," the medic said to himself as the wounded soldier's eyes began to flutter closed with the medication flooding his system. "Stretcher-bearers!"

"Go with them when they arrive," Everly told Bell.

"Forget that," Bell spat back and clambered up to the abandoned Vickers machine gun.

It was a large and complicated weapon with its heavy barrel shrouded by a water jacket that was needed to cool it during sustained fire. The jacket was attached to a one-gallon water can by a vulcanized hose. The box for the self-feeding ammo belt was on a sandbag next to the machine gun. In theory it worked automatically, but in the real world it needed a gunner's mate to help guide the chain of .303-caliber rounds into the receiver without causing a jam.

Everly joined him on the platform, but shoved him behind the weapon rather than the ammunition boxes. "Loading one of these is more art than science. All you need to do is push the button between the handles." As he spoke, Everly checked over the Vickers, making certain it was ready to fire after the mortar blast. "Short bursts only so we don't overheat the gun. Our sector is fifty yards wide. Don't search for targets beyond that. There are other machine-gun nests on the line for that, and for God's sake if you're not sure if a man running toward us is a German or one of ours, don't fire. Snipers will take care of them if it turns out to be a Hun."

Ready to face whatever horde was coming at them, Bell raised his head enough to look over the sandbag redoubt. The first thing he realized was that the night was much darker than before. There were far fewer flares burning in the sky with their phosphorus intensity. The battle was entering its second hour, and the British were running low on flares. They had to limit the number they launched. The second thing he noticed were the flitting shadows advancing from cover to cover across the ground between the two trenches. He couldn't tell who they belonged to, and yet Brits up and down the line were firing with abandon. They were tired and scared and wanted to keep the enemy at bay for as long as possible, even if that meant killing some of their own with friendly fire.

Bell let his gun remain silent. He traversed the barrel back and forth, his eyes never resting on one spot for more than a second. The cold turned his hands into claws clamped around the Vickers' handles. He watched three shapes emerge from a shallow crater, recognized their helmets were the distinctive German bucket style, and slammed his thumbs against the firing button.

Bell had fired machine guns before, but never like this. It was like holding a live electrical cable or a thrashing animal. The big Vickers jerked and bucked in his hand as the bolt ratcheted back in a juddering blur of mechanical precision. Flame shot from the barrel and twenty rounds went downrange in what seemed like the blink of an eye.

The ground around the three German soldiers came alive with bullet impacts, rocks and mud shooting into the air. Other rounds flew past them and dropped harmlessly to the earth many dozens of yards later. However, the majority of the slugs hit their targets, blowing back the men like they'd been yanked by an Olympic tug-of-war team.

He spotted two more Germans leaping up from another crater, assuming the machine gunner wouldn't notice them while his concentration was on the first group. They were wrong. He swiveled the Vickers a couple of degrees and let loose again, cutting them down with a far-shorter burst.

Heat washing off the gun's barrel was a welcome feeling as it hit his face and neck.

"Good, Bell," Everly said with enthusiasm. "Just like that."

Bell nodded, but didn't take his eyes off the battlefield. More and more soldiers were crawling toward the Allied position. Bell felt sure they were all Germans at this point, but held his fire until he was certain.

When he got confirmation he was savage in his action, shooting without remorse or regret at the men trying to kill him. As much as he fired at the advancing Germans, he and Everly became their prime targets. Bullets struck the sandbags with regular frequency, usually from an area outside their sector, since Bell was keeping the enemy pinned down under withering fire. He and Everly had some protection in the form of a metal shield placed around the gun that rang like a bell every time a round slammed into it. Still, being the target of so much gunfire made them feel conspicuously exposed.

N EARBY, BRITISH CONSCRIPTS POPPED OFF WITH THEIR BOLT-action rifles, often not even bothering to aim or expose much of themselves to the German advance. They were kids, their guts liquid with fear and their eyes clouded by tears they couldn't stop from falling. Terror made them shake as though in the throes of some terrible palsy. Corporals and more-seasoned privates were trying to stiffen their resolve, and in many cases the lads found some courage. In others, the fear paralyzed them as if they were already dead.

Before Bell realized it, they'd expended one belt of ammunition. Both men ducked low while Everly fed a new brass ribbon of bullets into the receiver, working the bolt twice to get the rounds to seat properly.

They were just about to start in again when the sky behind them flashed as though the entire horizon was ablaze with sheet lightning. A moment later came a thunderous roar unlike anything Bell had ever experienced. Seconds later came an even more fearsome sound; a thousand high-explosive shells landing one after the other on what had once been a no-man's-land and was now the staging area for the continued German offensive.

The ranks of Allied cannons nestled safely behind the line had roared to life.

Bell had lived through the Great San Franscisco Earthquake of 1906 and thought it was a mild tremor compared to what the artillery shells were doing to the ground less than a half mile from where he crouched behind the Vickers machine gun. Flashes of fire and smoke came with the suddenness of popping corn. But these eruptions were building-sized and chewed apart the German advance before they could fully secure even a single Allied trench.

"About damn time," Everly said with a mixture of frustration and pride.

The rolling artillery barrage went on for the best part of an hour, a tremendous pounding that reduced everything it touched into a sort of overworked loam made of earth and metal and men. Multiple shells exploded every single second, shaking the land as though the gods above were meting out their punishment. There was no pause, no lull. It was a slaughter on a scale Bell could barely wrap his mind around.

The Germans trapped between the current British defensive trench and the continuous pounding of artillery knew their war was over and broke from cover without their weapons and with their hands raised in the air, surrendering rather than face certain obliteration.

When it was over, Bell was left stunned, his ears aching from the sound and the increased air pressure caused by so many detonations in such a close area. Everly recognized the dazed look on his American comrade's face. He'd seen it a thousand times when a new recruit got his first taste of battle. Bell handled it better than most, but the look was still there.

The older Brit said, "When we go over the top for the spring offensive, the barrage will last days, not hours, and on a twenty-mile front, not this localized fracas. And for all the good it does, there are plenty of Huns left to bloody our noses when we launch the attack."

"What was this all about? Why did they do it?"

"To make us divert forces here and delay or even cancel our main assault. We got lucky that our lines held for as long as they did, so the gunners in the rear were able to re-aim their cannons. Had this trench fallen, the artillery wouldn't have been able to hit targets so close and we'd likely get routed. Good work with the Vickers."

"I can't believe you've been at this since 1914," Bell said. "It's inhuman."

"It's war."

11

B ECAUSE OF THE ELEVATED TRAIN TRACKS, DAYLIGHT NEVER really entered the bar on Manhattan's Lower East Side. For that reason the owner never bothered washing the single plate window and thus the interior was a murky gloom that made the faces of the few patrons look ghostly pale as they sought answers or oblivion in the bottom of a glass.

Hanna watched the door as customers came and went. This wasn't her regular place, or even neighborhood. She was here on her brother's behalf, tasked with meeting a man and taking him to meet another man, a man Hanna loved more each time she saw him. She was nineteen, practically an old maid among her people, with raven-black hair and dark eyes. Her independent streak ran wide, giving her a devil-may-care attitude that had attracted suiters since she was fourteen. Her late father had been indulgent and let her choose her own husband rather than arrange a marriage to a man twice or even three times her age.

She'd known the moment Balka Rath arrived from Europe that he was for her, and yet when she was in his presence, she felt like a gawky little girl, with cheeks that blushed red through her normally dusky complexion. She was certain he only saw her as her brother's little sister and not a woman who yearned to be with him.

She sipped from her glass of warm gin as two men who looked like regulars stepped inside and waved at the bartender. Finally the door opened for a single customer and Hanna knew even without the cheap cardboard suitcase clutched in his arms that this was her mark.

He had an innocence about him that she rarely saw anymore. He was maybe twenty, but had the wide eyes of a child and a coward's tentative demeanor. He didn't walk into the bar. He stood in the doorway as if he needed permission to be there. He glanced around, his eyes not making contact with anyone else's, his hands very white against his case's faux leather exterior. It didn't appear that he saw who he'd come to meet and stood at the entrance unsure and awkward. Hanna waited another beat, judging how long he'd loiter before fleeing into the mounting dusk.

She timed it perfectly, sliding off her barstool just as the boy reached for the saloon's door handle. She was at his side in an instant and spoke in an obscure Eastern language she knew he spoke. "Don't leave. You are here to meet Balka Rath?"

He startled, his doe-like eyes widening even further. He nodded.

"I will take you to him. Wait a moment." Hanna went back to the bar, downed the rest of her drink with a quick jerk of her head, and paid her tab.

Outside, she thrust her arm through the boy's, startling him. She liked to pretend to be out on an evening stroll with her beau. "What is your name?"

"Vano," he said in a soft voice.

"In America, that name is John."

"John," he said, as if tasting the word. He seemed to like it. "John."

"I am Hanna Muntean. Did you arrive this morning?"

"I did."

"And the crossing. How was it?"

"Not very good. The waves made me sick the entire time. I could barely eat."

She glanced at him. Even with evening settling over the city, he looked gaunt and drawn, his cheeks sunken and his Adam's apple protruding like a goiter.

"Do you have a place to stay?"

"I . . . I was told that Mr. Rath will take care of me."

She chuckled. "That one can barely take care of himself, but I'm sure he's charmed someone to take you in like a stray puppy."

They walked four blocks through neighborhoods that didn't improve. Kids as feral as dogs loitered on stoops and watched passersby like predators. Horse manure filled the gutters, and the streetlamps threw light that barely made a dent in the darkness.

The tenement she took him to was indistinguishable from a hundred other buildings in the city. Brick front, small windows, seven stories, no elevator or hot water. Privy sitting alone on a patch of weedy ground in the back. Hanna had grown up in a handful of identical places, moving whenever fellow tenants were getting wise to her father robbing them every chance he could. They climbed to the fifth floor and Hanna knocked at one of the four doors. Balka himself opened up. He wore a black peacoat with a dark watchman's cap perched on his head. Seeing his face gave Hanna a familiar twinge at the base of her belly.

"In," he said brusquely and ushered the two inside.

The apartment was sparse, the furniture mismatched, but there were curtains in the window and color pictures cut from magazines pinned to the walls. These were feminine touches. A woman lived here, Hanna thought. This wasn't Balka's place. He'd borrowed it for this meeting.

"Vano?" Balka said, and the timid boy from the old country nodded.

Rath turned his attention to Hanna. He peeled a ten-dollar bill from a roll he kept in the pocket of his moleskin pants and held it out for her. "Beat it."

She found courage at that moment and shot him a saucy wink as she took the cash. "For this kind of money, I'll throw in a couple of other services, just for you."

"Not if you were the cheapest whore in the world and I was John D. Rockefeller."

He'd already turned away so never saw the look of murderous rage on her face that lent truth to the saying about women scorned.

"What do you have for me?" Balka asked as soon as the girl was gone.

"Karl sends you his greetings and this." Vano set his suitcase down on the kitchen table and unwound the string ties that held it closed. He opened the lid. Nestled in the neatly folded clothes was the smallest radio transmitter Balka had ever seen. It was no bigger than a shoebox. Cased in black Bakelite, it had a couple of knobs and a window to display frequencies. There were insulated wires to connect it to a battery and a flexible metal antenna currently coiled up in the valise.

"What are my instructions?"

"Your brother wasn't very specific in terms of what he has planned."

"He never is," Balka told him.

"But he says you are to turn on this radio every night at midnight and listen in on the frequency he has preselected. He will contact you. He said it won't be for at least two weeks, so start listening in on the twenty-fifth of this month. He said you need access to a van and a reliable driver who will be available after the twenty-fifth no matter what."

Balka thought Hanna's brother, Hanzi Muntean, was perfect for that. He owned a box truck the family used to move stolen merchandise in and out of the city. Funny, he reflected, that when it came to an operation involving his brother, he would use only fellow Romani and not any of the trust-funded anarchists he knew.

He missed what Vano said next and asked him to repeat it. "Karl said you are to familiarize yourself with certain landmarks throughout the city, their addresses, and what is around them for several blocks."

The young Romani courier rattled off six names that meant nothing to him, but which Rath knew well. If Karl was thinking of attacking any of these places, his ambitions had grown in the months since the two brothers were together. Not grown, he thought. They were oversized. Balka had serious doubts that Karl understood the scope of what he was planning. He also thought that Karl overestimated the commitment of the American anarchists. These were effete intellectuals for the most part; men who were dissatisfied with being pampered and wanted to pretend they mattered.

Even with a hardened cadre of men from back in Europe, any assault on one of these targets was tantamount to suicide. There was no doubt Balka would do what he'd been tasked with, but he didn't understand it.

Again, the courier said something that Rath missed and had to ask him to repeat it. "Finally, your brother said that you are to treat me like you did Patrin back in Sarajevo."

That last sentence startled Balka. His eyes narrowed. "Are you sure he said Patrin?"

"Yes. Like you did in Sarajevo. He said you would know what this means."

It was one thing to use up local people, strangers. They meant nothing. However, Vano was one of them, maybe not of their clan, but of their people. For such a step, Karl had something big planned indeed. As he'd only made such an order once before.

Patrin Kirpachi had been the man to smuggle the gun from a Serbian paramilitary group called the Black Hand to Gavrilo Princip, who later used it to assassinate the heir of the Austrian empire, Archduke Franz Ferdinand, and his wife. For security reasons, the Black Hand demanded the courier be silenced—permanently. Karl had ordered Balka to do it himself. Balka, never one to shirk a direct order in furthering their cause of anarchy across Europe, subsequently garroted his best friend.

"I'm sorry, kid," he muttered under his breath and threw a right cross that the young man never suspected or saw coming.

Vano was unconscious before he collapsed to the floor with a thud that made the shoddily built structure shudder. His jaw was dislocated, and several teeth were loosened, but he was in a realm beyond pain.

Balka went to the small window and opened it up against its stop. He peered out and down. He saw no movement, and only a little light from the building on the opposite end of the courtyard. No one was heading for the outhouse. He lifted the courier off the floor by slipping his hands under Vano's armpits. The boy weighed less than a hundred and twenty pounds, and while Balka himself wasn't

particularly big, he was immensely strong. He dragged the unconscious man to the window and jockeyed him so that his upper chest
lay over the sill, his arms dangling into the night.

Vano's belt was a length of cord. Balka grabbed it and lifted at
the same time, pushing the young Romani farther out the window. In
moments the boy reached a tipping point and fell silently five stories
to the stony ground below. Enough bones broke that only a jigsaw
master could ever make sense of him.

Balka closed the window and looked around the apartment.
Nothing had been moved or disturbed. The couple that lived here
was in New Jersey visiting family and wouldn't return until after the
body had been discovered, taken away, and likely forgotten. He
picked up Vano's suitcase with the portable transmitter. He would
ditch the case once he found a secure place for the radio.

Stan the bombmaker from a couple of nights ago would be a
good candidate. For the time being he didn't want any of the other
Roma in the area to know he was on a job for Karl. Hanna and her
brother, Hanzi, thought he was meeting a simple smuggler and knew
nothing connected to his anarchist work.

He locked the apartment door behind him, heard a door close
many floors below, and went down himself, no more thought given
to the man he'd just murdered.

12

FRESH TROOPS WERE ARRIVING FROM THE REAR IN ORDERED ranks. The artillery barrage had halted the German advance, but the battle was by no means over. The British needed to retake their primary trench in order to prevent the enemy from consolidating their gains across the no-man's-land in this sector.

Officers were trying to organize a counterattack as quickly as possible. Sergeant Major Everly stayed in the thick of it despite his wounded ear. He'd at least allowed a medic to swath his head in white linen to prevent further blood loss. He berated, cajoled, screamed, and commiserated in equal measure to get his men ready to take the fight back to the Germans. He suspected resistance would be light since the Huns hadn't had enough time to fortify their position, but he had to believe there might be booby traps and other acts of sabotage.

For his part, Bell felt like a third person on a two-person date. He had no formal role other than to stick with Everly, and the NCO had nothing for him to do. He finally told Bell to make his way to the rear and find Major Fleming. Everly saw that Bell still wore clothes that had been soaked through.

It was one thing to borrow the helmet off a fallen soldier. It was another to plunder his uniform. Bell would rather freeze. Everly got some of the new arrivals to give up whatever spare clothes they had with them and soon enough Bell was wearing a mishmash of clothes, but at least he was dry.

"You put up a hell of a fight," Everly said and held out a hand. "Any idea what you're going to tell your President?"

Bell shook the man's hand. "As of this moment I'm going to tell him that he really doesn't want to know the truth, but he has to find a way to end this war."

"Fair enough. Good luck, Bell."

"You too, Evs."

He acted as a stretcher-bearer on the way to the rear. The going was treacherous because of so many men rushing for the front and their patient thrashed in pained delirium on the wood and canvas stretcher. The doctors had tents just beyond the third trench, with light coming from a generator as well as several trucks parked facing the makeshift hospital. There was no room inside for their patient yet and a medic directed them to a patch of grass where fifty stretchers were laid out in the darkness.

Through the open tent fly, Bell observed the doctors at work and thought grimly of how little medical progress had been made in the fifty years since the Civil War. The doctors were busy with bone saws, removing limbs they knew they had no chance of saving.

He took some solace that the wounded had been heavily sedated with morphine.

He moved along, asking the whereabouts of Major Fleming and

getting enough clues to keep him going for a half hour. He did pause when he was offered hot tea and a spot near a barrel filled with burning ammunition crates. He would have preferred coffee, of course, but the dark tea was heavily sugared and warmed him immeasurably.

Bell found Fleming near where they had corralled the hundred or so German prisoners. They had been stripped of all equipment and gear and stood huddled in their great coats, hands thrust in their pockets. They reminded Bell of penned-up cattle. Their expressions were dull, their manner sullen. A dozen Tommies watched the prisoners, plus there was a coterie of guards with Fleming as he moved among the Germans, searching for any officers. With the battle turned so quickly by the artillery, it was doubtful the Brits caught any high-value prisoners.

"Major Fleming," Bell called when the officer stepped out of the barbed-wire fencing surrounding the captured Germans.

Fleming's eyes goggled when he saw the American. "Bell. Where in God's name have you been?"

"Sergeant Major Everly and I were at an observation post in the first trench when the Germans came at us from tunnels dug under no-man's-land."

"And he got you evacuated right out of there, yes?"

"There was no time. We fought as best we could and then retreated to the second trench. He ordered me to keep heading for the rear, but I saw a need on the line and I filled it."

"Need?"

"A Vickers gun crew was hit by a mortar round. Everly and I took over the gun until the artillery chased the Germans back. He's still up there helping organize an assault to retake your trench."

"Already done," Fleming told him. "The Germans evacuated

back to their own line and our sappers blew up their tunnels. Seems you've joined the ranks of Americans fighting for us here in France."

Bell chuckled. "Call it temporary insanity. No matter what, this can't reach my wife. She would kill me."

"I'll tell Winston, of course, but your secret is safe," Fleming reassured him. "Any thoughts now that you've seen firsthand what we've been up to our necks in for the better part of three years?"

"Whether we enter the war or not, Europe is changed forever. There are rumors of revolution in Russia, and after this carnage no one will ever be willing to die for King or Kaiser."

"Do you think Wilson will enter the war?"

"I don't think he has a choice. Our humanity is at stake on these fields, and we need to find a way to claw it back."

"Are you satisfied, then? I can get you on a train back to Le Havre within an hour. You can be in London by dinner."

Bell gave the offer careful consideration. He hadn't been prepared to be thrown into the middle of a battle on his fact-finding tour for President Wilson nor was he expected to be. He was here as an observer, nothing more. He was tired, cold, and hungry, and he already knew what he was going to tell the President, but he didn't consider his mission complete until he'd achieved his goals. One was to see daily life in the trenches, for which he'd gotten a lot more than he'd bargained for, the second was to observe a large section of the front from the air.

He'd seen the war from an individual soldier's point of view. He wanted, needed, he believed, to see the vastness of it all and how the front stretched for endless miles. To accomplish that he had to see it from the cockpit of a plane ten thousand feet in the air.

At last, he said, "As much as I'd like to accept, I can't give Wilson my opinion until I've completed my mission. It would be like making an arrest without first gathering all the evidence. Just because I know someone is guilty of a crime doesn't mean I can prove it in court. I have to stay on this investigation, and to do that I need to head to the airfield Mr. Churchill mentioned."

Fleming nodded soberly. "I would have doubted my ability to read men if you'd said otherwise." He fished a creased piece of paper from an inside jacket pocket. "Give this to Wing Commander Crabbe when you reach the airfield. It lays out your mission and gives Winston's blessing. Sorry things got a little hotter around here than anticipated, but maybe that wasn't a bad thing after all. We need you Yanks, or this bloody thing will still be on when my sons are old enough to fight it."

Bell shook Valentine Fleming's hand. "Good luck, Major. To you and all of your men."

"Thank you. You too." Fleming then directed a corporal to escort Bell back to the rear encampment to get his bag, and when he was rested to drive him to the headquarters of the 22nd Aero Squadron.[1]

---

1 (Author's note: Valentine Fleming, father of James Bond creator Ian Fleming, died in an artillery barrage roughly two months after the events depicted in this book. He was thirty-five.)

13

B ELL DIDN'T ARRIVE AT THE 22ND SQUADRON UNTIL LATE AF-
ternoon the next day. He'd slept far harder and deeper than
he'd expected as a result of the adrenaline dissolving out of his system. After a meal of tinned meat, stale bread, and weak tea, he'd
headed out with a driver. On their way to the airfield, they passed
wagons being used as ambulances to transport wounded men from
the battlefield triage areas to a hospital ten miles back from the line.
Bell ordered his driver to stop and they jammed into the staff car
four men whose injuries weren't so severe they had to remain flat on
a stretcher.

They ended up making six such runs in the staff car, and by the
time the last of the soldiers wounded in the German raid had been
safely transported, the car's seats were sticky with blood and the
interior was thick with its coppery scent. An orderly at the hospital
gave them a galvanized pail with a weak solution of water and car-
bolic acid to clean up the mess.

The 22nd Squadron was deployed fifteen miles north of Valentine Fleming's sector and seven miles behind the main trench lines. It had once been a working farm and some crops still grew wild on the edges of the grass runway. The original farmhouse had been reduced to ruins during the constant back-and-forth artillery barrages, attacks, and counterattacks. However, the large stone barn fifty yards away had been built as stoutly as any modern fortification and had only lost part of its roof and its window glass. Once sheets of tin had been nailed in place to patch the holes and glazers repaired the wooden frames, it had become the squadron's HQ.

Nearby, Royal Engineers had erected dormitory-style buildings to house the pilots, bunkhouses for the enlisted men, and several open-fronted hangars so mechanics could work on the planes with some protection from the elements.

Arriving at the base, Bell was immediately struck by the aircraft lined up between the hangars and the runway. He recognized several from magazine articles he'd read back in the States, but others were unknown to him, especially a big two-person observation plane armed with a Vickers positioned to fire through the propeller and a Lewis gun on a Scarff ring mount for the observer station behind the pilot's cockpit.

The driver left Bell outside the barn after grabbing his leather bag from the staff car's trunk. The afternoon was warm and the sky nearly cloudless, making this as peaceful a moment as Bell could recall. He was even too far away to hear the incessant pounding of the artillery guns. A breeze made the tensioning wires on the nearby biplanes keen like an opera diva holding an impossibly long note.

The interior of the barn was a bit dim because there were so few windows, and while the manure smell had been erased with a thorough cleaning, it still had a scent of dried grass and loamy earth. To

Bell's right was a mess hall/recreation area with an upright piano against one wall and a beautifully crafted mahogany bar large enough for six stools. He guessed there was a story behind both items being hauled out here to the base. He also imagined both followed the squadron whenever they moved.

A couple of pilots lounged on the mismatched sofas and club chairs clustered around a low table that looked like it had come from the same venue as the bar. The men didn't look up from the newspapers they were reading or the game of chess two were playing. Mounted on the wall opposite the room's entrance was the top right wing of a German fighter plane. It was painted a mottled green with its distinctive Maltese cross done in gold-bordered black. The canvas wing showed at least a dozen bullet holes, testament to how it found its way here.

Partition walls had been erected by the engineers on the other side of the barn to create several offices off a central hallway. One was for a flight lieutenant named Baskers and another for the squadron leader, Geoffrey Crabbe. Bell heard two men in that office talking casually. He waited for a lull and knocked on the door.

"Come," a voice called from inside.

The office was spartan and had no ceiling so that light from the barn's high windows reached it. Behind a desk was a moppy-haired teenage boy wearing a proper Royal Flying Corps uniform. His upper lip had the barest shadow of a blond mustache. An older officer with a pipe clamped between yellowed teeth sat on one of the two chairs facing the desk.

"Help you?" the older man asked.

"I'm looking for Captain Crabbe," Bell said, realizing the teen boy wasn't quite as young as he thought and that he had three pins on each shoulder designating him a captain. "And I believe that I've found him."

"Indeed you have," the young airman said with a toothy smile. "And if I'm any judge of accents, you're the Yank Uncle Winston said to expect."

"Isaac Bell," the detective said and crossed the room to shake Crabbe's hand as the pilot got to his feet.

"Geoff Crabbe. This is our adjutant, Lieutenant Horatio Baskers. Everyone calls him Uncle. Though you're not much younger than he is, so I suppose calling him Cousin is more appropriate for you."

Bell was still a little off because Fleming and Churchill's friend was so young. It must have shown on his face because once they'd all sat down and Baskers had relit his pipe, Crabbe said, "I know what you're thinking. I'm too young to have served in the Queen's Own Oxfordshires with Val and Uncle Winston. Well, first, he's not really my uncle, but he is great friends with my father."

"Lord Chelmsford," the adjutant added quickly.

"Yes, yes, Uncle," Crabbe said dismissively at the unnecessary, in his opinion, mention of his father's peerage. "Mr. Bell doesn't care. It was Winston who got me my commission when I turned eighteen and had me posted to the Queen's Own. He and Val were reservists by then. I only stayed with them for a short time before catching the flying bug. And I know I look like I'm still eighteen, but I am actually twenty-four."

Bell finally caught the anomaly that had confounded him upon meeting Crabbe. He did have a boyish face, but he had a veteran's eyes, eyes not unlike Sergeant Everly's—eyes too young to have seen the things they already had.

"To further muddy the waters of my presence," the aviator went on, "a typical squadron is commanded by a major and I am a mere captain. Our last CO, Major Fairley, went a bit dotty in the head and tried to off himself by running into a spinning propeller. We await either a replacement from home or my promotion, both of which I dread in equal measures."

Crabbe pulled three shot glasses from a desk drawer along with a bottle of amber liquid. As he poured he asked, "Winston was rather vague in his telegraph, Mr. Bell. What is it you're here for exactly?"

While explaining his credentials and the presidential fact-finding mission to the squadron commander and his adjutant, Bell took a sip of what turned out to be rough country brandy that went down as smoothly as ground glass and hit the belly like a blast from one of those German flamethrowers. He had always had a strong stomach, especially for alcohol, but this stuff blew out his breath in an explosive whoosh. Baskers's eyebrow went up as he sipped his with the wariness of a mouse eyeing a cat. Crabbe gulped his like it was cold water on a hot day and offered a refill before topping off his glass once again.

Bell concluded by telling Crabbe that he was a pilot himself with nearly five hundred hours of flying time on a dozen different planes.

"No doubt every one incident-free," Crabbe said.

"Hardly," Bell said, grinning, "but I managed to walk away from every landing, so I have that going for me."

"I wrecked my plane so badly on my first solo landing, they had to cut me out of the cockpit," the young Englishman admitted. "Great times, eh?"

"If we have time, I'll tell you about me jumping from a plane's wing onto a moving truck in pursuit of some criminals."

Back came that toothy grin. "I think you're our kind of crazy, Mr. Bell."

"Isaac."

"Isaac," Crabbe said and saluted him with a now thrice-filled glass. "However, I can't lend you one of our planes. Regulations and all that. Simply can't be done."

"I wasn't even going to suggest it," Bell told him. "Since I don't know the terrain here, I'd likely end up miles behind the German lines or halfway to Paris before I realized it."

"Oh," Crabbe said, mildly surprised. "Most visitors we get here are pains in my arse. Aren't you refreshing. Tell you what, we've got dusk patrol in a little bit and then we bed down for the night. Dawn patrol is as it sounds, at dawn, and not conducive to fact-finding and President assuaging. I'll send you up with one of the lads an hour after we get back. Shouldn't take more than an hour of flying time to get a lay of the land and sneak a peek at where our intrepid artillery is turning good French mud into even better French mud."

"That works for me," Bell told him.

"Excellent. Uncle, find Isaac a bunk for the night, give him the penny tour, and make sure he doesn't wander onto the runway while we're taking off."

Baskers stood, his fifty-year-old knees crackling like dry leaves. "Mr. Bell, come with me, please." He led Bell out of the barn and ambled toward the pilots' housing units. He had a noticeable limp, but didn't use a cane. "First week in France," he said without being asked. "I was a reservist in a support role, typist for a brigade commander actually, when a cannon being test-fired caused a horse to bolt. Nag bowled me over and broke my leg so bad the sawbones had to . . . well, saw my bones.

"I wanted to stay in and do my part, so they promoted me once

I'd healed. I got assigned to babysit a bunch of post-teen boys who happen to know how to fly aeroplanes, first with the 53rd and now with this lot of rambunctious puppies."

"The couple I saw back in the barn do look young," Bell commented.

"Attrition keeps the average low. Old hands like Captain Crabbe and a few of the others are the exception. Most newly arrived pilots last just a couple weeks here."

"But there's no shortage of volunteers?"

"None. There are so many wanting to fly that the training back home gets shortened every couple of months to accommodate more pilots. Here we are, sir."

Baskers opened the door to one of the cabin-sized rooms in a long, hastily constructed building with a dozen such units. He closed it just as quickly. Bell caught a glimpse of a footlocker at the end of the bed, some clothes hanging in a cubby closet, and a few personal items on a small writing desk. "Sorry about that. McAllister went down a couple of days ago. I thought his batman would have cleared out his stuff by now. I need to have a word with him. No matter. We have others."

Two doors down, Baskers opened up another room. It was empty and smelled faintly of naphthalene and gun oil. As Bell stepped across the threshold and looked at the bare mattress with a bundle of sheets and blankets ready for use, he wondered how many deceased airmen had called this room home, if only for a short while. Baskers grabbed a folded towel off the pile of bedding. "There's a bath at the end of the building to the right, I'll have the bed made by the time you're done cleaning up."

"Best offer I've had all day. I had half a helmet of tepid water to rinse with this morning." Bell pulled his dopp kit and his last pairs of clean drawers and socks from his bag and headed out to find the bathroom.

He was back in his room twenty minutes later, the skin of his face tight from a straight-razor shave, his mustache neatly combed out, and his hair slicked back with a touch of a custom pomade Marion had made for him at a Fifth Avenue apothecary. His jacket had been hung over the back of the chair and he noted Baskers had sponged it clean.

The adjutant was sitting on a ladder-back chair leaning against the side of the barn, his hat pulled low and soft whispers of snoring coming with each breath. When Bell got closer he noticed the man's eyes darting like mad behind his closed lids. Like nearly everyone he'd met since his arrival in France, Baskers, too, was haunted by demons called up from hell on these battlefields.

Bell knew and understood that the decision to join the war in Europe was Wilson's alone, but he couldn't help feeling that his report put some of that burden on his shoulders, too. He would not claim any responsibility per se, but he was the type of man to accept the consequences of his actions, and for this mission they were the most dire he could ever imagine.

Baskers harrumphed awake and lowered his chair back to its four legs. "If you don't mind my saying, you clean up like a proper gentleman, Mr. Bell."

"That was my first shower in days," Bell remarked before adding, "I have great respect for those soldiers stuck in the trenches."

"They're why my boys take the risks they do," Baskers said as they started walking in the direction of the airstrip.

"How do you mean?"

"The air war is all about preventing reconnaissance aircraft from reporting back to the German command our troop disposition and movements. The first planes back in 'fourteen were unarmed and used solely for observation, but soon enough pilots started carrying pistols and taking potshots at each other. From there the modern purpose-built fighter was born. The men of this, or any other squadron, go after the Hun at every opportunity in order to prevent them from telling their artillery where to fire to do the most damage to our lines."

"They're willing to sacrifice themselves in the air—"

"To save those on the ground," Baskers said. "It's doubly true when the Huns put up observation balloons. They pop up and down as quickly as a vole coming out of his hole and give the enemy real-time intelligence on our troops' whereabouts. They usually have fifty or more big guns ready to fire as soon as the observer telegraphs our position and range down from his tethered basket. Devilish business."

They reached a split-rail fence that separated the base from the runway. There were eight planes taking part in the patrol. Mechanics were clucking around them like mother hens—tightening wires, lubricating parts, checking for any damage they'd missed from the morning sortie. The pilots were approaching. They were so swaddled in flight suits and heavy jackets that the cocky walk they all tried to affect came off as a comical waddle.

Bell spotted Crabbe. His face remained boyish, but his mouth was cast in a grim straight line. The young airman still managed to throw him a jaunty salute as he hoisted himself into the cockpit of a plane Bell didn't recognize. He asked Baskers about it.

"That's to replace the Sopwith Pups everyone else is flying. Called the S.E.5a. Single Vickers gun firing through the prop, and a separate Lewis gun on a Foster mount over the top wing. Captain Crabbe said she can out-turn and outclimb anything the Germans have in the air right now. We only wish we'd have more before the big blowup in Arras to the north gets into full swing."

"And the two-seater still in the hangar? It looks like a B.E.2," Bell said, thinking it was a reconnaissance aircraft put into service before the war.

"Actually that's a new kite to replace the B.E.2. Bristol F.2, she's called. She's a big beast of a plane, but I'm told she's nearly as nimble as the S.E. She can fly fifty miles per hour faster than the old B.E.2 and is doubly armed. She's a fighter more than an observation platform. We should be getting more of each over the next few weeks."

Bell thought back to some of the planes he'd flown, delicate things more suited for children's toys than actually flying. It was just seven years ago that he'd raced across America in an Italian monoplane that looked ready to fall apart without notice. It was laughable to compare that aircraft to these modern fighting machines, with their hundred-and-fifty-plus-horsepower engines and responsive flight controls. His pulse quickened at the thought of going up in the Bristol the next day.

The sun was sinking toward the western horizon when Bell heard the pilots shout, "Contact" to their mechanics and the propellers were thrown and the engines bellowed to life. The roar of the eight power plants sent another jolt through Bell's system. Soon the smell of raw unburnt gas and the planes' mildly familiar-smelling lubricant wafted over the two men.

Once the engines had sufficiently warmed, the mechanics pulled the wheel chocks, and the planes began jouncing their way from the apron to the grass landing strip. Geoffrey Crabbe led the procession of fighters, and as soon as he turned his plane onto the runway, he pushed the throttle to its stop and the plane picked up speed remarkably fast. The tail came up after only a moment and then the whole aircraft was in the air, climbing as swiftly as a hawk, shrinking into the sky as he gained altitude. The rest of the squadron followed suit, although their planes took far more of the runway to achieve flight and lacked the S.E.5's stupendous rate of climb.

The squad quickly maneuvered into a tight formation and turned eastward in pursuit of enemy planes.

"Well, that's the show," Baskers said around his pipe. "They'll be back in forty-five minutes, give or take."

14

ALL EIGHT PLANES RETURNED FORTY MINUTES LATER ACCORD-
ing to Basker's pocket watch, except one's engine keened at a
higher pitch than the others and it trailed a thin train of smoke.
Once they had all landed and taxied, the mechanics were there
again, swarming around the planes to check for damage and to give
the pilots help getting down from the cockpits. A forty-minute patrol didn't sound like a lot, but Bell knew the cramped confines and
unrelenting cold would stiffen their joints as though they were
old men.

It turned out that they hadn't come up against any German patrols and the damaged plane just had a faulty seal. Bell legged himself over the fence to join Crabbe as he debriefed his men in the
gathering darkness.

The squadron commander pointed to one of the pilots, a man
who looked even younger than his CO. "I'm sorry, what's your name
again?"

"Cotswold, Captain. James Cotswold."

"Since this is my first time up with you, I watched your performance. You fly straight enough and keep the formation, but you were staring straight ahead like you'd gotten ahold of one of those naughty daguerreotypes they sell in Paris. You've got to keep watch all around you, sides, above, below, everywhere and all the time. Head on a swivel, as they say. The sky's usually lousy with Huns and our best chance is to spot them before they get the jump on us. Got it?"

"Yes, sir."

"Speaking of Huns, I didn't see any at all. Anyone spot a stray one?"

His pilots all shook their heads in the negative.

"Damned curious," Crabbe remarked. "No Germans aloft since yesterday morning. Queer, to say the least. All right, lads, get cleaned up and we'll eat the ducks Bigalow shot this morning over on the millpond."

There were eleven men including Bell for dinner and only three ducks, so they supplemented their meal with tinned beef and locally made crusty bread that wasn't so old to have gone completely hard. Bell observed that even though they were all young, the pilots had picked up curious habits and tics like old men. Crabbe's was drinking without seeming to get drunk. The fellow who bagged the ducks, Bigalow, blinked so rapidly his lids were like a hummingbird's wings. Another massaged his fingers in the direction of their tips as though they had stiffened from arthritis. Several others had juddery legs or cracked their knuckles every few minutes.

They lived in the most stressful atmosphere Bell could imagine, risking their lives on aerial patrol twice a day, every day for months on end. It was slowly driving them crazy, and what Bell saw was only the outward signs. He could only guess what went on behind the fake smiles and easy banter and shuddered to think of the torture they faced in their sleep.

After dinner, they gathered around the bar and piano. One of them played some up-tempo rags while Crabbe's batman acted as bartender. Knowing he would need his wits for the next day's flight, Bell had only a single whiskey. The pilots were little more than boys and so Bell had no problem keeping them entertained with some of his adventures, especially his own flying tales and his stories about tramping around the deserts of the American Southwest.

He finally turned the attention away from himself. "Did I notice the smell of burning castor oil when you landed?"

"Indeed," Bigalow replied. Like Crabbe, he was an ace, and was the oldest pilot in the squadron at twenty-six.

"I thought by now you'd be using some of the new synthetic oils to lubricate your motors."

"Too expensive, we're told," Crabbe answered. "War Ministry says castor works just fine."

"It's one of the reasons for the silk scarves," another of the veteran pilots said. "Helps us filter out the worst of the raw fumes."

"Let's not fool ourselves, gentlemen," Bigalow said. "Since the laundress can't look any of us in the eye, we all know we breathe in plenty of castor fumes."

"On the bright side," one of the younger men ventured, "it's cleared up my acne in no time."

"I do love a diapered optimist," another drawled.

"Evening, gentlemen," a uniformed pilot called as he came into the room. Unlike the others, his clothes looked clean and recently pressed. He was wiry, with a thin mustache and an easy air about him.

"Thistledown," they called as one. Someone added, "I thought your leave doesn't end until tomorrow."

"It doesn't, but alas I spent my last sou and was asked to leave *mon petit hotel*. I'm now denied a final night in the embrace of a lovely coquette."

"Wait, you were playing lawn games?"

Someone handed Thistledown a glass. He said after a quick sip, "That's croquet, you philistine. I said coquette."

"I thought he was talking about hugging a ham sandwich," another pilot shot out.

"No, that's not right," said a third. "You're thinking of a croque monsieur."

"I thought he was fondling some swamp monster."

Thistledown replied, "That's a crocodile, and I've lugged my fair share in the form of matched luggage from Globe-Trotter." He spotted Bell. "Who's this, then, a new uncle?"

"An American observer," Crabbe told his second-in-command. "Isaac Bell, this miscreant is Reginald Thistledown, a middling pilot and lousy wit. Reg, can you take him up tomorrow in the Bristol after dawn patrol?"

"Sorry, bwana. My leave isn't officially over until noon, and I plan on sleeping until eleven fifty-nine."

Crabbe looked him up and down in a theatrical exaggerated manner. "You do look a bit piqued, old man."

"Oh, I peaked every single night of my leave." He chuckled at his own double entendre. "Besides, Whiddle is more qualified to fly the Bristol."

"God, that man is an insufferable prig."

"Also true. So that makes him a qualified insufferable prig."

"I'll tell him in the morning," Crabbe said.

"Problem?" Bell asked.

"No," Crabbe replied. "Lieutenant Whiddle is a flight instructor sent out with the Bristol to train pilots on its characteristics and the best tactics the Flying Corps has devised for her. He tends to think he knows more about combat flying than we do, even though he hasn't been on the front line in two years."

Bell nodded. "I've met the type before. In my line of work it's usually retired cops who work as bodyguards to rich nobodies and act like they still have the backing of an entire police department."

"That's our man, exactly," Crabbe said. "A sense of unearned superiority."

The pianist finally packed it in for the night and the pilots left the room in ones and twos, each reluctant to sleep for fear of their dreams. Bell remained behind with Crabbe and his friend Thistledown and accepted a second short whiskey.

"I don't know how you do it," Bell said, giving voice to that which should never be discussed.

"We do it," Crabbe said without looking at him, "because we have to."

Thistledown added, "And because if we don't, some other poor sod would be here in our place."

"We also do it," Crabbe said, his voice a little slurred from an entire day of drinking, "because the War Ministry was smart enough to promote men young enough to believe in their own immortality. At least we believed in it when we arrived. A few weeks of seeing squadron mates pancake into the ground or catch fire in the cockpit and jump rather than burn and you become all too familiar with mortality."

"By then it's too late," Thistledown said, knocking back the last of his drink. "You're at once horrified and desensitized to death and just carry on. You just try not to think that your number is ever going to come up, but know deep down that it already has. It's just that fate hasn't caught up with you yet."

"Also," Crabbe said with a gleam in his eye to turn around the solemnity of their previous answers, "and my man Thistledown can attest that nothing peels off a French girl's knickers faster than a man in a Royal Flying Corps uniform."

"Truer words have never been spoken. And also let's not forget the pay, Geoff. That twenty-five shillings a day makes it all worthwhile, eh?"

"A king's ransom."

Bell shook both airmen's hands. "I don't know if I will have a seat at the table here in Europe when America enters the war, but if I do I hope to face it with both your integrity and your humor."

"You think you will throw in with the Allies?"

"I don't think the Germans have left us much choice."

"Good." Thistledown grinned. "'Bout time you're the poor sods taking our place."

The following morning, Bell watched with Uncle Baskers as the patrol left the airfield. This time, the two-seat Bristol joined the patrol, though there was no gunner in the rear cockpit. The instructor, Whiddle, watched it fly off while leaning against the doorframe of the hangar across the grass strip. He noticed Bell standing with Baskers, shook his head, and turned away before the fighters flew out of view.

As before, all the planes returned in under an hour, and as before, they hadn't spotted a single German aircraft.

"Are the Huns taking a holiday we know nothing about?" asked one of the pilots as they huddled around Crabbe in the shadow of his S.E.5. "National Sauerkraut Day, or something?"

"I bet their new lederhosen are too tight," offered another.

"I say they got some bad food, and all the pilots have the schnitzel shitzens."

Crabbe chuckled before giving his opinion. "My guess is they were moved north in order to support their defenses against our spring push. They need to protect their observation planes and balloons as best as they can in order to blunt our attack. It's the only thing that makes sense."

The others nodded at their leader's assessment.

"Let's not look a gift horse in the mouth," Crabbe added. "If the Huns don't want to come up and play, that is perfectly fine with me. Gives the new boys more hours in the cockpit and our mechanics a break from having to fix up our kites. Oh, and Cotswold, much better today."

"Thank you, sir," the boy said, beaming.

Since dogfighting wasn't something best done on a full stomach, the pilots ended their meeting to go and get some breakfast in the big stone barn.

"Ready for your tour, Isaac?" Crabbe asked after a sip from a silver hip flask. "Won't be as fancy as a Thomas Cook outing, but you'll see the highlights."

Crabbe's batman, a lance corporal whose name Bell never caught, came out with a spare flying suit while mechanics topped up the Bristol's fuel and oil tanks as well as its radiator. Bell pulled the bulky fleece-lined suit over the clothes he already wore. He understood how cold it would be up at the operational ceiling of the Bristol fighter, somewhere above fifteen thousand feet. He was sitting on the grass putting on his boots over a second pair of socks when Lieutenant Whiddle made his way over at a leisurely pace.

His eyes gave Bell a dismissive flicker before turning to the squadron leader. "For the record, Captain Crabbe, I want you to know my opposition to this irregular request."

"Noted, along with your other protest at this morning's ops meeting," Crabbe said a little tightly.

Bell finally got his left boot on comfortably and stood. Bell was a tallish man at six feet, but when he stood he felt like one of the Brobdingnagian giants from *Gulliver's Travels*. Whiddle barely reached the level of his Adam's apple. He was reminded of some of the professional jockeys he'd known. He was also reminded how many of them resented a world in which they were forever looked down upon, literally, if not figuratively at times.

Bell extended his hand. "Pleased to meet you, Lieutenant. Bell is the name. Isaac Bell."

Whiddle reluctantly took it. "Know anything about flying?"

Crabbe answered for Bell. "I told you this morning that Isaac is a pilot. He showed me his card from the Aero Club of America. Claims five hundred–plus hours."

"Not only that," Bell said with a note of pride, but not boastfulness, "I've downed two planes. One from the deck of a ship with a Lewis gun like the one mounted there in the rear cockpit and the other in aerial combat." He omitted the fact that during the dogfight over San Francisco his opponent actually blew apart his propeller with a blast from his own shotgun.

Whiddle showed little interest. "The gun is loaded, but you are not to charge it or fire it. You're likely to blow off our tail or shred our upper wing. By the odd chance you spot another plane, tap me on the shoulder and point. Too much noise to shout back and forth. And just don't do anything stupid. Bloody civilians in a combat plane. What's next? A new iteration of the Children's Crusade?"

Bell let the pilot's gripes go unanswered. There was no point. Whiddle had his orders and in the British military that was final. A mechanic held a ladder steady for Bell to climb into the rear cockpit, while Whiddle vaulted up to the forward slot right behind the engine and the big Vickers machine gun.

Bell vs. The Baron

15

BELL HAD A POORLY PADDED SEAT IN THE TIGHT CONFINES OF the rear cockpit with the handle and pistol-style grip of the Lewis gun right behind his head. On each side of him were more of the dinner plate–sized forty-seven-round magazines mounted on pegs. Ahead of him, Whiddle worked the controls, checking for proper motion from each flap and aileron, as well as the rudder. Then he manually pressurized the fuel system and readied the magneto.

"Contact," he called to the two mechanics standing ready by the propeller.

They forced it around with a grunt as Whiddle sparked the magneto. The Rolls-Royce Falcon V12 exploded to life, hot exhaust blasting down the pipes that ran along the fuselage.

Bell had to contain a grin at the raw power he felt shuddering through the airframe. It was like the feeling just before a wild horse broke out from underneath a rider. The power was all there, ready to erupt, but still held in check by the flimsiest gossamer thread. When the engine was up to proper temperature and pressure, Whiddle advanced the throttle with his left hand and a bit more of that power was unleashed. The F.2 began to trundle forward across the uneven field, wobbly on its narrow axle. The two mechanics walked along with her to make sure a wing didn't dip too close to the grass.

By heading into the prevailing winds, the planes of the 22nd Squadron had formed bald stripes across the field in almost perfectly perpendicular lines. Today the wind had shifted a couple of points, forcing Whiddle to cut across some of the shallow ruts in order to keep the plane's nose directly upwind. The takeoff was fast, bouncy, and loud as the motor pumped out over two hundred and fifty horsepower. The tail skid had come up almost the moment Whiddle put the throttle to its stop, and just a short time later the plane became unbound by gravity.

This time Bell couldn't help but grin as Whiddle kept the plane level to build up speed and then they were rocketing for the heavens faster than Bell thought possible. He couldn't see over Whiddle's shoulder to check the altimeter, but he estimated they were climbing at almost a thousand feet per minute. Above the pilot on the top wing was a compass floating in a fluid-filled case. As they climbed, Whiddle set them on a northeasterly course to take them closer to the battle lines, but not close enough to attract any enemy interest.

They leveled off at twelve thousand feet. The sun shone bright, but did little to warm the March air. The bit of skin exposed around Bell's goggles grew numb until he adjusted his scarf to protect himself. The air was thinner at this altitude, but Bell was a man in his prime who enjoyed perhaps two cigars a year, and so he had little difficulty keeping his breathing as normal as if he were standing at sea level.

He saw no snow on the ground and that all the fields still wore their winter mantle of mottled chaff. The trees were still skeletal figures except for the pines, which carried their cloak of green needles. The terrain reminded him of upstate New York farmland or the areas settled by the Amish in Pennsylvania.

But then in the distance he saw something different, something his mind tried to reject out of hand. He no longer saw pastures and fields ready for the plow and tiller. Instead he saw a spreading cancer that was consuming the countryside, a brown stain that looked to be fifteen or twenty miles wide and stretching to the distant horizon, more than a hundred miles away. Smoke obscured great swaths of it as thousands of field guns lobbed high-explosive shells across the human-caused mire. Where they hit, fiery cotton balls erupted and sent geysers of mud and dirt into the air.

This is what the two sides had been fighting over for the past three years, Bell thought gloomily, a swath of ground so corrupted by war it looked like it would remain a suppurating wound forever. From this vantage, Bell couldn't see individual soldiers, but on the Allied side he saw convoys of vehicles stretching back many miles from the front, each bringing fresh shells for the insatiable gullets of the artillery. He imagined the Germans in their bunkers and trenches, hunkered down like moles waiting through a summer downpour, knowing that when the barrage finally ended the real gruesome business of war would begin.

Bell thought back to the optimistic opinion pieces he'd read as the war had gotten underway in the fall of 1914. The fools actually thought it would be over by that Christmas. Here it was, some three years later, and they were still at it, still wasting lives at such a prodigious rate that both sides' populations would be affected for a generation or more.

Just then the smoke began to drift away from the ranks of Allied artillery, carried away by a gentle breeze and not replaced by fresh gouts of smoke and fumes. The guns had gone silent. If doctrine held, the British soldiers would now run from their trenches and charge into a defense they'd been assured couldn't survive such a firestorm, but which invariably had.

Again the altitude was too great to see details on the ground and yet Bell strained to see any movement from the British lines. He thought back to the horror of the night attack by the German commandos and understood the fear striking the men on both sides of the front.

Whiddle's gloved hand suddenly pointed to the east. Bell had been so intent on the spectacle about to unfold down below that he had neglected to check his surroundings. They were a lone fish in a sea full of sharks and he hadn't been watching for fins.

He turned, expecting to see a flight of German fighters about ready to pounce on them. Instead he saw that, several miles behind the German lines, an observation balloon was being rapidly inflated with hydrogen. It was silvery and had a lattice of ropes across its skin like the strings around a sausage hanging in a butcher's shop. Bell recalled his conversation with Uncle and how the Germans used the balloons for spotters to concentrate artillery fire to where it would be the most deadly.

If they didn't knock down that balloon, the first waves of the British charge would be wiped from the face of the earth in a hellish maelstrom of fire and shrapnel.

Even as he cranked the rudder over to charge at the balloon, Whiddle jerked his hand over his shoulder at Bell and made a downward motion with his thumb. Bell looked down by his knees and saw the spare drums of ammunition for the Lewis gun. One of them had a daub of red paint on it. Bell intuited its meaning. Red meant fire. These were incendiary rounds, meant to ignite the hydrogen gas venting from a ruptured balloon.

He adjusted the safety belt around his waist so he could stand and released the lock holding the Lewis gun horizontal in its Scarff ring mount. Now he was free to train the weapon on any bearing in the sky. He popped off the drum of normal lead bullets and replaced it with the incendiary ammunition. After cocking the weapon with his right hand, he wrapped his gloved fingers around the grip, mindful to keep them away from the trigger.

He finally noticed that the plane was diving like a hawk, building up tremendous speed as it swooped downward over the German lines. The balloon was already the size of a barn, but not yet so buoyant that it had started to ascend. Bell saw that around it was a thick defensive perimeter of antiaircraft guns, both small-caliber cannons and machine guns on pintle mounts. The guns were already manned and ready, and even before the Bristol was within range, several opened fire, lofting shells with timed fuses that exploded in deadly clouds below and ahead of the hurtling fighter.

Soon enough the rest of the defenders let loose and the sky around the F.2 came alive with explosions of cutting shrapnel and strings of tracer fire that crisscrossed the sky in murderous ribbons.

They were still too far out of range when the balloon lifted off the ground, followed a second later by a wicker basket for the observer and a tether/communications line secured to a gasoline-powered winch mechanism. Bell had a brief flashback to a Long Island farm and a similar setup used by a German spy ring he'd recently broken up.

An explosion under the plane sent it tumbling for a moment and riddled the floorboards with a dozen whistling holes. Whiddle got the plane back under control and adjusted the nose a fraction to line up on the rising balloon. He was singularly focused and let neither flak nor machine-gun fire deter him.

He finally pulled the trigger on his Vickers. Although the gun was on a timing chain to prevent rounds from hitting the propeller, to Bell it sounded like a normal machine gun. The target was impossible to miss. The bullets puckered the silk envelope as they tore through it, but were going so fast they left behind tiny punctures that seemed laughable compared to the balloon's enormous size. It was like shooting an elephant with a spitball.

They roared past the balloon, barely five hundred feet off the ground. Germans down below fired up at them with their rifles from trenches dug around the balloon's encampment. Now it was Bell's turn. He placed his left hand on the Lewis gun's stabilizing handle and triggered the weapon. It came alive in his hands. White-hot phosphorescent bullets arced from the plane to the balloon in a continuous stream, while brass empties tumbled from the gun's ejector. He saw the rounds hit the envelope, rippling it like it was caught in a hailstorm, but the balloon wouldn't burst. He tracked around as they flew deeper into German territory, keeping his aim true, but still the balloon wouldn't catch fire.

And then he remembered the flammable hydrogen in the envelope wouldn't burn without the presence of oxygen. He raised his aim just as the Lewis gun was firing its last few rounds. Above the balloon was a perfect mixture of air and leaked hydrogen from the hundreds of holes the two guns had made. The tracers ignited the air in a blinding whoosh that burned through the top of the balloon in an instant, releasing a great mushrooming gush of hydrogen that exploded like a sun gone supernova.

The burning envelope immediately started falling to the ground.

The poor observer didn't even have the time to jump before the fiery shroud engulfed the basket and turned it into a pyre. Men on the ground scattered in stark terror as the flaming heap of silk and rope crashed on top of the winch in an incandescent shower of burning confetti.

Whiddle pulled back on the stick to reclaim the altitude they had lost and get them above the deadly flak. The ground fire had paused for a moment when the balloon went up like a Chinese lantern and now that the soldiers had regained their wits, the antiaircraft fire had returned with far deadlier fury.

The British pilot swung them around to head back west and the protection of the front lines when they were suddenly jumped from out of the sun.

There were three planes—all but invisible had Bell not looked up. As soon as he saw the fighters, he tapped Whiddle's shoulder to alert him of the threat. Whiddle went into immediate evasive maneuvers, snaking left and right, but he had very little altitude to work with. They were effectively pinned.

Bell didn't know German aircraft to recognize them as Halberstadt D.IIs. He didn't know the D.II was an older plane, but was being used heavily again while the more modern and far-deadlier Albatross D.III had been temporarily grounded in order to address a lower-wing defect. He didn't know the two planes flanking the leader, one painted in a red and white harlequin pattern and the other black with a yellow nose. What he did know was the identity of the pilot in the middle plane, with its coat of hastily applied red paint, which was about to open up with a kill shot on its first pass.

Manfred von Richthofen had been a cavalry officer at the beginning of the war, but soon switched to flight training. The godfather of German air tactics, Oswald Boelcke, had been a teacher and mentor. Von Richthofen gained an early reputation as a masterful pilot and aerial tactician, and then, in January of 1917, when he painted his Albatross a bright scarlet, did he gain the nickname used by both Allied and Central Powers—the Red Baron. He was just twenty-four years old and a few victories away from his thirtieth confirmed kill. Barreling in on the F.2, he must have been thinking this was going to be another easy one.

Unlike the German soldiers on the ground who'd gaped motionless while their observation balloon plummeted to the ground like a flaming comet, Bell had used those precious seconds to reload his Lewis gun.

Von Richthofen had made the same mistake Bell had when he'd first seen the Bristol fighter and assumed it was an old lumbering B.E.2. He came in straight and fast, believing his quarry was toothless.

Bell took aim, waited for as long as he dared, and let loose a ten-round burst. He hadn't realized the little vane on his gunsight automatically corrected for deflection and so his shots missed the leader of *Jasta* 11 and instead slammed into his wingman's Mercedes inline six-cylinder motor. The engine exploded in a shower of hot oil, burning gas, and scalding cooling fluid. Overcome by the savage pain of such severe burns, the pilot lost consciousness. The plane nosed over and began spiraling to the ground, a greasy corkscrew of smoke in its wake.

Whiddle threw the Bristol hard over, still trying to gain altitude, the big Rolls-Royce engine screaming above the wail of the plane's slipstream. The two Germans kept pace, juking and making micro changes in elevation to throw off Bell's aim. Farther east, the fight drifted, deeper into German territory. Whiddle was a good pilot who never let the German hunters gain an advantage, but he also wasn't able to press the fight to them, either. His combat style was always off the back foot, always defensive.

Bell didn't know that this cautiousness was the preferred tactic the Royal Flying Corps had devised for the two-seater and so his frustration mounted because the longer this went on, the greater the chances the Germans would find a chink in Whiddle's flying and exploit a mistake.

It happened two minutes after the initial attack. Whiddle nearly stalled the plane when he pulled back on the stick too hard. The Bristol paused for a second in midair before evening out, but it was enough for the Germans. Von Richthofen and his surviving wingman opened up with their 7.92-millimeter Spandaus. Bullets peppered the F.2, shredding its canvas skin and blowing splinters from its wooden frame. Amazingly, Bell wasn't hit as he swung the Lewis to give them another burst as they roared past.

He expected Whiddle to engage them with his Vickers, but the gun remained silent. Bell opened up with his Lewis as they looped back to take another pass. Then he took a second to check on Whiddle to see if his gun had jammed.

The pilot was hunched over, his head loose and lifeless. The back of his flight jacket had a line of bullet holes from waist to shoulder, obscene little craters of shredded leather and blood. By some miracle, his safety belts had kept him from interfering with the plane's controls, so they remained steady with a slight nose-up attitude.

The German fighters were almost back on them, coming in a little lower than before to make it more difficult for Bell to hit them from the rear cockpit. He had moments before taking another strafing run and he knew his luck wouldn't hold for a second time.

Bell shucked his seat belt so he could reach over Whiddle's corpse. Taking the full brunt of the plane's slipstream was like standing up to a hurricane and demanded every ounce of his strength. His fingers scrabbled to find the latch for the pilot's safety harness, but he couldn't quite get it. He lost a few seconds' time pulling off his glove with his teeth. He tried again and was able to spring the latch open. Whiddle was a small man, less than ten stone, as the Brits would say, but Bell had little leverage to pull him from the plane and so he would need some help.

He braced his knees as hard as he could against the side of the cockpit and reached around Whiddle with his left hand while holding on to the dead man's jacket collar with his right. With a gentle touch, Bell grabbed the stick and put the plane into a banking turn, mindful he had no access to the rudder pedals. As the horizon swung around and the two Germans were forced to compensate their attack run, Bell put the nose down in a steep dive. He went weightless for a second and would have been tossed from the plane had he not braced his knees. At that instant he heaved Whiddle's body from the seat and let him go. The last sight of him was as he flashed past the Bristol's tail and started tumbling to earth.

Bell felt no pride in his accomplishment, but held on to the grim notion that life was for the living.

He managed to pull back on the stick a little and regain his sense of gravity. He legged over the cockpit's coaming and lowered himself into Whiddle's seat. The fit was even tighter than in the rear manning the Lewis gun. He looked back over his shoulder. To his surprise, von Richthofen and his wingman were a good quarter mile back as they dove to keep on their target. The Bristol had a rate of descent far faster than the Halberstadt's. Bell would need to gain altitude if he was ever going to use that advantage again.

He checked the cockpit gauges as he eased the stick toward his lap. The engine was running smoothly and not showing any signs of overheating. He had hit a hundred and twenty in his dive and now that he was climbing up through two thousand feet, his airspeed was starting to bleed off, but nowhere near as fast as he'd expected. The Falcon engine was truly a marvel, he thought.

He looked up at the compass embedded in the trailing edge of the top wing to see it looked like an empty eye socket. It had been hit by one of the Spandaus' bullets and disintegrated.

Bell searched the sky for the sun, only to find it almost directly overhead. He didn't know which way was west. Behind him, the Germans were closing the gap. Bell studied the ground. The dog-fight had taken them too far for him to see the vast complex of front-line trenches. He recognized no landmarks, knew none of the roads or rivers snaking across the landscape below. It didn't bode well that von Richthofen seemed content to follow him rather than show concern that he was about to fly into Allied territory.

Bell suddenly threw the Bristol onto its left wing in a crushing turn that sent blood rushing from his head. The Germans assumed that with the pilot dead, the observer would have been paralyzed with uncertainty in the cockpit, since few of them had ever trained to fly. They never expected the Bristol plane to go on the offensive.

The nose came around in a flash. Von Richthofen reacted quicker than his wingman and flitted upward just as Bell's Vickers came to bear. The second pilot stayed at the same altitude for a beat too long. Bell hit him with a quick burst by triggering the lever on the fighter's stick. The synchronizing gear did its job and a dozen .303-caliber bullets raked the D.II.

The German quickly winged over into a dive and Bell went after him, his feet dancing on the rudder pedal in harmony with his hands on the stick. He hoped to see a trail of smoke, but his rounds didn't appear to have done any damage. He eased off the throttle so as not to overtake the German. Both men flung their airplanes around in the sky, the German trying desperately to shake his pursuer, while Bell tried to line up the Halberstadt with the center of his aiming reticle. He had very few opportunities to pull the trigger. The other pilot twisted and turned with the grace of an eagle.

Though larger, the Bristol was nearly as agile as the D.II and it was only a matter of time before Bell managed to get in a perfect shot. And just as the Vickers started to spit fire at the gamboling German fighter, a long blast from von Richthofen's Spandau laced Bell's plane.

Bell broke off from his pursuit of the German, having made the classic rookie mistake of not watching all around at all times. He'd been jumped, and that put him in serious danger. The German ace had him dead to rights and the reckoning was about to hit. Bell cursed his stupidity for not seeing the Red Baron coming at him to protect his wingman.

He rammed the throttle forward and dove hard, feeling the dynamic pressure building so that the Bristol's wings shuddered and the tensioning wires screamed in protest. Only then did he try to assess if von Richthofen had done any damage to the airframe or motor. The wings hadn't fallen off and there was no smoke boiling out of the Rolls Falcon. That was about the best Bell could hope for.

He looked over his shoulder. Both planes were in pursuit once again, diving at him like hawks. Just then, a spar on the wingman's plane suddenly splintered under the pressure of the dive. It was one Bell had hit with the last of his Vickers ammunition. The fighter's upper right wing collapsed in a spectacular failure that folded it back and ripped it free from the fuselage. The rest of the wing tore away and then the lower wings came off as if torn from the airframe by some unseen hand.

The plane went from a soaring, roaring mechanical marvel to a manned arrow arcing straight for the ground, its passenger's fate already set.

Bell's altimeter unwound through a thousand feet before he started pulling back on the stick. He'd gotten as much distance as he could from Germany's most famous pilot and now it was time to just run and hope he could figure out the direction of the Allied lines. The Bristol reacted far more sluggishly to his inputs than he'd anticipated and was still diving far too fast. He blipped the magneto to cut the engine so the big propeller stopped turning and became a source of drag to help slow him down.

The plane began to respond, but he could feel there was something wrong, a mushiness to the controls that told him von Richthofen had done some damage after all. The nose began slowly inching up even as the altimeter continued to unwind. Details on the ground quickly grew into sharp focus. He flashed through five hundred feet before he became certain he would pull out in time to avoid plowing into some farmer's field, though that truly hadn't been his major concern. The plane's sluggishness had allowed the Red Baron to eat into the lead he'd built.

The Bristol finally came out of the dive. He blipped the magneto again to refire the engine and looked back. Von Richthofen's red Halberstadt was so close it seemed to fill the sky from horizon to horizon. At any second he expected the black maw of the Spandau to start spewing fire and lead.

But the stream of bullets didn't come. Von Richthofen must have recognized something was wrong with Bell's F.2 because he didn't take the kill shot. Instead he pulled alongside so he and Bell regarded each other from a distance of only fifty feet. The Red Baron stuck his arm over the side of his plane and jerked his thumb downward.

His meaning was clear, and the severity of Bell's situation suddenly cut through the adrenaline jolt that had sustained him since he'd first been ambushed.

He was an American civilian. Flying a British aircraft. Over German-held territory. He was the very definition of a spy and as soon as he landed he'd be fitted for a blindfold and offered a last cigarette. He considered his alternative. The Bristol was flying like a limp noodle and the best fighter pilot in the world was ready to blow him from the sky if he didn't comply.

His choice was clear.

Bell threw von Richthofen a nod, not in defeat, but in the belief that for as long as he remained alive he could find a way out of this mess.

16

THE GERMAN ACE MADE HAND GESTURES INDICATING BELL
should follow him, presumably to whatever airfield *Jasta* 11
had been assigned, as it was now clear to Bell that the elite squadron
had been moved into the sector because of the Allied spring offensive. It was why Captain Crabbe's boys hadn't encountered any enemy patrols. The Germans had cleared their airspace so Baron von
Richthofen and his men could familiarize themselves with the area
with minimal Allied intervention.

Bell waved back that he understood, and just as the scarlet D.II
winged over to head back to base, Bell killed his motor by working
the magneto. He refired it almost immediately and then blipped it
once more. Von Richthofen came back to fly parallel to Bell's Bristol
again. Bell did an exaggerated shrug and then killed the motor a
third time by holding the stick with his knees and using his right
hand while his left was clearly in the German's line of sight.

Bell then pointed down with an urgent finger as if to say he needed to land immediately. Von Richthofen nodded in understanding and threw Bell a good-luck salute. He remained at altitude while Bell dropped low.

The landscape scrolling by under the Bristol F.2 was mostly open fields divided by hedgerows or lines of trees. Some farmland was rutted with frozen furrows left over from the fall, while others had become overgrown in the absence of their owners. Bell had to find one that appeared smooth and was large enough for the plane's roll-out, a distance he didn't know.

He saw a two-lane road, paved and engineered into long straight stretches rather than meandering along with the terrain like so many French country lanes. It would have made a perfect landing strip except it was clogged with German trucks heading to the front with men and matériel. Towed behind many of the trucks were long-barreled cannons on heavy-duty solid rubber tires. They were meant to be easily transported and looked like the guns Bell had seen amassed around the observation balloon he and Whiddle had destroyed.

It was going to be nearly impossible for Crabbe and his squadron of novices to hit the balloons the Germans were surely going to loft in the upcoming battle if they had to contend not only with antiaircraft fire but also the deadly precision of the Red Baron and his handpicked band of aerial hunters.

Bell put those thoughts aside, as his own situation was equally dire. He could see faces of troops in the convoy turned toward the two planes, one a distinctive red that brought waves of hero worship and the other with bull's-eye roundels painted on its wings signifying it as a British aircraft. German soldiers started cheering when it became clear that the Red Baron was about to capture an enemy fighter intact.

Bell spotted an appropriate field, one far enough from the road to give him time to act out the real reason for his charade about a dying engine. The controls remained loose in his hand as he shed both altitude and speed on final approach. Out of the corner of his eye, he saw a pair of Mercedes-Knight staff cars turn off the road at a farm tract and head his way.

Closer to the ground, the plane's nose refused to flare, and so the Bristol stayed stubbornly in the air, buoyed by a cushion of air caught beneath its lower wings.

With a hedge growing ever closer over the engine cowl and the Germans making good time in pursuit, Bell cut the motor entirely. The Bristol stayed aloft for a few more seconds before its wheels kissed the winter-hardened ground. Moments later, the rear skid touched down and dug into the soil enough to stop the plane with a snap that threw Bell into the control panel and bloodied his nose.

The open-topped staff cars were seventy yards away, kicking up dust as they raced to be the first to claim their prize. Von Richthofen buzzed the downed F.2 at less than fifty feet in a blatant display of his dominance.

Bell ignored him. He stood and turned so that he could swivel the Lewis gun in the rear cockpit close enough to pull its locking pin to the Scarff mount. With the heavy gun cradled in his arms, he leapt awkwardly to the ground and ran from the plane as fast as his bulky flight suit would allow. He ran in the opposite direction of the approaching German soldiers, but he heard their angry shouts when they saw him grab the machine gun.

When he deemed he was at a safe distance, Bell turned and opened fire with the Lewis, pouring a steady stream of rounds into a spot just behind the Rolls-Royce Falcon engine. The burst of .303 caliber shredded one of the Bristol's two gas tanks and splashed fuel over the hot manifold. The heat ignited the gas fumes, which ignited the liquid pouring from the ruptured tank. In seconds the brand-new, never-seen-in-combat, and oh-so-prized by Baron Manfred von Richthofen airplane was engulfed in a towering wall of flame that consumed her canvas skin in the first few seconds of combustion and then devoured the wooden airframe.

Bell knew the Red Baron had recognized the F.2 as a new aircraft type and that's why he hadn't shot him down. Capturing the plane in order to study it was a far greater prize than another tick mark on an already long list of kills. Had Bell landed at the German airfield, he wouldn't have had the time to destroy the plane before being swarmed by pilots and mechanics eager to see their commander's prize. He didn't particularly owe the Brits the courtesy of preventing their latest airplane from being captured, but he felt it was the right thing to do.

Until the Germans in the staff car started firing at him as soon as they came around from the far side of the burning plane. Bell tossed aside the Lewis gun, raised his hands, and dropped to his knees all in about a half second's time.

"I surrender," he said as clearly as he could, and added in halting French because he wasn't sure if he was right, "I, ah, *j'abandonne*."

One of the Germans raced up to him and tried to club him on the back of the head with the butt of his Mauser 98. He managed to hit Bell's shoulder with a glancing blow, but Bell went down like he'd taken a haymaker from a prizefighter. Lying on the ground with his bloody nose leaking into the soil, Bell fought the throb of pain with the happy thought that von Richthofen had been denied his trophy. He guessed that had he not been surrounded by German soldiers, the Red Baron would have gunned him down with an aerial strafing attack.

A moment later an officer took charge of the scene. The plane was obviously destroyed and rounds in the drum magazines were starting to ignite with a staccato. He ordered two men to drag the "unconscious" flyer back to their vehicles, all three keeping low in case a stray round somehow found them.

Bell was loaded into the back of one of the cars. He kept his eyes open to slits so he could get a sense of what was happening. The officer sat in the front seat next to the driver, a Luger 9-millimeter pistol in his hand and trained on his prisoner, while the soldier who'd clobbered him sat next to Bell with his rifle propped between his legs. The other staff car rejoined the convoy heading toward the front, while Bell and his escorts drove in the opposite direction, even deeper into German-held territory.

He didn't maintain his ruse of being knocked out for very long. Bell needed to see their route on the off chance he'd get the opportunity to retrace it during an escape. He moaned theatrically and massaged the back of his head as if feeling an egg-sized knot. The officer tightened his grip on the Luger, while the private straightened in his seat, his eyes trying to show some dominance, but ended up looking rather petulant.

They continued to pass trucks and other vehicles heading for the front, but the convoys weren't nearly so dense as before. The road had changed as well. It was no longer straight and level, but twisted along the bank of a small river that had carved a broad bed across the landscape. Stands of trees and thick bushes grew in the rich soil of each river bend.

The driver pulled the car onto a verge overlooking a small section of cataracts that turned the placid river into a stretch of white eddies and back currents. At the head of the cataract was a low dam made of stone and a waterwheel shed that had been blasted to rubble at some point during the war. The waterwheel itself lay broken on its side and partially submerged in the river, its upstream side a mass of tangled branches that had washed down and become enmeshed with its rotting paddles.

The men got out to stretch their legs and share a loaf of black bread and some hard sausage cut into manageable pieces with a trench knife. Bell was pleasantly surprised that he was given an almost equal share and allowed to drink a half canteen's worth of tepid, gritty water. The adrenaline that had sustained him during the dogfight had left him hungry and thirsty.

Three hours after they had started off once again, the driver turned from the road and the staff car started up a series of switchbacks hidden by a dense forest that had so far escaped destruction. Dominating the top of the hill, and thus the valley below, sat an enormous castle. It wasn't one of those Baroque fantasies that the French nobility built for themselves in the Loire Valley and in the process bankrupted prerevolution France. This was a medieval defensive fortification on a massive scale, almost large enough to be called a walled village. Approaching across a stone bridge that had been built over the broad moat, Bell estimated the stone walls were twenty feet high and the two visible corner towers, with their conical roofs, were another fifteen feet taller still. The car passed through the main gate under a portcullis that looked like it could drop at a moment's notice.

The inner courtyard was huge, like a military parade ground. Buildings, both ancient and modern, had been built against the castle's exterior walls, some with dark thatch roofs and others slate shingles, while the newer structures had sheets of metal as their roofs. Through its many open doors, Bell saw the largest of the outbuildings had been the stables and was now converted into a vehicle repair facility. A newer structure was a hospital judging by the bandaged men smoking near its entrance. Everywhere soldiers moved with purpose, some unloading trucks, while others drilled on an open field under the shouts and shrill whistle of a veteran sergeant.

The central keep was as large as a New York City office block, its crenellated parapet soaring twenty-five feet above the ground. Its closed doors were sized for a grand cathedral, though a human-scale door had been cut into one leaf for personnel to gain entry. A massive double-eagled Imperial German flag hung from the parapet.

Bell briefly pictured what the castle must have been like in its heyday, with knights on horseback, ladies in colorful kirtles, minstrels, and grand joisting tournaments. Not that he wanted to live in such a past, but it must have been a sight to see. His revery came to an end when the driver braked hard in front of the keep and the guard put a meaty hand on his shoulder.

The officer didn't bother menacing Bell with his Luger since it was apparent there was no place for his prisoner to go. They led him into the keep. The first room was large and high-ceilinged. Ancient tapestries adorned the walls and absorbed the sound of dozens of uniformed men pounding on typewriters or having shouted conversations through crackly phone lines. The castle had been electrified, but the overhead lights and table lamps did little to dispel the Gothic dreariness.

None of the workers gave the guards or the captive wearing a British flying suit a second notice.

Bell was prodded down a flight of circular stairs and assumed he was being led to the old dungeon, now converted to a prisoner holding area. The air grew mustier and there were a few wet patches on the walls. Lighting was even poorer here and Bell kept a hand on the wall as he negotiated the uneven steps.

At the bottom was a receiving area ahead of a bunch of iron-barred cells. A pair of guards came forward when Bell and his minders reached the basement level. Bell stumbled into one of them as he negotiated the last of the stairs.

He was ordered to strip and place his clothes on a wooden table in front of a pair of noncommissioned officers. As each item hit the table, the Germans inspected it minutely, turning out pockets, feeling along hemlines, making certain there was nothing hidden between layers of fabric. A gold pen given to him early in his career by Joseph Van Dorn vanished into one of the soldiers' pockets. His wallet was emptied of all its cash, which was a significant amount. The men gave Bell a look, daring him to object to the obvious theft. Bell knew he'd get a rifle butt in the kidneys if he uttered a sound and so he kept his face blank and made sure his anger never touched his eyes.

Once the inspection was complete, Bell was allowed to dress again. He didn't bother to put on the heavy flying suit, but carried it draped over his arm. The basement guards walked him down a hallway between jail cells. As they approached one of the cells with a half dozen men already inside, Bell changed which arm he was carrying the bulky flight suit and accidentally jostled one of the guards. The man scowled at him with open hostility, but didn't think the infraction warranted handing out a beating.

The door to the cell was locked. The prisoners inside had been here long enough to know the drill. They backed up to the far wall with their hands on the backs of their heads as the guard jangled a set of heavy keys to open the door.

Bell was pushed inside, and the door was shut and locked behind him.

The men lowered their arms and appraised the newcomer as Bell gave them a once-over of his own. They were all young, fit-looking for the most part, and dressed in various bits of flyers' uniforms. He rightly assumed they were all downed pilots, gunners, or observers. More than one had bruises on their faces.

"Welcome to the rest of your war stuck in a German cell," said the oldest of the pilots and likely the ranking officer. "When did they get you?"

"A few hours ago," Bell replied, and his American accent caused a bit of a stir.

"Yank, eh? Lafayette Escadrille?"

"No. I was an observer in the back of a new Bristol belonging to your 22nd Squadron."

"Ah, Major Fairley's outfit."

"Not sure how long you've been here, but Fairley tried to off himself not too far back. He's been relieved. Captain Crabbe is currently in charge."

The officer smiled and held out a hand. "That was a test. I know all about Fairley trying to tango with his Sopwith's propeller. Every once in a while the Germans sneak in one of their own in a British or French uniform in hopes we spill some vital intelligence in front of them. Hasn't worked because their English is so poor, but I was cautious that one of them could pull off an American accent to throw us off our game. I'm Captain Liam Holmes."

"Isaac Bell. What's the indoc around here like?"

"Indoc?"

"Sorry. It's a jail term for when a new prisoner arrives."

"Ah. In a short while they'll bring you upstairs to the commander's office. He speaks passible English. He's going to ask a bunch of questions about where you're posted, type of plane you fly, and any strategic or tactical knowledge you might have. Chances are he won't like your answers and a guard named Schmidt with hands like hams will take a few whacks at you. Nothing too brutal, but none too gentle, either."

Grimly, Bell said, "Since I know nothing about anything, I suppose Herr Schmidt and I will get rather well acquainted. Afterward?"

"Back down here. They lock us in pairs at night, but let us stay together in this cell during the day. Meet your fellow prisoners. We have John Denton, John Fox, Andrew Longtree, Lanny Logan, and William Baltimore."

Bell said hello to each man and shook hands. When introductions were complete he asked Holmes, "How long have you been here?"

"Five days," Holmes replied. "They interrogate each of us a couple of more times, and then after a week, poof. Gone."

"Where?"

"We assume to a prisoner of war camp back in Germany, internment for the duration and all that."

"I don't think that'll be my fate," Bell said and explained, "My pilot was killed shortly after we took out an observation balloon. I am a flyer myself and managed to get into the cockpit. But I was in the middle of a fight with planes from *Jasta* 11."

"Dear God, are you sure?"

"It was the Red Baron himself that forced me to land, but not before I downed two of his men." Bell paused as a thought struck him. "Looking back on it they had to have been novice pilots that he was training. I doubt very much I could have gone toe-to-toe with a couple of veteran dogfighters. Anyway, you can see my predicament."

Holmes nodded. "Noncombatant shooting down two German

planes and a balloon. Sorry, mate, but you've got a date with the hangman."

"Yup."

Before Bell and Holmes could further discuss the situation, guards started down the hallway from the reception area, their boots clacking loudly on the old stone floor.

17

WITH JUST SECONDS BEFORE BEING TAKEN AWAY FOR WHAT
had been described as light torture, Bell pulled his boot
knife from his jacket pocket and handed it to a startled Liam
Holmes. He'd snuck the weapon into the lockup by slipping it into
the pocket of a guard's overcoat when he'd arrived in the basement
and then retrieved it on the way to the cell when he'd jostled the man
a second time with his flight suit. He'd always been of the mind that
being a putpocket, able to secrete something onto another person,
was far trickier than being a pickpocket and taking it away. Still,
he'd practiced both for many years as a way to better understand the
criminal mind.

"I'll take it back later," he said as the prisoners moved to the back
of the cell and raised their hands. "And tell the men to be ready,
we're escaping tonight."

There were two guards, neither the one who'd unknowingly
smuggled the knife. Once the door was open, one stayed just outside

the cell, while the other came in with a pair of heavy manacles. He secured them around Bell's wrists and led him out. The cell door closed with a crash behind them.

One guard kept a hand clamped on Bell's arm as they escorted him out of the basement, past the main working room, and up another flight of stairs, these broad and elegant, but still dim. The second floor was a long hallway with doors on either side and a window at the far end providing light. The sun was moving closer to the horizon and actually made the passage glow. The guard knocked at what would be a corner room, waited for a bid to enter, and then opened the heavy wooden door.

Inside was an antechamber with an arrow slit for a window. A young soldier was behind a tidy desk sorting papers into open folders. On the desk was a small sign identifying him as Erich Cussler. The assistant stood and knocked on the door of an inner chamber and opened it when instructed.

The room was broad and well lit, with heavy timber beams in the ceiling and wide plank floors. The Gothic windows had ancient glass that let in light, but weren't fully transparent. Behind a desk large enough to land a dirigible sat an officer in a dark beribboned uniform. He was in his fifties, with salt-and-pepper hair cropped close to his skull. He had a Teutonic bearing that he clearly cultivated, what with the monocle like the Kaiser sometimes favored and the walrus mustache.

Standing in the corner of the large office was the guard Holmes had warned Bell about, Schmidt. He was a slab of a man with an almost square head and his hands reminded Bell more of anvils than hams.

Bell set himself the task of surviving the next hour or two and drawing up a plan to escape.

"You are the new flyer shot down today by Baron Captain von Richthofen?" the major asked, his English accented but understandable.

"Not exactly. I was given the choice of surrendering or being shot down. Obviously I chose the latter, and for the record, though I am a flyer, I wasn't the pilot."

"What is your name?"

"I am Archie Abbott, a reporter for the *Toronto Sun*. I was being given an aerial tour of the battlefront for my readers back home when we were jumped by your Red Baron."

The major's eyes flicked over to Schmidt in an oft-used signal and the man came at Bell with a lightning-fast slap to the face that nearly corkscrewed him into the floor. The detective worked his jaw to realign it properly and massaged away the worst of the sting.

"That was a warning about lying. Do it again and he will close his fist. Keep it up and he will use brass knuckle-dusters and finally a wooden baton. Clear?"

"Yeah, ah yes, sir." Bell's jaw finally clicked into proper alignment.

The German continued. "My name is Deiter Kreisberg. I am commander of this facility and in charge of interrogating downed pilots before they are processed back to Germany. I already have reports of an observation balloon being destroyed and the deaths of two pilots from *Jasta* 11. Tell me the truth."

"I really am a reporter," Bell said. "And I was being given a tour of the front. That is the whole truth. During our flight, my pilot spotted an observation balloon being sent aloft on your side of the line. I guess it's standard procedure to go after them no matter what because the next thing I knew we were strafing it with everything we had. It was after it exploded that we were jumped by your fighters. My pilot managed to shoot down two of them before he himself was killed.

"I've been a pilot for several years now and understood what I had to do to save myself. I managed to dump his body from the plane and took the controls. I knew I had no chance fighting a combat pilot let alone a legend like von Richthofen. He recognized my predicament and like a gentleman allowed me to land unscathed."

Bell saw Kreisberg's flick to Schmidt and had time to prepare for the punch swung at his head. He managed to turn enough to only get a graze, but the punch would have been one of the hardest he'd ever taken had it struck clean. Schmidt followed up with a shot to the gut that Bell didn't think he had the time to really throw and so was unprepared. He dropped to his knees. It almost wasn't an act.

He gasped and wretched for nearly a minute, using the time to catch his breath. He had to survive this with relatively little damage if he hoped to make it out of the Germans' grasp. Schmidt seemed to tire of his weakness and hauled Bell back up to his feet.

"That was the truth," he wheezed at the commandant.

"Perhaps," Kreisberg said mildly. "Perhaps not. When I was informed of the destroyed balloon and fallen airmen, I was also told that Baron von Richthofen himself will be coming here tomorrow after the dawn patrol. If his narration of the events differ from yours, Herr Abbott, you will likely die at sundown as a foreign spy. What squadron were you flying from?"

Bell had a split second to answer and weighed his options. This facility was clearly part of German intelligence with a focus on aviation and would undoubtedly know the disposition of enemy forces in the area. It seemed to Bell that Captain Crabbe and the rest of his pilots had been using the old farm as an airfield for some months at least. Surely Kreisberg would know of them and so there was no need for subterfuge.

"The 22nd Squadron," Bell told him.

He missed the signal because the next thing he knew he was back on the floor again with an aching kidney that would doubtlessly pass some blood the next morning. Schmidt's meaty fist would also leave a bruise the size of a salad plate.

"Next time, don't think before answering me," the German officer scolded.

That Kreisberg caught Bell's slight hesitation told him the German interrogator was a formidable opponent and that he had to keep his wits if he wanted to walk out of the office on his own steam. He climbed back to his feet.

"Sorry. I was just told that I might die tomorrow. It took me a second to process that. I'm no spy. I was a passenger in the back of that plane when the pilot took off after the balloon. I am a victim of circumstance."

"What was the pilot's name and the type of aircraft?"

"Whiddle, Weddle, Wendall, something like that. I met him just moments before we took off. They called the plane a Bristol. Beyond that I'm not sure."

"A newer plane?"

With the wreckage burned to ashes Bell saw no reason to lie. "I believe it was a new model, yes."

"I was told by your arresting officer that you shot up the plane in question after you landed. Why is that?"

"I may not be a combatant, Major Kreisberg, but as a Canadian, I am a loyal subject of the king's. I felt it was my duty."

To Bell's surprise, that answer actually seemed to impress the German. He had probably been raised since birth to always do what his nation asked of him. He seemed to have accepted Bell's story about being a journalist because he didn't ask much about his background. He had a few more questions about the 22nd Squadron, which Bell deflected by pleading ignorance. Thankfully Schmidt wasn't called in for any more of his special brand of TLC.

"Very well, Mr. Abbott," Kreisberg said after thirty minutes or so of questioning his newest prisoner, "Baron von Richthofen will be here tomorrow around ten, and your fate will be in his hands. If your story deviates from his I will shoot you myself. Do we understand each other?"

"Your meaning is quite clear, Major."

As Bell was led back to the dungeon cell, he knew that he would either escape successfully tonight or die trying. There was no way he would let that German have the satisfaction of executing him.

18

SERGEANT JURGEN SCHMIDT REMOVED HIS CAP AT THE BOTTOM of the stairs leading to the Ratskeller in the little village down the hill from the castle. This particular tavern wasn't in the basement of the town hall, as was typical, but in a building next door. The atmosphere was smoky and loud. Having such a large military presence in such a small town had made the villagers rather prosperous over the past year, and with no other entertainment for miles around, the pub was usually busy.

He scanned the room for his contact and saw him sitting at a corner table with the woman who accompanied him at times. A half-full pitcher of beer and two glasses sat on the tabletop. Karl Rath saw him, but didn't acknowledge him.

Schmidt grabbed an empty glass from the bar near the taps and went to the table. There were no extra seats, so he hunkered down next to the leader of their anarchist cell. Despite the burns on one cheek and half his forehead, and the eye patch, Karl Rath remained a rather striking person. Not handsome, but masculine and forceful, a natural leader others gravitated toward without understanding why. The woman was pretty, in that French willowy way. Though he had seen Rath in the tavern every three days for the past two weeks, as had been prearranged, this was the first time they'd spoken.

"Who is she?" Schmidt asked bluntly as he filled his glass from the pitcher.

"A woman of no consequence," Karl Rath said. The sergeant looked at her and saw she obviously understood German because his words had stung. Her pouty lower lip quivered and tears welled up in her lovely eyes. Rath added, "She's just cover I brought from Belgium. Locals here leave me alone if she's with me."

"She not part of the cell, then?"

"No. But she knows the consequences if she were to ever betray me."

"As long as you deem it safe to share the news."

"What news?"

Schmidt said, "Another pilot arrived today. We now have the three you said we'll need. But there is a problem."

"Tell me," the anarchist said.

"It is likely he will be shot tomorrow morning."

"What? Why?"

"He claims to be a reporter from Canada, but I have my doubts. So does Kreisberg. He said he was a passenger in a British observation plane when the pilot crossed the line to shoot down one of our balloons."

"You said he's a pilot," Rath protested, his remaining eye glaring.

"He is. They then got jumped by von Richthofen's *Jasta* 11 and the British pilot was killed. This so-called journalist said he dumped the body and took the controls himself. He claims that von Richthofen forced him to land the plane so it could be examined by our people. The Red Baron himself is coming to headquarters tomorrow to give his account of the events. Kreisberg knows the two stories won't corroborate and that the man's a spy."

Rath sat back to consider his next move.

Schmidt knew his place within the cell was precarious. He'd been recruited because of where he worked and because he was infinitely corruptible. He wasn't a true ideologue like Rath and his band of cutthroats. Still, he dared to give a little pushback. "Karl, it's not worth it. The real mission is with the admiral. Your plan with the plane is brilliant, but it's a sideshow, a distraction we don't need. Why take the risk? We can leave now, tonight."

The woman's eyes shot to Rath's face. It was clear she didn't know he was planning on leaving. He pinned her back with an angry stare, as if defying her to speak. She couldn't meet the glare for even a second before her gaze dropped to her lap.

"You just want to save yourself, Schmidt," Karl Rath said, turning back to the sergeant. "You want us to take you to America so that when this war is over, you are not tried for torturing and even murdering captive Allied airmen. A chance for freedom and a little money to help start a new life is a fine motivation for a man like you."

Schmidt didn't exactly like how Rath said that so dismissively, but he wasn't wrong. That was all he wanted.

"Do you know what I want, Jurgen? I want to tear it all down, all of the European monarchies and royal families and anyone else who lived like a parasite off the rest of the people for hundreds and in some cases a thousand years. Kaisers, tsars, queens, and kings. All of them need to be swept aside, abolished, and abandoned."

"Why?" Schmidt asked, not grasping the scope of Rath's ambition. "I mean what's it to you?"

"You understand that there is no opportunity here, no place for a man to better his station in life beyond maybe owning one more suit than his father ever had, or buy an extra hectare or two for the family farm. That's what I want to create."

Schmidt was clearly confused. "A farm?"

"No," Rath said, hiding his annoyance. "Opportunity. Out of the ashes of the old Europe will rise a new one, one where people can achieve anything provided they are willing to work for it."

"You're doing this for the people?"

"Don't be naive. I'm doing it for myself and a group of like-minded men from all over the world who will pull the levers behind the scenes when peace is finally declared, and will mold the world as we see fit."

"So your cell . . ."

Rath didn't respond, believing he'd said too much, though a dullard like Schmidt wouldn't understand. He looked to his female companion, Magdalena. She was a tavern keeper's daughter, not particularly bright and easily controlled. He needn't worry about her, either.

"Enough," Rath said to get the conversation back on track. "I will send her back to her father in Belgium and we will proceed as planned, only we will bump up the time frame." Rath got to his feet and pulled Magdalena from her chair. "Be ready to come with us, Jurgen, and start your journey to America."

19

FOUR HOURS LATER, THE JAIL CELLS WERE QUIET EXCEPT FOR
the occasional snore or soft grunt of a man being tortured by
his dreams. Liam Holmes had arranged for Bell to share his cell that
night. He'd given back the knife as soon as Bell had returned from
his interrogation and together they had sketched out the bare minimum of a plan to get them all out of the prison castle.

Three guards remained on duty in the basement at night. They
usually slept in shifts out of boredom and only occasionally left the
reception area to check on their prisoners in the back cells. Since
returning from Kreisberg's office, Bell had been moaning theatrically and occasionally retching. The guards knew well Schmidt's
handiwork and gave it little thought.

"It's time," Bell whispered to Holmes, who was on the bottom of
the bunk beds.

Bell started crying out as if his very life was in the balance. "Help
me, please," he wailed. "Something is wrong inside of me."

It was an old ploy and usually wouldn't work, but the guards here knew they had high-level prisoners, officers, and that there would be severe consequences if one died while under their eye.

Two guards quickly appeared at the door. Holmes moved to the rear of the cell with his hands over his head. Bell remained curled on the cold floor next to the slop bucket. The door was opened. One guard remained just outside the cell, his rifle in hand, but not particularly concerned. The guard that crossed over to Bell had left his weapon out in the main reception area.

He came to Bell and asked something in German. Bell moaned a pained response and gave the guard no other option but to gesture for Liam Holmes to help lift him to his feet. Holmes came over and together they got Bell to stand. He swayed with an arm over both men's shoulders and them taking most of his weight.

In lockstep they crossed back to the cell door. As they neared, Bell lurched through the doorway into the guard standing outside. In the same instant, Holmes used all of his strength to jam the razor-sharp knife through that guard's uniform coat and shirt, and in between his third and fourth ribs. His heart stopped almost instantly, but even so he would have been able to cry out had the Englishman not clamped his left hand over the man's mouth.

While this was happening, Bell had gotten his other hand onto the back of the first guard's head for leverage and used the one draped over his shoulder to snap his neck around in a spiral fracture that severed his spinal cord.

To keep up the ruse for the guard out in the main part of the basement, Bell moaned a few more times. They quickly searched both guards for keys and anything else that could aid in their escape. Apart from a small pocketknife and the Gewehr model 98 bolt-action rifle, they found nothing useful. Bell left those to Holmes and took back his boot knife, which Holmes had cleaned off on the dead guard's tunic.

Bell left Holmes to drag the bodies into the cell. He padded down the hallway with his knife in hand. The third guard wasn't behind the counter, but there was light spilling from around a partially closed door to a room behind it. He crossed to it and peered inside. The third guard happened to be looking toward the door at that exact second and saw an unfamiliar face. There was an alarm button wired to the wall a few feet from where he sat. He turned to activate it as Bell reversed the grip on his knife and threw it in a well-practiced maneuver. Even as the blade tumbled through the air, Bell was rushing in after it.

The tip of the knife sliced between the delicate bones in the back of the man's hand a moment before he reached the alarm and emerged through his palm with enough force to slam the weapon's small hilt against his skin. Bell was there a moment later, gripping the knife and using his momentum to plunge the dagger into the man's chest. He eased the dying man to the floor and waited for him to expire before yanking the boot knife free.

He took the guard's Luger pistol and jammed two spare magazines into his pants pocket.

By the time he returned to the cell block, Holmes had the other doors open and the other five men freed. They had discussed earlier that while Bell had no choice but to escape tonight or face certain execution, the others had no desire to spend the rest of the war as prisoners of the German empire. Better to risk recapture or death than to meekly accept such a fate.

They didn't know how the drafty castle was used at night, if there were dormitories inside or roving guards, so Bell told the Brits to wait in the basement while he reconnoitered the old keep.

He climbed the stone steps on the balls of his feet, the Luger at the ready, his index finger just outside the trigger guard. Bell suspected that if anyone slept in the building it would be on the upper floors, but still he kept to the shadows when he reached the main level. A single lamp had been left on, a beacon in an otherwise inky black room. He listened. All he heard was silence, as if the thick walls absorbed sound the way they blocked light.

Then came the merest whisper of something. Not so much of a sound but a lack of utter silence. Bell crouched, turning his head to determine the direction it was coming from, if it indeed was a sound and not his imagination. Then came a barely perceptible glow from the big staircase up to the castle's upper stories. A few long seconds later, a guard carrying a feeble flashlight glided down the stairs, the leather of a rifle sling chafing against his jacket being the only sound he made. At the base of the stairs, he paused, training the light left and right.

Bell was hidden behind a desk. Not the best spot if the guard performed a systematic search, but good enough if he just had a quick look around. He kept his breathing shallow and even.

The soldier started ambling about, not looking for anything in particular, but weaving about the large open space as if he had a few minutes to kill. He even started whistling some Germanic opera Bell thought he recognized. The guard approached where Bell lay hidden, his light and gaze swiveling back and forth. Bell tensed, ready for a surprised exclamation when he was discovered. But he wasn't. The man passed close enough to Bell that, had he wanted to, he could have grabbed his leg.

He continued walking around the great chamber for another couple of minutes and then left via the wicket gate cut into one of the massive main doors.

Bell let five minutes trickle by before going back down to get the others. He had been right in scouting ahead. Despite their best efforts, the airmen made more noise than the brass section of an orchestra as they crossed the empty hall.

Bell had them pause at the door. He opened it slowly, staying low so that anyone watching wasn't likely to notice him. The vast courtyard appeared deserted under the silver light of a waxing moon. The castle complex's thick perimeter walls looked black and as capable today of protecting those inside as they had when they were built a thousand years ago.

He kept watch for several minutes. There didn't appear to be any sentries on patrol or anyone up on the walls looking inside. This far back from the lines, the Germans must have felt they were completely safe.

Bell took his first step outside when a teen dressed in chef's whites appeared from around the keep's corner. He and Bell looked at each other in surprised confusion, neither expecting to see anyone out in the darkness. Then the cook's assistant noticed the gun in Bell's hand and recognized that he was in danger.

He turned on his heel and took off like a frightened rabbit, vanishing back around the corner like a white wraith. Bell had no choice but to take off after him. If the cook raised an alarm he and his companions were as good as dead. Captain Holmes had been close enough to Bell to see what happened and took charge of the escape. They had always intended on stealing a vehicle, so with Bell in hot pursuit of the cook, he led the other flyers toward the motor pool.

Bell swept around the corner of the keep, moving as fast as he could. He admitted to himself that he wasn't in top form, especially with his kidney still aching, but he ran with a desperation born of necessity. The cook was ahead, but not really pulling away despite his youth. He had an awkward gait that cost him some speed.

The cook crossed from the shadow of the massive keep to the side of another stone building that looked to be the same age as the rest of the compound. His arms were pumping and his feet slapping at the hard ground as he continued to flee in terror. Thankfully it hadn't occurred to him that he should be shouting his lungs out right about now.

There was a break between two buildings ahead, an extremely narrow alley, a remnant of stoneworkers being given just enough room to erect a second structure as close as possible to the first. Such alleys were common all over Europe.

The cook hooked an arm around the edge of the wall of the alley to turn himself down it as quickly as possible. Bell was perhaps five seconds back. He took the sharp corner as though it were a racing line on a track and shaved another second off the fleeing chef's lead. Bell's shoulders were a hand's span away from either stone wall, which rose three stories and almost looked like they met above, as it was so dark.

He was grateful to be chasing a chef in white and not a soldier in a dark uniform.

Ahead, the cook reached an unseen ramp because he started rising up from the alley floor in an odd, jerky fashion. The ramp seemed to slow him because Bell caught up in just a couple of long-legged paces. It was then that he realized there was no ramp. The young conscript was climbing the walls using a foot on each side to propel himself upward. Bell saw the man had a destination in mind. There was a window opening halfway up that was a shade darker than the stone.

The teen had momentum to help him make the climb. Bell didn't have time to backtrack, so he shoved the Luger behind his back, found a toehold against the mortared stone wall on his right, and used his hands as a brace as he lifted himself off the ground. He found a spot higher up on the left wall and repeated the process, bracing himself with the muscles of his legs while maintaining balance with his hands.

Above him, the soldier was nearing the window. He'd run out of momentum by this point and was forced to climb like Bell. He might have been younger, but Bell had him on strength and sheer determination. Bell found perfect holds each time for his feet as though he could see what he was doing rather than making the climb by feel. It was obvious the cook had done this before, a game he'd likely played with others stationed at the base, but fear made him cautious and Bell was gaining on him once again.

The kid reached the window. It was wooden framed and from the outside he could swing it open toward him. The frame barely missed the opposite wall. He slithered through less than fifteen seconds ahead of his pursuer. Bell redoubled his effort, taking higher steps each time. He had no idea what lay on the other side of the window and needed to prevent the young soldier from taking advantage. He ignored the burning pain in his thighs and the scraped skin off his hands and kept climbing.

In his haste, the cook hadn't closed and locked the window, maybe it couldn't be. It didn't matter. Unlike the German, who'd crawled through the window like a snake, Bell kicked off the opposite wall with everything he had in order to launch himself into the building.

And he nearly fell to his death.

The planks of the second-story floor had been removed at some point in history, so the building was now an open-plan space with soot-blackened wooden columns and a lattice of massive joists where the second floor had been. Bell had landed on a narrow shelf that ringed the building some eighteen feet above the floor and nearly rolled off. A few lights had been left on in what was obviously a large warehouse full of all manner of military supplies. Below the spot where he clutched at the shelf were stacks of razor wire in tightly coiled loops.

If the fall hadn't broken his neck, he would have suffered the death of a thousand cuts.

Bell got to his feet. Like a tightrope walker, the chef was crossing the warehouse on the heavy beams that once supported the second floor, his arms out and his feet dancing like a gymnast's. Bell considered using the Luger, as he suspected the thick stone walls would trap the sound, but didn't know if there were others in the building.

He took off after the cook. Whenever he came to one of the vertical columns that barred his way, he had to stop, grab on to it with both hands, and feel around it with a foot. Once he found the next beam, he used his shoulders to pivot himself around the column and ran after the chef once again. Here he was slower than the cook, and any advantage that Bell had made during the climb soon evaporated.

At the next column, Bell tried to slingshot around it using momentum and almost toppled from his perch into a bin of obsolete *Pickelhauben*, the iconic spiked helmets the Germans issued their soldiers until they realized they were useless on the modern battlefield. He went back to his tried-and-true slower technique at the next column.

The kid had nearly reached the far wall. Bell didn't see anything of note in that direction and wondered what the endgame of this chase would be. That's when the chef came to a complete stop, looked back in Bell's direction, and then allowed himself to topple backward off the beam, his arms outstretched. He looked like a falling crucifix.

He landed flat on a six-foot stack of mattresses for army cots. They more than absorbed the impact and he rolled off the mound with a cat's agility. That was the game he and his buddies had invented—climb the alley walls and cross the warehouse in order to jump onto the mattresses. Young men would do anything to alleviate boredom. Hell, Bell had once stolen a train when he was about the same age as the cook.

Bell didn't wait until he was directly over the mattresses. He leapt and rotated in mid-flight so that he landed on his back with enough force to launch him off again and back in pursuit.

The cook raced for a door that exited the building on the opposite side from the alley. He had to unlock it and Bell nearly got a hand on him, but he squirted through just beyond Bell's fingers.

The soldier darted left toward another building, a long, low affair that had been erected by the German army when they'd taken over the castle. It had light spilling from every window and aromatic smoke coiling from several chimneys. The last leg of the chase was a footrace across a courtyard and the cook found a final burst of speed because he reached the door to what was apparently the kitchens ahead of Bell, though not by much.

The kid nearly yanked the door off its hinges when he reached the building and started yelling in excited German as soon as he was inside the industrial kitchen. Bell bounded in a few seconds later and came to a sudden stop. There were a half dozen men in whites getting ready to feed the garrison their breakfast. Some were stirring huge vats with what looked like boat oars, others were feeding split wood into stoves and ovens, while a pair were working mounds of dough with floured hands.

They all looked up from their tasks as their young assistant tried to explain what was happening in between great asthmatic breaths. The cooks seemed utterly bewildered by what the lad was trying to say, but in a corner near a little potbelly stove a man enjoying a coffee, and the first of the day's strudel, lowered the two-day-old paper he was reading. Bell felt the stare as if he'd been physically poked. He turned just as Sergeant Schmidt tossed aside the paper and came out of his seat as though he'd been launched by a catapult.

20

BELL BARELY HAD TIME TO BRACE HIMSELF. HE TOOK THE charge as though he were accepting being tackled, but then turned just at the last second, grabbed one of the thug's arms, and tossed him over his hip. Schmidt hit one of the heavy prep tables on a shoulder and rolled up onto it, scattering bowls, spoons, and jars of honey.

Bell's hand went to his lower back and the Luger, only to come up empty. It had fallen out when he'd hit the mattresses, but he hadn't felt it because the jolt upon impact had been so strong.

The German rolled over to the other side of the table and stood, his big hands balled into hammer-like fists, a sneering snarl curling his lip. The cooks rightly scattered. As Schmidt turned right to come around the prep table, Bell dashed left to keep the heavy piece of furniture between them. He was in no condition to fight this guy. Schmidt had him by forty pounds of muscle and Bell had been put through a meat grinder over the past week. He needed a weapon. When Bell's back was to the row of stoves, he reached behind him and grabbed an iron saucepan full of some dark bubbling liquid. He hurled it at the German.

Schmidt had seen the attack coming and dodged the heavy pan, but was hit with a spray of boiling beef stock that scalded half his face and cut vision from one of his eyes. In response he threw his full weight against the table in an effort to pin Bell against the hot stoves.

Bell jumped straight up to land on his heels atop an oven door handle and leapt again just as the two-hundred-pound table slammed into the stoves with a mighty crash. Schmidt hadn't expected Bell to be so quick, and so he wasn't ready for the solid kick Bell landed right in his mouth. Had he been wearing the tall leather boots pilots were issued, the fight would have ended then and there. But Bell had been given some insulated boots to help ward off the cold of flying at altitude and the padding at the toe cushioned the blow.

Schmidt was staggered by the kick, but didn't go down. He spat a gob of blood on the floor and rushed at Bell once again. Bell jumped from the table, pulled the paddle from the vat of oatmeal, and brandished it like a baseball bat, clots of porridge scattering off the blade as he swung.

He lined up on Schmidt's head and let fly a one-handed strike. The German didn't flinch. He raised an arm in defense and absorbed the impact on his hard muscles. The paddle just didn't have the weight to turn momentum into force. But that wasn't its purpose. As Schmidt had been watching the paddle in Bell's right, he hadn't noticed him pick up a heavy cleaver in his left.

Bell jumped toward Schmidt as he took the hit with the improvised stirrer and brought the cleaver down in an overhead strike that came with everything he had. The edge of a cleaver doesn't need to be particularly sharp to be effective. Efficiency comes down to the weight of the blade and the strength of the user.

Bell hit the German torturer a fraction of an inch from where his thick neck met his left shoulder. The blade cut through the clavicle like it was a chicken wing, tore its way through the first rib with little trouble, and hacked deep into Schmidt's lung. Bell yanked the blade from the gruesome injury as his follow-through.

The German made to scream, but his lung was already filling with blood. Shock quickly overwhelmed his nervous system and he collapsed to the floor. He'd be dead in moments.

And moments was something Bell had run out of. The cooks were doubtlessly raising the alarm about an escaped prisoner and a fight in the kitchen. He ran out the door he'd entered and saw two sentries rushing toward the building. One shouted and started running at him. The other stopped and shouldered his rifle. Bell was around a corner before he could get off a shot.

Bell had always been gifted with rarely ever getting lost. He had an innate sense of direction that could help him navigate places he'd never visited, often with the confidence of a native. This night was no different. Though he'd never laid eyes on the castle and its complex of buildings until that afternoon, he knew how to reach his rendezvous point with the British flyers.

The first shots rang out seconds later as another patrol spotted him. Bell dove behind a parked truck and searched for the shooters. They were perfectly positioned to block Bell from reaching his target. He backtracked, keeping low and hugging walls where he could. Losing his pistol had been an unforgivable rookie mistake, one that could end up costing him his life.

Searchlights were being turned on, their long beams lancing

through the night as they swept the compound. Bell circled away from the lights and got his first bit of luck since escaping the cell. A soldier had stopped to tie his boot on his way to join the search. He was alone and preoccupied. His rifle was on the ground next to his bent knee. Bell snatched it up and hit the hapless soldier before he knew he was being stalked.

He pulled two spare clips from the unconscious German's bandolier and raced off once again. He spotted another patrol hunting for him, two men walking cautiously side by side, their rifle barrels in constant motion. He couldn't go around them, so he took aim. The first man went down, and as Bell swung to aim at the second German, he raised his own rifle rather than seek cover. It was a fatal mistake.

As was inevitable in a situation like this, frightened conscripts with poor training and a genuine fear of death began firing at shadows. First it was one gun, then two, and soon it seemed everyone had opened fire at imaginary targets. No doubt some of the guards were firing at their own men. Levelheaded NCOs were trying to quell the fusillade, their whistles piercing the night.

Bell stuck to the shadows and avoided areas where the guns seemed the loudest. He was forced to backtrack several times to avoid roving patrols. He had to end this soon, as more and more men were turning out of their barracks. He was at the back of the keep, crawling on his belly because he was so exposed, when someone spotted him. The shot blew chips off a stone block an inch from his head. He wriggled to face the gunman, swinging the rifle to his shoulder in a classic prone shooting position. The gunman had just finished cycling the bolt closed when Bell spotted him and fired the only bullet he would need.

Bell got to his feet and started running. There were just too many

Germans out hunting him for him to try for stealth. He could only hope the Brits had done their part. At the corner, he paused. The old stables that the Germans had converted to a motor pool sat directly across from him, its doors sealed for the night. That was his destination. He'd tasked the flyers with getting a vehicle to make their getaway. He just hadn't expected the whole castle to be awake to make that task all but impossible now.

Five soldiers stood in front of the main door to the space, their rifles held at their waists, but they appeared alert. The back of the stables was the castle's main perimeter wall, so there was no sneaking around the building looking for a rear entrance, and from where Bell crouched he couldn't see a side door, either.

This wasn't a stalemate because eventually the Germans would recapture him. He had to move, even if a frontal assault was tantamount to a suicide charge. He replaced the clip in his rifle with a fresh one and was about to take out the first German when the tall door behind them suddenly exploded outward in a burst of splintered wood.

Emerging through the carnage like an enraged bull after a matador was a captured Mark II tank, one of Britain's latest weapons. It was a beast of a machine, some twenty-six feet long, thirteen feet wide, and eight feet tall. It weighed in at just under thirty tons. To accommodate crossing wide trenches, the vehicle was essentially a large rhombus with the tracks on the very perimeter and its guns mounted in big boxy sponsons that jutted out from the sides.

Four of the Germans had fast-enough reflexes to leap out of the way of the charging tank. One poor fellow didn't and vanished under its heavy steel tread.

Liam Holmes emerged from a hatch at the top of the massive vehicle brandishing a Spandau light machine gun, its ammo belt swaying like a shiny brass ribbon. Accustomed to firing from a moving airplane at other moving airplanes, he had little trouble mowing down the stunned German guards while atop a lumbering tank.

The gun threw long tongues of flame as he raked the guards in the immediate area, clearing the way for Bell to break cover and rush at the tank. The side hatches were closed because the Brits didn't know what they'd be facing once they escaped the motor pool, so he raced to the back of the crawling tank and leapt onto one of the moving tracks. It swept him upward with a jerk that nearly threw him back to the ground. He found his balance as he reached the top of the tank and jumped onto the armored decking just behind Holmes.

"A tank?" Bell shouted incredulously.

"Only Fox and I are pilots. The others were all gunners who got their start in the tank corps," Holmes replied. "And when we heard all the gunfire we figured better safe in one of these than in some open truck."

As they rumbled across the inner courtyard, Bell and Holmes climbed inside the steel monster. Two of the former tank crew were at the back of the vehicle working the mechanical clutches that controlled each track in order to steer the vehicle. They were taking cues from one of the other former tankers up in the front of the vehicle who was looking through a periscope.

It was already hot in the surprisingly cramped interior. There was just barely enough light to see. The engine was placed in the center of the crew compartment and leaked exhaust at dangerous levels. Bell's eyes watered at the chemical stench. He decided then and there that the inside of a tank was a hellish place.

Now that Holmes was no longer firing the Spandau, German guards began taking potshots at the Mark II, their bullets pinging harmlessly against the armor. However, the sheer volume of their

fire made it sound like they were trapped inside a continuously ringing bell.

The Mark II was notoriously underpowered, and thus slow, capable of barely moving above a walking pace. The Germans who'd
captured her, forever the great tinkerers of Europe, had replaced the
Foster-Daimler engine with a Mercedes power plant with twice the
horsepower. The driving was erratic because of the increased speed
and the unfamiliarity of its new crew, but they got the tank across
the courtyard and were quickly approaching the main gate.

It was then that the huge portcullis dropped from the gate tower
with a solid crash and now blocked the castle's only exit. The tank
braked to a stop. Bell and Holmes rushed forward to peer through
the driver's periscope. The wood that comprised the latticed gate
was far too thick for the vehicle to crash through like they had back
at the motor pool. And remaining stationary would make them vulnerable to hand grenades or a carefully placed satchel charge.

Holmes and Bell rushed back to the sponson-housed 57-millimeter
Hotchkiss cannons. Bell had never fired such a weapon before, but
it was a straightforward design and he could intuit how it all worked.
He slid one of the heavy high-explosive shells into the breach and
closed it by rotating a lever and put a hand around the grip/trigger
assembly. He sighted through the brass telescope atop the gun and
moved it via a long, padded handle.

He quickly lined up the gun at the stonework just above the portcullis and fired. The sound inside the tank was an assault to the ears
that was physically painful. The explosive shell detonated almost
immediately, cratering a barrel-sized hole in the stone. Debris
crashed to the ground amid waves of dust. Holmes took his shot as
Bell reloaded his gun. More of the stone and wood framing that kept
the gate upright was blown away.

One of the brakemen had taken the Spandau back through the roof hatch and was hammering away at any Germans daring to approach the renegade tank while Bell and Holmes fired salvo after salvo until the top of the gatehouse was a shattered ruin and the portcullis swayed like an unsecured garden gate. One last shot from Holmes's Hotchkiss six-pounder blew the last remaining link between the portcullis and the castle and it crashed to the ground atop a pile of rubble.

The tank lurched into motion, a signal to the topside machine gunner to get back into position. They lumbered through the ruined gate, climbing up the mountain of debris until the tank reached a tipping point at the top and crashed down on the far side in a jarring collision that nearly sent Bell tumbling. Unharmed, they continued on. The left sponson scraped against the side of the gate because they weren't perfectly centered, but they made it through as the Germans pummeled the rear of the tank with rifle fire.

They started across the long stone bridge, accelerating to get out of the reach of the pursuing German soldiers. The tank wasn't fast enough, even with its new engine. They were taking too much fire and someone was bound to go after them with an anti-tank gun capable of shredding one of the caterpillar treads.

Bell tapped the driver's shoulder and made a rotating gesture with his hands. The man understood and signaled the clutch operators in the rear. He then slowed the tank to barely a crawl and had the right-side tread stop completely. The Mark II turned on its own axis, coming around in one long smooth arc. Bell was already back at his gunner's position. He lowered the gun's aim and fired. The high explosive slammed into the roadway in between two of the bridge's anchoring piers.

Ears ringing, he shouted over to Holmes, "Hit the same spot."

The Brit caught what Bell was up to and together the two sent a dozen high-explosive shells into the ancient structure. Each explosion tore more stones out of position, adding to the load the rest had to carry for the bridge to remain intact. Three more shells slammed into the structure and it was all the punishment the old span could take. As if in slow motion, mortared rocks began falling from under the arch, first in ones and twos and then more. Finally, in a catastrophic moment the section of bridge between their solid supports collapsed into the moat, sending waves expanding outward like miniature tsunamis.

The driver spun them around once again and continued their journey of escape. For good measure he rammed several telephone poles that stood on the edge of the remaining bridge sections, knocking them flat and snapping the wires. The Germans at the castle were effectively cut off.

They trundled along for another few minutes, Bell and Holmes sitting on top of the tank to get away from the unmuffled engine's roar and stink. Bell spotted something up ahead and was about to shout a warning, when a blast erupted from a hidden bunker and a cannon shell shrieked through the night.

21

WHAT BELL HAD SPOTTED WAS A SANDBAGGED REDOUBT FOR a sentry gun. It was a Krupp FK 96, an older-model field cannon that was being replaced in frontline units because of its poor range. But firing this night at the rampaging tank, the range was point-blank.

The 77-millimeter armor-piercing shell hit the left track just below its return roller. The tread came apart in a spectacular shower of shrapnel, some of which penetrated the Mark II armor, but fortunately didn't hit any of the men. The tank slewed hard to the left as the right tread kept working, while the left was torn off the vehicle.

Knowing how quickly he could load and fire the tank's cannon as a rank amateur, Bell assumed a trained German gun crew could get another round into the tank in a handful of seconds. He and Holmes jumped free of the vulnerable Mark II just as the door in the left sponson was thrown open and the men came out in a diving rush. The field gun spat once more, and this time the shell tore through the half-inch armor and slammed into the engine block with enough kinetic energy to tear it from its mounts.

Gasoline gushed from the ruptured line, igniting seconds later, so the last man out of the tank was chased by a roiling ball of flame. Fire and smoke billowed from the hatch the Germans had installed to swap out the engine and very soon the buildup of heat caused the ammunition to reach a critical temperature. Fifty-seven-millimeter rounds started going off, their propellant charges and warheads detonating with enough force to rip the tank's armor like paper. Bell and the Allied flyers raced for a ditch along the side of the road and hunkered down as the tank lit off like some nightmare fireworks show.

Two hundred yards down the road, the German gun crew sheltered behind their cannon's splinter shield until the last of the ammunition had gone off and the tank sat quiet save the flames still eating away the paint and the last of the engine oil.

Bell looked at the woods a hundred yards off and thought about making a run for it. It was still dark enough to give him some cover, but it was too much of an obvious plan. The Germans would be on him like a pack of dogs before he got halfway. Better to wait for a better opportunity in whatever chaos the night still held.

The escapees rose to their feet and raised their arms when six armed guards rushed past the tank and surrounded them. They were then marched to the gun emplacement.

While the FK 96 needed a five-man crew, the sandbagged defensive position was big enough for a ten-man complement to guard the road leading to the castle. They had gotten word from the German headquarters about the renegade tank before the telephone wires came down because the field cannon usually pointed up the road and not back at the castle, as it was now.

With a rifle barrel, one of the guards told them where to sit and he and another guard stood over them while the crew returned their gun to its proper position and swabbed out the barrel and lubricated the breach. Bell could tell they were unsure and apprehensive without direct contact with their superiors back in the castle.

Holmes noticed it, too, and whispered, "There is opportunity in disarray."

Bell nodded and watched.

After a few minutes with nothing to do, the squad sergeant, who looked young enough for this to be his first command, sent a private and a corporal back to the castle to assess the situation there and possibly receive fresh orders concerning the recaptured airmen.

A couple of the gunners ate an early breakfast of slightly molded bread and cheese. Bell wasn't particularly hungry, but the water sloshing in their canteens worsened his thirst. He pointed to a canteen, but was ignored.

A truck arriving from the main road at the bottom of the valley started lumbering up the access road, its engine struggling with the gradient. They couldn't yet see the vehicle, nor its headlights in the darkness, but they could follow its progress by the sound of its overtaxed motor.

When it finally hove into view around a final bend in the road, the young sergeant was on his feet to greet the newcomers. The truck was a typical three-ton Daimler with a four-cylinder engine and solid rubber tires that made riding in one a bone-jarring experience. It braked to a stop. The sergeant approached the driver's door, saw the rank of the man behind the wheel, and snapped a crisp salute.

They spoke for a few moments, the officer in the truck pointing to Bell and his group of captives and asking about them. The sergeant gave him an answer that somehow displeased the driver. He stepped out of the truck. Bell could see he was a large man, a commanding presence that made the sergeant take an involuntary step back. The light from the sentries' fire was erratic, but it looked to Bell that the man's face was scarred, and he had a patch covering a missing right eye.

What happened next took Bell several seconds to process. The big driver pulled a gun from his hip holster and shot the sergeant in the chest as four men leapt from the back of the truck and began gunning down the rest of the soldiers. Bell felt bullets passing over his head as he sat under the watch of the two guards. They were the next to die, struck multiple times and collapsing in formless heaps. The remainder of the gun crew weren't armed, so they put up no resistance. Raised hands and pleas for mercy were ignored.

It was over in seconds, and in its aftermath, the echoes of gunfire faded just as quickly.

Bell and his companions remained where they were, struck dumb by the surprise and savagery of the massacre. It was then that Bell saw blood seeping through John Fox's shirt and that his boyish face had gone as white as marble. He managed only ragged sips of air. Bell scrambled over to check on the young pilot. The bullet had hit his shoulder, and when he peeled back Fox's flight jacket, he could see the joint looked like it had been smashed with a hammer.

The truck's driver, seeing that one of the captives had been wounded in the melee, glared at the men who'd killed the two guards until one couldn't meet his malevolent stare. The driver crossed over to the guilt-ridden killer and pistol-whipped him across the face hard enough to open a gash in his cheek so deep the bone was briefly visible before the wound filled with blood.

The driver approached the captives. Bell and Holmes got to their feet, letting the former tankers tend to Fox as best they could with no medical supplies. The approaching driver was several inches taller than Bell's six feet. He was broad across the chest and thick-necked. Not as big as Schmidt, but a formidable opponent if it ever came to that. He wore an eyepatch and the upper right side of his face was made shiny and tight by an old burn scar. Bell noticed the ear on that side was a gnarled stub.

"You are the pilots?" he asked in English. His accent wasn't German.

"For the most part," Holmes said. He gave a salute. "Liam Holmes. Captain, British Royal Flying Corps. Despite the uniform you're wearing, I take it you are not part of the German army."

"My name is Karl Rath. We are partisans trying to bring an end to this war. We were on our way to Falkennest to rescue you."

"Falkennest is the castle?" Holmes asked.

"Yes, where the German intelligence is headquartered in this sector. We also know it is where newly crashed pilots are interrogated."

"Can we hurry this along?" Bell said. "There are two more men from this gun crew who could be back with reinforcements at any time and we have a wounded man here who needs a doctor."

"Yes, we must." Rath hesitated. "I have a man in the prison who was to help us. His name is Schmidt. He was to come with us."

"He had an accident," Bell said without a lick of guilt. "He won't be going anywhere."

Rath caught his drift and nodded.

Two of the Brits helped Fox up into the back of the truck. The bleeding had slowed, but he was growing more unresponsive as he sank deeper into shock. Rath got behind the wheel, while the rest of his men packed themselves into the covered bed. Bell understood how sardines felt.

The ride over the dirt roads was spine-crushing and every deep rut made Fox moan in his delirium. They motored for hours, stopping once to fill the gas tank from one-gallon tins stored in a compartment between the front and rear tires. Bell suspected they were on an old smugglers' route and had crossed out of France and into occupied Belgium.

The sun was beginning to pink the horizon when they approached the outskirts of a large town, or perhaps small city. Traffic was light at the early hour, mostly delivery drivers in one-horse carts.

With no firm plans on how to escape German-occupied lands once they'd gotten out of the castle, Bell was content to let events unfold rather than try to control them. He was wary, of course, but had no better option than to allow Rath and his guerrilla band take them where they were headed.

With an eye pressed to a small tear in the canvas side of the Mercedes truck, Bell saw they passed through the town's medieval central square. There was a large bronze fountain at one end and encircling buildings that looked unchanged for hundreds of years. Past the old town, they entered a more industrial area that was built along wharves that fronted a broad river. The truck finally came to a warehouse made of brick with a metal roof that looked to be a hundred years old. A guard swung open the fence gate surrounding the structure and another was there to open one of the big doors.

Bell joined the others, jumping down from the truck on knees that had gone stiff over the long ride.

Rath was already out of the truck, issuing orders in a language Bell didn't recognize. By the speed with which his men moved, his authority was absolute.

The interior of the building was gloomy, its distant corners in heavy shadow. Rather than a large open space full of cargo ready for transshipment on river barges, it looked like small buildings had been constructed within the echoing volume. A man with a medical bag, though perhaps not a medical license, came out of one of the buildings at the urging of the partisan who'd accidently shot Fox, eager to get back in his commander's good graces. A pair of men carrying a canvas stretcher also appeared, and in moments Fox was out of the truck and on his way to what Bell assumed was the guerrillas' makeshift surgical dispensary.

Holmes, as the ranking British officer, nodded to Logan and Baltimore, the two clutchmen from the tank, to follow and make sure Fox received proper care. Rath came over to Holmes and Bell, as they both knew he would once he'd gotten his men settled in.

"I think breakfast is in order, yes?" Rath read their expression. "He is not a doctor, but he has been looking after my crew for months now. He has seen many bullet wounds and knows how to treat them. Come. There is much I would like to discuss with you."

The big freedom fighter led the pair to another of the wooden structures built within the large warehouse. It had a door and a single window, and when Rath gestured for them to precede him inside, it showed that it had no roof and was open to the high ceiling above. The building was laid out like an apartment, with the appropriate furniture including a dining table, though there was no kitchen or bathroom visible. A bedroom lay beyond a partially closed door. A woman had been sitting on the couch when Rath had thrown open the door and she guiltily leapt to her feet.

She was pretty, about twenty-five, with dark hair and eyes. She crossed to Rath and he kissed her cheek. The light touch made her wince ever so slightly. He was twenty years her senior and his bulk made her appear so small and fragile.

Fragility, Bell thought. That was the exact word. She had a fragility about her that he had seen a thousand times over the course of his career. Women too scared of their man to ever leave. Living in constant fear made them timid and unable to express themselves for fear of retribution. He had known agents who'd tried to rescue such women from their psychological captors only for them to physically resist being taken away or, more disturbingly, returning to their abusers at the first opportunity. Bell didn't understand the dynamic himself, but knew each one, abuser and victim, exploiter and exploited, fulfilled some dark need by staying together. It made his blood boil because in such an uneven relationship the man generally flourished, while the woman withered away.

He looked at her more carefully and noted the color on one of her cheeks was slightly more yellow than the other, the final stage of a fading bruise.

"Magdalena, be a good girl and get us breakfast. See if you can find tea for our English friends."

"Mr. Rath, I want to thank you for our rescue," Liam Holmes said rather stiffly. He'd also sensed an uncomfortable undercurrent just then, even if he couldn't quantify it the way Bell had.

"It is not without price," the man said bluntly.

"I figured that. What exactly do you want from us?"

"First, I must know how it was that you ended up in a tank. A most interesting, ah, escape vehicle."

"We broke out of our cell by pretending Bell here was ill with the intention of stealing a motorcar or truck. We were discovered during our escape and everything went to pot with guards shooting left and right with little regard to target. We figured we'd be safe from their small-arms fire in that behemoth."

"It had the added bonus of enough firepower to knock out the only bridge across the moat," Bell added.

Rath cocked his head like a dog who'd heard an unfamiliar sound. "Your accent. It isn't British."

"No. I'm an American civilian. From New York."

Rath's rather moody demeanor changed and a smile creased his face. "I sent my brother to live in New York. How is it you were captured by the Germans?"

"Long story short, I ended up in the rear seat of an observation plane that found its way across the lines."

Rath suddenly looked very concerned. "You are not a pilot?" He looked to Holmes. "You are, yes? And the others?"

"I'm a pilot," Holmes assured him. "Bell is one, too. Though I've not seen him fly. The wounded man, Fox, is also a pilot. The others are observers and rear gunners."

"You really can fly a plane?" Rath asked Bell.

"I learned back in 1910 in order to participate in a cross-country air race from New York to San Francisco."

Holmes looked at him with incredulity. "What on earth for?"

Bell didn't want to get into the details of how he was protecting one of the participants from a murderer, so he simply said, "For the fun of it. Oh, and a fifty-thousand-dollar first prize purse."

"Good Lord. Did you win?"

Bell gave him a sad grin. "Afraid not."

Holmes shook his head and once more addressed their mysterious host. "I can safely guess that you rescued us for our ability to pilot an aircraft."

"Is true," Rath said. "I told you we are fighters who want to end the war. We want to go back to our homes, pick up our lives again, and put all this ugliness behind us. But we are a small band of like-minded men. Yes, we find sympathizers in towns and villages up and down the front lines, but most are unwilling to risk themselves in order to end the bloodshed.

"Because of this, we have had limited success. We have ambushed a few trucks, derailed a train, and stolen supplies. Like a gnat to an elephant is our efforts against a juggernaut like the German army. We want to do something greater. Something that will really hurt the Germans and also aid the British gearing up for the spring offensive."

Holmes made to protest. Rath held up a forestalling hand. "It is not exactly a secret that you have amassed three armies near the town of Arras, with supporting artillery. And the French have an even bigger force to the north."

Magdalena appeared just then with a wooden tray of food. There was bread with butter, and cheese, hard-boiled eggs, and a hunk of salami as thick around as Bell's calf.

"*Je suis désolé*," she said in a soft voice before switching to English. "I am sorry. We have no tea, only some, er, imitation coffee."

Bell made note that her eyes were downcast as she made this admission, fearful of Rath's anger at even a minor infraction that wasn't her fault. He wanted to conduct a test and said to her in poor French, "As an American, I prefer coffee to tea."

She looked up at him in surprise and smiled at his attempt to speak her language.

Bell said, "Your English is better than my French. Where did you learn?"

"Before the war, my father's tavern was very popular with tourists."

Out of the corner of his eye, Bell saw Rath's scowl deepen. He made a noise deep in his barrel chest that was almost too low to hear and yet Magdalena picked up on it and the smile dropped from her face and her shoulders sagged inward. Bell gave her the most empathetic look he could muster, and it must have struck home because she regarded him for an extra beat before fleeing the room.

Perhaps not a lost cause after all.

22

LIAM HOLMES HAD BEEN EATING PRISON RATIONS FOR THE BETter part of a week, so no sooner had the tray been set on the table, he'd popped one of the peeled eggs into his mouth and chewed as if in ecstasy. Though only in German hands for less than twenty-four hours, Bell was overjoyed to help himself to a slice of bread slathered in tart apple butter.

"Tell me, Mr. Rath, what is it you want from us exactly?" Holmes said with a hunk of cheese in his hand that was ready to follow the egg.

"There is a railway yard here in occupied Belgium. Eighty percent of all German supplies to the northern section of the front lines pass through it. It is too large for us to attack on the ground, but aerial bombs would make a mess of it."

"One plane wouldn't make a difference if the facility is as large as it sounds," Holmes said, and Bell nodded. "You'd need a fleet of aircraft to do any real damage."

"This is where you are wrong. One aircraft is enough, and we have access to it thanks to a sympathizer in the German air force. It is a Zeppelin."

Bell and Holmes exchanged a bewildered look. Holmes laughed and said, "A Zeppelin? As in an airship? Mate, you've lost the plot. I've never seen one, let alone know how to fly it."

"Besides, it takes a crew of a dozen or more men to fly one of those floating gasbags," Bell added.

"No, no, no. You misunderstand. I am talking about a four-engine bomber built by the Zeppelin company. That you can fly, yes?"

Holmes and Bell looked at each other once again. Though they hadn't ever laid eyes on such an aircraft, both were confident enough in their abilities that they felt they could fly it.

"More than likely, yes."

Karl Rath beamed at the idea that his plan was going to work. "Excellent. And the best part is there will be no artillery or machine guns firing up at you. The entire mission is so far behind the German lines that there is no antiaircraft defenses."

"When would you have us make this raid?" Holmes asked.

"Tonight," Rath said. "That is why we went to break you out of Falkennest. The moon is full and my man at the airfield tells me the rest of his comrades are attending a special dinner with their *Kommandant* at a beer hall. Upon your return, I will turn you and your comrades over to a different group of partisans who will smuggle you across the border into neutral Holland. From there a ship can take you back to England."

"You make it all sound rather easy," Holmes remarked as he pushed away his empty plate.

"Is easy," Rath said. He lit a cigarette. Upon seeing it, Holmes asked if he could have one as well. The partisan handed his pack and a book of printed matches to Bell, who passed them along to the Englishman. Rath continued after Bell returned the pack. "I send one of my men with you on the plane to help find the railyard. He worked for railroad before war and knows which lines to follow."

Holmes asked Bell, "What do you think?"

"I hate to admit that I don't know the geography of the area well enough to have much of an opinion," Bell answered. "How far away is the target and what's the plane's range?"

Rath said, "My man at the base said the plane can carry two thousand kilos of bombs and fly eight hundred kilometers."

"Five hundred miles," Holmes converted for Bell's sake. "We've more than enough range and that's almost two and a quarter tons of bombs. More than enough in that department, too, I would say."

Bell rubbed his chin. "So in a war I have no business fighting, I've defended a trench against attack, shot down an observation balloon, been involved in a dogfight with the Red Baron, and escaped a POW camp in a stolen tank. Hell, I might as well bomb Belgium to complete my grand European tour."

"Is good," Rath said.

Bell had little doubt what would have happened to them had he and Holmes refused to fly the mission. Rath had an edge to him, a ruthlessness that he didn't bother to hide. He recalled the pistol-whipping of his own man the night before at the ambush site. Rath hadn't hesitated for even a moment before scarring one of his men for life.

The partisan added, "The planes are usually based at a big airfield near Ghent. Several were flown to a much-smaller field near here two weeks ago. It is that which gave me idea to rescue pilots and bomb railyard. I say this so you know they are common in skies over Belgium, and you will not be attacked on return flight."

Holmes wasn't impressed by this last comment. "Not unless the Germans are on the ball, which my experience tells me they are, and alert their antiaircraft batteries about us bombing their choo choo. We'll have the cover of night on the flight there, but on the way back we might be the target of a good old-fashioned turkey shoot."

"You have those in England?" Bell asked.

"We mostly shoot pheasants. I said turkey for your sake."

"Appreciate it," Bell said with a wry grin. He became serious again when addressing Rath. "Listen, breakfast was great and all, but we need some shut-eye before tonight, and I'm sure Captain Holmes would like to check in on his men, especially the wounded flyer, Fox."

"Of course, of course," Rath said, getting to his feet and crushing out his cigarette in an overflowing glass ashtray.

They left the room. Bell noted that most of the lights inside the warehouse had been turned off and he saw none of Rath's men about. He assumed they, too, needed rest after their rescue raid. Rath first showed Bell and Holmes the room they would sleep in. With the exception of John Fox, the other Englishmen were asleep on cots in the Spartan, windowless, and roofless space. Bell let Holmes go on alone to check on his wounded man.

When the door closed behind him, he turned. There was no handle on this side of the door. He was trapped.

23

ISAAC BELL WAS IN POSITION TO THE LEFT OF THE DOOR WHEN HE heard Liam Holmes and who he now considered their captor, Karl Rath, approach a few minutes after locking him in the dim room.

"He will need a long time to heal," Rath was saying as he approached the door, "but my man knows what he's doing."

"Can't thank you enough," Holmes said.

Bell imagined the polite Englishman wanting to shake Rath's hand once again.

The door was pulled open from the other side.

With just his fingertips, Bell reached around and pressed the cover he'd torn from the matchbook he'd stolen back in Karl Rath's office over the strike plate protecting the hole in the frame for the latch. He used his own blood as an adhesive that he got by rubbing two knuckles raw against a poorly smoothed section of the room's concrete floor. The trick was to let the blood congeal for a few moments.

The move was lightning fast and he had already stepped a pace away and had crouched down when Holmes came into the room. The pilot didn't see him as he studied his comrades asleep on their cots. Rath closed the door. Bell had to be quick. He dropped flat to the floor and worked his fingertips into the slight gap between the floor and the door.

Rath would sense something wasn't right when he closed the door, and so when he inevitably tugged on the outer handle, Bell had such a tight grip on the bottom of the door that the guerrilla leader was certain his charges were locked in their cage until he was ready to send them on their mission.

Holmes finally noticed Bell sprawled on the floor at the base of the door, his face contorted with the effort to keep it closed against Rath's not inconsequential tug. To his credit, he said nothing until Rath gave up and his footsteps receded from their room and Bell let out a breath as he shook feeling back into his fingertips.

Bell got to his feet and motioned for Holmes to follow him away from the door. Their ensuing conversation took place slowly as each man had to turn his head to present an ear so they could whisper at the lowest level possible.

"There's no handle on our side of the door so we're locked in."

"Why on earth?"

"Not sure, but I intend to find out. I put a piece of cardboard against the frame to keep the latch from engaging. In a few hours I am going out to reconnoiter. I don't trust Rath."

"What about our mission? The flight?"

"Not sure yet. He has another agenda. Money, I assume. My guess is they are smugglers."

Holmes nodded in agreement. "People have been getting rich off wars since Hannibal came over the Alps. Elephant food can't be cheap. Are you coming back?"

"I'm not leaving you guys in the lurch. Better we stick together. I'll only take a quick look around. It'll be fine. Get some sleep."

They each took a cot. Bell was exhausted, drained down to near the bottom of his reserves. This was supposed to have been a quick fact-finding tour for President Wilson, a few days, a week at most. For the hundredth time, he wondered what Marion was going through. She was used to him heading off into danger, but not in-ured to it. He could only hope that Churchill had given her what updates he could. Marion was the type who'd rather know he was missing over enemy lines than know nothing at all. It was her faith in him. So long as he was missing, she believed that he would find a way to be found.

As much as he wanted all the sleep he could get, he mentally gave himself three hours before he'd awaken. Marion's face was the last thing on his mind when he succumbed to his exhaustion.

One hundred and seventy-eight minutes later, Bell's cold blue eyes snapped open as if he'd heard a pair of cymbals crash. He remained utterly motionless, reaching out with his hearing to discern the slight-est noise. He heard his British cellmates breathing and snoring, and making small movements as they twitched through whatever visions haunted their dreams. Beyond the room's lathe-and-plaster walls he heard nothing. No conversations, no footfalls, not even settling noises. A building this old had done all the settling it ever would.

He got off the cot as silently as he could. He'd earlier removed his boots and he left them standing at the side of his bed so he could pad silently in thick wool socks to the door. It opened without a sound and he peeled his telltale matchbook cover from where he'd pressed it against the frame. There were only a few lights still on and just a bit of moonlight streaming through the building's clerestory win-dows. For Bell, it was enough.

He headed out, keeping low and slow. At the next of the buildings the men had built inside the warehouse, he could hear men sleeping. Judging by the size of the structure and the volume of snoring, he guessed well over twenty. It was far more than he'd seen on their rescue and made him wonder what else Rath had in the works.

He moved on.

The next space he checked turned out to be a communal bathroom with multiple stalls and showers. The size led Bell to double his estimate of Rath's force. It appeared he'd assembled a small army.

The next open-topped building within the warehouse was laid out like a classroom, with rows of wooden desks facing a lectern. He scanned the floor for any lost papers to give him an idea of what was being taught. They'd been swept clean, but he found a scrap of paper with writing on it crumpled in a wastebasket. It was too dark to read, so he folded it and put it in his pocket. He turned to leave and nearly bumped into one of Rath's men.

He had obviously just gotten out of bed, as he wore only a pair of white drawers. He had a large tattoo of a compass rose on his chest and several more smaller ones on his arms that were too indistinct to decipher. He said something to Bell in Rath's language. It sounded Eastern European to his ear, but he couldn't be more precise than that.

Without knowing the language, Bell still knew what he'd been asked. "I'm looking for the bathroom. Er, toilet." He made a universal pantomime that all men would understand.

The man's suspicion faded and he beckoned Bell to follow him to the big washroom. When they'd finished up, the man escorted the American detective back to his room and made certain the door was locked behind him with a firm rattle of its handle.

Bell was chagrined. He'd barely begun his investigation and yet he'd been caught flat-footed by some guy on nature's call. He felt like a rank amateur. And worse, he knew nothing more about Karl Rath or what exactly he was doing. The size of this place, the number of guerrillas he guessed the man had under him, and the fact they had a large classroom did not equal a small band of partisans interested in ending the war.

His first guess about smuggling could still be true, but again the number of men stationed here would indicate some other goal. Bell wished Archie or James Dashwood or even old man Van Dorn himself were around to spitball ideas and theories. In detective work, it was too tempting to listen to your opinions echo in your head when it came to a favorite hypothesis. Working with a tried-and-tested team was essential. He hoped to have the time to springboard some things past Liam Holmes. The man had a good head on his shoulders, but he doubted they'd get a chance to talk.

Lying down on his cot once again, Bell heard a guard's footsteps approach their little building and come to a stop just outside the door. The man had been quiet, but not overly so, and Bell didn't know if his presence was a warning or just a precaution.

Yes, nothing was quite what it seemed.

24

ACCORDING TO HIS INTERNAL CLOCK, IT WAS THREE IN THE morning when Karl Rath sent two men into the room where Bell and the others were asleep to wake them. The men singled out Bell and Holmes and indicated the others were to remain behind. Bell didn't know if the remaining Brits realized they were prisoners and bargaining chips.

They were led to the washroom and then taken to the far side of the big building, where Rath waited with a couple of his goons plus a sad-faced kid in his early twenties who looked like he was processing the worst news imaginable.

Magdalena was there with a carafe of ersatz coffee, which she poured into tin mugs for Bell and Holmes. There was thick cream, but no sugar, which would have helped mask the taste of roasted acorn. She handed Bell a paper sack. Inside were two objects wrapped in wax paper.

"Sandwiches for your flight," she said without looking up.

"*Merci*," he said softly.

"I hear one of my men found you outside your room last night," Rath said darkly.

"I needed the bathroom," Bell said, the picture of innocence. "Is that a problem?"

"I . . ." Rath didn't want to admit he'd locked them in their room, so there was really nothing further that he could say. He let the matter drop. "Are you two ready to fly? We leave in a few minutes. It has been timed so you will arrive over the railyard just after the sun comes up."

"Your cot is vastly superior to the ones in the castle," Holmes replied. "First morning my back hasn't ached since the crash."

Rath pointed to the grim-faced man. He was worrying at the collar of his jacket like how some people work a rosary. "This is Georgi. He knows the way to the railyard and will fly with you."

"Isaac Bell," he said and held out a hand.

Georgi didn't stop fingering his coat until Rath prompted him with a thumb to the ribs. He shook Bell's hand. His was slick with cold sweat.

"Liam Holmes." He looked at his wet palm after shaking Georgi's hand. "You okay, mate? You're a little green about the gills."

Rath quickly said, "This will be his first time in an airplane. Also his English is not so good."

"Ah, right. Tell him he has nothing to worry about. I've already had my allotment of crashes this week."

Rath looked at him queerly.

"It's a joke, mate," Holmes said. "Just tell him he's in good hands."

"I do have a question," Bell said. "Once we're through attacking the train yard and return here, we can't exactly land their stolen bomber back at the German's airfield."

"Yes, yes, yes. I will show you. The airfield is ten kilometers from here. There is a big open field only two kilometers away, where you have enough room to land the plane. We pass it on our way. Once you are down, set the plane on fire. I will have men waiting to take you back here."

Bell nodded. "Sounds reasonable."

"Good. Then it is time. Come with me."

Rath led the party outside to their truck. Bell and Holmes went in back with the two goons. Georgi helped crank the Mercedes to life and rode in the cab with Rath. The streets were even more quiet than when they'd arrived in town. They didn't pass the old town section again, but left heading south. Bell kept his eye to the small rip in the canvas despite the warning scowl on the goons' faces. In case things didn't work out upon their return, he wanted to know the way back to Rath's lair.

A few minutes later, Rath brought the truck to a stop. The town had ended abruptly a mile back and around them was nothing but open land ready to be planted in a few weeks' time. "Will this be to your liking?" Rath asked from the cab.

Bell and Holmes surveilled the area by opening the rear flap of the truck's canvas top.

"Looks good," Holmes told him.

Rath said, "The river is just over that rise. Is easy to find from the air."

"Better and better."

They lit out once again and drove for a half hour. Bell took note that a barbed-wire fence had appeared on their right side, anchored by a forlorn guard tower. Moments later, they passed a cluster of buildings, some of them large enough to be hangars for multiple aircraft. This had to be the airfield. They continued on for a bit, Rath keeping the truck at a slower pace. He turned off the road and they entered the restricted military installation through a cut section of fence. A soldier was there with a powerful flashlight. He hitched a ride on the truck's running board while giving directions to Karl Rath.

They finally came to a stop. Bell felt the truck shift slightly when the soldier jumped free. A second later, Rath's door squealed open. One of Rath's men opened the tailgate and waited for Bell and Holmes to step down onto the cool grass field.

The two moved around to the other side of the Mercedes and stopped in utter astonishment at what basked in the truck's head-lamps. Even if they weren't seasoned pilots who had a long-standing love affair with aircraft, the machine in front of them would still stir their blood. The Zeppelin-Staaken R.VI was a spectacular piece of engineering of such a staggering size it almost defied belief. With a total wingspan of one hundred and thirty-eight feet, each of the wings was the length of a tennis court. The bracing between the up-per and lower wings was a complex network of struts and wires that kept them in place with at least ten feet between them. There were pods flanking the fuselage placed between the double-stacked wings. Each nacelle housed a pair of Maybach Mb six-cylinder engines with one propeller facing forward and the other prop aft. These nacelles were the size of automobiles. Like the main wings, the tail was also of a bi-wing configuration, with two separate vertical rudders.

The fuselage stretched seventy-two feet, about the length of two city buses. It was one of the first fully enclosed airplanes in the world. There was room in the cockpit for two pilots, a navigator, and a radio operator, but the interior was laid out so there was in-flight access to the nose gunner's position as well as the tail gunner's compartment. She normally carried two flight engineers, who each had a place in the nacelles between the engines out on the wings and had access to additional machine guns on top of the pods.

When sitting idle, the plane rested on sixteen individual tires on four separate trucks. As she was a taildragger, the front tires needed for taking off were currently off the ground at head height, while the top of the cockpit was some fifteen feet in the air.

"What do you think?" Bell asked.

"She's a monster all right, but the principles are all the same, right?"

"Are you asking or is that rhetorical?"

Holmes chuckled. "Not sure, actually."

The German mechanic loyal to Karl Rath said something to Bell and Holmes. Since neither man spoke German, they looked to Rath to translate. "He says not to be intimidated, but also do not underestimate, either. She is big and heavy and needs two men to wrestle her around in the air."

The German spoke some more. "He says on a long flight they have relief pilots on board to take over for when the first team become too tired. Your flight won't be so long, but you will still feel the effects."

"How is she to land?" Holmes asked.

The mechanic looked away for a second before replying. "She wants to float above the ground for a long time when you try to land. Be prepared for that."

"Ground effects," Bell said.

"I've experienced it a few times," Holmes assured him. "If we bring her in hard and fast, who cares if we break an axle? It's not like she'll ever fly again."

"Good point."

"Come," the German said in English. He led Bell and Holmes to a ladder leaning against the left wing's leading edge. They climbed up, with Rath joining them to translate. Georgi stayed behind, flanked by Rath's muscle.

The cockpit was like a cozy room ringed with large windows. The two pilots sat next to each other behind large control wheels rather than stick controls, as found in a fighter. A large compass was between the seats on the dash as well as clusters of instrument gauges.

There were two other seats farther aft, and beyond those were two rows of steel drums for the plane's three thousand liters of gasoline.

The mechanic pointed to some controls and explained their purpose. Rath listened and then repeated it in English. "The plane is equipped with self-starters for the engines. You fire up the lead motor in each nacelle and use it to jump-start its partner. Other than that everything is standard, just big."

"Okay, then," Holmes said. "We should be about set. I just want to do a full walk-around."

"There is no time," Rath said. "You must arrive at sunup."

"Sorry, mate. I don't fly a kite I haven't eyeballed for myself."

"Same," Bell said.

Rath's anger was plain to see, but so, too, was the resolve of his two pilots. "Fine," he said between gritted teeth.

Bell and Holmes spent ten minutes inspecting the exterior of the giant plane, making sure the control surfaces had free motion and there was no obvious damage to her canvas skin. Bell wrapped a knuckle against one of the bombs held in racks below her belly for luck. The final part of the tour was a look into the engine pods atop the wings. Rath stayed with them the whole time, as if his presence would hurry them along.

Frustrated to not have any time alone to strategize with the Englishman, Bell finally muttered, "There is an *et tu Brute* moment coming. Let it happen, but when I touch your shank, make us an elevator to Hades."

"Huh?"

"What was that?" Rath asked, unfamiliar with the words Bell used.

"Airplane jargon," Bell told him, eyeing Holmes to see if his presumably boarding school education would pay off. "The elevator is the control surfaces in the tail."

"And the shank and brute?"

"The shank is the hinge pin that holds it on," Bell answered.

With a wink to Bell, Holmes said, "The brute is what we call the double cross of bracing wires between the tail wings."

Kudos to a classical British education, Bell thought.

They returned to the ladder. Rath said a few words to Georgi that seemed to make him feel a little better about the flight. He gave a small smile and vanished into a bear hug from his mentor before climbing up onto the wing to take his place in the seat behind the pilots.

Rath turned to Bell and Holmes. "This is a real blow you are about to strike. Be proud of yourselves, and by tonight we will have you and the others safely over the border into the Netherlands. When you take off, fly due north. Georgi will know when to turn to find the rail line to the marshaling yard."

"Thanks. We'll be back before you know it." Bell shook Rath's outstretched hand.

The partisans returned to their truck, while the mechanic stood by to remove the wheel chocks once the engines had fired. Bell led Holmes up the ladder and was in position to turn his back on the cockpit door and hold a finger to his lips just as the Brit was about to ask a string of questions. Holmes looked puzzled.

Bell tossed his head in the direction of their passenger, who was within earshot. "Could be the same trick the Germans tried to pull back in your cell."

His suspicion was that Georgi could speak English and was along for this mission to prevent the pilots from deviating from Rath's mission. He wouldn't understand the context of what Bell had just said, but wouldn't divulge his secret for something so innocuous.

They entered the massive bomber and secured the cockpit door. Bell shot Georgi a thumbs-up, which the young man didn't return. He was playing with the collar of his coat again. Bell gave Holmes the command seat on the left side of the plane and settled into the right-hand seat. Turning the wheel and moving it forward and back took some effort. In the air, with an eighty-knot slipstream making the control surfaces even more sluggish, flying this beast would take some serious muscle.

They strapped themselves in using the lap belt provided and Holmes repeated the instruction on how to start the plane. When Bell concluded he had it right, he began working the toggles and switches that primed the engines with fuel and prepared them for the ignition process. With a final push of two buttons, the leading engines on both the starboard and port sides roared to life in a blast of noise and exhaust.

Neither man could help but grin at the raw power now coursing through the airframe, and when the other two motors started, the grins became toothy smiles, for that power was now double. They had a tiger by the tail.

Though the cockpit was enclosed, the noise of the big engines was near deafening. Any conversation now would have to be shouted.

Holmes worked the throttles to even out how the motors were running before giving the mechanic a signal that he could pull the wheel chocks. He vanished under the fuselage for what seemed like an inordinate amount of time before finally emerging from under the nose with the big wooden chocks in hand.

With that final task complete, Holmes edged the throttles a bit, drawing more power from the plane's four engines. The noise and vibration grew, but hadn't yet become unbearable. The prop blades no longer looked like solid things. They were now just a blur that confused the eye when witnessed from any distance. At last the heavy bomber started to trundle over the grass, slowly at first, but steadily building speed. When he deemed their speed fast enough, Holmes hit the rudder to turn them toward the runway. Bell could see the strain it put on his leg, and added his own strength to the task.

The Zeppelin-Staaken came around in a ponderous quarter loop that left the plane rocking a bit when they aligned with the runway. Bell looked back. Georgi was staring out the window and playing with his lapel. He had a pocket watch in his other hand, which rested in his lap. He didn't look particularly afraid of flying, but he was definitely concerned about something.

Holmes set the throttles against their stops. What had been a throaty roar turned into an echoing thunder that made the hairs on Bell's arms stand up. He and Holmes exchanged another boyish grin. The plane started accelerating down the field, jolting and bouncing like an unbroken horse, picking up speed with each passing moment, but it certainly wasn't an exciting level of acceleration.

Halfway down the long grass strip, the tail had enough lift to unstick the rear skid plate. The nose dropped down so that the front landing gear hit the earth. The ride became a little smoother and their acceleration grew noticeably quicker. The plane was nearing full gallop now. Holmes gave the wheel a gentle tug to judge if they were going fast enough, waited another fifteen seconds for that last bit of speed, and then fully eased back on the wheel. As before, Bell assisted by pulling back on his synchronized wheel, but always making sure Holmes was leading the effort.

The jouncing ride evened out the moment the wheels left the ground and the wings took up the burden of holding the plane aloft. She climbed like an overweight goose, slow and stately. A minute after taking off, they were less than four hundred feet above the ground. Holmes still felt comfortable enough to put her in a shallow turn until the compass pointed north. It would take twenty minutes or more to reach ten thousand feet.

"She feels lighter than I expected, but a slow climber," Holmes yelled over the engines' roar.

Bell looked back to see Georgi studying his watch. "Kid's acting like he's waiting for a date."

"Odd duck, that one."

Bell looked at Georgi every couple of minutes, and each time he was checking his watch. Whatever appointed time finally came and he stuffed the pocket watch in his jacket and stood. He came up behind the pilots so he could stand in between them.

"Change of plans," he shouted in a high, breaking voice. He pointed to the compass. "Forty degrees is your new heading. Do not deviate from it."

"That'll take us toward Holland," Holmes shouted back, surprised that Bell was right and Georgi was like one of the English-speaking spies the Germans tried to intermix with their captives.

A snub-nosed revolver appeared in Georgi's hand. "You will follow my order or one of you will die."

Bell and Holmes exchanged another look. This time there was no boyish smile, but the acceptance of the grim reality that the betrayal Bell anticipated had arrived. Holmes's look also conveyed that he hoped Bell had more than just good predictive skills and actually had a plan to take control of the situation.

Georgi jammed the gun's barrel into Bell's neck. His finger was on the trigger. "Turn now!"

With no other choice, the two flyers banked the aircraft to starboard, not knowing that they were experiencing history's first hijacking.

25

OF THE MANY MISCALCULATIONS BELL HAD MADE ON THIS MIS-
sion, the one he feared would get him killed now was how
slowly the big Zeppelin-Staaken bomber could climb. The higher
they flew, the thinner the air became, and the less lift the monstrous
wings provided. Eventually they would hit her absolute ceiling of
around fourteen thousand feet. Bell's quick mental calculation based
on their current altitude and rate of climb told him it would take
nearly three hours.

The very thought of a nervous twentysomething with poor trigger discipline holding a pistol pointed at his head for that much time
was a recipe for disaster. Still, Bell needed as much altitude as they
could manage for his plan to work.

On they droned over Belgium, climbing at a slowing pace with
each mile they put behind them. Georgi no longer pressed the gun
to Bell's neck, but it was never more than a foot or two away, and

the young partisan's finger never lost its tight curl around the trigger, an obvious sign the weapon was in a novice's hand.

The juddering altimeter needle finally pointed to an altitude of three thousand meters, or close enough to ten thousand feet, that any delay on Bell's part was him merely stalling. Moving a hand at an infinitely slow pace so as not to draw Georgi's attention, Bell eventually hooked a finger under his lap belt's metal buckle. There was no need to worry that unbuckling it would alert their captor, but Bell kept himself buckled in when he reached over to point at one of the gauges on the central part of the cockpit's dashboard. He sensed Georgi lean forward to see what had caught Bell's eye.

Bell tapped Holmes's leg and the cockpit seemed to explode.

The Brit had been expecting the signal and was ready to put everything he had into nose-diving the giant bomber. He pressed hard on the wheel, using all of the muscles in his back, chest, and arms, and the response was sharper than he'd expected. It was as though the plane no longer wanted to be in the air. The nose dropped while the engines continued to roar, and for the next few seconds the plane was falling faster than its passengers, and so they experienced complete weightlessness.

Holmes was still strapped in, so he remained in his seat. Georgi wasn't prepared at all. He had only a tenuous grip on the back of Bell's seat. He was lifted off his feet and started drifting aft, his hands flailing uselessly. The big Zeppelin-Staaken did nothing very quickly, so the young partisan was moving almost gently, like a leaf caught in an updraft, and had plenty of time to brace himself before he hit the double row of cylindrical metal gas tanks.

Bell anticipated his moves even as the barn door–sized elevators tipped the plane into a dive. He'd experienced weightlessness before while flying, and he knew what to expect. He launched himself out of his chair as soon as he saw Georgi floating away, the gun no longer pointed at his head. He used a piece of the cabin's tubular frame as a handhold to hurl himself at their hijacker. With no gravity acting on his body, he flew like a missile and had aimed himself perfectly.

He slammed into Georgi just as they reached the gas tanks with an impact that caused the younger man's breath to explode from his body. The blow also broke a couple of ribs. Somehow, he managed to keep control of the pistol. Bell was a little staggered by the violence of the impact himself and was a fraction late in blocking the revolver from coming around. He deflected Georgi's arm at the last second.

The gun went off with a sharp painful bark. The bullet struck one of the tanks a glancing blow that sent it ricocheting through the plane's canvas skin and off one of the engines.

Bell clamped a hand around Georgi's wrist as he tried to aim it at him once again. It was a test of strength that the younger man should have lost in moments, but he was driven by a fervid belief in this mission and fought with strength he didn't know he possessed. Even with Georgi hyperventilating to reinflate his lungs, it was all Bell could do to maintain a stalemate. They were like two evenly matched arm wrestlers. They each fought with both hands and neither could find an advantage.

Rather than maintain the fight until one of them tired, Bell took his left hand off Georgi's arm and jabbed his knuckles into the man's ribs, twisting them in against the broken bones. Georgi screamed in pain and Bell pressed his advantage, bending the man's wrist sharply and looping a finger over his trigger finger. The sound of the gun going off was muted by their bodies pressed so closely together.

Bell felt a searing pain when the muzzle flash burned a patch of skin on his stomach. It was nothing compared to the damage the small-caliber bullet did to Georgi. The round tore through diaphragm and lung and cut a pencil-thin tunnel through his heart, stopping it immediately. The roar of pain at the jab to the ribs died on Georgi's lips as a new sensation short-circuited his nervous system. His gaze turned to Bell as if there were an explanation to be found in the American's cold blue eyes.

Bell didn't wait to see him take his last breath because, as they were fighting, he became aware of the banshee-like shriek of wind over the wings and through all the plane's supporting guy wires.

The bomber was shuddering and shaking and seemed to want to tear itself apart. A new sound joined the unholy chorus as bits of canvas covering the wings began to tear away. A tension wire snapped and fouled one of the pusher props for a moment. Bell let Georgi collapse to the deck and crawled his way toward the cockpit, using whatever protrusion was available for foot and handholds. With the plane still in a dive, it was like climbing with a hundred-pound sack on his back. He finally made it to his seat and flipped himself into it.

Holmes had already cut the engines back to idle and was pulling on the stick even harder than he'd slammed it earlier to drop them out of the sky. Bell added his strength to the controls, pulling until his neck corded up and sweat burst from every pore.

The altimeter needle spun passed a thousand meters in a blur like a compass sitting too close to a magnet. Their rate of descent didn't appear to be slowing for several long moments. But then, ever so slowly, their efforts began to pay off. Their strength moved the elevators against the slipstream enough to start to bring the nose out of its screaming dive.

At five hundred meters, the plane was nearly out of its dive. Airspeed had bled off some and it became easier for them to wrestle the bomber onto an even keel.

They finally leveled out at three hundred meters, or about a thousand feet. It sounded like a healthy cushion, but to Bell and Holmes it felt as though the bomber's belly was about to scrape the earth. The two pilots shared a look of relief haloed by incredulity that the big plane hadn't lost a wing and augered into the ground in a crumbled heap.

Holmes fed more power to the motors and they started the laborious climb all over again. He banked the plane to take them back over the front lines and into Allied territory.

"Why not carry on to Holland?" Bell shouted over the riotous din filling the cabin. "We're closer."

"I can't imagine the Dutch being too keen on a British officer flying a stolen German plane into their neutral territory," Holmes shouted back. "Safer to get as much altitude as we can and head home."

Bell couldn't argue with his logic. He changed topics. "I believe the bombs we're carrying are dummies. I tapped one during our walk-around and it rang hollow."

"That explains why this old girl is lighter on the controls than I expected. She'd be a right pig with a couple thousand kilos of bombs under her belly."

Bell didn't ask the logical follow-up question because Holmes wouldn't know the answer, either. If they weren't going to bomb a German-controlled rail depot in Belgium, what was their mission? The answer wouldn't come to him, no matter how he tried to glean any meaning from what he knew of Rath and his merry band of cutthroats. Why fly to Holland? They weren't going to bomb it, that was for sure, so there was something else.

Did Georgi have a specific mission he'd been ordered to carry out?

Bell dismissed this idea as soon as it formed in his mind. The kid fought harder than he'd expected, but he was such an awkward person to be considered for a solo mission that Rath put so much effort and sacrifice into. For something critical, like perhaps a meeting at a Dutch airfield, Rath would likely go himself or send a more senior man, not a callow boy who had no idea how to properly handle a gun much less himself.

If it wasn't Georgi then it was something else. Something in the aircraft, perhaps.

Bell called over to Holmes. "Are you okay for a couple of minutes?"

"Yes, but make it quick. I'm going to need you to spell me for a bit. My arms are dead."

Bell left his seat and made his way aft. Georgi was dead, lying broken on the floor, an unearthly white hand pressed to the entrance wound in his chest, as if that could keep in the blood. Bell knelt next to him, but rather than close Georgi's sightless eyes or arrange his limbs in a more respectful pose, he rifled through his clothes with an expert's touch.

Georgi carried nothing but a pocket watch and a cashless wallet with an identification card that said he was an Austrian named George Jaeger, but the ID was fake in Bell's estimation. A good forgery, but not the real thing. It was in the embossing. It was slightly off. There was no notebook or envelope. He carried nothing that looked like he was acting as its courier.

If not the man, Bell thought, then the plane.

He performed a methodical search, opening the drawer under the navigator's tiny desk, feeling along seams in the canvas walls for hidden pockets, looking on, under, and around everything he could.

He crawled between the two rows of tall gas cans, feeling around each for anything that had been stashed away. Nothing.

Beyond the tanks was a little room with two storage lockers on the floor. On the far wall was a canvas flap snapped in place with brass fasteners. Bell left the lockers for now and opened the cloth door. The sound of the slipstream grew sharper. Bell crawled through the doorway and stood. He was in the Zeppelin-Staaken's rear gunner's station. There were mounts for a pair of 7.92-millimeter MG-14 light machine guns. Neither gun was aboard. Bell did a quick visual sweep and backed out when he saw there was nothing of note. He refastened the flap to cut down on the noise and opened the first metal locker. There were some spare parts, a couple of oilcans, and various tools a mechanic might need during a long bombing run.

The second locker, the last place Bell could check, was where he found a heavy steel case, like a piece of luggage, only more industrial looking. He opened it and saw it was full of asbestos sheets packed around another, smaller case. This was made of conventional leather and looked old, but well cared for.

Bell opened this case. It was stuffed with official-looking papers written in German with fanciful crests and stamps and the words *Streng Geheim* on each sheet. He guessed it meant "top secret."

Mindful of Holmes still flying this big plane solo, he closed up the case and hurried back to the cockpit. He slid into his seat and placed the case between them. Putting his hands on the wheel, he said, "I have the controls."

Holmes blew out a breath, flicked his wrists to loosen them up, and slumped back. "Thanks, mate."

"How's your German?"

"Schoolboy mostly."

"See what you can make of the contents of that case," Bell said, his eyes scanning the dials and compass and then returning to the windscreen.

Dawn was breaking behind them and the landscape below was starting to emerge from the darkness. They were just now climbing back up through eight thousand feet. The front was still fifty miles away, which would give them another few thousand feet of altitude at their predicted rate of climb. It wasn't as high as Bell would have preferred. Remaining over the German side of the line wouldn't be a problem. It was when they crossed into Allied territory that they would be potential sitting ducks for dawn patrols.

They didn't have enough fuel to wait it out over German-claimed land until the Allied patrols had returned to their airfields. They would just hope their luck held. Bell occasionally turned to Holmes to see what progress he was making. The airman's face went from confusion to understanding to concern with nearly every sentence he read.

Bell couldn't take the wait and finally yelled over the plane's rattling and the wind's howl. "Well, what is it?"

"You're not going to believe it," Holmes replied, as though he wasn't quite sure he did, either. "These are the detailed plans for a German invasion of Holland. They're going to ignore Dutch neutrality and execute a lightning raid all the way to the port of Rotterdam. The Germans figure they can seize enough warehoused supplies like steel, oil, and gas, as well as chemicals and food for them to keep fighting until 1920. They think they can wear down the Allies in a continuation of the current trench war stalemate. It'll be the biggest heist in history."

Bell knew that wasn't true, but was duly impressed anyway. It was audacious, but also brilliantly calculating. "When?"

"Ten days' time." He pointed at the open case on his lap. "In here are troop numbers, railroad dispatch tables, air-cover plans. The works."

Bell remained silent, his mind working furiously even as he continued to monitor the aircraft and the brightening sky around them.

"Lord knows how Rath and his thugs got their hands on this stuff," Holmes continued, "but it appears our flight was meant to deliver a warning to the Dutch government. He is true to his word about wanting to end the war."

Bell still kept his own counsel. The numbers didn't add up. Georgi was a lousy choice to act as a courier and emissary. He was what generals called cannon fodder, an expendable soldier of little consequence in the grand scheme of war. Rath was too cunning to send the wrong man, so Georgi's role was something else. The asbestos was the key, and when Bell realized it, his blood pressure spiked because his heart went into overdrive.

"Had we stayed on the route Georgi laid out, would we have flown over Amsterdam?"

Holmes caught the urgency in Bell's shouted question. "Near enough. Why?"

"What time would we have arrived?"

"Hard to say. About now, really."

"No time to explain. Take the controls. Slow us down as much as you dare. Hang her right above stall speed." Bell jumped to his feet.

"What's going on?"

"There's a bomb attached to the undercarriage."

Bell saves the Staaken R4

26

LEAVING LIAM HOLMES WITH A STUNNED LOOK ON HIS FACE, Bell ran from the cockpit and raced aft to the starboard side-exit door. As soon as he got it ajar, the wind took it and slammed it back against the plane's fuselage. The pod holding the two engines was only a few feet away, looking like a monstrous oil tank on thin legs with thrashing propellers on either end.

Despite his surprise, Holmes had followed Bell's orders. The Zeppelin-Staaken had slowed noticeably and the bellow coming from the tandem motors had diminished. Still, the wind was a force to be reckoned with. Bell dropped to his belly and started sliding out into the slipstream, his hair and then his clothing flapping furiously in the gale. There were plenty of guy wires and bracing spars between the two wings for him to maintain a firm grip at all times, but one slip out here would mean a minutes-long plummet to the unyielding earth below.

Thinking through each move before he executed it, Bell crawled out until he was directly behind the tractor-style propeller pulling the plane through the air. The noise and back draft physically shook his body as he found places to brace his feet. A mistake here would be just as fatal, but mercifully shorter. The pusher prop beat the air directly behind him, and if he lost his grip he'd go through it like a tree limb through a wood chipper.

He slowly bent over the wing's leading edge, mindful of the whirling prop two feet from the back of his head. He saw the bomb straight away, as he knew he would. It hadn't been there when he and Holmes had done their visual inspection. It was a package about the size of a loaf of bread and was attached to the main landing gear's support strut. He clung to the wing with one hand, his feet hooked around two spars. He reached out with his other hand, stretching so that more of his body was being pummeled by the wind. At the full of his stretch his fingers closed around the bomb. It was tied to the metal strut with some cord that allowed him to slide it closer to his torso. Once he had it at the top of the strut, just behind the wing's lead edge, he managed to slide a little farther back and use just his feet to hold himself against the deafening wind. Now he could use both hands. It took him only a few seconds to untie the thin rope.

He simply let it go and the device vanished into the burgeoning dawn. For about three seconds.

The bomb was designed to sheer off the plane's wing and so wasn't particularly large, but it detonated in a bloom of fire and smoke close enough for the pressure wave to lift the big bomber like a kite in a gust. Bell was nearly thrown into the leading propeller when one of his feet slipped, but managed to avoid the spinning disc by digging in hard with his other leg.

Once he got his other foot hooked around the spar once again, he pulled himself back toward the middle of the wing and retraced his path to the aircraft's door. He couldn't close it against the slipstream, so the noise and gusts of wind blowing into the cabin were one more in a long list of annoyances.

"We were that close?" Holmes said when Bell took his place in the right-hand seat.

"It went off about two seconds after I untied it from the landing gear," Bell replied.

"How did you know?"

"The asbestos in the outer case was meant to protect the inner case and the documents from fire. The only way Rath would think fire would be such a hazard is if he planned on us crashing and the plane's fuel igniting. No matter what happened to the plane, or us for that matter, the documents would be found by the crash investigators and quickly find their way up the chain of command."

"This was a suicide mission for Georgi?"

"That's why he was such a nervous wreck," Bell answered. "Rath needed a man on board so we didn't just steal his plane for a joyride back to our side of the lines. Georgi pulled the short straw and was a dead man walking when he boarded the plane."

"A true fanatic."

"People generally only sacrifice themselves for religion, family, or politics. My money is on the latter. Rath and his men don't want to bring about peace. I think they're anarchists who thrive in the chaos of war and want to see all of Europe burned to the ground, Holland included."

"Do you think the discovery of these battle plans are enough to get the Dutch to declare war on Germany preventively?"

"I know next to nothing about Holland, so I can't say. But Karl Rath risked his life and the lives of his men to rescue us so we could fly this mission. And he sent Georgi on a suicide run to make sure we didn't double-cross them. You don't make those kinds of sacrifices unless you believe in your ultimate success."

It was an opinion Holmes found himself agreeing with and so he said nothing more on the topic. Instead he asked, "How did you know where the bomb was?"

"Oh, that. Remember just before takeoff, the mechanic who snuck us onto the base took a long time pulling the wheel chocks? He knows pilots always do a preflight walk-around. He needed to wait until after we did our inspection to secure the bomb to the plane. That was his only opportunity."

Holmes looked at him with a mix of admiration and suspicion. "Who the hell are you?"

"I'm the lead detective for one of the largest private detective agencies in the United States, the Van Dorn Agency. We even have a small branch in London," Bell said, and then added the grim news he'd also realized moments earlier. "I don't believe Rath is going to let your men live. With us dead from a crash in a neighborhood outside of Amsterdam, he doesn't need them for anything. They're a liability. I am sorry."

Holmes clearly hadn't considered that and the horror of it cast a shadow behind his eyes. He and the others had been strangers until just a short while ago, but they were all part of the Flying Corps and shared a bond not bound by the duration of their acquaintance. Their loss was a lance to the heart, and yet he couldn't let it pierce through to his soul. His was a grim business and he knew the risks. He shook his head as though to slough off the melancholy and clear his mind for the task at hand.

"Bloody war," he said just loud enough for Bell to hear.

Not long after, they spotted the muddy mire that was the Western

Front, a loathsome stain on an otherwise beautiful countryside. What they hadn't spotted were any German patrols. They were north of the armies skirmishing around Arras before the main battle got underway and so air cover appeared to be nonexistent.

They had managed to claw their way to eleven thousand feet. It was bitterly cold and both men felt like a horse sat on their chest and prevented them from completely filling their lungs with the thin, oxygen-poor air. They droned on over the battle-scarred land, just able to make out lines of trenches amid the churned soil. It took only a few minutes to cross from the German-occupied side of the line to the Allied portion, and while it was a relief to be almost home, the danger of being attacked actually increased, since they were clearly flying a German bomber.

"Stay high or go low?" Holmes asked.

Bell considered the question and finally said, "Not too many pilots loiter above this altitude, so the chances are we won't be jumped. Best stay up here until we spot an airdrome. The danger comes when we try to land."

"I agree."

Fifteen minutes later they both spotted an airfield at the same time. The runway was clearly marked out with signal flags, and two large hangars had been erected along the flight line. Near them were a clutch of smaller buildings. Several planes were flying in a loose formation in the direction of the field following their morning patrol. The planes looked like insects from their altitude.

"Here we go," Holmes called and eased back on the throttle, at the same time putting the big plane into a circling dive.

It was just bad luck that the lead fighter heading in for a landing took one last look around the sky and spotted what he assumed was a German plane intent on bombing their airfield. He put on speed, and the two planes lined up with him also aborted their landing and began a furious climb toward the bomber.

Bell and Holmes increased pressure on their respective wheels in order to steepen their dive and thus reduce their exposure. Holmes also gave the bomber a little more throttle, but not like their earlier near-suicidal dive.

The Allied fighters were climbing as hard as they could, approaching the plummeting German plane with the speed of a knight in a joust. They would only get one crack at using their machine guns before flashing past. By the time they got turned back around, the bomber would have had time to unleash its payload, by their reckoning.

Holmes and Bell watched the planes grow larger through the windscreen. They were rushing at each other at a nearly two-hundred-knot closure.

"Nieuports," Holmes said when he recognized the model. "French kites. Very good."

They waited as long as they dared as the range shrank at a frightening rate. Just seconds before the lead plane opened fire with its Vickers machine gun, Holmes and Bell worked the wheel to slew the Zeppelin-Staaken out of the direct line of fire. Their move made the pilot miss entirely and left him with no time to adjust his aim before the two aircraft rocketed past each other.

They successfully avoided the attack run by the second plane, but the third managed to pour a half dozen 7.7-millimeter rounds into the bomber. Most of the bullets slammed into the starboard engine and lower wing. Two shattered the windows on Bell's side of the cockpit, but thankfully missed both men.

The lead starboard motor seized a moment later, as all its lubricant had drained away through a crack in the oil pan.

The asymmetry of the thrust made the plane crab through the sky as it continued its descent. They countered this by each stomping on the rudder pedal in the opposite direction. Holmes quickly reduced power from the port engines to compensate. In just a couple of seconds they'd fully recovered the plane.

"Where are those Nieuports?" the Brit asked through bloodless lips.

Bell looked aft as best he could. "The lead plane is coming into a dive after us. I can't see the other two."

They remained tense as the altitude bled off. It was a race to the ground. Bell kept trying to track the lead fighter, but the Nieuport had to be directly behind them and hidden. The others had yet to show themselves again. They swerved the giant bomber through the sky as they descended, trying to foul the pilot's aim as his quicker and far more nimble fighter swooped down on them like a hawk.

Moments later they were too low for evasive maneuvers and were forced to hold her steady as they lined up on the runway. They were less than thirty feet above the grass field when the trailing Nieuport had them in his sights and opened up with his Vickers. It was like a buzz saw against a balsa-wood toy. The Zeppelin-Staaken's tail took the brunt of the stream of lead slugs that the pilot directed for maximum effect. Wood and canvas and yards of control wiring came apart in a spectacular failure that saw nearly the entire assembly disintegrate.

The result was instantaneous. Without the double horizontal stabilizers countering the main wing's natural rotation, the plane's nose dipped. There was nothing either pilot could do. The front landing gear hit the ground hard enough to crack the axle. That impact knocked the nose up once again and then the main gear struck the field. Both men were slammed into their seats by the force and shaken like rag dolls as the plane barreled down the runway with zero control.

There was more torque being generated on the port side because both engines were still functioning and so the plane started a ground loop, turning in a long arc that nearly flipped it onto a wing tip. The pressure against the landing gear drove the two sets of main tires to collapse. The props still spinning flew apart when they came in contact with the ground, sending wood splinters the size of daggers through the cabin just aft of the two battered pilots.

The remaining engines ceased working and the wreckage came to an ignoble stop.

As much as Bell wanted to leap from his seat and get as far from the downed plane as he could in case there was a fire, he couldn't bring himself to move for nearly a minute. His spine felt like it had been wrung out like a wet rag and the base of his neck like he'd been hit with a tire iron. He managed to look over at Liam Holmes. He was unconscious, blood oozing from his forehead where he'd cracked it against a window frame.

The sight of the unconscious pilot galvanized Bell into action. He shucked off his seat belt and knelt next to the Brit. As he got close, Holmes moaned and pulled himself upright.

"You okay?"

"I wish this was the worst hangover of my life," he said. "It would feel better."

"You'll live," Bell replied with a smile at Holmes's very British humor.

He helped the man out of his seat and supported him by an arm as they shuffled out of the cockpit toward the still-open starboard door. There was no smoke outside the aircraft, just a cloud of settling dust. In the distance uniformed men were running from the hangars toward the downed plane. Bell gestured for Holmes to wait until he was on the ground in order to catch him.

Bell tossed down the incriminating briefcase and sat on the wing's trailing edge. He slid aft until he tumbled off of it. He hit the ground after a five-foot fall and dropped to his knees as if in prostration.

When he looked up, it was into the glowing tawny eyes of a juvenile lion that was staring at him from no more than two feet away.

27

⸙

THE INCONGRUITY OF HIS SITUATION FROZE BELL IN THE POSI-
tion in which he'd fallen, on his knees, his chin inches from the
ground. The lion's tail twitched in agitation and a rumble built deep
in its throat. Its mouth opened to show a pair of inch-long fangs. It
took a tentative step toward him. Its claws were still retracted, which
he took as a good sign.

And then Bell saw boots and heard voices.

"Whiskey, get away from him, you bad cat." The voice was pure
American upper crust. "Raoul, do something about this mangy
beast."

Bell looked up, now even more confused. Several pilots and mechanics had arrived from across the airfield. They wore a patchwork
of uniform coats, riding breaches, overalls, and all manner of non-
regulation hats. The pilot who'd spoken was on the short side, and
despite the thin mustache, possessed a classic baby face. No one

seemed to show any animosity toward the pilots of a German bomber that had crashed their home turf. If anything, they showed amused curiosity.

Another pilot arrived. The lion immediately padded to his side, and he gave its dark mane a couple of affectionate strokes.

Bell chanced getting to his feet.

"I say, chaps, I could use a hand," Liam Holmes called from his perch atop the plane's wing.

Two mechanics quickly got into position to catch him as he slid off of it. "Thanks, boys." He accepted a handful of cotton waste to wipe the worst of the blood from his face. He managed to merely smear it and looked even more demonic.

The squadron that had strafed the plane were on final approach.

"My name is Isaac Bell. Where exactly are we?"

"American? What do you know?" said the baby-faced flyer. "Welcome to the Lafayette Escadrille. Home to a mad bunch of American pilots willing to go at it against the Boche on behalf of the Allies. I'm John Drexel."

Bell was very familiar with the volunteer American flyers. If not for Marion, he probably would have joined up as well. Then the young pilot's name rang a cord in his memory. "Are you Tony Drexel's little brother?"

"Dear God," he said with a toothy grin. "The world's a small place, but I still wouldn't want to pay to dry-clean it. Bell? I know who you are. You've flown at a couple of events around New York with Tony. He's mentioned you to me. How the hell did you end up here flying this . . . pterodactyl?"

Just then another pilot approached, this one better turned out, with shined boots, a pressed uniform, and his cap at a rakish angle. He had a typical Gaulish face and the obligatory mustache.

"*Bonjour.* I am Captain Thenault, commander of the Lafayette."

Holmes came to attention and saluted. "Captain Liam Holmes of the Royal Flying Corps."

Thenault returned the salute and looked to Bell. Bell stretched out his hand for a shake. "Isaac Bell, chief detective of the Van Dorn Agency. I'm a civilian on a fact-finding mission for our President, Woodrow Wilson. I was briefly attached to the British 22nd Aero Squadron on the request of Winston Churchill, the former Lord of the Admiralty and current Minister of Munitions."

Bell knew he was laying it on pretty thick, but he had a sense of urgency coursing through him like electricity in a high-voltage wire, and the sooner he established his bona fides the better. He wanted to get back into Belgium on the jump because his interest in Karl Rath was far from over.

"Perhaps we should go to my office to talk. Captain 'Olmes, do you require medical attention? I can send for our corpsman."

"It looks worse than it is, but it's not going to stop bleeding without a dressing. One would be greatly appreciated."

"*D'accord.*" He spoke in French to one of the mechanics, who dashed off in the direction of the airdrome HQ.

Ten minutes later, the three men were enjoying coffee in Thenault's office overlooking the airfield. In the distance, mechanics and off-duty pilots were crawling all over the Zeppelin-Staaken like ants over a dead bird's carcass.

Bell told the Frenchman about his mission on behalf of the President and how he came to be shot down over German-held territory and captured along with Liam Holmes, who'd been shot down a few days earlier. He told him about the escape and subsequent recapture by Karl Rath and his men. He kept his tale as dry as possible so as not to push the captain's credulity. He then handed over the briefcase and explained the circumstances around their flight and escape back over the Allied lines.

"Is this genuine?" the Frenchman asked, pawing over the sheaf of documents.

"Not remotely," Bell assured him. "They are very good, to be sure, but they're forgeries. But I don't think that matters. I've been thinking about this for a bit. The Dutch have been surrounded by war for three straight years. Their people are suffering. They want it to end just as badly as everyone else. This gives them an excuse to open a new front against Germany and accelerate the end of the conflict."

"Why would this anarchist, Rath, want that?"

"No country that has fought in this war is going to look the same once it's over. An entire generation of young men have been gunned down. That alone will change demographics for the rest of the twentieth century. Empires are crumbling. I believe the monarchies of Europe, the Hapsburgs, the Romanovs, the Ottomans, Prussia's Hohenzollern, are all going to be swept aside in populist uprisings. Maps are going to be redrawn in ways no one will recognize. Into all that there will be power vacuums that men like Karl Rath know how to exploit. The greater the chaos, the better he will do when the guns finally fall silent."

Thenault and Holmes nodded in silence at Bell's grim assessment because neither man had a counterargument for what could happen to Europe in the foreseeable future.

"Captain Thenault, I need to return to occupied Belgium."

"What?" This was the first Liam Holmes had heard of Bell's plan and his eyes goggled.

"I don't believe our flight was Rath's only operation." Bell pulled out the crumpled piece of paper he'd found in the trash in Rath's headquarters. He'd given it a glance during the flight. He straightened the scrap and held it out to Liam Holmes. "What does your schoolboy German make of this?"

Holmes took it. There were two columns of words, one in a language he didn't recognize but looked Slavish. They were apparently then translated into German. "Ah, let's see. *Anker* is anchor. Um, *Munitionaufzug* is an ammunition hoist or elevator. *Vollgas* means top speed or maybe full speed. Not positive about *Dampfrohr.* I think it's some kind of pipe." He handed it back to Bell. "What is this?"

"I found it in what looked like a classroom back in Rath's warehouse. I figured out the meaning of *Anker* pretty easily. It made me realize the significance of the tattoo I saw on the guy who caught me snooping around. It was a compass rose. That's a sailor's tattoo. Your translation now confirms my suspicion that Rath has some operation in mind involving a warship, something so big it needs a hoist to get ammo to its guns. I need to go back and find out what he's up to next."

Holmes stared at him for a moment. "No offense, mate, but what's your stake in this? What do you care what some anarchist hothead is doing in bloody Europe when your country's not in the fight?"

"Because his last operation was about embroiling a neutral country into the war, and Rath mentioned he sent his brother in New York. I can't risk that being a coincidence."

"What would you like of me?" Thenault asked.

"First I need to contact Captain Crabbe at the 22nd and tell him I'm alive, but that his plane and pilot were both lost. Even with a map I doubt I can give any meaningful location as to where it happened. Then I need to send cables to Churchill in London and my office back in New York. We have our own coding system, but I don't know how you encode communications between the Allied forces."

"We do not have a telegraph here at the airfield," Thenault told him, "but there is a headquarters not far from here with what you will need. I will issue you permission to use their facilities under the escadrille's authority."

"And I hate to ask, but I could really use some new clothes and the use of a cot for a few hours."

"You are too tall to borrow any of the French pilots' clothing, but I'm sure your American comrades can help with that."

"Thank you."

"And Captain Holmes? How may I help you?"

"That cot sounds jolly good, and if you could, I'd like a lift back to the 56th Squadron. We're about fifteen miles south of Arras, unless they've moved us since last Tuesday."

"After you've slept, I will lend you a dispatch rider and his sidecar motorcycle and you shall find your unit together." Thenault gave a dismissive wave. "Now, out with you. I need to write a report for my superiors about how a previously unknown German heavy bomber ended up in my custody."

Both men got to their feet. At the door, Bell paused and turned. "Just out of curiosity, how is it that you have a lion?"

"We have two, Monsieur Bell. Whiskey has a companion named Soda, and we have them because your countrymen are all quite mad."

T HIRTY HOURS LATER, BELL GOT OFF A TRAIN IN THE PORT CITY of Calais and hailed a taxi to take him to the harbor. As the closest point to England, the Calais region had always been a bustling place, but with the war on, the port was a scene of pandemonium. A troopship had just arrived and fresh-faced recruits were marching off the gangways in ordered ranks. Even at a distance Bell could hear the sergeants' bellows. Elsewhere were vast parking lots for trucks that had been sent across the channel and big horse corrals filled with animals. A cruiser of some considerable size was just ahead of the troopship, its main batteries turned out to the sea and no doubt manned all day, every day, on the chance a submarine or other German ship approached.

His destination wasn't these reserved military docks, but a commercial area for fishing boats. This section of France was known as the Opal Coast because of the pearlescent quality of the light. It had attracted artists and poets and writers for generations. Bell found the sky leaden and full of coal smoke and the stench of rotting fish and old hemp.

He eventually located the right fishing pier and the boat hired to take him to Holland. It was a newer trawler, smallish but well-maintained with an A-frame crane over her flat stern. Though a French boat, she flew the red, white, and blue horizontally striped Netherlands flag as a safeguard against a U-boat attack. In truth, the German submarines cared little for the nationality of their victims. They had already sunk over a hundred neutral Dutch fishing boats and killed over a thousand members of their crews.

Bell paused at the quay until he caught the eye of a sailor coiling rope on the forward deck, just under the pilothouse. He noted the time by the angle of the watery sun and nodded.

Bell stepped aboard the boat, mindful the deck was slick with fish oil and slime. A door to a small cabin located under the pilothouse swung open as if haunted. Bell stepped through into a dim, cramped space. Another man was there, dressed in tweeds rather than work clothes or a proper suit. He was shorter than Bell—most men were—and heavier around the middle. He had the soft and long-suffering look of a bureaucrat sent out into the field against his will.

"You must be Bell." His accent was in imitation of an Etonian graduate's.

"I am."

"Wife's maiden name?"

"Morgan."

"Name of the man who rescued her in Panama?"

Bell chuckled at the memory and how she liked to tell the tale. "Teddy Roosevelt."

"Her favorite color?"

"The same blue as her eyes," he said without hesitation.

"And indeed you are Bell," the man said rather more cordially and stuck out a hand. "Thomas Wrightsmith, Naval Intelligence. Winston still has some clout in Room 40, so I got the call to come over to meet with you." He looked around at the tiny cabin as if seeing it for the first time. "Not exactly luxurious, is it?"

"You didn't cross the channel on this boat?"

"Oh, heavens no. I came over on a destroyer parked on the other side of the port. This rattletrap is taking you to Rotterdam, while I head home with the next convoy." Wrightsmith indicated the two pieces of luggage at his feet. "Your wife and Mrs. Churchill didn't think one of your regular suits would work with the cover we've devised for you, so they went shopping. You should have everything you need for a couple of days in German-held territory."

"And the other case?" Bell asked.

Wrightsmith lifted it onto a small table between two bench seats bolted to the deck. It took a little more effort than Bell thought necessary and it hit the table with a solid thunk. The British spy worked the latches and opened the leather case's lid. He had to open a second flap that covered the main part of the case. The insides were divided into nearly sixty individual cells, like a bee's honeycomb. In each little cubby were various-sized ball bearings.

"Since no state of war exists between your country and the Germans, you get to keep your name, but from here on you're a representative for the Fullerton Forge of Pittsburgh, Pennsylvania. It's an open secret that the Kaiser underestimated the number of these little balls needed to prosecute a modern, mechanized war, and their supplies are dwindling. If you are stopped for any reason, the authorities should look favorably on your mission and will likely give you a pass."

"Good thinking."

"You're not the first spy we've sent in using a similar cover," Wrightsmith confessed. "Rest assured, they all made it back out again."

The spy handed over a leather billfold of documents. Inside was a visa to enter Germany, letters of introduction to several industrial suppliers inside Belgium, business cards for the Fullerton Forge, and sample order sheets.

"Very thorough," Bell said.

"We have some of the best forgers in the business," Wrightsmith said with some pride. "Now, there is a bicycle factory one town over from where this Rath character is based out of. It's been converted to make motorcycles for the German signal corps, meaning your presence in the area peddling ball bearings won't arouse suspicion."

"Okay, good. What about transport? A car?"

"Too conspicuous, even for a traveling American. Best if you use trains. Tickets have already been bought." Wrightsmith paused to make certain he had Bell's full attention when he added, "I don't need to remind you what would happen should the United States enter the war while you're in Germany. The Germans not letting you leave will be the least of your worries. They will be suspicious of the timing of your visit and you'll likely end up in Berlin in front of a man named Walter Nicolai."

"Who's that?"

"He heads up Department IIIb. Counterespionage. A real nasty piece of work by all accounts. Rumor has it that he personally outed Margaretha Zelle as a German spy to the French."

"I'm not sure I recognize—"

"Better known as the exotic dancer Mata Hari. Story we're getting from our own spies is he grew annoyed that all the intelligence she gathered was about boudoir-hopping French officers and their various conquests and is letting the Deuxième Bureau do his dirty work. Mark my word, the frog-eaters are going to put her up against a wall soon enough, sans blindfold and last cigarette."

"Grim," Bell remarked.

"My point being is that if your lot does declare, get yourself out as fast as you can and assume that legal checkpoints are out."

"Got it."

"That's about it, then, Mr. Bell. Consider yourself briefed. The boat will be met in Rotterdam, and you'll be escorted to the station for a train into the occupied territories." Wrightsmith shook Bell's hand and doffed his hat. From the door of the little cabin he said over his shoulder, "Good luck and all that, Yank."

28

———⚬✄⚬———

Aᴼᵀᴱʀ ᴛʜᴇ Eɴɢʟɪꜱʜᴍᴇɴ ʜᴀᴅ ɢᴏɴᴇ, Bᴇʟʟ ᴏᴘᴇɴᴇᴅ ᴛʜᴇ ꜱᴜɪᴛ-
case to find a suit of decent rather than luxurious wool and
a shirt and tie of matching quality. The shoes on the bottom of the
case were used, with just the right amount of scuffs and polish for a
busy salesman on the go. The few other items matched his cover
story costume and he could imagine Marion having fun with
Clementine Churchill picking everything out. As his Cartier wrist-
watch was back in England, they had included a Swiss pocket watch
by Doxa.

He checked it against the ship's chronometer above the table and
gave it a quick wind. He cleaned up as best he could in the galley's
pump sink, using his old shirt as a towel. As he was dressing himself,
the tone of the fishing boat's idling engines deepened as lines were
cast and they began to pull away from the pier. He didn't bother
with the tie just yet, but gratefully slipped on the sweater the two
women had thoughtfully packed. His eye caught what looked like

253

moth holes on the bottom hem. Closer examination revealed them to be knitting needle–sized punctures to make the new sweater appear older and more lived in.

He loved his wife all the more for her attention to detail.

He stepped out onto the rear deck to watch the harbor pass by. On some unconscious level he could still smell the loamy mud in the trenches and the stench of death that oozed up from beneath it. It was good to purge his lungs with deep drafts of the tangy sea air. It also served to clear his head.

Bell well knew he was about to risk his life on the belief that President Wilson wouldn't declare war on Germany until he heard his full report from the front lines. Through Winston Churchill he'd sent some preliminary notes to Washington on the conditions American troops would face and his belief that the war was being fought with twentieth-century weapons but seventeenth-century tactics, and a continuation of this blunder would kill scores of American soldiers unnecessarily.

He hadn't added that he believed Europe would not enjoy a meaningful and lasting peace at war's end unless America had a place at the bargaining table. To bring that about, the United States needed a hefty military presence on the battlefront ahead of time.

Bell made his way to the pilothouse. The captain and his mate greeted him with silence. Whatever they were being paid to transport him to Holland clearly wasn't enough to buy a little courtesy.

It was a ten-hour journey to the port of Rotterdam, a trip that saw fair weather and no German U-boats or bobbing anti-ship mines. The only moment of interest on the voyage occurred when the first mate spotted a pair of massive Zeppelins on their return leg from a bombing run to London. The airships were trundling along at about five thousand feet and looked as big as ocean liners. The two Frenchmen had a quick excited conversation about the dirigibles.

"What is it?" Bell asked, his curiosity piqued.

The captain thought for a moment, translating into English in his head before speaking. "These are different, bigger, and they are painted black. That is new. We will report this when we return to Calais."

The docks at Rotterdam were a frenzy of ships, vehicles, and men—a riotous chaos of chugging tugboats, swinging cranes, and lumbering trains accompanied by a tin-eared symphony of ships' horns and steam whistles. As the Netherlands remained neutral, much of Germany's international trade came through the port, including most of its imported food. The Allies had a treaty in place to curb some activity, but the temptations of smuggling meant the Germans remained supplied and shipowners and captains were getting rich.

Rotterdam was also a hotbed of espionage, with cadres of spies from both the Allies and the Central Powers prowling the docks and the streets of the ancient central city. It was from here that British intelligence ran spy rings throughout Germany and occupied Belgium. The city was also home to a large number of Belgian refugees as well as deserters from the French and German armies.

Bell stood at the rail of the fishing boat as it approached a wooden pier that looked ready to collapse at any moment. As a precaution against German spies, he wore a battered peacoat over his suit and his luggage was slung over his shoulder in a dirty canvas seabag. He stepped onto the dock and the boat's skipper immediately pulled away into the channel to swing back around and return to France.

Bell walked to the end of the pier, where a man was waiting next to an empty truck.

"Welcome to the Netherlands, Mr. Bell," he greeted in Oxford-accented English. "Needn't worry about disguising yourself as a fisherman today. The Germans who usually watch this part of the port were tipped off about some fiction of British agents arriving today aboard a Spanish-flagged schooner. We're quite alone."

Bell shook the spy's bony hand and shrugged out of the salt-rimed peacoat. "Glad to hear it. This jacket smells like a seal colony my wife made me visit in La Jolla." He tossed it into the truck's bed along with the unnecessary seabag. "And you are?"

"No one of consequence or whose name you should worry about. I have your train tickets and will be your chauffeur to the station. The return tickets are all open-ended, so take all the time you need."

"Fair enough. What about getting back to England?"

"When you get back here to Rotterdam, just buy a bloody ticket to London. Passenger liners aren't running, of course, but you can cross on a freighter braving the Boche and their U-boats."

The nameless driver needed the better part of an hour to get them out of the sprawling port. A short while later found them at one of the city's four principal train stations. "You have a bit of a journey ahead of you, as there are no trains currently crossing into occupied Belgium, your final destination as I understand it."

"That's where I was taken after escaping the German prison."

"Didn't need to know that," his British minder said. "Anyway, you have tickets to Amsterdam, and from there south into Germany and across into Belgium. Good luck, Mr. Bell, and I hope to hell it's worth it."

Bell hoped so, too.

An hour later he was in a crowded carriage on the first leg of his journey into occupied Belgium. The train car was dirty, with soot ground into the wooden floor and litter gathered in the corners and under the seats. The people themselves were quiet, stoic, even. Though they were neutral, the strain of massive armies fighting to the death just across the border was clearly leaving its mark on the Dutch people. No one made eye contact or offered to chat up a neighbor.

Bell changed trains in Amsterdam. He had time for a sandwich at a café as the shadows lengthened with dusk's impending arrival. The bread was good, if not exactly fresh. He couldn't determine the origin of the meat by taste alone. It was fatty and shot through with gristle and only made palatable by the honey mustard that had been spread across the whole of the sandwich. The coffee was little more than hot water stained black.

He was jolted awake hours later when his southbound train reached the German border and came to a coupling-crashing halt. Powerful lights on tall poles gave the scene a garish, brassy glare that cast stark shadows of barbed-wire fences and men with dogs on tight leashes.

All of the passengers were ordered off the train by German border guards armed with Mauser rifles. They were told to bring their luggage. When Bell stepped down onto the ballast stones next to the tracks, he saw that the train had entered an enclosure made of barbed wire with doors at either end that could be closed while the carriages and locomotive and its passengers were examined. It felt like a prison.

While inspectors went through the boxcars at the end of the train, customs agents checked the two dozen or so passengers headed into Germany. Many were German citizens on day trips to Amsterdam and were quickly let back aboard the train.

"*Name*," Bell was asked when he reached the little table the Germans had set up next to the lead carriage.

"My name is Isaac Bell," he said as casually as possible.

The customs man looked up sharply, sucking air through his teeth. Two nearby guards moved closer, their grip on their weapons a little tighter.

"I'm an American businessman," he added in hopes of cutting the thickening tension. "I plan to make some sales in your beautiful country."

The customs man took the visa and studied Bell's identification. It was a company ID from the Fullerton Forge company and thoughtfully included a photograph of Bell. He recognized it as half of a couples picture that Marion liked to keep in a silver frame on their bedside when they traveled. She'd cropped out herself and the fact Bell was wearing a tuxedo.

"What do you sell?" the German asked, his eyes like slits in the harsh light.

Bell lifted his sample case from the ground and shook it. "Ball bearings, the finest America has to offer, in fact." The agent indicated Bell was to open the case on his desk. He did. The man poked around the little cubbies of steel balls with the tip of his pen. He waved away the case, which Bell secured and closed.

The man started writing information on his ledger sheet. It seemed to be more information than Bell had provided and the silent scribblings went on while the locomotive chuffed nearby.

"Is there a problem?" Bell finally asked, his concern genuine.

The man shot him a bloodless stare. He had the power to deny Bell entry on a whim. Bell kept his face open and friendly. The customs agent eventually closed his ledger without looking at it further, sat impassive for several more seconds, and then said in a dismissive sneer, "Welcome to Germany, *schwein* American."

Bell didn't react at all. He simply took his cases and mounted the stairs back into the first-class carriage. Had the light been more natural, the Germans would have seen that his ears had gone beet red with suppressed rage.

Dawn found him in another station inside Germany. The pastry he had for breakfast was better than the sandwich dinner, but there was no improvement on the coffee. The Germans waiting for the next train with him were even more grim than the Dutch, and Bell could see that everyone's clothes seemed a size too large. The German people were eating, but not nearly as well as a few years earlier. Another toll being taken by the populace was that there were no young men about unless they were in uniform and headed back to the front or going home on leave.

Because of that, Bell noticed that many young women were dressed to do work that had been traditionally men's jobs. Even the ticket taker on the train to occupied Liège was a pretty blond girl who looked like she was playing dress-up in her father's conductor's uniform.

The border into occupied Belgium was even more fortified than the one between Germany and the Netherlands. As before, the entire train was boxed inside a barbed-wire enclosure and every car and passenger was checked. There were more guards, more dogs, and a heightened sense of watchfulness.

It took twice as long to clear the checkpoint as the night before. Bell once again had to show his ball bearing samples as well as having his luggage rummaged through and standing still for a thorough pat down. Bell wasn't sure if there had been problems that necessitated such paranoia or if it was merely Teutonic efficiency.

In truth the only thing he knew about what was happening in Belgium was that an American mining engineer named Herbert Hoover had been instrumental in getting relief supplies into the country to stave off widespread famine and starvation.

As they pulled away from the frontier outpost and entered the first Belgian town, he saw the contrast immediately. The people may not have been on the brink of starvation, but he was shocked by the hollow cheeks and the sunken eyes and the fact that people were gray. Not pale, not wan, but an ash-gray color that made them look like gaunt living statues. He saw no children playing, no old men chatting over coffee at cafés, no ladies out shopping for their families. He saw misery and defeat and a pall of joylessness that hovered over the town, permeating every nook and cranny as if these people all existed in purgatory.

The German military presence wasn't overwhelming, but to know your nation was under the boot of another was so demoralizing and dehumanizing that it looked like it wouldn't take more than a few soldiers in each town to keep the population in line. To think of a country with such vast overseas colonies being brought to its knees in a few short months and now in its third year of occupation made Bell shudder. America hadn't had foreign soldiers on its soil since the British were routed at the Battle of New Orleans more than a century ago.

The train continued on, chugging lethargically from the border as if it, too, had been affected by the social and economic malaise that had ground Belgium into the dirt. No one was in the fields preparing them for the spring planting season. The few roads he could see from the carriage had been ruined by the passage of heavy German cannons and mortars when they transected the country on the way to France. A couple of farmhouses he noted had been destroyed during the invasion and now sat abandoned, the adjoining fields overrun with scrub.

They rolled into Liège at lunchtime. Bell was eager to get out of Belgium as quickly as possible and so he bought some black bread and liverwurst at the station and ate while he walked to his final destination. There were no taxis, though he managed to hitch a ride on the back of a wagon carrying milk urns for the final mile into the town where Rath was holed up.

Bell found a hotel first thing. He wasn't sure how he was going to go about getting information from Rath or one of his men. He hadn't planned that far ahead, but he figured it would take a couple of days at the least for something to come to him. Best he rent a room. Bell stowed his luggage under the twin-sized bed and then headed out to find the warehouse. The town wasn't all that large, and he'd seen some of it on the ride to the German airfield, so it took him only a short amount of time.

His nose led him around the last few corners through a run-down industrial part of the town. The smell of burnt wood and charcoal was overwhelming.

He rounded the last turn and saw what he already knew he would see. The warehouse had been burned to the ground. Only a few brick half walls and the stumps of toppled chimneys remained upright. He could see some plumbing fixtures coated in soot among the rubble, but everything else had been reduced to ash. No doubt Rath had doused the building in kerosene or gasoline before putting it to the torch.

There was no evidence that the local fire brigade tried to douse the flames, no puddles of filthy water or wet pieces of crocodile-skin timber. They had likely faced a raging inferno and thought it best to just let the fire do its worst.

Knowing it was a waste of time, Bell was ever the consummate investigator and spent an hour sifting through the wreckage. A few times he kicked up a pile of wood that was still smoldering even though the fire had been days ago, probably the same day he had taken off in the Zeppelin-Staaken with Liam Holmes. He found nothing useful and so dusted off his suit pants and strode from the site.

29

BELL HAD ONE HOPE OF SALVAGING THIS MISSION. MAGDALENA
hadn't given him the name of the tavern her father owned, but
it stood to reason that the matchbook he'd swiped from Rath's office
had been a promotional item from there. Bell recalled the establish-
ment's name and after fetching his luggage from the little inn and
getting directions from the innkeeper, he soon came to the place. It
was late afternoon by this time. Too early for the after-work crowd
and well past the late lunch takers.

A little bell tinkled gaily when Bell opened the heavy oak door
that was likely two hundred years old. The interior of the tavern was
dim, but not dark, the perfect level of light for intimacy or bonhomie
depending on what one was looking for. There were a half dozen
tables, as solid and ancient as the door, and a long bar running along
the rear wall that had places for a dozen drinkers.

A man with an apron wrapped around his waist had just left the room through the door to the kitchen. That left a woman bent over a table with a rag in her hand. Bell had only seen Magdalena on two brief occasions, but he was a master of recognizing people even at angles he'd never seen before.

"Magdalena," he called softly.

She turned. No amount of makeup could hide the black eye she'd been given. She quickly moved her head so that her coils of hair partially covered the ugly bruise even before she recognized the stranger who'd come to her father's bar. "You?"

"Like the proverbial bad penny." He crossed to her, and they both took a seat at the table. Besides the black eye, her lower lip was swollen. Her fingers worked at the threadbare bar rag in her hands.

She could not meet his eye. "Karl said you and the Englishman died when your plane crashed."

"That was the fate he had in store for us, but we had other ideas." He cupped her chin gently and raised it so she had to face him.

"Why are you here?" she asked.

"I need to find out what he has planned next. I also need to know what happened to the other English flyers. The three men we left when we took off in Rath's bomber."

"I am sorry. He had them killed. I saw their bodies when the police recovered them following the fire."

Bitterness scalded the back of Bell's throat. He had guessed their fate straight away, but the confirmation struck deep. He would make sure word got back to the Royal Flying Corps of their fate.

"And Rath's plans? Where did he go? What is it he hopes to accomplish?"

"He took all his belongings for a long trip, but I do not know where," she said. "He left not long after you that morning, with all of his people except one, a man they call a *pyromane*."

"Pyromaniac," Bell guessed.

"He likes fire. A short while later, the warehouse Karl had rented burned down and the *pyromane* vanished."

"Yes, I was just there. A rather unsubtle case of arson. But surely Rath gave you some idea of his intentions. All those men? How many did he have and what were they training for?"

"There were forty-five men in total," she said, very sure of herself. "He said it was the bare minimum, but he never told me for what. They did, ah, *callisthenie*." She pantomimed someone lifting weights over their head.

"Calisthenics."

"Yes, that. They had classroom instructions, too, but I do not know what they were taught."

Bell said, "I saw one of the men on the night I stayed in the warehouse. He had a tattoo on his chest that made me think he was a sailor. Did anyone else have sailor's tattoos?"

Her eyes lit up for the first time as if she were happy to be of some use. "Yes, many of them did. They liked to show them off to me when Karl wasn't around. Some were very, ah, risqué. Nude women and mermaids with big . . ." Another pantomime.

"I get the idea."

"That helps me remember now. When Karl left, he said he was going on a voyage, one that would start a new world."

Bell arched a brow at the comment. Her information was further proof he was on the right track about Rath's preparations, though not his exact plan.

"What did he mean by start a new world?"

Magdalena shrugged. "I can't say for certain. Karl was angry and bitter over the murder of his parents. They were killed by the Hungarian police, apparently over some business dispute. Their farm and lands were taken as a result."

"Karl is from Hungary?"

"No, further east, high in the Carpathian Mountains where there are no real borders. He and his brother became brigands. But they only attacked and robbed aristocrats. Karl hates royalty. He espoused that all of Europe's crowned heads be decapitated at war's end, most especially the Hapsburg monarchy."

"He wants a new world order without dynastic rule."

"It is more than that. I overheard many conversations where he discussed subverting troops to march against their own governments, then to destroy the banks and other institutions." She looked away a moment with a hardened stare. "Karl lives to destroy, but thinks he can rise from the ashes of the ruination like a phoenix, to rule all. He is very forceful. Maybe he can do it."

"Not while I'm breathing," Bell replied. But he knew history's cold lessons. Revolutions needed a guiding figure to lead the masses after the destruction ended. Amid the chaos and confusion, the rise of autocratic rule was an all-too-common aftermath.

He shook away the thought, as there was another thread he needed to tug. "Rath's brother. Did you ever meet him?"

"Yes," she said, and the melancholy returned. "Balka."

"Why did Balka go to New York?"

"Karl sent him to live in America. I don't know why, but it had to be for something important, because he was more like a father to Balka than a brother. He raised him from the time their parents were killed."

"He was here with Karl and the others?"

"Yes, for a time. They had a radio in the warehouse that Balka operated. He was always practicing on it with another man before he departed."

"What is Balka like? Big like Karl?"

"No. He is thin and delicate and beautiful. You are a handsome man. Balka is different. He is beautiful, like a woman, but he is still all man. Do you know what I mean?"

"I think so," Bell assured her.

"He is who every girl believes she loves, but also who their mothers and grandmothers desire as well."

"Got it."

"But he is only beautiful on the outside. Inside he is rotting. He has no soul, only cruelty. In that, he is like Karl. He cares only for himself."

"It sounds like he hurt you."

"No," she denied quickly. "I was Karl's woman by the time Balka arrived in town."

"I'm sorry he . . ." Bell made a vague gesture toward her blackened eye.

"If only that was the worst Karl left me with," Magdalena said and laid a protective hand across her belly in a gesture as old as motherhood.

"Did he know?"

"It wouldn't have mattered if he did," she told him matter-of-factly. "He was finished here in town and finished with me."

"I'm sorry," Bell said sincerely. "What will happen to you now?"

"I have two aunts in Antwerp. They are *célibataires*. They never married."

"We call them spinsters."

"My father is sending me to live with them. I can return some months after the baby is born and claim the father was a former soldier who was killed resisting the Germans."

"There will be a lot of women in that exact same situation in the coming years and a whole generation of fatherless children." Making such a statement made Bell think about what he was going to report to Wilson. The more he worked on this, the harder a recommendation became.

"At least those women can talk about their husbands' nobility, their sacrifices. My child will not hear such tales about his own father." Anger pinched her voice.

"I know I already asked, but it is important. Is there anything, anything at all that Rath let slip about his plans?"

"I am sorry, monsieur. He told me nothing. I realized too late that I was his servant and plaything, nothing more. Wait, in Germany on the night he was to rescue you from the castle, he mentioned there are other men like him from all over the world who wanted to shape the future how they saw fit. I did not know what it meant."

That wasn't exactly a revelation, he thought. The world was filled with megalomaniacs who thirsted for power and control. He kept the disappointment off his face. Magdalena had proved helpful in her own right, but not to the detail Bell had hoped. He asked, "Do you have access to the black market?"

"Monsieur?"

"I only have a little bit of local money, but I have plenty of British pounds. If I give you some, can you get it exchanged?" Marion had packed him far too much cash and so he felt it was the least he could do.

"I can, but it is not necessary."

"I don't know how much longer this war is going to go on, so you will need it. If not for yourself, then for the baby." He gave her a smile. "I hear they grow expensive very quickly."

She looked like she was going to refuse again. Bell pulled some notes from the wallet Marion and Clementine had provided and thrust them into her hand. He closed her fingers around the bundle. With the Belgian economy in ruins, it was probably the most money she'd seen since the Germans rolled across the frontier back in August of '14.

Her eyes went limpid with tears. "*Merci*, monsieur. You are very kind. I saw that right away."

Bell settled his hat back on his head. "Take care of yourself and good luck."

Bags in hand, Bell walked out of the bar. The train station was over a mile away, but he had plenty of time. He went down the street for no more than a half block when he spotted a narrow alley. He looked back and saw nothing untoward, but still he darted into the alley, set down his bags, and waited for his quarry.

He needed only a minute before the aproned man from the tavern rushed by. Bell reached out a hand to grab his arm and pull him into the shadowy alleyway.

"I figured you wouldn't talk in front of your daughter," Bell told the startled tavern owner. "But I sensed you have something to tell me."

The two men sized each other up. Magdalena's father had salt-and-pepper hair and mustache, a slight gut, a slouch, and tired, tired eyes. He was a man who now merely existed rather than lived. Bell suspected his daughter's pregnancy at the hands of a bastard like Karl Rath was the last straw on his trail of defeats.

Bell wasn't sure what the Belgian saw in him, but whatever it was it seemed to pass some internal test. "That man who . . ."

"No need to say it," Bell assured him.

"Will you kill him?"

"He tried to kill me and a friend as well as executing three inno-cent airmen. For those crimes alone, I plan on killing him. As for the rest of his villainy, that will be between him and God."

The barman studied Bell's eyes, and he nodded. "I believe you. He would come in occasionally on nights when my Magdalena wasn't working, drinking with some of his men. They would sing folk songs in their native tongue and get drunker and drunker. They scared away other customers, but I was powerless. They had been known to beat shop owners, and they had stopped paying rent on that warehouse after threatening the owner's family if he tried to evict them. We have no police and no one would dare tell the Ger-mans, so there was nothing we could do."

"I'm sorry, but how does this help me find him?"

"*Je suis désolé.* I am sorry. I talk too much, according to Magda-lena. When they were ready to leave my café, they would always toast a man. He sounded important to them, like they worked for him. If you can find him, maybe he can lead you to that . . . savage."

"And the name?"

"Joaquim Marques Lisboa. Does it mean anything to you?"

"Not at all. Sounds Portuguese."

"I do not know, but they all seemed to respect him a great deal. I know it is not much, but I hope it helps."

As he did with the man's daughter, Bell didn't let his disappoint-ment show on his face. The lofty-sounding name of some foreign gentleman wasn't exactly a hot tip. "Thank you," Bell told him. "In my line of work, one never knows where a clue will lead."

They shook hands, and the Belgian ambled back to his quiet little tavern in an unimportant little town in the middle of the greatest war mankind had ever fought.

30

B ELL ATE HIS DINNER AT A CAFÉ NEAR THE SMALL TRAIN STA-
tion. It was potato and leek stew that was unsurprisingly watery. He washed it down with a pale Belgian beer that was remarkably
good, if a little sweet for Bell's American taste. He chuckled at people's priorities. Thin gruel all day, every day is fine so long as it's
accompanied by a decent beer. He assumed the people in France
weren't scrimping on their wine, either.

He considered dumping his luggage in the trash at the station—
the attaché of ball bearings weighed the better part of twenty
pounds—but decided to keep his salesman's cover until he was back
in the Netherlands.

The train pulled into the station right on time and Bell found a
seat in the first-class carriage. He stowed his two cases on the overhead shelf and got as comfortable as he could. The sun had set,
though there was still light in the sky. Bell tipped his hat brim low

over his eyes and tried to shut down the constant swirl of ideas and insights that kept his brain firing at all hours of the day and night.

An hour after crossing the border back into Germany, Bell roused himself to use the facilities at the end of the passenger car. He heard loud voices coming from the next car. It sounded like quite a party. Instinct told him to go back to his seat and sit until the train pulled into his transfer station sometime after dawn, but he was bored and restless. This trip had been a waste of his time, and his investigation into Karl Rath had cratered before it even started. He felt he deserved a consolatory drink.

He passed through the windy vestibule between the two cars and entered the next one up the line. The back half of the carriage was a dining/bar car with white-jacketed waiters and an upright piano against one wall. The group was mostly men in gray/green high-collared army uniforms, with tall black boots and matching belts around their waists. Each one was armed, and judging by the length of their holsters they carried the fabled P-08 Luger pistol.

There were a few women in dresses, likely the wives of the handful of civilian men toasting their army officers.

Bell was only a few paces into the car when he knew he'd made a mistake. Not that he had anything to hide, but mingling with high-ranking German soldiers while he was technically in the country as a spy wasn't his smartest move.

Not knowing if anyone was paying him any attention, he acted like he realized he'd forgotten something, patted his pockets as if to verify it wasn't there, and was about to turn on his heel and return to his seat.

Bell knew exactly one German, so the odds of being recognized were low, but not precisely zero. Afterward, when he had a chance to reflect, it wasn't all that coincidental. This was the only train running in this part of Germany and it looped westward after leaving Belgium, which made it the logical mode of transportation back home from the castle German intelligence had made their sector HQ.

Deiter Kreisberg was at the far end of the car, effectively screened by the crowd. He had noted Bell's entrance, and for reasons his conscious mind didn't understand at first, he couldn't take his eyes off the newly arrived civilian. In the blink of an eye he realized he knew the man, but couldn't place from where. It was just as the stranger was about to turn away that the synapsis in the major's brain produced the spark of recognition.

He almost dismissed the thought as being too ridiculous, but his memory was one of his better assets. It *was* the American calling himself Abbott, the man who had escaped the castle and killed scores of men, who had put such a black mark on Kreisberg's reputation that he would likely never be promoted again. As it stood, he was lucky not to be court-martialed for the debacle.

Bell had turned and was a step away from opening the car's connecting door when a German shouted a terse order behind him.

"Stop that man!" Kreisberg bellowed in German while fumbling with the holster flap securing his Luger.

Most people would have frozen in that moment, at least for a second or two. It's why police yell vocal orders when trying to apprehend a suspect. A quirk of human evolution makes people pause to better process where the threat is coming from before reacting to it.

Not so Isaac Bell. Even before he registered that he recognized Kreisberg's voice from their meeting in the German castle, he was flinging open the vestibule door as his shoulders hunched to reduce his size as a target. He was through the door before a quick-acting young lieutenant swiped at his arm, but failed to get a grip.

Bell tore open the door to his car just as the fair-haired soldier started after him in pursuit. Bell reached his compartment and hooked an arm against the open door so that his momentum threw him into the compartment while slowing him down. His hand locked around the handle of his attaché case just as the German reached him. Bell swung the case like an Olympic hammer thrower. The confines were tight and the target close, but Bell had enough power behind his swing to batter the side of the soldier's head and drop him unconscious to the compartment floor.

Bell lost seconds looking for the man's gun, only to find he was one of the few in the bar car not strapped with Germany's signature 9 millimeter.

Bell looked back down the length of the car to see Deiter Kreisberg bull through the interconnecting vestibule with a savage look on his face. Unlike the soldier at Bell's feet, the German officer had a pistol clutched in his right hand. Bell caught a break as a passenger opened his compartment door to see what the fuss in the hallway was all about.

Kreisberg used his left hand on the man's face to shove him back into his compartment. It was a small distraction, a couple of seconds at best, but Bell made the most of it. He'd unsnapped his case's clasps and unhooked the inner cover. Like he was at the lanes near the Knickerbocker Hotel, Bell released the contents of his case in an easy underhand roll.

The companionway was narrow, and so the thousands upon thousands of various-sized ball bearings made a virtual carpet across the entire floor that shifted with each tiny motion that transferred up from the tracks through the train's wheels.

Bell turned to flee as more men poured into the car to aid their comrade running after who they assumed was a thief, deserter, or spy. Kreisberg fired off a snap shot that shattered the oil lamp sconce just above Bell's shoulder.

The oil caught fire as it fell to the floor in an incandescent cataract that spread when it hit the floor. The curtain of flames temporarily shielded Bell from his pursuers, but wouldn't last long, as there was little easily combustible material to help the fire grow, nothing like curtains or a cloth suitcase.

Behind Bell, the chase turned into farce.

The Germans all wore stiff-soled jackboots that were especially susceptible to slipping on the countless skittering ball bearings. Kreisberg was the first to go down. His feet came out from under him so suddenly that he didn't have time to brace for the fall. He landed flat on his back and his head hit the floor with the sound of a melon falling off a table. The man right behind him went sideways when he lost his footing and smashed an elbow through one of the train's windows.

When he tried to right himself, he stepped on more of the elusive little balls and went down yet again. Unfortunately for him he reached out to steady himself and ripped open his hand on the jagged glass shards still attached to the windowsill. He screamed and clutched the bloody member to his chest as he fell the rest of the way to the floor.

Behind them, more German officers had their feet kick out from under them. They often took down the man next to them in a desperate bid to stay upright. The ball bearings were as effective as a layer of grease spread across the car's floor. No sooner did one man get back to his feet, he either stepped on more ball bearings and went down again as the car swayed and lurched or was taken down by a comrade who was trying not to tumble himself.

Bell had already fled the car, raced through the next one, and stopped in the windblown vestibule. The coupling linking the carriages together was nowhere near as complex or substantial as the ones back in the States. It didn't even have safety chains. As he pulled a pin from the decoupling handle, he guessed that with everything being poured into the war effort, old stock was once again rolling on German rail lines.

He looked up just as the coupling opened and the train's last three cars started to fall away. He could see shadows rushing down the hallway of the final car. In seconds he witnessed the hatred on Deiter Kreisberg's face as he reached the door. Already thirty feet separated Bell from the slowing compartments. Too far for the German to jump, but close enough for the Luger he still wielded.

Bell scrambled away as Kreisberg threw open the door. He took aim, but Bell had already vanished into the next carriage. The German still fired a full clip in angered frustration that accomplished nothing.

At the next station, Isaac Bell was the first passenger off the train. He didn't recognize the name of the city, but judging by the number of uniformed men milling about, he guessed there was a large army base nearby. Seeing a string of military staff cars waiting outside led him to further deduce that this was Kreisberg and the other officers' destination. There were a few taxis waiting for officers who didn't rank a government vehicle.

Bell approached the first in line, held up the Doxa pocket watch Marion had provided and said, "Netherlands, *ja*? Holland? Dutch?"

The elderly driver got where Bell wanted to go, noted the make of the expensive Swiss watch, and jerked a thumb to the rear passenger compartment while he stepped from the vehicle to crank the engine. Just as it fired, a commotion started to build in the halls of the glass-roofed station when the stationmaster tallied that the newly arrived train was missing three cars. Whistles were blown, conductors began shouting, and drivers waiting to take their charges to whatever meeting had been planned looked about with uncertainty.

Bell's driver looked to the station for a second, turned to look at Bell in a moment of indecision, and finally shrugged as if to say it wasn't his problem.

Two hours later, Bell passed through the border post into the Netherlands on foot, raising no suspicion from either side as he crossed. He was able to convert some of his remaining British pounds into guilders and pay for transportation in the back of a truck heading to Amsterdam. From there it was a quick trip to Rotterdam and then a boat across the English Channel to London.

He'd figured it would take him about eighteen hours in all. He ended up doing it in twelve.

31

MARION BELL RUSHED OUT THE DOOR OF WINSTON CHURCHILL'S sprawling Tudor manor house and into her husband's arms as soon as he stepped from the car sent to fetch him from London. She'd been a guest of the Churchills the entire time he'd been away. Winston and his charming wife, Clementine, waited with more decorum by the front door.

Bell greeted them with Marion still clinging to his arm and her beaming face turned to his.

"Welcome back, old boy," Winston said with a firm handshake. Marion and Clemmie, as Marion had been given the privilege to call her, had become friends enough for her to allow Bell to kiss her cheek in greeting.

"Good to be on friendly soil again," Bell said as the Churchills led them inside their newly acquired home.

They settled in a large informal library and Churchill had a servant pour champagne all around. Churchill lit an enormous cigar.

"Was the trip worth your time?" he asked.

"I don't think it was, to be honest. Karl Rath and his men had moved on as soon as they sent Holmes and me on our one-way flight. I spoke to the girlfriend he left behind, in the family way, I might add. She confirmed that Rath had more men than I ever saw, forty-five to be exact. She also shared he and his men would often toast someone named Joaquim Marques Lisboa. Mean anything to you?"

"Can't say that it does. Give me a moment." He pulled a discreet chain attached to a summoning system to alert a servant. When he arrived, he whispered instructions into the man's ear. Churchill tuned back to Bell. "I always have my computer on hand, even when I'm out in the country."

"Computer?"

"Maths whizz, but my girl is a bit of a prodigy and knows practically everything about everything."

While they waited, Bell told his tale of his time in Belgium and about his escape from the train. Marion admonished him for being reckless, even though she admitted it was just bad luck that Kreisberg was on the same train and it was not Bell's fault. He knew not to sugarcoat the dangers of his profession, but he vowed to deliver an edited version of his time in France and Germany when the time came. Some things, like flamethrowers and artillery barrages, need never be spoken of again.

A woman in a plain white blouse and simple brown skirt came into the room as his tale was winding down and stood in front of Churchill. She was in her early sixties, plump but not overly so, with the classic British peaches-and-cream complexion, horn-rimmed glasses of considerable thickness, and her hair done into a bun with such expertise that not a single hair managed to escape it.

"You wanted to see me, sir?"

"Yes, Davida. Question for you. Does the name Joaquim Marques Lisboa ring any bells?"

"Lisboa?" She paused as if to think, but Bell could tell by her eyes that the answer had come to her in an instant. "Ah yes, Joaquim Lisboa is considered the father of the Brazilian Navy."

The British statesman and the American detective traded an intrigued glance. Churchill said, "Navy, eh? That's a step in the right direction. Is he still alive?"

"No, sir. He died twenty years ago. Almost to the day."

"Damn." Churchill grunted. "Looks like that's a dead end after all. I thought this chap could have been helping your anarchists."

Bell played poker well enough to keep his own sense of disappointment off his face.

"Thank you, Davida. That is all."

"Yes, sir." She turned to go, but then paused at the double doors leading to the house's main entry. "Not sure if this is anything for you, but the Brazilians named an old dreadnought they bought from the Germans after him."

This time, Bell's poker face failed him completely. His grin was wide and wolfish.

"When?" he asked.

"It's a bit of a muddle. Archduke Ferdinand was killed during the middle of the deal. Knowing war was inevitable at that point, the Germans wanted to cancel the sale to keep their fleet reinforced, but the Brazilians refused to give it up. The Brazilians named her after Admiral Lisboa about this time to bolster their position.

"As the ship happened to be in the Azore Islands at the time of the sale, the Portuguese government offered to mediate, but as things here in Europe went from bad to worse, nothing ever got resolved. The Germans ferried all their stranded sailors home on U-boats.

The ship has remained under impound at Ponta Delgada since the autumn of 'fourteen, presumably with a skeleton crew of Brazilian sailors aboard to keep up her maintenance."

Bell asked Churchill, "Could forty-five men crew a battleship?"

"Not if she's coal-fired. How about it, Davida? This ship, oil or coal?"

"I'm good, Mr. Churchill, but I'm not that good. I'm sure somebody at the Admiralty would know. Her German name was *Saarland.*"

"Thank you, Davida. You're a tremendous help, as always. Please follow up on this for me and contact our chargé d'affaires in Ponta Delgada to confirm the ship is still there."

"Yes, sir. Right away."

After she'd gone, Bell said, "Quite a remarkable woman."

"A second cousin of mine. She has what they call an eidetic memory. Never forgets a thing."

"Invaluable in this instance. Consider the *Saarland.* A German ship would have German signage throughout. That explains why I saw evidence of Rath's men being taught German nautical terms. He must have learned of a battleship being impounded in the Azores and it inspired his whole mission."

Churchill nodded, his cigar cradled in his fingers. "If your anarchist is going after this ship, what do you think are his ultimate goals?"

"Could be anything," Bell admitted, and then something occurred to him. "Thinking aloud, I had the feeling he regretted mentioning to me that he'd sent his brother to New York. So maybe New York is a target. I need to know more about the ship and its capabilities."

"I just remembered I have exactly what you want." Churchill got off his sofa and ambled over to one of the floor-to-ceiling book-shelves. His hand went unerringly to the book he wanted, as if he'd memorized the location of every tome on the shelves. "This will do. Jane's *All the World's Fighting Ships*. It's an older edition, but it should suffice."

He began thumbing through the thick book, repeating under his breath the German name of the battleship, *Saarland*, until he found it. "Here we go. The *Saarland* is her own class of ship, a one-off the Germans laid down in 1907 when they got wind of the construction of our HMS *Dreadnought*. So, Davida got one wrong. The *Saarland* would technically be classified a pre-*Dreadnought*."

"Pardon the interruption, Winston," Marion said as politely as possible. "I hear talk about this *Dreadnought*, but I don't under-stand its significance."

Clementine Churchill, dutiful wife and chief confidante of the former Lord of the Admiralty, answered for him. "She was built as the largest battleship ever, back in 1906 or so. She was the fastest, best-armed, and best-armored ship of any fleet in the world and completely changed how such capital ships are conceived and constructed."

"At a cost of just over one point seven million pounds," Churchill added, "it makes her the most expensive as well. It set off an arms race unlike any before, as she made all other battleships immediately obsolete."

"Thank you." Marion smiled prettily, thinking, but not mention-ing, that the arms race the Brits started had been a huge determining factor in the current war.

"Okay," Churchill said, his head wreathed in fragrant cigar smoke. "Back to the *Saarland*. She's four hundred and sixty feet long, seventy-four wide, and displaces a little under sixteen thousand tons. She carries four of the German SK L/40 main guns in two turrets. Eleven-inch bores and the ability to hurl a quarter-ton shell about twelve miles, as well as a bunch of six-inch guns in broadside barbettes.

"And, Marion, in comparison, the *Dreadnought* displaces twenty thousand tons. She's five hundred and thirty feet long, is armed with ten main guns, and can launch a shell some fourteen miles."

"Wow," she replied, understanding Churchill was trying to impress her. "I guess that is quite the difference."

Churchill went back to his reference book and within just a couple of seconds exclaimed, "Well, that certainly explains it."

"What?" asked the three others simultaneously.

"They miscalculated her propulsion. She is slow, only about fifteen knots. They converted her to oil in 1911 in hopes of boosting her speed, but to no avail. She can't keep up with the rest of Germany's High Seas Fleet. She's useless to them. I wager they just wanted her big guns back when they tried to cancel the sale."

Bell couldn't remain in the plush chair he'd been occupying. He got to his feet and began to pace, his brain racing with ideas and possibilities. "Winston, you said Rath couldn't operate a large ship with only forty-five men if he needed to feed coal into the boilers. The *Saarland* is now oil-fired. Do you believe he and his crew could steal the ship from impound on the Azore Islands and sail it to New York in order to bombard the city?"

"Why on earth would they do that?" Clementine asked in her thick Scottish brogue.

Bell answered straight away, even though the idea had just struck him. "For the same reason they wanted to plant false invasion plans in Holland. They want to draw yet another belligerent into the war, sow more carnage, weaken Old World institutions so that he and his ilk can implement their vision of what Europe should be when it's all over, some twisted form of Bolshevism, I would imagine."

"Oh my."

"Indeed. How about it, Winston?"

Before the seasoned statesman could respond, his aide, Davida, knocked on the library door as timidly as a church mouse.

"Yes," Churchill called. "What is it?"

"Mr. Churchill, the *Admiral Joaquim Lisboa* was built to burn coal, but was converted to oil in 1911."

"Yes, we know. I recalled there is an old Jane's reference book in here."

"More importantly, sir, the telegraphs to the Azore Islands are down, both from our end and coming in from North America."

"Since when?"

"Three weeks, sir. News reached us a week after a storm tore up the cables running into the capital, Ponta Delgada. No news yet on when a cable-laying ship will be able to recover the cables and effect repairs. Until then all communication is via mail service aboard ships calling on the port."

Churchill and Bell exchanged worried looks. The Englishman ground out his cigar. "Thank you again, Davida. Please give us a minute."

Marion stated the obvious. "That means there's no way of knowing if this Rath character is trying to steal the ship and no way to alert the locals."

"I need to get there," Bell said, also stating the obvious.

"He has a few days' head start," Churchill pointed out.

"We have no idea how he's getting to the Azores. He might need to travel overland some distance to reach a ship willing to take him. It could take a week or more. He seems to favor smuggling routes, which are safe for him but notoriously slow. And moving forty-five men inconspicuously isn't all that easy, either."

Again Churchill played the spoiler. "He set up a clandestine training facility right under the Germans' noses. The man is resourceful."

"I grant you that," Bell conceded, still thinking on the deviousness of Rath's plan to goad the Dutch into the war. Diabolical. "That doesn't mean I don't have to try. I know all the fast liners are either laid up in port or serving as troopships, but there must be a speedy freighter in some English harbor."

"What are you going to tell President Wilson?" Churchill asked with nonchalance as he poured the last of the champagne into his flute.

The question came out of left field for Bell and rendered him momentarily speechless. He quickly gathered his wits. "I mean no disrespect, Winston, but I believe that information should remain confidential until I issue my report directly to the President."

"No disrespect taken. If I am going to divert vital war material for you yet again, I'd like to know what I'm getting in return."

"I beg your pardon?"

"We have dozens of destroyers lying about, what with the German High Seas Fleet unwilling to have another scrap like Jutland."

"You'd let me aboard one and send it to the Azores?"

"I'm considering it, but there is a quid pro quo attached, I'm afraid."

Bell considered his position. On the one hand, Churchill was his only option of getting to the Azores quickly enough to make a difference. On the other, the Brit was Machiavellian enough to use what was in Bell's recommendation to some advantage, an advantage Bell couldn't possibly fathom as of yet. In the end, he went with his gut. Rath was the enemy here, not Winston Churchill, and no matter what he recommended to Wilson, it was still the President's call to declare war.

Out of the corner of his eye, he saw Marion nod imperceptibly. It wasn't that he needed her approval, but it was reassuring that they were of a like mind.

He said, "I'm going to recommend that the United States enter the war, that we integrate our forces with the seasoned troops already deployed on the front, but under no circumstances are we to place our men under the command of a French or English general."

Churchill considered the words for a moment. "Just about exactly what I would recommend if I were in your shoes. Let me ask you, why?"

"Simple. A peace deal needs to be negotiated that doesn't see Europe back at war in another generation, which seems to be the cycle the continent has been on since the Middle Ages."

Churchill grunted. "And before, I assure you."

"I believe having the United States at the bargaining table is the best way to make that happen. We aren't saddled with all the past grievances that would sour an armistice. We could be the voice of reason in an otherwise highly charged negotiation, one that absolutely must succeed. I shudder to think of the carnage of the next war if Europe doesn't agree to a sensible and lasting peace."

"Again, you and I are in agreement," Churchill told him.

Bell looked to Marion. "This means I have to cut our reunion short."

She gave him a little pout, but nodded in understanding.

Churchill went to his study to set things in motion. He was no longer the Lord of the Admiralty, but still carried considerable sway, though not with the fleet's current commander, John Jellicoe. He made no mention of anarchists when he secured Bell an escort, but told of a spy learning that the Germans wanted to recoup their battleship from its current purgatory. He didn't need to explain the significance of such an occurrence. The main German fleet was bottled up by a blockade maintained by the Royal Navy that only their U-boats could slip past. They were menace enough. The very thought of a single battleship let loose in the Atlantic would be as devastating to civilian shipping as a whole armada of submarines. Such a ship could literally change the outcome of the war.

He explained away Bell's need to travel aboard the destroyer as an extension of his fact-finding tour on behalf of Woodrow Wilson.

Bell wasted, in his estimation, a good chunk of his limited time with Marion composing telegrams for Archie Abbott at Van Dorn's New York office as well as his contact in the Navy, Franklin Roosevelt. He wrote a third to Woodrow Wilson with his official endorsement of the United States entering the war, his reasons for it, and his confession that he'd told a ranking member of the British government. He felt Wilson should know about that sooner rather than later if for no other reason than Bell hadn't liked being forced to divulge it to Churchill.

He put down his pen and turned from the writing desk to where Marion was propped up against a wall of pillows on the guest room's four-poster bed. He said, "There, finished."

She held out a hand, her eyes hooded. "Oh, Mr. Bell, you're not finished until I say you are."

32

A DAY LATER, BELL THANKED THE YOUNG ESCORT WHO'D driven him from the gate of the Royal Navy's side of Southampton harbor to the gangway of his ship. There, an ensign was waiting, and it looked like he was fighting the urge to salute even though Bell was just a civilian.

"Welcome to the HMS *Mastiff*, Mr. Bell," the ensign said with a hand halfway to his forehead before he caught himself.

Bell held out his hand for a shake to make it less awkward. "Glad to hitch a ride with you boys."

Tied to the quay behind the sailor was a greyhound-lean Thornycroft M-class destroyer. The warship was two hundred sixty-five feet long, but less than thirty feet at her widest. She carried three four-inch Mark IV cannons in open turrets, one fore, one aft, and another on a platform between the last two of her three circular funnels. She also sported a complement of antiaircraft guns as well as a suite of torpedo tubes. Down in her engine room lurked three steam boilers and a pair of Brown-Curtis turbines that could drive her up to thirty-four knots or nearly forty miles per hour.

She was fast, capable, and deadly.

"Captain's compliments, sir. He's on the bridge and would like you to join him when we cast off. He said to get you situated first." The man made to take his bag, but Bell held on to it. "Follow me, please."

They entered the ship through a doorway just under her bridge and descended a flight of stairs. The interior of the ship was painted white, but there were few lights, meaning much of it was cloaked in shadow. The ship had a complement of only seventy-six sailors and officers, but it seemed they were all bustling through the corridors in preparation for departure. Bell and his guide had to keep pressing themselves against the cold steel walls to let others pass by.

"Sorry, we don't have a proper visitor's cabin," the young sailor said, looking over his shoulder. "Thing is, we don't have many guests."

"It's fine."

The sailor opened a plain door and stepped aside. Bell entered the room. It was the ship's infirmary. There was a single narrow bunk, a desk, and cabinets he presumed were full of medical supplies. Through an open door at the rear of the room, Bell saw he had a phone booth–sized head with a sink basin that folded down from the wall.

"We don't rate a proper doctor, of course, but our third officer has had some formal training. He can stitch up a wound, has this great salve for burns, and once set a broken wrist."

Bell tossed his hat onto the mattress and slid his bag under the bed. He also shrugged out of his overcoat and found a peg attached to the door to hang it up.

"All set, sir?" the sailor asked.

"Lead the way."

A minute later, Bell and his escort entered the bridge from a door at the back of the pilothouse. There were a number of sailors present as well as two officers. Bell recognized the stripes on the elder of the two's sleeve and presented himself with his hand outstretched.

"Captain, I am Isaac Bell, and I want to thank you for assisting me on my mission."

"Ah, yes," the man said with an amused spark in his dark eyes. He had a hatchet face and prominent Adam's apple, but had a competent and calm air about him. "Old Winnie might be out of the Navy, but the man's owed favors from Surrey to Siam." He shook Bell's hand. "Reginald Finch. Welcome aboard the HMS *Mastiff*. Got him settled in, Seaman Cairns?"

"Yes, Captain."

"Then off you go. You've other duties."

"Yes, sir." The escort vanished the way he'd come.

"Mr. Bell, this is my XO, Tony Whitman." Whitman wasn't yet thirty, huskily built with a grip he obviously tempered when they shook hands.

The captain led Bell and his executive officer to a small day cabin behind the bridge reserved for his private use. The dishwater light coming in through a small window indicated the weather was worsening. Finch poured tea from a vacuum flask. "Could you elaborate on the need for our mad dash to Ponta Delgada? My orders were rather vague."

"There is reason to believe the Germans are going to try to retrieve an old battleship that's been impounded since the war began from the Azore Islands. My mission is to alert the authorities so they can beef up their security and stop them."

"And if we're too late? You don't expect us to go after them solo, do you?"

"No, Captain."

"Thank the Lord for that. We'd need a squadron of tin cans to go after a Boche battlewagon, even an obsolete one."

"If the ship is already gone, our mission is complete, and we return to England at best-possible speed. We need to alert the Admiralty that there's a new hunter on the open Atlantic far deadlier than any U-boat."

Bell added this last bit to maintain the fiction that he was in pursuit of Germans and not anarchists bent on seeing the world turned to ashes. If his hunch was right, Rath and his crew would still be at sea by the time the *Mastiff* made it back to Southampton. He would have to admit to his and Churchill's fib to the Navy and suffer whatever rebuke they were due. On the bright side, it also meant he could give Archie and Roosevelt an accurate estimate of Rath's arrival time if New York was his intended target.

There was a knock on the door.

"Come," Finch called.

A sailor stepped into the cabin and announced the harbor pilot was here, the extra fuel was aboard, and they were ready to cast off.

"Very good. Mr. Bell, a couple of rules. You're permitted on the bridge provided you stay well back from my men. For meals, you'll dine with the officers. And if we have to go to battle stations at any point on the voyage, your action station is your cabin in the sick bay. You are to wear your life jacket and remain there until the all clear is signaled. Is that understood?"

"Yes, Captain. My cabin, in a life jacket."

Bell enjoyed watching competent people doing their jobs. It didn't matter the job. A pizza chef tossing pie after pie over his head could be as satisfying as watching a mason build a straight wall by sight alone. Captain Finch had a very competent crew, and watching them take the *Mastiff* out of the harbor under the guidance of a civilian pilot was a treat. Not a word was wasted nor an order missed.

Once the pilot was disembarked onto a tender that had shadowed the destroyer, Finch ordered the *Mastiff* up to speed. Bell loved speed, be it car, plane, or boat. He looked forward to the sensation of such a nimble ship cutting through the waves at nearly forty miles per hour. The swells outside the harbor were moderate, and the *Mastiff* took them well. Soon Southampton was well behind them and there was no traffic around, and yet the destroyer never accelerated past sixteen knots.

By this time Finch had left the bridge and his XO, Whitman, had the con.

"Begging your pardon, XO," Bell said, standing at the man's shoulder. "I thought the ship was much faster than this."

"She is. She can do double what she's running now. The problem is she can't sustain it for long. Burns too much fuel and kills our range. As it stands, we'll be close to dry when we reach Ponta Delgada."

Bell did the calculations in his head. They had a journey of two thousand miles, and at sixteen knots it would take just over five days. Anxious about the lead Karl Rath already had, Bell knew he'd feel like a lion in a cage for every minute of the trip.

33

ARCHIE ABBOTT WAS ONE OF THOSE RARE CREATURES THAT was a natural at just about anything he did. The first time he tried golf, he shot seven-over. The first time in a bowling alley, he rolled a two hundred. He won his first boxing match on a dare against someone who'd been training for years.

He never let the ease of his success go to his head. He was truly grateful. That was the reason he'd given up a career as a stage actor to follow his friend Isaac into the world of the private detective. He was good at it, for he was smart, observant, and had a knack for guessing people's motivations. More important, he'd seen how Bell made a difference for the people he helped and sought to do the same.

Most people who came to the Van Dorn Agency had nowhere else to turn, no other recourse open to them. They were frightened, usually embarrassed, and most definitely desperate. And when the agency solved the client's problem, no matter the outcome, usually the person was relieved to finally have answers. It was a good feeling making that happen.

His current client was his best friend, Isaac Bell, and he wasn't going to be happy with the results of his investigation because there were none.

The job was a simple missing person's case. All he had to do was locate a man and keep him under loose observation. It should have been a snap, especially because the guy was described as handsome to the extreme. In Archie's experience, handsome men liked to be around beautiful women. Lord knows before marrying Lillian he spent more than his share of time in the company of some beauties.

The job was even easier in that he had a name, Balka Rath. He'd sent junior agents out to canvas dance halls, brothels, and the night-clubs that vaudevillians frequented after their shows. He got a big fat goose egg. Bell had said the man came from the Carpathian Mountains. He put out feelers in Easter European neighborhoods. There it was always a little tricky because recent émigrés didn't like the police in any form and so they were reluctant to talk.

People were talking about a kid newly arrived from Hungary who fell from the window of an apartment of some other Hungarians who were out of town at the time. It was all very suspicious because he was seen in the company of a young woman shortly before his death.

Archie didn't think this had anything to do with his case, but he personally went down to the bar where the kid had met the woman. A few dollars were passed around. The bartender remembered the girl because she was dark and pretty and that he'd never seen her before or since. He was the person who recognized the photograph of the kid's face the cops had put on flyers around the neighborhood.

He knew nothing more. Archie made sure to give the man his business card.

Back at the office on the second floor of the Knickerbocker Hotel, Archie reached out to one of his police contacts, a detective in the First Precinct named Al Tanner.

"Tanner."

"Al, its Archie Abbott. How's life down at 100 Old Slip?"

"Archie," Tanner said with genuine affection. "How are you doing?"

"I'd complain, but I know you wouldn't believe me."

"You've got a beautiful wife, a pile of dough, and work for the best agency in the country. What do you have to complain about?"

"She's too pretty, I'm too rich, and the Van Dorns are all too good," Archie answered with a laugh. He then turned serious. "I might have something for you about the bombing at the post office."

"Agh, that fiasco. Postal police out of Washington want to run the investigation themselves. They must have brought up a dozen inspectors."

"They getting anywhere?"

"No, not really. The bomb was homemade with dynamite that's virtually untraceable. The night supervisor who was blown up when the truck went off had been stabbed in the heart just before the blast. The explosion made it impossible to tell the size of the blade, or much else for that matter. He was the only fatality. A couple of the drivers waiting to unload their mail that night sustained minor injuries. No one saw anything prior to the blast.

"The truck's real driver was found dead out on Long Island about twenty feet from the road that was his normal route. He'd also been stabbed. The pathologist said the blade was about four inches long and thin."

"Like a stiletto?"

"Maybe. I think even thinner, actually."

"Any witnesses there?"

"Nothing. Our contact at the post office says the driver would've been in that area at around three in the morning, so it's no surprise no one saw anything."

"These guys knew what they wanted and where to get it."

"Appears to be the case," Tanner agreed.

"Listen, I'm on a missing person's case that might be connected to a suspicious death."

"And?"

"Bell put me on the case. He's in Europe right now and came across a plot involving anarchists from somewhere in the Austro-Hungarian Empire. They're a sophisticated outfit with deep pockets and real bad intentions."

"Okay," Tanner said, clearly not getting to where Abbott was heading.

"The leader of the group is a guy named Karl Rath. R-A-T-H. He sent his brother here to New York not too long ago. His name is Balka. He may have set himself up with anarchists here in the New York area."

"Hold it right there," Tanner interrupted. "The postal dicks already pursued this line. They had us drag in a few so-called anarchist agitators. They're all a bunch of pseudo-intellectuals better suited to a college campus than fighting in the streets. They talk a good game and carry signs with the right logos, but they're all paper tigers. Trust me."

"That's my point. This Balka Rath could be the real McCoy. A true revolutionary who isn't afraid of getting his hands dirty. He might be the kind of guy who would have no problem shivving a couple of civilians and blowing up a federal building."

"Got a description?"

"Early twenties, likely dark hair and eyes, and said to be very attractive in a feminine way."

"Pretty boy."

"Yeah."

"Like you." Tanner laughed.

"Watch it."

"How do I know you're not feeding me this so I spend my time trying to find your missing person for you?"

"In truth, you don't, but I've got a hunch. Bell thinks the older brother, Karl, and his men are heading to New York. I believe that the guy who took a header out of a fifth-story window, who was from Hungary by the way, was sent from Europe as a courier by Karl Rath to alert his little brother to be ready for their arrival. According to what I've been able to piece together, this kid, Vano Hetzko, had arrived in the country less than six hours before he died."

"Thin."

"Absolutely gossamer," Archie agreed. "But it makes some sense."

"We had that down as a suicide."

"Of course you did. Less paperwork. But my money says he had help going through that window. Balka Rath's help."

"Do you have any leads on finding him?" Tanner asked rather noncommittally.

"The dead kid was seen meeting a young woman in a bar on the Lower East Side."

CLIVE CUSSLER THE IRON STORM

"Which bar?"

"Good Gotham's."

"Little out of my precinct, but I know it."

"I'm sure you do."

"Funny."

"Anyway, the dead kid was found only four blocks from it."

"Description of the girl."

"Same as Balka Rath. Young. Dark hair and eyes. Pretty."

"I don't know, Arch. All you got linking them together is an Eastern European background. If it even was murder, she could have been a working girl and lured the kid to her pimp and he tossed him out the window."

"He'd been in America for just a couple of hours, Al. He was definitely meeting someone. Someone who didn't want to be seen meeting him. The girl is a cutout."

Ever a dedicated cop, Tanner said, "If Rath is as dangerous as you think, that could put her at risk."

"All the more reason to look into this."

"I don't like being manipulated."

"Then you never should have gotten married. How about it, pal?"

Tanner blew a breath like he was a long-suffering victim. "Fine. I'll get some men to poke around. We've got a rookie from somewhere in Hungary or one of those places. Maybe he can make some headway."

"Thanks, Al. I owe you one."

"More like four or five by now, but who's counting?"

"Only you," Archie said and hung up the phone, a wide grin on his face.

Once set in motion, he figured his plan would need a day or two to work.

34

THE HMS *MASTIFF* CRUISED TWO MILES OFF THE SOUTH COAST
of São Miguel Island, the largest of the Azores and home of the
largest city, Ponta Delgada. The spine of the island was formed from
several volcanoes, now covered with forest and some open mead-
ows. The sea turned a frothing white when waves crashed into the
rock ramparts that protected the isolated bit of land.

Bell enjoyed his last few minutes on the bridge. Captain Finch
was taking no chances. When they neared the harbor, he wanted
his destroyer battle-ready. That meant hatches battened, guns
manned, and their only guest stuck down in his tiny cabin until
Finch determined it was safe for him to come out. Bell had tried
to talk the man out of imprisoning him as they entered port, but to
no avail.

A lookout on the bridge wing glassed the shoreline with binoculars bigger than wine bottles. He lowered them and stepped inside. "Captain, I can see the breakwater. It's clear of shipping."

"Very well. XO, sound the alarm."

The XO nodded to another sailor, who flipped a switch on the ship's internal communications system. Throughout the ship, speakers mounted in nearly every compartment started wailing. Bell looked to Finch for a last-second reprieve, but the man was focused on the task at hand and never even gave him a glance.

The stairwells and corridors were scenes of controlled bedlam as the men got their ship in fighting shape. He kept tight to the walls to let each one pass as easily as possible. They were all young, but appeared well-drilled and ready for whatever came. Bell could sense the centuries of British naval tradition in each and every one of them.

He didn't put on his life jacket when he got to his cabin, but he did pull it out from under the bed and set it next to him. He wanted to leave the medical bay door open as well, but an NCO inspecting that the ship was at battle stations admonished him with a sharp look and closed the heavy door tight.

Bell felt caged.

The harbor of Ponta Delgada was protected by a massive seawall that hid most of the coastal town from a ship as low to the water as the *Mastiff*. They could see the hills dotted with houses and villas rising up the mountains behind the small city, but until they cleared a dogleg into the harbor they were blind as to what ships lay at anchor.

Finch had been here once before early on in his career and knew about entering the harbor blind. It was why he'd put the ship on alert. Until they made that turn, he acted as though the Germans had already captured the *Saarland* and were coming out ready to fight.

"Make your speed one-quarter," he called to the helmsman.

"Speed one-quarter, aye." His hand went to the brass engine telegraph. He ratcheted the handle to alert the engine room and then set the needle to "One-Quarter."

The seawall was off the port side. They could now see the western side of the harbor. There were several fishing boats at anchor as well as a small freighter having cargo in net slings pulled from one of its holds. Everything looked normal, to Finch's relief.

That's the moment when the hulking prow of the German battleship came into view. She was absolutely enormous, but it wasn't that she was more than twice the *Mastiff*'s length or two and a half times her width, it was that she was sixteen times her weight. It was like the ship had its own gravity to draw in the attention of anyone who looked at her. She towered above the town like a cathedral over a medieval village.

A moment passed. Nothing seemed amiss. There was smoke coiling from only one of her three funnels, but that wasn't particularly alarming. The Brazilian skeleton crew needed lights and heating and needed to keep the ship in good order if they were ever to take full possession of it.

It looked to Finch that they'd beaten the Germans to the island. Bell could warn the local authorities about the plot to steal the ship and they could go home knowing they'd kept a deadly marauder out of the Atlantic sea-lanes.

Just then a great gush of smoke erupted from the *Saarland*'s second and third amidships funnels. Those boilers had been lit all along, but now someone was calling for a full head of steam.

Finch went a little pale, but his voice was sure and steady. "Helm, full reverse. Keep us straight and mind that seawall."

They only had to reverse for a few seconds to put another harbor wall between them and the *Saarland*'s massive main guns. Once safely out of view, they could keep backing out of the harbor and then pour on the speed in the open ocean. The battleship might lob a few shells their way, but the *Mastiff* was as agile as a mongoose and should get away clean.

Just a couple of seconds, the captain prayed in his head. "Lord just give me a couple—"

The range was only a few hundred yards, so the flash of the eleven-inch cannon firing and the impact of the quarter-ton high-explosive shell came so close as to be imperceptible. The destroyer's armor was too thin to activate the shell's impact fuse, but when it struck a solid bracing column within the hull, the main charge went off in a devastating explosion just below the pilothouse that ripped the *Mastiff* in two.

A blooming cloud of fire, smoke, and shrapnel boiled up from beneath the shredded decking and a concussion wave tore across the water faster than the eye could track.

In his tiny cabin, Bell observed the steel wall opposite his bed actually rippling an instant before the concussive force of the blast tore through the ship. He was thrown from his cot and crashed into a wall up near the ceiling. Had the room been much larger, the impact would have broken bone. He crashed back to the deck, dazed and deafened, even as the banshee roar of the explosion continued to echo and re-echo around him.

Smoke began to coil out through the sick bay's tiny ventilation grate.

Bell didn't need to know what had caused the explosion, though he could guess. He just knew that such a massive explosion was a fatal blow to a ship many times the size of the plucky little destroyer. He staggered to his feet. He hadn't yet fully regained his wits, but knew to strap on the kapok-filled life jacket.

He touched the back of his hand to the door, testing it for heat. The metal was cool. Still, he ducked low and opened the door slowly. A cloud of black smoke roiled over his head and created a noxious fog clinging to the sick bay's ceiling. Just then a sailor ran past. He was screaming in agony. He'd taken a jet of superheated steam to the face and hands and the sight of what had been left behind would haunt Bell's dreams for the rest of his life.

He could hear metal rending as the ship came apart further and the chilling sound of water gushing into the hull. This wasn't the first sinking ship he'd been aboard. That honor went to the *Lusitania*. But just because he'd survived didn't mean his heart rate hadn't spiked or that he didn't feel the icy grip of panic trying to cloud his mind.

The *Mastiff* was sinking by the bow and in the few seconds he'd stood in the hallway outside the infirmary, he could feel her angle steepening. He had just a handful of minutes. More men were rushing past him. Scared kids who'd forgotten all their training, going on instinct to always seek higher ground.

Bell didn't give in to panic. He turned and started striding down the deck, toward the sinking bow and away from what logic said was the safer option. He could feel the heat building and the smoke growing thicker, but he didn't see any flame.

Without warning, the destroyer suddenly shifted, rolling at least fifteen degrees to starboard, settling there for a moment and then revolving completely onto her side. The wall suddenly became the floor. Bell had grabbed on to an overhead conduit and managed to keep himself from being slammed into yet another unyielding metal surface.

He lowered himself and felt heat transfer through the soles of his boots. The room next to him was an inferno. He went farther down the corridor. Ahead, he could see water slowly creeping toward him as the ship slid beneath the waves.

He was up to his knees when he came to the stairwell that would lead him to the main deck. He'd just turned into the vestibule when water burst into the burning room behind him. When the seawater hit the fiery-hot metal, it turned to steam in a flash reaction that tore through bulkheads like tissue.

Bell was just far enough away, and partially shielded, to not get burned, but it spurned him on with added urgency. The lights flickered just then and suddenly went dark. Bell turned his attention to the stairwell. It was narrow, which meant he had little headroom. He had to negotiate the space on his hands and knees, constantly slamming his shins on the unforgiving handrail as he rushed through the darkness.

He reached the "top" of the staircase and found the door to the outside impossible to open no matter how hard he pushed on it. Water seeped from one corner of the doorframe, telling him the whole thing had been warped by the explosion.

The men running toward the stern had been right all along.

Bell wasted no more time. He turned without another thought of being wrong and retraced his steps. He stayed low once he reached the long hallway, as steam from a ruptured pipe continued to gush from the destroyed compartment. He edged around the spears of metal that had been blown outward like the petals of some nightmarish plant. The heat was nearly unbearable. Sweat poured into

Bell's eyes, forcing him to close them to slits. The emergency lights gave off a feeble glow, so in effect he was moving blind.

Once past the damaged bulkhead, Bell kept crawling, one arm outstretched and sweeping back and forth like a blind man's cane. Once he was able to wipe the sweat from his eyes, he got to his feet. The ship was shaking and bobbing like some demented funhouse ride, forcing Bell to run a hand along what had been the floor to keep steady.

He came across a sailor slumped on the deck, his legs outstretched, one at an unnatural angle below the knee, clearly broken. He'd crawled as far as he could.

"I've got you," Bell said when he reached the sailor's side.

The man blinked, not believing his eyes that there was someone to help him.

Bell got an arm under the man's shoulders and lifted him up so he stood on one foot. The movement caused the broken ends of his tibia and fibula to grate at his already damaged flesh.

He screamed and Bell said, "Yes, let it out. Scream all you want."

After a few more seconds, the man turned his head to look Bell in the eye. He nodded with fearful resignation, knowing more pain was to come.

With Bell acting as his crutch, the pair continued down the hallway, climbing up an ever-steepening ramp as the ship settled farther into the sea. There were pipes and handrails and door flanges to help find purchase against the metal wall, but still the going was slow. Air blew past them in a gusty wind as water forced it out of the parts of the destroyer already underwater.

They finally reached another stairway. This time, it was on the port side of the hall. Bell had to climb up and into the vestibule and then gave the sailor a hand to lift him up. The man was of average build, but was so wasted by the ordeal that he could offer little help. Bell had to deadlift him up into the little crawl space, straining his shoulder almost to the point of tearing muscle. He finally got him up, the sailor's face blistered in the sweat of agony, but he hadn't screamed.

"Almost there."

The ship shuddered again, its plates creaking and groaning as she neared the moment of her death spiral to the bottom of the harbor.

"Come on!"

Urgently, because they didn't have the time to lose, Bell dragged the sailor through the disorienting stairwell. The man's leg warped and twisted every time it hit the handrail. There was no help for it, and he screamed at the top of his lungs between blubbering pleas for Bell to just let him die. They reached the head of the stairwell and, to Bell's surprise, there were three men waiting for them.

"Ahoy. Heard him screaming and came back," said the only officer present, a young Welshman named Awbrey. He put his face close to the injured man's. "Good set of lungs on you, Bobby. Likely saved your life."

The two sailors with Awbrey relieved Bell of his burden by each lifting one of the injured man's legs and draping his arms over their shoulders.

Awbrey and Bell followed as they went down one more dimly lit corridor to where a hatch had been opened to the outside. Soft sunlight poured in like the rays through a cathedral's windows.

They emerged on the port side of the ship, thirty feet from the fantail, which was fully out of the water by then. Bell could see one of the ship's propeller shafts and bronze screw. Out across the harbor, the *Saarland* was building up speed, disregarding all maritime safety rules on her quest to be free. Seeing her charging from her anchorage with smoke pouring from her tall funnels was all the proof Bell needed to know his guess about the explosion had been correct.

Had they so chosen, Rath's band of cutthroats could have put another round into the *Mastiff*, but they didn't. Instead, the battleship steamed past the stricken destroyer, her massive bow wave further destabilizing the already mortally wounded ship. Two men lost their balance when the wave struck and fell into the water below. One surfaced, sputtering. The other never came up.

"We've got to get away before her final plunge," one of the dozen or so survivors said.

"Not to worry," replied Awbrey, wise beyond his years. "The *Mastiff* is longer than the harbor is deep. Any minute now . . ."

Just as those words left his lips the bow struck the bottom of the harbor, sending a shiver through the hull that nearly sent another man tumbling off had a buddy not yanked him back by the arm.

"She'll be steady for a bit," the officer said, his eyes down the channel to where the *Saarland* continued to steam away.

Bell, too, looked after the fleeing battleship, the bitterness of failure like ash in his mouth. Awbrey believed the deadly vessel would be used to further harass shipping trying to reach his island nation in an effort to starve the British into a peace deal. Bell knew that wouldn't be the case. He felt certain Rath was heading to New York in order to shell the city and push the United States into joining the war, not knowing Wilson was about to make that decision anyway.

He also felt certain that if the American people believed the Germans had launched an unprovoked attack on the homeland, they would not settle for a negotiated armistice, but would demand the war not end until Germany had been burned to the ground.

He had to find a way to stop Rath, but his only real chance lay mortally wounded in a harbor more than two thousand miles from home.

35

The girl held out for three days. Archie Abbott was impressed. With Al Tanner's cops beating the bushes for her, he figured she would have gone to the bar a day or two ago. He knew she'd go there. It's why he left his card with the bartender with instructions to give it to her when she showed up.

"Who told the cops about me? You?" she asked when he'd picked up his phone and identified himself. She had an accent that couldn't mask her anger.

"It was easier to flush you out than for me to hunt you down. What is your name?"

"Hanna Muntean."

"It's nice to speak with you, Hanna. As you know from my card, my name is Archie and I'm a private detective, but not police. Do you understand?"

She ignored his trying to charm her. "You knew I would come to the bar? How?"

"It's the only public place connecting you to Vano Hetzko. You had to go back to find out who convinced the police Vano's death was murder and not a suicide."

"I didn't kill him," she said at once.

Archie took it as a good sign that she didn't want him to think she was a murderer. It was clear that she already cared what he thought of her.

"I never believed that you did. Neither do the police, now that I've talked to them."

"I didn't know he was going to kill him."

"Balka Rath?"

"Yes."

"What is he to you? How do you know him? Is he your boyfriend?"

"No," she spat. "Never. Not if he was the last man on earth."

It was clear from the vehemence of her denial that she once harbored strong feelings for him, love or her version of it, but now felt betrayed. This is good, Archie thought. He could use that.

"You need protection from him."

"Now I do, thanks to you," she shot back at him.

"You always did, only now you're a priority because the police are involved. He can't take the chance of you being interrogated. He's hunting for you even as we speak."

"No. He is on a mission with my brother."

"What mission?"

"Do you think they tell me anything?"

She was scared and getting defensive. Archie had to be careful, or he'd lose her.

"Let me help you. We can protect you."

"I can take care of myself."

"Normally I would agree with you, but I don't think you quite understand how dangerous Balka Rath really is. He's part of a group back in Europe who will kill without a second's thought. My partner is over there now. He's seen them kill at least ten people, several in cold blood, one of them an injured soldier. They are savages, Hanna, and we believe they are on their way to New York led by Balka's older brother, Karl. Even if Balka has a soft spot for you, his brother does not, and he will order your death as soon as he finds out you exist."

This was met by silence.

Archie continued. "Please, Hanna. Let me help you. We are going to round up Balka, his brother, and all the rest, and then you will be safe. Until we do, though, you need protection. Can we meet?"

"I . . ."

"Do you know the carousel in Central Park?" Every New Yorker did.

"Yes."

"Meet me there at three. I will be carrying an umbrella." There wasn't a cloud in the sky, so he'd be the only one. He was sure he would have recognized her by her body language alone, but it was important that she approach him as part of him winning over her trust. It was like trying to befriend a stray animal. You had to make them want to come to you. "If you help me, Hanna, we can put this all behind us that much quicker. Three o'clock."

He hung up without giving her time to answer.

"What's that all about?" asked James Dashwood, one of the permanent agents in the New York office. He'd once been Isaac Bell's protégé, but was now a top investigator in his own right.

"A girl who can help me track down an anarchist tied to the group that Isaac fell in with over in Europe."

"I heard Isaac's on his way back."

"Not exactly. He's going to the Azore Islands to make sure these nihilists haven't absconded with an old German battleship."

"And if they have?"

"Heaven help us all."

Archie arrived at the park several minutes early. The air was still a little cool so there weren't that many children waiting to ride the park's famous carousel. Still, it was a city favorite, and so there were always kids, usually with their mothers or nannies, willing to fork over the nickel for a ride. It wasn't that long ago that the power to turn the merry-go-round was provided by a horse or donkey tied to the central pole down in the basement under the ride. They were trained to stop and start when the operator tapped the floor with his foot. Now it was powered by electricity, and old-timers said it smelled so much better than before.

Central Park was the city's great equalizer. Anyone, from grandee to guttersnipe, used the park, so no one really stuck out as not belonging. Not knowing Hanna's circumstance and not wanting her to feel uncomfortable or, worse, have her barred from entering, Archie couldn't have invited her to the Knickerbocker Hotel or a nice restaurant. Here in the park, Archie looked as in place in his bespoke suit as the young nanny in a threadbare dress and secondhand coat pushing a pram, while another of her charges talked excitedly about the make-believe race he'd won on the carousel.

Archie spotted Hanna Muntean before she saw him. She was dark-haired with a dusky sort of complexion. She was about twenty, pretty, but Archie could see that life was already taking its toll. The way she slouched made her look like she carried the weight of the world on her shoulders. She wore a black dress and coat clutched tightly at the throat for warmth, but also for psychological protection. She didn't fidget much, but she was actively watching her surroundings, making certain that no one was approaching her from behind.

He was reminded of a little mouse coming out of its hole at the first whiff of food, at once tentative and determined.

He strolled past her, his incongruous umbrella in hand for her to see. She didn't show any sign of recognition, which he didn't think she would. She was young, but had been around long enough to know how to protect herself. He walked to a nearby bench and sat, the umbrella upright between his knees.

Hanna didn't approach directly, but circled around a little bit so her joining him didn't seem so obvious.

"Hello, Hanna. I'm Archie Abbott. Thank you for meeting me."

She didn't say anything. He understood why. Talking to him and potentially helping him was an act of betrayal to her and all those like her—not exactly criminals, but not citizens, either. She and her friends lived by their wits and had to trust each other with their lives. Talking to outsiders was simply not done unless they were a mark for some scam.

"Were you there when Balka killed Vano?"

"I . . . No. I had left the apartment, but I waited downstairs. I heard something hit the sidewalk. I looked out and saw him on the ground. He was . . . broken. I ran out the back of the building."

"How do you know him, Balka Rath?"

"We are the same cla—" She was about to say clan, but stopped herself. "From the same part of Hungary."

Archie had already guessed she was Roma, what others derisively called Gypsies for the misguided belief the people had originated in Egypt. They were hated across much of Europe because they were so clannish and resisted integrating into whatever country they im-

CLIVE CUSSLER THE IRON STORM

migrated to. That hate had come over on the migrant ships to America's shores and so she was naturally reluctant to discuss her family's past.

"He came here last fall. Sent by his brother. Karl is famous, even here. He is a strong leader who has dedicated his life to protecting our people. Karl knows my father and so he sent Balka to us. My papa is dead, so my older brother became his contact here. He was so handsome and mysterious. I . . ." She caught herself and went quiet.

She had clearly fallen under Balka's spell, and just as clearly that love had soured, perhaps over the murder of Vano Hetzko, perhaps something else. It didn't matter.

Archie asked, "What was Balka's mission?"

"I don't know."

"No one has discussed it around you?"

"I am a woman. Nothing is discussed around me."

"I need to find him, Hanna. A short while ago, Karl Rath forced my friend Isaac into a dangerous mission that could have made the Dutch enter the war. And just so you understand the stakes, the Germans would roll through Holland with ease, killing thousands in the process. We think Karl may be trying to do the same thing here. Engage in some monstrous act that will compel America into joining the war."

"But the President said that the United States will never enter the war in Europe."

"Depending on what Karl Rath does, he might not have a choice." Now for the hard sell, Archie thought, the make-or-break moment. "Balka is likely part of that plan, Hanna. From what you've told me, your brother is, too. I need to stop them before they hurt anyone, themselves included. The police are now looking for Balka, but they don't know the kind of man he is. He'd rather die than get captured. He'd likely get your brother killed, too."

Hanna sat very still on that park bench, her delicate hands in her lap, fingers interlaced, like the knots in her mind that she needed to tease apart to discover what was right.

"I need to find Balka before it's too late, before Karl arrives and they unleash whatever hell they have planned for New York."

She remained silent for a minute, wrestling with her clan loyalty, her love for her brother, her newfound hatred of Balka. Archie saw a strength in her that was well beyond her years. That meant there was another element swirling in her mind. She was brave and independent, but had been marginalized her whole life by her gender. He was giving her a chance at her own agency and she was wondering if she had the will to take it.

She gave an unconscious little nod when she'd made up her mind. "If I knew, I think I would tell you. You have kind eyes and are very, ah, earnest, but I do not know where they are. I haven't seen Hanzi or Balka in a week, maybe ten days. I've asked around. No one knows where they are or what they are doing."

Archie believed her. That made his disappointment all the worse. He'd gotten through to her, but she had nothing to offer. A guy like Balka Rath would be a ghost. Al Tanner and his boys at the First Precinct would never find him, and now it looked like neither would he.

"My brother has a truck," Hanna said after a few moments. "I think whatever they are doing will involve it."

"Can you describe it?"

"It's a truck. Old. I don't know, but I would recognize it if I saw it."

Archie thought about the nearly five hundred miles of roads on

Manhattan Island and the odds of coming across one particular vehicle. About as high as winning a lottery on the same day you find a
four-leaf clover and get struck by lightning. Still, it was an offer to
help, and keeping her close would also keep her safe.

"I think that might be helpful," he said, slapping his knee as if it
were the best idea in the world. "I'm sure we can come up with some
ideas on how to narrow the search. I have no doubt you've learned
things you don't even realize you know. That's where I come in. A
good detective has instincts about which are the right questions to
ask. In the meantime I'm going to introduce you to my wife, and
she'll get you settled."

"In your home?"

He looked her square in the eye. "You've placed your trust in me,
Hanna. It would be dishonorable of me not to afford you the same
courtesy."

"But . . . you're a gentleman. I'm nothing. A nobody."

"And that is the last time you will ever think of yourself like
that." He stood, extending a hand. "Come on."

Hanna looked up at this tall, attractive stranger who made her
feel comfortable despite not knowing anything about him. He had
charm, but it was no grift. He really was a gentleman. She held up
her hand and he helped her to her feet. "Okay."

36

THE FISHING BOAT TIED TO THE PIER AMID DOZENS OF OTHER craft was larger than the one that had ferried Bell from France to the Netherlands, but not much. She was a ketch-rigged motor sailer, meaning she had a main mast amidships, and a shorter mizzenmast toward her blunt stern, as well as a gasoline-fueled engine for when the wind was lacking. She was older, but appeared in good order, a working boat rather than a rich man's toy. What had grabbed Bell's attention was the Stars and Stripes hanging from her jack staff. As far as he could tell, she was the only American boat in Ponta Delgada.

A man in a black watch cap and farmer-style overalls over a wool shirt was seated near the transom repairing a section of netting. His hands were blunt, but quick.

"Ahoy," Bell called to get the sailor's attention.

The man looked up and squinted. The sun was directly behind Bell. He moved to his right so as not to blind the man.

"What can I do you for?"

"Gloucester?" Bell thought he recognized the man's accent.

"Close. Ipswich."

"Boston. Isaac Bell."

"Beacon Hill?"

"I won't deny it."

"And I won't hold it against you. Vernon Grimm."

"Any chance you're returning to the States soon?"

"I'm the master of the *Alice N.*, but we're on a charter now, so I go where my client says."

"Is he around?"

"Yup."

Grimm set aside the net and tools and got to his feet. He ambled across the stern to the boat's cabin. He opened the door and called out a man's name in a muffled voice. Grimm was back at his task by the time a second man emerged from inside the fishing vessel. He appeared to be about a decade older than Bell and wore blue denim jeans and a corduroy shirt. He had a well-worn cowboy hat perched on his head. He wasn't particularly tall, but he had a lean strength about him. His eyebrows were full and his face long with a strong jaw.

"Good morning," Bell said. "Sorry to bother you. My name is Isaac Bell. I'm a detective with the Van Dorn Agency and have been recently marooned here thanks to a German battleship."

The stranger looked impressed. "You were on that destroyer?"

"In a manner of speaking, I'm the reason she came out here, Mr. . . ."

"Oh, sorry." He crossed the deck and stretched his hand up so Bell could shake it from where he stood on the quay. "Zane Grey."

Such was his nature that very little surprised Isaac Bell, but meeting the famous author on a speck of land in the middle of the Atlantic wasn't something he'd ever expected. "*Riders of the Purple Sage*," he blurted. "I don't read much fiction myself, but my wife absolutely loved that book. She's a movie director and she's often mentioned adapting it for film. I'm pretty sure she read the sequel, too."

"*The Rainbow Trail*," Grey said as if he were a father naming one of his children.

"I don't picture you out at sea, Mr. Grey. On a horseback in some desert canyon, yes, but not way out here."

"Please call me Zane. My passion, above baseball or writing, is fishing. I fish wherever and whenever I can. Grimm's taking me out for bluefin tuna this time, and in these waters lurk some real monsters. Five hundred pounds and up. Do you fish?"

"As a kid. I grew up in Boston, so we were always around water, but I have to admit it was never my thing."

"I imagine as a Van Dorn you get all the excitement you need." Grey stepped back and made a sweeping gesture with his arm. "Come aboard. I have coffee on. And I was about to rustle up some lunch if you don't mind fried tuna steak sandwiches."

"Thanks. I can always use more coffee and I'm absolutely starving."

The lounge of the *Alice N.* was worn but tidy, with a small functional galley and a hallway leading forward to where Bell could see doors for four tiny cabins. He accepted a mug of black coffee from a battered percolator on the stove.

Grey got busy making lunch for them. "I assume you're here for a reason."

"I am," Bell told him. "I need to get to New York as fast as possible. I am convinced that the men who stole that battleship are planning on bombarding the city. I've already learned this morning that they arrived here two days ago, that many of them spoke German, and people saw a few wearing German naval uniforms. They want to make us think it's a German attack and force the United States to declare war on the Central Powers."

Grey looked skeptical. "Sounds a bit far-fetched."

"I would agree with you if they hadn't already tried to get the Dutch into the war by planting false evidence that a German invasion of the Netherlands was imminent. I have firsthand knowledge of this because myself and a British pilot were the ones ferrying the fake invasion plans. Sowing discord is their stock-in-trade."

"Who are they?"

"Their leader is a man named Karl Rath. A real nasty piece of work who would make a great villain for one of your books. He kills people as easily as you and I would swat a mosquito. Rath and his men, they're anarchists. They want to see the world destroy itself, eliminating all structures of governance in the process. They then expect to rise to power in the ashes that remain. Roping us into the war means more chaos, more destruction spreading farther and wider. They want to make this a true world war.

"Now, you must be aware that the transatlantic cables to the Azores were damaged in a storm. Had they not, I could get warning to our government and relax here for a few days. My only option is to chase after them and you're my best shot."

"Not so sure about that. The *Alice N.* is a fine vessel and all, but you won't see her in next year's America's Cup."

"Here's the thing, the battleship is severely underpowered. She's slow. It's why the Germans opted to sell her prior to the war. She can't keep up with the rest of their fleet. She has a maximum speed of fifteen knots, but far less than that if they need to conserve fuel, which they no doubt have to do. Maybe this boat can't catch and pass her, but we can keep pace and arrive in New York not long after."

Grey handed Bell a plate with his food. His face was unreadable. They ate a couple of bites of their tuna sandwiches in silence.

"You're not pulling my leg." It was a statement more than a question.

Bell said, "You have to head back to the States eventually, right? All I'm asking is you cut short your trip. When we reach the city I will hand you a check so you can charter this boat all summer long if you'd like."

The two men stared at each other, one confident in what he knew and deduced and the other asking himself if his instincts were right. The author finally put his food down and said "Okay" to himself. He was at the door in seconds.

"Grimm, when's Caleb due back?"

"Anytime now, I suppose."

"All right, good. Soon as he's here and we get the provisions aboard, move us over to the fueling bowser and top off the tanks. We're heading to New York as fast as this old girl can carry us."

The grizzled master looked like he'd been gut-punched. He thought he had another two weeks' charter. "What's the problem, Zane? Fish are still running and the price we're getting per pound is practically paying for your charter."

"It's not that. It's the battleship that sank the British destroyer and snuck on out of here this morning. This man is a Van Dorn detective who says they're headed to New York in order to shell the city. They could potentially kill hundreds. Thousands, even."

"The hell, you say."

"Just make ready."

"We could use an extra hand if you want us there quickly."

"I can sail," Bell told him.

Grimm scowled. "We aren't day sailing out to P-town, Beacon Hill."

"I've seen my share of nor'easters, Captain Grimm, and I'm not a man who can't back up his boasts. I'll be crew enough for you."

Grimm's eyes flicked over to his paying customer. "Zane, your charter, your call."

Grey didn't hesitate. "He's a Van Dorn man. Most-trustworthy detectives in the country, by all measure. If Isaac says he can sail, I'll take him at his word."

Fifteen minutes later, the *Alice N.*'s mate, Caleb, arrived seated next to the driver of a one-horse flatbed wagon. He was about twenty-five, tall and lanky, with a chin so weak it was practically nonexistent. He wore a Boston Red Sox cap, in honor of their World Series win the year prior.

With all four men pitching in to unload crates of food, ice blocks, and gallon tins of fresh water, it took only minutes before the taciturn and unhelpful driver was off again. Grimm fired the fishing boat's engine and ordered Caleb to cast off the lines. He spun the boat to head deeper into the marina in order to tie up next to the fuel pumping station. While they puttered across the water, and passed more fishing boats, Caleb, Bell, and Grey set about stowing all the provisions. The ice and perishables went into a cold storage locker installed under a hatch in the main salon's floor. Grey and Caleb had a system for where everything went, so while they stocked shelves, Bell lugged it all in from the deck.

The fueling station consisted of a five-hundred-gallon tank set on a wooden frame several feet above a cement pier and a hand-operated suction pump. The tank had a narrow graduated-glass window to mark how many gallons had been pumped. A Portuguese boy of no more than twelve with a grubby Greek fisherman's cap covering a mop of unruly hair worked the pump, his skinny arms showing remarkable stamina.

Grimm had a wooden stick he could push to the bottom of the *Alice N.*'s fuel tank to check its level. After thirty minutes, in which the kid's pace never slackened, he was satisfied the tank was full. He paid the kid's father, who'd sat on a chair and watched the whole process from under a slouch hat, with a hefty handful of silver coins from various nations' mints.

A dozen small boats still puttered around the remains of the *Mastiff.* She'd sunk lower into the harbor as more trapped air escaped from the deep reaches of her hull. Bell could see Lieutenant Awbrey, the ranking survivor, directing salvage teams trying to save anything they could before the ship fully sank to the bottom. Bell tried to catch his eye, but the Welshman never looked over.

As they motored past the coastal city's seawall and into open water, Bell reflected that he couldn't have done any better. Just six and a half hours had passed since Karl Rath had sunk the *Mastiff* and stranded him in the Azores, and here he was, already in full pursuit.

Captain Grimm kept the motor running for the first couple of hours of the journey. The engine was small and so they barely cracked seven knots. Bell tried not to keep recalculating how much farther ahead the *Saarland* sailed with each passing hour. It did him no good to agonize over it, but agonize he did.

As the sun dipped lower toward the horizon, the winds picked up. They worked as a team to hoist the main sail, followed soon by the jib out over the little boat's prow, and finally a mizzen sail over her stern. The difference was immediate and dramatic. A bow wave curled off the hull in a long-running V, while the ship heeled to port and accelerated to eleven knots at least.

"She's quicker than you let on," Bell said to Grey and Grimm as all three stood in the small enclosed cockpit under the mizzenmast.

"I think old *Alice* is showing off for you, Bell," Grimm said, still unconvinced that Bell was a sailor despite the ease he showed putting up the sails. "She's at her top speed straight out of the gate like she's giving her favors to a man in a hurry."

Bell felt his first glimmer of hope.

37

AMONG ALL THE WORKS CREATED BY MAN, NO OBJECT GREATER personifies "form follows function" more than the modern battleship. Her function is to bring the largest and greatest number of guns to a naval engagement in order to defeat the enemy, and this alone determines every aspect of her form. Nothing about the design deviates from that. The hull is streamlined for efficiency not grace. Apart from some wood paneling in a few officers' cabins and their wardroom, every surface is made of steel. The vessels are cold, industrial, brutalist, with little consideration given to the men who serve aboard, as they are effectively cogs in the great machine themselves.

The *Saarland* was no different. She didn't cut through the water, rather, her high bows tossed the ocean contemptuously aside as she raced across the Atlantic for her date with destiny. The seas weren't particularly rough, but even then the battlewagon refused to roll with the swells. She was like an unmovable force of nature.

Standing on the bridge of the *Saarland*, Karl Rath had never felt so powerful in his life. They'd just executed his most audacious plan yet, and it had gone off without a hitch.

Escaping out of occupied Belgium had been easy. They knew all the established smuggling routes and all forty-five of them had made it to Rotterdam without incident. There waited a small steam freighter whose captain was sympathetic to the anarchist cause and vastly reduced his charter fee. They had sailed with the tide after the last of his men reached the port. The trip to the Azores had been uneventful. Rath used the time to further drill his men on how to operate the *Saarland* once they took her from her Brazilian minders.

Rath was in overall charge of the mission, but he lacked the experience to effectively run the ship herself. For that he had two former Italian naval officers, who'd been drummed out of the Navy for dereliction of duty. One had even spent six months in the brig before being dismissed. They were both bitter and resentful of their treatment and more than willing to be recruited into Rath's gang. It was his chance meeting with them at a political rally in Switzerland that had given him the idea for this mission.

Under them were a motley assortment of men, some with naval or artillery training thanks to the ongoing war, of which most had deserted. There were Germans, a few more Italians, Eastern Europeans like Rath himself, even a couple of radicalized Frenchmen who were more communist than anarchist, but were willing to sign on.

They had made certain to get noticed when they arrived in Ponta Delgada. Those that spoke German did so at every opportunity, though never about why they had arrived on the island. It took only a handful of days to learn the dull routine of the twenty Brazilians stuck in the Azores looking after their all-but-forgotten ship.

They lived aboard, of course, but at any time half of them were in town. In order to support themselves, these men had taken jobs at the fish-processing plant. It was up to the others to keep one of the ship's boilers up and running and ensure that every moving part had been properly greased and any rust that started to show through was scraped down to bare metal and repainted.

It was little wonder that such a small team hadn't been able to keep up on the repairs of such a massive ship. When Rath and his men hit town, the *Saarland*'s paint looked scabrous with rust spots and streaks, and the smoke chuffing out of her forward funnel appeared to be far oilier than it need be.

They had struck at midnight. The Brazilians hadn't even posted a night watch. As suspected, the sailors had availed themselves of the officers' cabins. Rath trusted this part to his Roma compatriots. They knew the way of the knife and worked with a single-mindedness that abolished any thought of compassion. The entire crew aboard was dispatched within a matter of minutes.

The plan was to dispose of the bodies after they were out at sea.

The following eight hours was a frantic rush to make the ship ready to depart. Two of Rath's men had experience working at power plants and they needed a dozen others to ramp up the salt-water evaporator for a greater supply of fresh water and then to light the idled boilers. Their task was made more difficult because the dampers for the aft two funnels had to remain closed and all smoke vented through the forward stack. They were lucky in one regard: The Brazilians had rotated between all of the engine room boilers during their extended stay in Ponta Delgada.

While this was going on, others among the crew, guided by the two Italian officers, checked over the battleship's mechanical systems, steering gear, and auxiliary generators. The men with artillery experience examined the main guns and inventoried their ammo supply. Still others needed to head back into town for provisions. The caretakers kept only minimal stocks, since their ship was never leaving port.

Karl himself looked over the ship's radio array to make certain it functioned properly. Without it, the guns would be firing blind. He was relieved to find that one of the Brazilian caretakers must have had a real love for electronic devices. The sets were in perfect order and kept covered by custom-sewn cozies.

They had just completed everything only moments before the British destroyer pulled into the harbor. The leader of the team in the forward gun hadn't waited for orders. He'd taken the initiative to fire that devastating point-blank salvo that utterly destroyed the British ship.

Rath's most trusted adviser was a man named Pesha Orsos. As a teen, he had been press-ganged into the Austro-Hungarian Navy for two years and had been stationed as a gunner's mate aboard a heavy cruiser until he'd jumped ship while they were at anchor in Istanbul. He was in charge of the lead turret and had ordered the shot that sank the *Mastiff* and most of her crew.

He knew to approach Rath from the right, where he still had an eye. "Karl, we've finished the ammunition inventory. It's not good. We have plenty of powder. That isn't the problem. What we don't have are a lot of shells for the main guns. It looks to me that the Brazilians sold a lot of them off as scrap to help pay their way in Ponta Delgada."

"How many are left?"

"Just thirty. Most are high explosive, which I doubt any local junk dealer would touch with just a couple of solid armor piercing remaining."

Rath absorbed this news, calculating. "It should be enough, but it's more pressure on Balka as our spotter. We have six targets. The two train stations, the Stock Exchange, the Woolworth Building—the city's tallest—St. Patrick's Cathedral, and finally the Brooklyn Bridge, arguably the hardest to hit. If we need four or five rounds to dial in on each target and destroy it at least partially, that still leaves us enough ammunition to hit the bridge."

"It may take more than four or five rounds, Karl," Pesha replied. "Yes, your brother can tell us how many blocks east or west we missed by, but these guns are unfamiliar to me. They will have quirks I do not know. And there is no guarantee each bag of powder we use is exactly uniform. It takes eight ten-kilo bags to fire one of those shells. If even one bag is a little deficient the shell will land short no matter how accurate I am."

Rath clapped his friend on the shoulder. "You worry too much. Do you think if we destroy the first five targets and leave the bridge standing the Americans won't be any less eager to add their soldiers to the list of the dead in Europe? They will be clamoring for blood if just one of our targets is leveled and the finger points to a German sneak attack."

"You think so?"

"I do. But that doesn't mean you don't drill your men every day, so we don't squander one of our precious shells on a mistake, yes?"

"Of course. These guns are much bigger than the ones I fired in the Navy, but the principle is the same. We will be ready."

"I know. Have you thought about afterward?"

They planned to abandon the *Saarland* as soon as the attack was over. During the crossing to New York, a team was making two of the utilitarian lifeboats look like pleasure craft that would be completely anonymous as soon as they were launched. Once ashore, the lion's share of Rath's men wanted to remain in America. Most of them had family in the United States, many in New York, in fact. They might be anarchists, criminals, and malcontents, but they were also human and liked a soft life of creature comforts that America appeared to provide.

Rath wanted to return to his homeland. Plunging Europe into war would see the end of the hated Hapsburg dynasty. And that was the lofty goal he and others had set out to accomplish. But there were personal scores to settle, too, petty functionaries all through-out the bureaucracy who had wronged Rath and his family in one way or another. Policemen who'd harassed them. Tax collectors who'd overcharged them, a particular mayor who had seized valu-able property. All of them had to pay as surely as young Charles I would lose his throne.

Pesha hadn't yet said what he would do afterward. Karl would love to have him return with him and Balka. It would be like old times. But Pesha was more of a humanist than the others. Karl knew that his old friend had become disillusioned with Europe. He hated how eagerly they turned to war and how stubbornly they refused peace. He feared Pesha would decide not to return.

"When this is over, I will know in my heart where I belong. But not until then," he had told him.

"Fair enough," Rath had said.

"What are you two on about?" asked the captain, Luigi Valenza, in English, their common language. He'd come over to them from his elevated seat on the corner of the bridge. Behind them a helms-man stood at the wheel and another of the crew stood ready for whatever was needed.

"We only have thirty shells for the main gun, and I was assuring my pessimistic friend that it will be enough."

"How fast can you fire them, do you think?" Valenza asked Pesha Orsos.

"That depends on my brother," Rath replied for him. "As our spotter, the quicker he tells us where our shells landed versus where we aimed them, the quicker we can adjust and fire again."

"I just worry about the American Navy. Once we open fire, we'll be a sitting duck."

"Bah," Rath scoffed. "Unless they happen to have a heavy cruiser or battleship in the area we are perfectly safe. Besides, that's the risk we all knew ahead of time. But the odds are small, and we're exposed for an hour, maybe an hour and a half. Right, Pesha?"

"At the most."

"See, nothing to fear, Captain. You just worry about getting us there, and we'll do the rest."

38

THE TROUBLE DIDN'T START UNTIL THEY WERE FIVE DAYS OUT OF Ponta Delgada. The sky had been bright blue and the seas calm with a steady breeze that made the stumpy *Alice N.* cut through the water like a clipper ship. On the morning of the fifth day, dawn revealed the western horizon to be a towering wall of gray from the sea to the top of the sky. It was some miles off, but Captain Grimm knew just by looking at the clouds that the storm was intense and absolutely massive.

From the fishing boat's little bridge, he called to his crew, who were below preparing their morning meal. "Zane, finish up making breakfast—double rations for everyone. It's going to be a piece till we get another hot meal. Then I want you to make us a mess of sandwiches and wrap 'em in wax paper. Also brew up as much coffee as you can find a container for. We're gonna need it. Oh, and break out our slops."

"Slops?"

"Foul weather gear. Caleb, you and Bell batten everything inside and make sure the bilge is clear. After that start hauling down the sails and be ready to set the storm jib and the trysail."

"Why not just reef the main?" the young mate asked.

"No, lad. That storm's gonna hit like a polar hurricane and would rip the mainsail from the mast no matter how she's reefed. Best we show her as little canvas as possible. Gentlemen, we're in for a miserable time, make no mistake, but the *Alice N.*'s a fine boat and she'll see us through."

The first squall ripped at the ocean's surface as if it were being raked by machine-gun fire. The wind puffed a strong chilled gust just then, died for a moment, and came roaring at the boat like an icy avalanche. The seas dropped away from under them like the first big dip at a Coney Island roller coaster and rose again in a spine-compressing swoop just moments later. After that, the rain came in earnest, slashing in every direction including up when the wind twisted into spiraling vortices. As the men and the storm raced at each other, the sky overhead grew steadily darker until it was as if they were in deepest twilight and Grimm's only sense of how the seas were running was by watching the lines of white spume that rode on the crest of each black wave.

Thirty minutes into the teeth of the storm, Grimm was forced to admit a mistake. He'd called for the larger of his two storm jibs, thinking he'd prefer to have better steerage, but the wind was just too strong, and it was only a matter of time before the storm tore it away.

"Sorry, men," he said with rumbling reluctance. "That jib has to come down."

"You want the white one up instead?"

"Aye."

Bell and the young mate exchanged a look, one that said it was a tough job, but both felt confident of their abilities. Caleb pulled the sail from a locker down below. It was smaller than a twin bedsheet, but incredibly strong. The two men already wore rain jackets and pants. They each tied on their sou'wester hats, nodded to each other again, and Bell opened the door to the deck. The wind tried to wrench it from his hand as rain filled the small enclosed cockpit. He pushed through, shoulders hunched, knees flexing with each wild gyration of the *Alice N.*'s hull. Caleb came out on his heels.

The wind pressed against them like a solid force and when it gusted it was like being shoved by a football lineman. They stayed low, their chests against the deck as they slithered toward the bow. Rain and salty spray found every chink in their protective clothing, sending icy fingers across their skin. The sound of the storm was a visceral presence that made their bones vibrate. Maintaining a grip to the boat's deck was like riding an unbroken stallion, a wild unpredictable series of bucks, kicks, and lunges.

It took several minutes to crawl the thirty feet to the forestay, where the too-large storm jib was as tight as the head of a drum because of the storm's intensity. Bell turned his back to the bow and remained seated. He took the smaller sail from the *Alice N.*'s mate. Caleb uncleated the sail running up the forestay and started lowering it. Bell gathered it up as it came down the wire brace, twirling his arms around each other like a mechanical mixer so the wind never had a chance to snatch it away. He switched the sail he'd been sitting on with the new one and tied on the head of the smaller storm jib.

He had just finished tying the tack of the sail to the line when a wave came over the bow like a runaway locomotive. Bell managed to keep hold of the stay, the thin wire digging into his palms until they bled. Caleb lost his footing and washed across the deck, slamming into the railing with his back. He was pressed there for many long seconds until the boat heaved itself out of the wave's trough and water drained off the wooden plank deck.

Bell let momentum carry him over to check on the young New Englander. Caleb was soaked through and moaned when he straightened his limbs, but was otherwise all right. They waited for the boat to rock again and returned to the unfinished task of raising the small storm jib. The wind took it as soon as it could, billowing the cloth with a sound like a cannon. It took both Bell and the mate to raise it against the wind as it bellied out.

Once up and secured, they ran the jib sheet back from the clew corner of the sail to the protected cockpit. Bell ran it through a jib block and secured it to a sheet winch.

"Are you okay, boy?" Grimm asked as Caleb dumped water out of his waterproof hat.

"Aye, Cap. Breath knocked out of me is all."

Grimm turned a weathered eye to Bell. "Fine job you done, Beacon Hill. I guess you know how to sail after all. That was a neat trick to bundle the sails. Very efficient. Where'd ya learn it?"

Despite the compliment and what sounded like a touch of grudging respect from the captain, Bell couldn't help digging at Grimm's belief in a working class/upper class false equivalency and said with a smile, "Oh, that. The sailmaster at the Boston Yacht Club."

T HE STORM RAGED FOR A TOTAL OF THIRTY HOURS, PUSHING ALL four men to their physical and mental limits. They partnered off in four-hour shifts, Bell and Caleb as one team and Captain Grimm and Zane Grey the other, but when it was all over the four were as tight a crew as had ever sailed together.

Luck or Grimm's skills at estimating their course had been with them during the storm. It had pushed them only a hundred or so miles off course. That small miracle did nothing to allay Bell's concerns. The *Saarland* might have been slowed some by the storm, but not nearly as much as the *Alice N.* The battleship's lead had widened incalculably.

Bell had explained to Grimm and Caleb the stakes of their mission on their first day at sea and so they wasted no time setting progressively heavier sails as the storm abated. Rain was still falling and the wind remained fierce when they hoisted a tightly reefed mainsail, only to keep letting more and more of it out as the storm continued to peter out.

Grimm kept their tacks crisp and precise, and eked every knot out of his trusty boat as he drove her ever westward. By this point, he trusted Bell to take the helm when he was off watch down in the salon, so it happened to be Bell who spotted the tip of Long Island just as dawn cracked behind them. He'd been steering for it by the pulse of the Montauk lighthouse for some time. Not only was Grimm an amazing sailor—they'd made the crossing in just under ten days, averaging an astonishing nine knots despite the storm—he'd proved himself to be a master navigator as well. They'd arrived exactly where they'd intended.

Bell noted the time and penciled in an entry on the meticulous log Grimm maintained.

He turned the helm a few points to the south so they would keep the island to starboard as they sailed for New York. Soon the beaches were scrolling by. There was the occasional beach house, too, but all were still shuttered for the now-ending winter. Bell rued that there were no proper harbors on Long Island. Had it been summer and the population at their elevated levels, he could have hitched a ride on the Long Island Railroad at Southampton or paid a driver to take him to the city. On more than one occasion he'd taken his Simplex Crane Model 5 to nearly seventy-five miles per hour on the Long Island Parkway. It could have saved him hours. Instead, this part of the island was all but abandoned for another few months and the trains only ran once a week. He was stuck with the *Alice N.* giving her best, but managing only seven knots as the breeze started to falter.

In his mind's eye he saw the *Saarland* creeping through New York Bay, low and menacing like a jungle cat, her big guns trained and elevated, while the great city off her bows lay as supine as a sacrificial victim on some pagan altar. Every second brought Manhattan closer to the range of those massive cannons. He could imagine the first salvo, fire belching from the barrels and quarter-ton shells hurtling through the sky. He saw the impact, saw buildings blown apart so that bricks turned into shrapnel that scythed down pedestrians in every direction. He heard the panicked screams and could feel the chalky dust on the back of his throat.

The images filled Bell with impotent rage. There was nothing he could do but keep the fishing boat trimmed and on a tack to maximize every bit of the wind hitting her sails.

"Hey, gents," he called down into the salon. "We're parallel to Long Island now. We've no reason to think the *Saarland* hasn't beaten us here by days, but I think we should keep a watch for her just in case."

"Prudent idea," Grey said. He popped up from below a moment later with a pair of binoculars hanging from a strap around his neck.

As New York was America's busiest port it was little wonder there was so much shipping funneling into the lower bay. The size and type of vessels was countless, but traffic was mostly dominated by freighters trailing long tethers of dissipating coal smoke. Notably there were no large passenger ships heading into New York from Europe or going eastward toward the deadly ring of U-boats attempting to blockade the British Isles.

It was twilight by the time they reached the lower bay leading into New York Harbor. There was too much shipping to keep the sails out, so Bell and Caleb dropped them for the final leg of the journey.

"What's it mean that we haven't heard those guns?" Caleb asked as they furled the sails for storage in the large locker. "Did we actually beat them?"

Bell was contemplating the exact opposite; that Rath had already come and gone and once they reached the harbor proper they would see parts of the city aflame against the backdrop of the nighttime sky. The other thought darkening his mood even further was that he'd been wrong about Rath's intentions all along, that he'd never intended to attack New York and that he had some other nefarious mission for the infernal machine he'd stolen. Rath could have his sights on another city, or maybe he had gone after shipping, as Churchill had intimated to his government to obtain their cooperation.

He voiced none of this to Caleb, who so wanted to win this race even if he didn't fully grasp the consequences of losing. He'd never witnessed the horror of a modern artillery attack, as Bell had firsthand. Instead he said, "I doubt it, unless they had some major mechanical failure."

They soon passed between Staten Island and Brooklyn through the Verrazano Narrows and entered the upper bay. Everything seemed normal. The two boroughs were well lit, there were no people trying to flee, no unusual boat traffic of gawkers looking for a better angle at the destruction, nothing at all to indicate the city had been attacked.

Bell wasn't sure what to make of it.

Finally lower Manhattan came into view and Bell let out a breath of relief. The city blazed in all its glory, the high-rise buildings were all aglow as they stretched into the darkened sky. There were no fires. There were no panicked throngs. There was no monstrous warship just off Governors Island making ready to open fire with her eleven-inch cannons. There was nothing but the hustle of the city, which many said never slept.

"What say you, Beacon Hill?" Grimm asked, using the nickname he'd dropped after the storm. Zane Grey noticed, but said nothing.

"Not sure," Bell replied. "I doubt we beat them here and I am almost positive I deduced Rath's intention. Let's stick to our plan. Put me ashore at the ferry dock, find someplace to berth the *Alice N.*, and make your way to the Van Dorn offices at the Knickerbocker Hotel. That's on Broadway and Forty-Second. I appreciate you gents supporting me on this."

"We've come this far," Grey said. "There's no way I'm not sticking around to find out how it ends."

"Let's hope with egg on my face," Bell said, "and that battleship sold for scrap."

39

BELL CALLED THE VAN DORN OFFICE FROM THE STATEN ISLAND Ferry Terminal in lower Manhattan using a nickel he'd borrowed from Grey. The few dollars in his pocket to pay for the cab ride he'd soon take to Midtown had also come from the legendary writer. If Grey took Bell up on his offer about chartering the *Alice N.* for the rest of the summer, this was little more than chump change.

"Van Dorn Detective Agency, how may I help you?" a young woman answered when the call went through.

"Betsy?"

"Yes," she replied warily.

"Bets, it's Isaac Bell."

"Oh, hi, Mr. Bell," she said, her voice going up an octave.

"Has anything unusual happened recently, anything about a German battleship?"

"No, sir. People are talking about the Zimmerman telegram—"

Bell cut her off. "Listen, I want you to call up a team. I need Archie,

James Dashwood, and Eddie Tobin, if he's back. Have them come into the office pronto. Has there been any communications from Franklin Roosevelt? The assistant secretary of the Navy?"

"I don't know, Mr. Bell. I only answer the phones at night and rarely talk to the others."

"Never mind that. I also want you to send a telegram to Lullenden Manor." Bell forgot to get the phone number. "It's in Surrey, England, and belongs to one Winston Churchill. The Western Union man can get the address. Marion is there. Tell them I am back in New York. No sign of my quarry, but I'm still hunting. Got all that?"

"Yes, sir, Mr. Bell. You can count on me."

"On the jump, Betsy, I'll be there soon."

Bell hung up. From a ferry terminal concession stand, Bell ordered a hamburger steak, but rather than eat it on a plate with breadcrumbs, he asked the counterman to put the patty between two pieces of toast and add some mustard and extra onion. He drank two glasses of water while he waited for his food, the first that hadn't tasted stale and a little briny since leaving the Azores.

He was handed his burger in a pocket of folded newspaper. He liked tuna as much as the next guy, but nine days in a row was well past his limit. The first bite of beef made his salivary glands work overtime.

He was still munching away when he reached the head of the taxi line outside the bustling Beaux-Arts terminal on South Street. He told the attending valet his destination, which was relayed to the driver in the front seat of a Model T. The liveried man held the rear door for Bell and received a quarter tip for his troubles. Bell usually overtipped, but his funds were limited.

Traffic was light, allowing them to make it to the Knickerbocker Hotel in a little over fifteen minutes, faster than the subway, even.

He paid off the cabbie and rushed into the hotel lobby. There were just a few guests about, two reading quietly on one of the deep sofas and a couple dressed for the theater talking about how much they didn't like the play they'd seen. Bell nodded to the hotel detective, who was in fact a Van Dorn agent, as were most in-house security personnel at the city's better hotels.

In long-legged strides, he climbed up to the second floor and let himself into the Van Dorn's New York office. It was all so familiar, the large wood-paneled bullpen that was usually a hive of activity during the day, the back wall of offices, one of which was his, the smell of cigarette smoke, and the easy glow of shaded desk lamps. It felt like he hadn't been there in months, but at the same time he was almost sure he'd just been away a few moments.

"Mr. Bell." Betsy Singer had been at her desk in one corner of the large room and sprang to her feet. "Mr. Abbott and Mr. Dashwood are on their way, and the telegram has been sent."

"What about Eddie Tobin?"

"I talked to Diane from the day shift. She told me Mr. Tobin has returned from England, but he didn't answer my call. I'll keep at it every fifteen minutes until he does."

"No need for him to come in, but I need to talk to him. I'm running upstairs for a few minutes."

"Yes, sir."

Bell had lost his keys somewhere in France and so grabbed a spare set from his office and took the elevator to his floor. The rooms he and Marion occupied looked out over Times Square, but were high enough to filter out most of the noise. They were tastefully appointed, neutral for the most part, but with some pleasing feminine flourishes that made it feel like home. Bell stripped out of his clothes and stuffed them into a trash can in the bathroom. He'd have room service empty it as soon as he was finished. He could almost see the odor wafting off of them.

He took his first shower in days, soaping his lean body and lathering his hair twice in order to cleanse himself of salt and the stench of fish oil and bad cooking. He dressed in a pair of casual herringbone slacks and a black cashmere pullover. From a drawer of various holsters and weapons tack, he grabbed a shoulder rig for his spare Browning automatic pistol. Since the weather appeared unseasonably mild, he covered it up with the lighter of his two leather flying jackets.

He was back down in the office within fifteen minutes.

Bell went through the correspondences on his desk that had grown into an impressive stack during his absence. He was dismayed that there was nothing from Franklin Roosevelt. Surely he'd gotten the cable he'd sent from Churchill's country estate concerning the possibility of an attack on New York. At least there should have been a receipt that he'd received the cable, but there was nothing.

A creeping sense of horror filled the pit of Isaac Bell's stomach. His race across the Atlantic had been for nothing. It had all been for nothing. He was more than willing to do whatever it took to stop Rath from carrying out his attack, but he'd worked off the presumption that the Navy would have the primary task of destroying Rath's ship. He'd been thinking of his team in the secondary role of apprehending Balka Rath, Karl Rath's brother, while on the streets acting as a spotter.

The phone rang out in the bullpen and Betsy called to him that it was Eddie Tobin.

"Thank you," he called back and picked up his phone as Betsy jacked in the line. "Eddie, glad you're back safe and sound. How was the crossing?"

"No problem," the grizzled investigator told him. "What about you?"

"You wouldn't believe me if I told you."

"With you, I'd believe anything."

"Listen, there's no time for small talk. I believe there is a captured German battleship on its way to bombard New York."

"Huh?"

"You heard me right. It's a dreadnought-style ship sporting eleven-inch guns. She was taken by a group of very motivated anarchists, and I believe their mission is to shell the city."

"You're not one for elaborate jokes in the middle of the night, so I'll bite. What do you want from me?"

"Reach out to all your contacts, every pirate, fisherman, smuggler, scow captain, anyone you can think of. I need to know when the ship is approaching New York."

"Okay, then what?"

"I don't know. Up until a few minutes ago, I thought the battleship would be the Navy's problem and not ours. Bloodhound this for me, Eddie. A lot of lives are at stake."

Bell dropped the microphone onto its cradle and called out to Betsy again. "Can you call Joe Marchetti over at the Brooklyn Naval Yard? I—"

"Helen Mills's fiancé?"

"I thought you said you didn't talk to the others."

"Not about work, but gossip is always fair game."

Bell rolled his eyes. "Tell Joe I need him here. Tell him to go AWOL if he has to. It's that important."

"On it."

Marchetti was a young Navy officer who'd been invaluable on a case the year before involving German spies operating in and around

New York. He was smart, kind, and to everyone in the office's delight, he'd caught the eye of Helen Mills, one of the few female agents currently on staff in Manhattan. They'd announced their engagement at last year's Christmas party.

Bell leaned back in his chair, his fingers laced behind his head. He looked calm, relaxed even, but his mind was a kaleidoscope of ideas forming, changing, and vanishing only to pop up again in a slightly altered form. He was of the mind to break down complex problems into manageable parts, solve them individually, and then fit it all back together again to formulate a master plan. It wasn't really a revolutionary technique, but it had given him the edge over countless criminals in his storied career and he approached a plan to deal with the Rath brothers and their threat to the city in the exact fashion.

"You asleep?" Archie Abbott asked, his broad shoulder leaning against Bell's office doorframe.

Bell didn't open his eyes. "Didn't it bother you that Roosevelt never responded to my cable containing a warning?"

"Not even for a second. The Navy is under no obligation to inform a civilian firm of their intentions even if said firm provided them the warning."

"I still think it's odd he didn't leave even a simple message of receipt."

"Mr. Bell," Betsy called from the outer office again. "Joe Marchetti would like to talk to you before he agrees to go AWOL."

"Patch him through." Bell picked up his phone. "Joe, are you guys under any kind of alert right now?"

"Not that I should divulge Navy secrets, but no we're not. Why?"

"Any idea where Franklin Roosevelt is?"

"I believe he's with Navy Secretary Daniels. It's a big inspection tour of the naval base at Pearl Harbor, Hawaii, before they plan to expand it."

"In Roosevelt's absence, who responds to his communications, things like telegrams?"

"I'm sure he has a secretary of his own, but I have no idea who, a confidant no doubt. Why? What's this all about?"

Marchetti was a no-nonsense type of guy and so Bell laid out his case as plainly as he could.

When Bell finished and Joe had a taken a few seconds to process the information, he said, "If Roosevelt had gotten your cable on time and convinced Daniels of its veracity, they might have been able to get some assets to New York to counter a ship like you've described. But right now all we have here at the Yard are a couple of twenty-year-old destroyers that are about as toothless as a day-old infant and a battleship that's only halfway through construction."

"Then it's up to us," Bell said, already including the lieutenant in his plans.

"What are you thinking?"

"Since there's nothing we've got that would penetrate the *Saarland*'s protective armor, we sneak aboard and blow her up from the inside."

"Is that even possible?" Archie asked, having overheard Bell's side of the conversation.

"How about it, Joe?" Bell said into the handset. "Is it possible?"

"A bomb placed anywhere near the powder magazine would open her up like a tin can," Marchetti replied with confidence. "The problem is getting away. That means a long timer, which increases the chance of the bomb being discovered. Also if we're spotted, even if we get away, they will know what we were up to and find our bomb."

"So we give them exactly what they expect to see," Bell said cryptically. He then said, "Listen, Joe, I don't need you on this mission, but you've got more explosives training than any of my people. We've got all the gear, but I would appreciate if you assembled the bombs."

"Do you know your way around a modern battleship?" Marchetti asked a little hotly.

"I don't even know my way around an old battleship," Bell admitted.

"That settles it. I'm coming with you. No argument. This is my decision, so not another word."

"Thank you, Joe. I think I could manage this myself, but having you along just tripled the odds. Do you know the police armory on Eighth?"

"No, but a cabbie will."

"We rent out part of it and keep a lot of equipment and arms there, including some dynamite. I'm sending an agent to meet you. He'll have our key." Bell gave him some specific instructions and told him to wait at the armory for additional instructions.

"You're really going to sneak aboard a battleship?" Archie asked with a skeptically raised eyebrow.

"That's probably the least crazy thing I've done in the past few weeks. What about you? Where are you with finding Balka Rath?"

"Thanks for assigning an impossible task, by the way," Archie said, his voice dripping with sarcasm. "So much to go on. Really handsome, maybe dark eyes and hair, probable foreign accent. Give me a break."

"So you got nothing?"

"Did I say that? In what only can be described as brilliance on my part, I found a girl who'd met him on the night he killed a courier who'd just gotten off a boat from Europe. Hanna Muntean is her name. She's a waif who runs errands for criminals, mostly Romani as near as I can tell. She's all but admitted to being in love with Rath, but turned against him recently. Again a guess on my part but I don't think she realized how dangerous he was until he hurled the courier out a tenement window. She's been helping me find the truck Balka is using along with her brother."

"Where is she now?"

"My place."

"Is that wise? She may be a waif as you say, but even street kittens have claws."

"Relax. Everything of real value is in the safes. She never leaves the house without an escort and someone from the staff is always up and about no matter the hour. And since she's set eyes on Master Dashwood of the quick smile and flashing eyes, she's been on her best behavior."

"Fickle little thing."

"At that age, everyone is."

"No luck locating the truck, I take it."

"Big city, few hundred miles of roads, the odds were long, but I needed to keep her safe since she's on Rath's list of loose ends and she needs to feel she's maybe putting her old life behind her."

"I'm actually surprised he left her alive when he killed the courier," Bell remarked. "But don't worry, you'll get your chance to nab him if we're too late and the *Saarland* opens fire. Balka will have to drive close to the targeted firing sites in order to radio adjustments back to the ship."

"And by nab you mean . . . ?"

"Arch, even if we stop Karl Rath from leveling the city, I won't consider this a success if Balka escapes. He's worse than his brother according to a woman who knew them both. You get the chance, you put him down like a rabid dog."

"Woof woof."

40

As the night wore on, more and more moving pieces were put into play. James Dashwood had arrived shortly after meeting Joe Marchetti at the armory and accessing the explosives. Zane Grey and Vernon Grimm showed up an hour later. They'd berthed the *Alice N.* at a commercial slip on the East River near Fortieth Street. Grimm had already had her tanks filled and had a mechanic lined up to inspect her engine in the morning. Both men renewed their vow to see this through to the end. Bell got them rooms in the Knickerbocker for the night.

For himself, he managed to get some sleep on the couch in his office.

A little after dawn, Eddie Tobin phoned in. He had dozens of people keeping a weather eye out for any sort of warship, but so far no one had seen a thing.

Betsy's shift had ended at midnight and had been replaced by Fred Wright, a probationary employee only on his second month. He was astute enough to have a fresh pot of coffee brewed by the time Bell ended his call with Tobin and emerged from his office yawning broadly.

Bell poured himself a mug, sipped, and told Wright, "You just earned my vote for your probation meeting. Put a call through to Mr. Van Dorn in Philadelphia. It's early, but it's why he gets paid the most. He's staying at the Bellevue-Stratford."

At nine, Archie returned with his new charge, Hanna. She wasn't at all what Bell had expected. He'd assumed she'd be shy and tentative. Instead, she shook his hand with a firm grip and looked him in the eye when she said it was a pleasure to meet him. She had an accent, but it was more charming than distracting.

"Why are you helping us?" Bell asked when the pleasantries were over.

She darted a glance at Archie, but turned back to Bell. "My people," she started, but then faltered. Bell saw her clench her jaw to give herself strength. "My people have been hated across most of Europe for centuries and that hatred has taken root here, too. If it is ever learned that Roma were involved in something as terrible as what Balka is planning, that hatred will only grow worse. I fear there will be pogroms here as there have always been back home."

Bell scratched at the stubble on his chin. "Wise beyond your years, I see. And Balka Rath?"

"He has led my brother astray and treats me . . ." Her face flushed with embarrassment. "I would rather not say what he thinks of me."

"No need," Bell assured her. "I think I understand. When the attack comes, you and Archie are going to be in real danger. You'll be rushing to the area near large explosions with more possible at any time. You could even be killed. Do you think you can handle that?"

She gave her answer some thought before saying, "I have only ever learned how to take, Mr. Bell. Mr. and Mrs. Abbott are teaching me what it means to give back. It is important and it is what makes us human. If my fate is to die giving back, I can think of no better death."

Bell nodded. "You already think like a Van Dorn."

At eight, James Dashwood called from the armory. He had everything Bell requested, and the bombs were ready. Bell told him to sit tight. There was no need bringing high explosives into one of the city's finest hotels just so they could all wait together.

At nine, Zane Grey called from a pay phone on Forty-First Street. The mechanic had finished tuning the boat and he and Grimm were ready. Bell got the *Alice N.*'s exact location and phoned Dashwood at the armory. He told him to take all their gear to the fishing boat and have Joe Marchetti wait with the men already there. He wanted Dashwood back in the office to ride shotgun with Archie as backup.

Just twenty minutes later came the call Bell dreaded, but which also shot a load of adrenaline through his system like he'd never felt before. Edie Tobin said without preamble, "The ship was spotted ten miles north of Eatons Neck by some oystermen who just got in."

"What time?"

"Dawn."

"That's three hours ago."

"Like I said, the oystermen just got back into port and dropped a nickel to me."

Bell realized he wasn't familiar with the location. "Remind me again where Eatons Neck is."

"Long Island Sound in Huntington Bay."

The news rocked Bell back on his heels. For whatever reason he'd always assumed that Rath would arrive in New York through the Verrazano Narrows. It was how shipping traditionally arrived and so he'd never considered any alternatives. Now that he knew the truth, it made some sense. There was far less boat traffic along the northern shores of Long Island, and if he and his men abandoned the *Saarland* after the attack rather than risk being hunted down, there were far fewer witnesses to the north than in the harbor proper. And Lord knew the guns on the battleship had the range to hit just about anywhere in the city from the top of the East River.

"We don't have much time," he said to Eddie. "Keep calling in updates as you get them, okay?"

"Will do, boss man."

All morning, Bell had had secretaries calling in every agent on the books, including hotel detectives and guards not on duty. He needed manpower for the next phase. The bullpen was filled to almost over-flowing, and the din of conversation was like a locomotive passing by. Bell climbed up onto one of the desks, placed two fingers in his mouth, and whistled around them so shrilly that the crowd instantly fell silent.

"Ladies and gentlemen, I just heard from Eddie. The *Saarland* was spotted at dawn in Long Island Sound about forty miles from the East River. They should be within striking distance in another two hours or so. It's time for you all to head out. Check the sheet by the door for your assignments. Each of you will stay close to one of the likely targets—but not too close in case they get lucky with their first salvo." That drew a couple of grim chuckles.

"And not too far in case they're lousy shots," someone called from the back to more laughter.

Bell continued. "The moment you hear or see anything, call the office and tell us where. That will be James and Archie's cue to head out and hunt Balka Rath. We have only one chance to get this right or a lot of innocent people are going to die today. Now let's go. On the jump."

Bell took Archie and James Dashwood aside by the door to the outside hallway. "You watch yourselves. Once Hanna points out the correct truck, have her get out with cab fare back here. She doesn't need to see your takedown if her brother might become a collateral kill."

"I was already planning on it," Archie said.

"That's likely a lie, but I'll let you get away with it. Good luck and happy hunting." Bell shook both their hands and dashed out of the office.

The uniformed bellman on duty saw him striding through the lobby and recognized the look on Bell's face. He didn't bother holding the door but instead rushed out onto Forty-Second Street with his whistle to hail a taxi. The cab was at the curb just seconds after Bell exited the hotel.

"Thanks, Carmine," Bell said as he ducked into the back of the idling Ford.

He gave the cabbie the address where the *Alice N.* was berthed and tried to clear his mind for the short ride. He had his own near-impossible mission to worry about. Archie and James were more than capable enough to deal with Balka Rath. But like any good leader, he hated ordering men into danger that he himself wouldn't face.

The commercial marina at Fortieth Street was just a handful of slips, mostly small lightering boats to take cargo from wharf to wharf or out to a ship that hadn't yet gotten a berth. He saw that Grimm had removed his boat's masts. They both lay on the dock next to the fishing craft. There was no sign of Joe Marchetti or Grimm and Grey. He guessed they were below checking gear. He paid the cabbie and gave him an exorbitant tip rather than wait for change and rushed down to the *Alice N.*

"Ahoy, the boat," he called as he jumped aboard. "Captain Grimm, we need to leave."

The three men came up from the lounge.

"They here?" Zane asked.

"Long Island Sound. We have maybe an hour, two tops."

"Then it's a good thing you brought me a real sailor, Beacon Hill," Grimm said with good-natured gruffness and backhanded Joe playfully in the chest.

"Funny." Bell shook Joe Marchetti's hand. "Been a while. How are you?"

"Grateful Helen wants a long engagement."

Marchetti had classic Italian looks with olive skin, dark hair and eyes. He was just a couple years out of Annapolis, but still looked young enough to be a midshipman. Bell knew his youth and slim build hid a sharp, penetrating mind and a fierce competitiveness that was beginning a meteoric rise within the Navy's ranks. He was the first from his class to be promoted to lieutenant junior grade.

Grimm already had the engines fired while Grey cast off the lines.

"Thanks again for agreeing to come with me," Bell told Marchetti. "Your help will be invaluable. Did you get everything?"

The engine's rumble deepened as Grimm backed the fishing boat out of her slip and into the East River. The river wasn't really a river at all, but a part of Long Island Sound that wrapped around the western tip of the island close to Manhattan. There was no current, but it did experience the ebb and flow of the tides. The tide was flowing out, which gave them another bit of speed, while at the same time slowing the *Saarland.*

"Bombs, weapons, clothes, ladder, the lot," Joe assured him.

"Good, because—"

The boom hit them just then, a concussive burst of noise that while distant rattled their chests. It was followed a moment later by a scream that seemed to be tearing the atmosphere apart. It was a scream that ended with another distant blast that rose above the buildings of New York in a cloud of white smoke and black, sooty dust.

Not that he could have moved any faster, but Bell cursed himself for already being too late.

41

ARCHIE ABBOTT AND JAMES DASHWOOD WERE SITTING IN A conference room inside the Van Dorn headquarters. Archie was sipping a coffee. James was cleaning his Colt pistol. Hanna was on the couch thumbing through a magazine from the waiting room. They were all three bored.

Then came the sound like a sharp thunderclap followed by the unmistakable noise of an explosion.

Abbott and Dashwood looked to each other and said at the same time, "Penn Station."

All three leapt to their feet and rushed for the exit. They were outside in a handful of seconds. One of the agency's highly tuned Ford Model Ts sat at the curb. A pair of agents had been assigned to fire up the car at the first sign of trouble or if they saw Archie and his party rushing out of the Knickerbocker. The engine was running by the time they reached it. One agent held the door for Archie, while the other opened the rear door for Hanna.

They were away from the curb long before the cloud of dust thrown into the air by the blast began to resettle back on the ground. They raced past pedestrians who continued to stand still, unsure of what had just happened. Closer to the epicenter, they encountered crowds of panicked people running from the explosion. Traffic became a snarled mess.

Archie and James shared another look that conveyed they were thinking the same thing. If the streets were already this jammed, Balka Rath and Hanna's brother, Hanzi Muntean, would get entangled in traffic and would be unable to do their job.

"They'll be a couple blocks further out than we thought," James said.

"Yeah," Archie drawled. "My bet is Hanzi will stay with the truck, while Balka scouts the scene on foot and runs back with the necessary adjustments."

Before they encountered full gridlock, Archie steered the car down an alley, nosing aside several trash cans in his bid to find a clear street. The next block was far less pandemonium, though faces were etched with concern and people were still fast-walking away from the explosion.

Archie parked the Ford in a dedicated loading zone. "Stay here with Hanna. I'm going to get over to where the shell hit and see if I get lucky."

He made sure his pistol was secured in a holster under his jacket and the Ford's key remained in the ignition. On the sidewalk, Abbott was like a salmon swimming against the spawn. Everyone was moving west while he bulled his way east. He was well above average in height and he'd been a boxer and knew how to twist and torque to keep himself protected. Despite the throngs of people he knifed through, he bumped into no one.

He finally reached the area where the big naval shell had plowed into the city. For the most part, they'd been lucky. The shell had hit the street just four blocks from Penn Station—a remarkedly accurate opening shot. The crater it left continued to billow noxious smoke as did the remains of two cars that had been blown more than forty feet when the warhead detonated. Clear-thinking pedestrians were giving aid to the injured. Others had taken the time to drape the bodies pulled from the cars with rumble seat lap robes or overcoats. Archie counted five dead and assumed that number would climb as the most grievously wounded succumbed.

What he didn't see was anyone matching Balka Rath's description in the area. Nor anyone making note of where the shell had slammed into the street. He continued scanning the crowd for another two minutes on the off chance Rath had been farther from the blast and would just now show up.

At last, Archie had to cede defeat, and he rushed back to the car.

"We were too late," he announced. "The shell hit north and east of the station right in the middle of the street. I saw five dead."

Hanna gave a small choking gasp and Dashwood muttered a quiet oath. He said, "We now know the target, so I think we should get closer to the station."

"Agreed," Archie said. He opened the car's rear door. "Are you up for this, Hanna?"

"More than you know," she replied with anger.

BALKA NODDED TO HANZI AS HE WALKED PAST THE PANEL truck's cab. He opened the rear door and crawled inside. He had hooked up the transmitter to a truck battery and attached it to an aerial that poked out through a hole drilled into the van's roof.

The top of the antenna had been clamped to the third story of a fire escape in the alley where Hanzi had parked. Light came from a lamp attached to a second, smaller battery.

He had practiced diligently with the telegraph arm that sent messages over the airwaves, but he hadn't developed much proficiency. He didn't have what amateur radio enthusiasts called "fist."

With slow deliberation he tapped out instructions to his brother some miles distant on the bridge of a stolen battleship. They didn't use any fancy codes, but just a simple straightforward set of instructions. THREE BLOCKS EAST ONE BLOCK SOUTH. That would put the first of several shells through the roof of the vital Pennsylvania Station.

Balka yanked on the antenna wire sticking through the van's roof to pull it free from the metal fire escape and drew its full length into the van's body. Once it was secure, he rapped on the bulkhead separating the cab from the cargo area.

The truck's engine had been idling. Hanzi put his van in gear and drove them away from the curb. He had told Balka that it was possible for a radio transmission to be tracked back to its source. While unlikely that someone who heard the open-air broadcast would inform the police, it was a smart move to relocate after each time he called to the ship.

Of course he'd seen the bodies and had arrived at the blast zone in time to hear one of the victim's wails of agony go silent when she died. His brain wasn't wired for him to care. That they'd died, that anyone died, didn't register to him the way it did to any other human being. Someone was alive and then they were not. It was that simple to him.

His brother, Karl, could feel sympathy. Pain and loss motivated him. But not Balka. He knew how to make the appropriate expressions and say the right things, but his heart remained unmoved. He never understood grief because he never really understood loss. When he was a boy and was told his parents were dead, he'd kept sharpening the little knife Karl had given him without pause.

Traffic remained a snarled mess. Hanzi used the van's fender to exploit any advantage in order to get out of the area. A block away from where they'd parked, cars began to move in a more orderly fashion. It was still crawling, but at least there were no abandoned vehicles blocking their path.

A clap like thunder shook the city once again, followed seconds later by an eleven-inch naval projectile falling from the sky. Balka expected it to land almost seven blocks from where they were. Instead it hit close enough to rock the van on its suspension as it exploded in the iron skeleton of a nearby ten-story building under construction.

Rath had been thrown to the floor by the concussion. He got to his knees and pushed open the van's doors in time to see girders beginning to rain from the sky as the building began to collapse. Pedestrians were screaming, construction workers were trying to flee the fenced-off lot. The sound of collapsing steel was a combination of roaring destruction and the ringing clang of metal careening off metal. The building folded in on itself, pancaking into a thirty-foot-tall tangle of bent steel and dead workers shrouded in a veil of concrete dust that billowed for several blocks.

Balka lost a full minute staring at the devastation and listening to the screams of trapped and dying men. He finally roused himself. He leapt from the van and raced up to Hanzi, who was leaning out the driver's side window, his mouth agape.

"This is a disaster," Balka said.

"I'll say," Hanzi replied, still eyeing the wreck that had once been the bones of a skyscraper.

"No, you idiot. Karl missed by at least half a mile. I don't know what went wrong but we have to warn him before he fires again. Find us a place to put up the antenna." He ran back into the cargo bed and slammed the doors shut.

Hanzi made no pretense of his intentions to leave the area. He used his truck's powerful engine to push aside a smaller car and did it a second time when the driver wouldn't pull to the curb as he stood on the street, his Ford's door open at his side. The man cursed at Hanzi as he drove by. The Roma threw him a rude hand gesture and ground his way down the block.

They turned down a tree-lined side street and found an alley much like where they'd parked before. Balka shoved several feet of the antenna wire out through the roof, enough for Hanzi to grab a handful and begin to climb a fire escape. He wasn't halfway up when another shell streaked over the city from the north and detonated less than fifteen feet from the ruins of the building the ship had already leveled.

The explosion destroyed a storage shed but by this time all the workers who'd survived the initial blast had evacuated the construction site.

While Hanzi clamped the aerial to a fire escape railing, Balka calculated how far off his brother's shots were landing. He tapped out, BOTH LANDED EIGHT BLOCKS EAST THREE BLOCKS SOUTH.

Karl had two sets of coordinates and would now figure out the proper targeting. Rush hour was winding down, but there would be enough people at the train station to make this the greatest tragedy since the paddle steamer *General Slocum* sank in the East River, killing more than a thousand people.

42

APTAIN GRIMM COAXED EVERYTHING HE COULD OUT OF THE *Alice N*. Her engine was revved to just below its redline, making a deafening racket while smoke boiled out of her skinny funnel. Whoever had tuned the motor early this morning knew what he was doing. Bell estimated he'd wrung an extra two knots from the tired old fishing boat.

Bell had changed clothing and was now on deck with Joe, checking over the weapons and gear.

"You sure about that gun, Isaac?" Grey asked. "It's the oddest-looking thing I've ever seen."

"You should see the guy who designed it. Khristofor Ovlovey. Master mechanic, machinist, and gunsmith who lives on a farm on Long Island. This is his answer to trench warfare. Semiautomatic 12-gauge shotgun with a folding metal stock and a ten-round box magazine that feeds from the side."

"Why not the bottom?"

"Without a long clip hanging under the receiver, a shooter can hunker a little lower in a trench while firing. It increases his chance of surviving. This type of weapon also makes anyone using it far deadlier than an ordinary rifleman. This beast can lay down nearly a hundred man-stopping pellets in about fifteen seconds."

"Nasty. Has he sold the design?"

"No takers. To make it reliable, the tolerances need to be very precise. That makes the gun horribly expensive to manufacture. Khris has made a lot of one-off items for the agency over the years. He thought of me for this gun when he knew he'd never get to make a second one."

"Expensive?"

"Eye-wateringly."

Bell and Marchetti both wore black one-piece suits, with padded and reinforced knees and elbows. Each man carried a pistol in kidney holsters as well as backpacks loaded with the bombs and other gear. Joe would also carry a chopped down 20-gauge shotgun loaded with buck rather than birdshot. It wasn't as powerful a weapon as Bell's piece, but he freely admitted the recoil from a sawed-off 12-gauge was too much for him.

Bell's head snapped up when he heard the full-throated roar of the *Saarland*'s main battery firing for a second time. They were far enough up the East River to the see the muzzle flash reflected off the low clouds blanketing the city. It was like distant lightning. A moment later came the freight train–like roar as the huge shell split the sky. And a handful of seconds later came the sound of the shell exploding in Manhattan. Bell watched as a fresh plume of dust climbed into the sky very near where the first had impacted. They were both in Midtown and he guessed that either Penn Station or Grand Central Terminal was the target.

He clenched his fists to keep them from trembling in rage.

Moments later they were motoring through Hell Gate, the once deadly narrows at the top of the East River. The *Saarland* fired a third round just then. It had come so much faster than the second that Bell knew that Balka Rath had zeroed in the range and trajectory for his brother aboard the battleship.

"He's north of Rikers Island," Bell shouted into Grimm's ear. "Take us to the east and we'll come up behind him."

They lost some more time circumnavigating the island with its disused Union army training ground, and Bell felt each second ticking by. His gut was clenched with anticipation of more shells being lobbed at the city in a rapid-fire bombardment, but minutes crawled past, and the big guns remained silent. He was confused but grateful for the lull.

They finally came around the north shore of Rikers and got their first look at the anarchists' battleship as she menaced New York. Her aft turret looked inert, the two big cannons extending straight back and parallel to the deck. Her forward turret was turned and one of the guns was elevated to a great degree. Bell studied the massive warship through binoculars. He saw no one on the deck and no one standing on the bridge wing high above. It was impossible to see into the bridge itself and yet Bell's imagination put Karl Rath in there near the glass windscreen, his binoculars trained on the city to which he was laying waste.

The *Alice N.* raced across the open water and tucked alongside the ship near her fantail. Being this close changed their perspective on the battleship. She seemed to take up the entire world, her gray hull curving up and over them, so the fishing boat was draped in shadow.

In order to keep the ship on station, one of her three propellers spun slowly to maintain tension on the anchor that had been dropped into the tidal estuary.

Now that they were invisible to anyone on deck because of the hull's curvature, Grimm slowed his boat. They were so close to the *Saarland*'s hull that Grey kept having to push them off so they didn't scrape the steel plates. Everyone kept an eye toward the sky. If an anarchist noted their approach now, he could reach over the railing with a machine gun and shred the sturdy little boat.

Bell and Marchetti moved to the *Alice N.*'s bow. Bell's hybrid shotgun was slung across his back on a thick webbed cotton strap, while Joe's sawed off 20-gauge fit in a special holster belted around his waist and tied off around his thigh. They had brought a lightweight aluminum ladder to ease in boarding the battleship, but with the anchor down, they could clamber up the chain and squeeze through the hawsehole.

It had been at least seven minutes since the last salvo was fired at the city. That respite ended with a crashing explosion, the loudest any of the men had ever heard. Had they not earlier fixed wax plugs in their ears and been under the long gun tube, they would have all lost their hearing. Still, the noise left them reeling and with the feeling they'd been punched in the lungs without the protection of their ribs.

The men took a few seconds for their bodies to recover. The *Alice N.* had drifted a little from the great warship. Grimm made a quick correction. Grey grabbed on to the *Saarland*'s anchor chain when they got close enough. Bell and Marchetti exchanged a brief nod. They had never seen combat together but had helped each other escape the doomed liner *Lusitania,* and knew neither lacked courage and would remain calm under the most hellish conditions.

Bell gave Joe a thumbs-up and started climbing the sofa-sized chain links.

43

I've got it!" Archie shouted and gave the Ford's steering wheel a fingertip drum solo.

"What?" asked his two passengers.

It had been a minute since the third shell had exploded at what a passerby had told them was a construction site on Sixth Avenue.

"They have the grids reversed," he said as he put the car in gear and merged into traffic. "They had the number of blocks correct when they adjusted after the first shot, but the gunner thought New York City blocks are nine hundred feet wide and two hundred long when in reality it's the other way around, on average. That's why the second two rounds were so far off."

"So the next one?"

"Since it hasn't already been fired, they're realizing they've miscalculated. They'll work it out eventually and put the next high explosive shell right through the roof of Penn Station."

"And Balka will be nearby to tell his brother he's made a direct hit," Hanna said from the back seat, her eyes reduced to angry slits.

"And that's where we nab him," Archie told his companions, his hunter's instinct telling him he was right.

It was only a couple of blocks, but they were going against traffic trying to flee the area and many times their lane was taken up by oncoming cars driving illegally on the right. At one point a stampede of four fear-crazed horses raced past, the big animals' eyes showing mostly white while their bodies were covered in sweaty lather.

Eventually they made it to the massive white-columned station. Traffic here had thinned out, as if people were coming to realize the explosions weren't random, that their beloved city was under attack, and the likely target was the gleaming new station. They turned from Thirty-First onto Seventh Avenue, each looking for any kind of van or truck. There were several but Hanna was sure none of them belonged to her brother. They kept on circling the sprawling station, peering down side streets and alleys in hopes of spotting their quarry.

Then came the gut-clenching sound of a fourth incoming projectile, that long rolling crack that grew louder as it drew closer. They saw the shell hit high up on the train hall's exterior wall near where it met the roof. The round bored through the granite façade and plowed aside interior layers of stone and brick and structural steel.

It then shot across one of the tall passenger galleries before plunging through the floor, subfloor, and twenty feet of compacted dirt before screaming into a vacant train tunnel and finally embedding itself in the filthy ballast stones between the rails.

Rather than waste another precious high-explosive shell, Karl

Rath had ordered one of the armor-piercing rounds be fired to make certain they had corrected their geographic error. Once Balka confirmed a hit, the building would be reduced to a smoldering pile.

Archie, James, and Hanna waited for the rendering explosion that never came, none of the trio breathing for many long seconds.

"A dud?" James asked at last.

"Looks to be," Archie agreed.

Hundreds of people were rushing out the station's multiple doors. Men in suits or work clothes, women in long coats and dresses, kids in school uniforms all fled from the building in a panicked rush. Archie could hear their screams of fear from a half block away. He saw a couple of cops give up trying to tame the chaos and instead allow the crowds to bear them along.

This was the critical moment. They had seconds to find Rath before he reported to his brother it was time to fire at will.

"Mr. Abbott," Hanna squealed from the back seat, her arm shooting over his shoulder to point down an alley they were just passing. "There. That is Hanzi's truck. I'd know it anywhere."

Archie braked hard. The tuned brakes nearly stopped the car on a dime. The car behind them tried to brake in time but ended up smashing into their rear bumper. Archie ignored the accident, dropped the Ford into reverse, and pushed the other car backward enough for him to make the turn into the alley. The front of the Ford hadn't been hardened like a couple of the agency's pool cars so he couldn't ramp up to a hefty ramming speed as he'd wished. As it was, he smashed into the rear of the covered cargo truck hard enough to throw whoever was in the bed up against the cab and break the hinge of one of the rear doors.

Hanzi had been watching through the wing mirror and had seen the black car racing down the alley with the look that it wasn't going to slow. He hadn't been fast enough to get the truck moving to avoid being hit, but he had them rolling seconds later.

"Everyone all right?" Archie asked, his palms stinging from holding the wheel during the collision.

"Yeah, I mean yes, I'm unhurt," Hanna said.

"James?"

He wiped a trace of blood from his forehead from where it had hit the dash. "It's nothing."

Archie saw that the van was already pulling away. He revved the engine to see if he'd damaged it. It sounded fine. He took off after his prey, mindful that he should drop Hanna off but not daring to lose the time.

"Mr. Abbott, my brother, please don't hurt him."

"That'll be up to him," Arch said as they burst from the alley onto Thirty-Third Street.

As long as he kept Hanzi driving as though his life depended on it, Balka couldn't use his radio's telegraph key to transmit a message. That equipment needed a flat, steady surface in the hands of an expert, which he doubted the anarchist was. Archie didn't exactly back off but knowing they couldn't broadcast to the battleship allowed him to relax into the chase.

B ELL HAD TO PULL OFF HIS PACK AND PASS HIS GUN THROUGH the hawsehole when he reached the top of the thick anchor chain. Only then could he slither through the gap and land inside the *Saarland*'s chain locker room. He took Marchetti's gear and helped pull him through the hawsehole. They resettled their equipment and went to the room's only door. There was no lock and so Bell eased it open, mindful that the hinges made the sound like nails down a chalkboard.

The hallway beyond was curved along the lines of the exterior plating and appeared to run the entire length of the ship. Overhead, the ceiling was a snake's nest of wiring and conduits. There were lights in stout wire cages every five feet and shin-breaking coamings for watertight doors every twenty feet or so. The walls were rust-streaked and the deck dirty. Bell felt the interior of the ship had the sinister atmosphere of a haunted mansion, all the deep shadows and murky corners and the feeling of long abandonment. The distant thrum of the ship's steam engine and generators made it feel like the whole ship was breathing a dark, malevolent breath.

Despite the winter chill, Bell's flanks were slick with sweat, and he had to dry his palms against his thighs.

With such a small crew of anarchists, neither Bell nor Joe Marchetti expected there would be any guards posted but they lit out as silent and as vigilant as possible. They swept each open room they passed as they patrolled aft. Most were empty, save for old metal bunk frames or piles of trash the Brazilian caretakers had left behind back in the Azores. They heard a few rats foraging amid the piles of refuse.

As they neared midships, Bell slowed their pace even more. He knew time was his enemy as much as Karl Rath, but they had to be cautious until the bombs were planted. This was a must-win fight like no other, with hundreds of New Yorkers' lives in the balance.

Joe pointed to a stairwell and jerked his thumb downward. Bell nodded and led them down the stairs, his trench-sweeping shotgun at the ready. He heard voices when they reached the next deck, orders shouted and acknowledged. He padded out of the vestibule, keeping low and slow until he reached an open watertight door that gave him a measure of concealment. He peered around.

A man in work clothes stood outside a room where the light spilling from it appeared diffused. He said something to a man or possibly men inside. To Bell, it sounded like the language Rath spoke back in occupied Belgium. A moment later two men emerged from the room pushing a cart that had rubber wheels. The cart was loaded with two dozen silk-wrapped objects that reminded Bell of Marion's smallest hat box.

Bell didn't need Joe's naval experience to recognize propellent bags for the *Saarland*'s main battery. The men were wheeling enough explosives to level an office building. Apart from the rubber wheels, Bell noted the cart was coated in bronze so that even if it struck a bulkhead, it would produce no sparks. They moved about fifteen feet down the corridor before steering the cart into a waiting elevator. All three rode up together.

Bell rushed from his hiding spot and into the powder magazine, Joe on his heels. The storeroom reeked of strong acidic chemicals as there were thousands of propellent bags stored on row after row of open wooden shelves. Thick glass covered the few lights as a precaution against one of the bulbs exploding and igniting one of the bags. The glass gave the lights the diffused look Bell had noted moments ago.

He dropped to his knees so Joe could easily reach into his pack for a bomb. It was only a single half-stick of dynamite wired to a clock timer, but it didn't need to be larger or more elaborate. Bell started shifting the propellant bags in a corner of the magazine as far as possible from where the anarchists were depleting the store. Joe placed the bomb against a bulkhead and set the timer.

They'd just completed burying it under the bags they'd just moved when a shadow crossed the room's open hatch.

"Oi!" shouted a bearded crewman.

Bell whirled and brought the shotgun to his shoulder before realizing a discharge in here would blow the battleship in half. The crewman took off running.

Bell shrugged out of his heavy pack and gave it to Joe. "You know what to do. Good luck."

He sprinted out of the magazine and stopped. He looked fore and aft. The man had vanished. Bell held his breath and strained his ears. He heard a soft noise to aft and took off running. He saw a shadow flicker in the stairwell vestibule. Bell raised the shotgun, but there was no target. He raced for the stairs, climbing them two and three at a time, not knowing if the other man was armed and laying an ambush. At the top of the stairs, Bell peered out into the hallway. It looked very much like the one below. He heard feet slapping against the metal deck and gave chase, running for the ship's bow this time.

He leapt over the door coamings like a steeplechaser, his shoulder and head hunched so as not to hit the top lip, his gun cradled in both hands. Bell spotted his man as he tried to slow himself and turn a sharp corner. It gave him all the opportunity he needed.

The shotgun roared twice with two quick pulls on the trigger. Twenty pellets sprayed from the weapon in an expanding arc that literally filled the hallway with lead. The anarchist made it out of the line of fire, but many of the pellets ricocheted off the steel walls.

Bell heard the man scream and fall just out of view. He ran up, the shotgun swung around his back and an automatic pistol now in his right hand. He darted his head around the corner. The anarchist was on the deck, but he wasn't down by any count. It didn't look like he'd been hit at all. He was sitting with his knees bent to help stabilize the big revolver in his hands.

Bell ducked back an instant before the man fired. The slug hit a bulkhead and left a golf ball–sized divot. Bell fired blind at the wall near where the anarchist sat to distract him enough so that he could reach around the corner with his Browning. He emptied the clip at where he knew the man sat, cycling the pistol as fast as he could, knowing muscle memory was bringing the barrel back at his target following each shot.

He switched the pistol to his left and held the shotgun one-handed when he chanced another glance around the corner. He hadn't hit the man with every shot, but there were enough holes in him and in the right places for him to stay down, permanently.

Bell took a second to get his bearings. Up ahead he saw the curved wall of the barbette, the armored structural support for the ship's forward turret. The hallway the dead man took led to some officer's quarters. There was a great deal of wood paneling and tarnished brass accents and better-quality light fixtures. This was where the Brazilians had been living. It smelled of dirty laundry and unwashed men.

He turned to retrace his steps when he heard men coming toward him. They were running hard. His gun battle had drawn their attention. He dashed from the corridor, his gun aimed down the main passageway. He saw three men running abreast, all armed. Bell ran in the opposite direction, trying to get out of their range. A few shots were fired his way, but none came close. He turned a corner and went a dozen paces before finding a stairwell. He went down it by lifting his feet and sliding on his hands. At the base he turned and raised the shotgun. The anarchists were smart, they fired down the steps before they could see him, forcing Bell to retreat.

He ran into a room off the ship's central corridor. It was a vast dining area, with heavy round tables bolted to the floor and a kitchen visible through a pass window. He waited by the door, wishing he had a small hand mirror. He had to trust his hearing and instincts. He'd been hunted so many times before he knew that the need for caution by the hunter balanced with the desire of the kill produced a certain pace. He waited, imagining the men reaching the bottom of the stairs. He could almost see them exchange glances and point to the open dining room door. They would feel a sense of confidence. They knew the ship better than the man they hunted. They would know there was no place to hide.

They'd start striding faster and faster.

With a shout Bell swung around the door and opened fire, charging at them for added confusion as it was the opposite of what they'd expect. They were exactly where he'd thought they would be. He emptied the shotgun's magazine, filling the hall with a scything gale of lead shot. Each man was hit multiple times at almost point-blank range. It was as if the deck had vanished under their feet when all three men went down, limbs like rubber, pistols clattering to the floor.

After jacking a fresh magazine into the side of the shotgun's receiver, Bell went to check on the men. They were all dead. He recognized one as the man who'd caught him sneaking around Rath's training facility, the one with the compass rose tattoo.

A pistol shot rang out from down the corridor and a bullet came close enough for Bell to feel its motion. He whirled, dropping so his chest was on the deck, and returned fire. His attacker had vanished around a corner. Bell thought about giving chase but the clock running in his head told him he'd wasted enough time. His mission had been accomplished.

He climbed up three flights of stairs before he reached the main deck. Bell walked down yet another corridor, looking for a way to get outside so he could get off the ship. Before he could find a hatch, he froze as he heard yet more men ahead.

44

THE CHASE HAD ONLY GONE A COUPLE OF BLOCKS WHEN THE rear van door suddenly burst open. Archie got his first look at Balka Rath and understood why everyone said he was so handsome. Even with a cruel sneer to his mouth, his looks were otherworldly, truly like an angel come to earth. Then the man whipped a pistol into view. Hanzi had been watching the mirrors and alerted Balka that they were being pursued.

He opened fire. The Ford's windshield spiderwebbed and then collapsed onto Archie and James's lap in a cascade of daggerlike shards. Archie swerved, managing to sideswipe a city bus but dropping out of Balka's immediate line of sight. He waited then fired again, trying to either hole the radiator or the driver.

Dashwood had to ignore the glass cutting into his waist when he punched out his side window with the butt of his pistol and thrust his torso outside the car. He was one of the best shots in the office, but the angle of his body sticking out of the car made accuracy all but impossible. He fired once but when he saw that his bullet missed the van entirely he stopped shooting. Unlike Rath, he wouldn't needlessly endanger civilians.

Archie slowed to increase the range and Hanzi took advantage, accelerating hard in an attempt to get away. Archie could have caught him with no trouble, but he'd put himself square in Balka's range again. They turned onto Seventh Avenue and Archie finally saw an opening. He punched the gas and swung around the side of another bus and used its bulk to shield them from Rath. He was doing fifty when he reached the front of the bus directly abreast of Hanzi's khaki-colored delivery van.

With a deft touch on the wheel, Archie crossed in front of the bus and hooked the Ford's bumper into the van's front spoked wheel. The wood splintered like it had been hit with a grenade. Hanzi kept the now three-wheeler stable by jamming its left side against Archie's sedan.

Archie turned the wheel to slam the Ford into him and then quickly swung away. Hanzi was too slow to match the maneuver and the van's left front collapsed onto the road in a shower of sparks. Hanzi lost all ability to steer his van. He hit the brakes, threw open his door, and vaulted from the driver's seat before they'd come to a complete stop. He hit the sidewalk, rolled over on one shoulder and leapt to his feet to sprint away.

Archie had also slammed the brakes, but had done so without realizing he hadn't pulled far enough away from the double-decker bus he'd just overtaken. Its brakes and tires screamed in a valiant attempt to stop, but to no avail. It slammed into the Ford hard enough to accordion the trunk. Hanna was thrown into the back of the front seat with enough force to break her collarbone. A piece of the broken windshield the size and shape of a steak knife was driven two inches into Dashwood's groin, barely missing his femoral artery.

In the second-long gap between hearing the bus's brakes lock and the vehicle hitting the Ford, Archie launched himself from his seat over the steering wheel and through the now-empty windscreen frame. The impact knocked the car forward but Archie jammed his foot on the top of the steering wheel, and he fell flat onto the Ford's hood.

He rolled off onto the roadway, groping for the pistol under his suitcoat. He staggered to his feet in time to see Hanzi start running. Pedestrians were already on edge because of the four mysterious explosions that had rocked the city. Seeing a man running from an accident ramped up their anxiety and as a result they parted as if by Moses. Archie aligned himself in a proper firing stance and pulled the trigger.

The .45-caliber slug hit the fleeing anarchist in the right buttock and lodged against the outside of his pelvis. The kinetic impact of the heavy bullet kicked his right leg out from under him, so he went down on the sidewalk without any chance of bracing himself. The impact of his skull against the unyielding concrete was like a melon dropped from a table. He'd be out for hours.

Just then Balka Rath jumped out of the back of the van. Archie tried to line up a shot, but the crowd was in full-blown panic because of his first shot. They gave the anarchist perfect cover and Rath seemed to disappear. Archie caught a glimpse of him running down the street and he took off in pursuit. It was like running through a herd of stampeding horses. People were scattering in all directions, some trying to get onto the roadway, others trying to find a lane to run on the sidewalks, others dashing into storefront doorways and others emerging from the shops. It was bedlam and Archie felt he was losing his target.

He pressed on, his mouth a tight grim line as he edged people out of his way as gently as he could. Up ahead, he saw a tall man suddenly lurch right with enough force to dislodge his hat. He knew Rath had just pushed the man out of his way. He wasn't as far behind as he feared.

All at once the crowds seemed to thin and Archie caught sight of Rath. The anarchist must have sensed him. He looked back, his cherubic face a mask of both fear and anger. His eyes widened when he saw his pursuer. Rath suddenly juked left through the door of a hardware store. Archie raced for it, his gun at the ready.

The store was laid out in long aisles running toward the back. Each was lined with shelves displaying all manner of tools, plumbing supplies, bins of nuts and bolts, and anything else someone in the building trade would need. Archie lost a few precious seconds because Balka hadn't run down the aisle directly behind the door. He had to check three of them before he saw his man nearly at the other end. He raised his pistol but couldn't fire as there were two men in overalls examining lengths of copper pipe for sale. Rath dashed through a curtain to the back of the store separating the customer's area from the private domain of the employees and owner. Archie was hot on his heels and burst through the curtain a second later, stooping as low as he could just as he parted the dark fabric.

Rath was waiting just behind the curtain with a balisong knife, which he thrust at Archie with a lightning strike. Had the detective been standing upright, the blow would have split his ribs and pierced his heart in a fatal blow. Instead, the stiletto-like blade sank to its hilt into Arch's well-developed trapezius muscle. Archie's shock at the sudden explosion of pain down his right arm made him drop his gun.

Since Rath hadn't expected his pursuer to be hunched over and his attack not lethal, he hesitated at pulling the knife and correcting his aim. It was a fatal mistake. Archie caught his dropped pistol with his left hand, raised the barrel slightly, and put one of the big .45 bullets into Balka's heart. Rath had a moment to stare into the eyes of the man who'd shot him. He saw nothing but determined satisfaction.

Archie had seen the glint of a blade in Rath's hand when he raced through the curtain, though he was certain it hadn't been there seconds earlier. Rath's only hope of winning the fight was an ambush as quickly as possible. Since Archie couldn't slow his pursuit, he'd protected himself as best as possible and ran in hunched over like an old man.

He left Rath where he'd fallen and staggered back to the Ford almost a full block away. Blood was soon snaking down his arm and dripping from his fingers.

"What have you done to Hanzi?" Hanna screamed at him. She'd gotten herself out of the car and was standing over her brother with her bad arm cradled in her good, her face gone pale and glossy with perspiration. "You've killed him."

Arch Abbott left the knife embedded in his flesh and slowly lowered himself to the curb. Through the pain, he managed to say, "No, but he won't be sitting down comfortably anytime soon."

"You don't move, mister," said a portly man looming over Archie. He wore a grocer's apron and was brandishing a wooden truncheon.

"It's okay, I'm with Van Dorn," Archie said, showing the would-be hero his empty palms. "Those two jokers are connected to the explosions near Penn Station."

"Really?" said the grocer, lowering the baton.

"Just proving the Van Dorns always get their man," Archie called up to James Dashwood who remained in the front seat of the demolished Ford. "You doing all right up there?"

"Big piece of glass is stuck where it shouldn't be and I don't want to move until there's a doctor or two hovering over me. You?"

"About the same, but mine's some sort of floppy-handled knife."

"What about Rath?"

"He took his to the heart from my .45 so he's not coming back from that one."

"Where'd you wing Hanna's brother?"

"Keister."

"Nice." James paused for a moment. Despite leaving the shard in place, he was still losing blood. When a wave of nausea passed, he asked, "Do you think this is the end of it? Karl Rath's spotter is dead. There will be no more radioed instructions."

Beat cops blowing whistles were starting to show up. Ambulances wouldn't be too far behind.

Archie answered James's question. "I think when enough time has passed and Rath still hasn't heard from his brother, he's going to fire at random to do the maximum amount of damage he can."

"I was afraid you were going to say that."

"It's up to Isaac and Joe now. All we can do is hope."

B ELL WAS NEVER ONE TO SLINK OUT OF A SITUATION, BUT HE knew discretion was the better part of valor in this instance. He turned as soon as he heard the group of approaching men. He found a ladder to the next deck and climbed. Now above the main deck, where presumably there was no need for Rath to have any of his men, Bell ran aft. The rooms he passed served functions he didn't understand, presumably to do with aiming and firing the main guns or perhaps damage control.

He found a door to the outside and opened it. He found himself on an observation platform just aft of the bridge, near one of the ship's countless tertiary artillery installations. He looked up toward the bridge and saw that his arrival had caught the attention of two men standing on the wraparound bridge wing just above the forward turret. Bell recognized Karl Rath instantly, but it took the anarchist a long second to realize the man he'd sent to his death aboard the Zeppelin-Staaken aircraft had not only survived the flight but had somehow managed to follow him across the Atlantic.

The range was too great for the shotgun and before Bell had time to draw his pistol, Rath and his companion opened fire with pistols of their own. Bell just managed to duck through the door when the bullets arrived in an angry swarm.

"I will kill you myself," Rath shouted down to Bell, his voice like the bellow of an enraged animal.

Pesha Orsos, Rath's childhood friend asked, "Who was that?"

"The man from back in Belgium, Isaac Bell," Rath said, feeding additional bullets into his revolver while keeping one eye trained on the platform below. "Listen, Pesha, we've waited long enough for my brother to radio in. Something must have happened to him. Get back to your station and fire at will on the city. Aim as best you can from this range, but fire quickly. We may not destroy their landmarks but thirty quarter-ton shells raining down on New York will still get our desired results."

Another of Rath's men ran out onto the platform. He was winded. "We found it, no problem."

"A bomb?"

"A small one in the powder magazine where Pesha said it would be. It was easily disabled. I had the parts thrown over the side just to be sure."

"This man Bell is not as smart as he thinks he is," Rath said. "Good job, Pesha."

Rath's confidant beamed. "As soon as I got word that there was an intruder aboard, I knew right where they were heading and why. The powder magazine is the only place that a bomb small enough for one person to carry would do any good."

"Bravo. Go now. I will make certain the lifeboats are ready to launch. How long will it take to fire the remaining rounds?"

"Twenty minutes."

"Perfect. When you're done, we will motor over to the Connecticut side of the Sound and make our escape." Rath handed his pistol to the new arrival and said, "Stay here and watch that gun platform down there. The American may still be just inside the door. If you see him shoot him. I'll get others to hunt him from inside the ship."

"Yes, sir."

ONE OF THE BULLETS HAD GRAZED THE OUTSIDE OF BELL'S CALF. The bleeding wasn't so bad, but it hurt like he'd been burned with the long edge of a fireplace poker. His shotgun had fared even worse from the quick encounter. When he'd leapt back through the door he had slammed the weapon into the frame and managed to knock the magazine out of alignment. He couldn't pull it free and couldn't trust that it would feed new rounds into the receiver. Without a second thought, he left the expensive weapon behind. His

Browning pistol had gotten him out of a great many scrapes in the past and he trusted it wouldn't fail him this time.

Bell saw that he was leaving a trail of blood spatters in his wake. He took another moment to tie a bandage he carried in one of his suit's numerous pockets around his leg to staunch the flow.

He descended the ladder he'd climbed earlier and ran aft as hard as he could. He wanted to put distance between himself and where Rath knew he'd been. He was also aware of the ticking timer on the primary bomb in the magazine. There was about ten minutes to go, and it would be a stupid death to be killed by his own detonation.

Bell dropped down another deck, noticing a small placard affixed to a wall at a juncture in the corridor. The universal pictogram told him that there was a lifeboat station at the end of the branching passageway. Joe would already be back aboard the *Alice N.* with orders to leave five minutes before their time bomb went off, no matter what. Bell had too many men searching for him between his location and the chain locker, so returning there was no longer an option. Escaping on the lifeboat was his best hope.

At the end of the corridor was another watertight door. On the other side he found an alcove overlooking the water with a thirty-foot lifeboat hanging on steel davits. The lifeboat wasn't matte gray like the rest of the ship, but had been painted white with a gaudy red stripe along its hull. Part of the bow had been decked over and a fake cockpit installed to make it look like a rich man's toy rather than a piece of naval equipment.

Bell climbed a small ladder to reach the lifeboat's gunwale. He noted the craft's actual controls were in the aft at a small stand-up console with just a wheel, an engine RPM gauge, a throttle, and a starter button for the motor. To save himself time, he went to the console and pressed the starter. Since the anarchists had taken the time to disguise the boat, his assumption that they'd made certain it worked was correct. The two-cylinder motor buried deep in the boat's hull came to life and the brass screw whirred like an electric fan.

Bell was backing down the ladder when a pair of arms encircled him from behind and ripped him from the rungs. He was tackled in a takedown that sent him crashing to the deck with the other man on his chest. The speed and violence of the attack left him stunned and gave his opponent the chance to grab the sides of his head and prepare to dash the back of his skull into the metal decking until it cracked open.

Bell caught sight of the man's eye patch and knew his opponent. Even fighting for his life, part of Bell's mind deduced that Karl Rath must have followed Bell onto the platform, hiding in the lifeboat recess while he was on the boat.

As his head was yanked up, Bell tightened his stomach and did the fastest sit-up of his life. His forehead collided with Karl Rath's nose. The blow lacked the power to break it, but it watered the man's eyes and made blood rain from his nostrils. It was enough of a distraction for Bell to lever up a knee and push the bigger man off of him.

As Bell scrambled to get to his feet, his left hand lay flat on the deck for an instant. Rath was only partially to his feet but still had the leverage to slam the heel of his boot down on the back of Bell's hand with the force to break bones.

The *Saarland*'s main gun fired just then, a great roar of smoke and flame belching from the barrel in the wake of another high explosive shell aimed at the city. The sound drowned out Bell's own roar of pain. In all his years of boxing and working as a detective he'd never had a broken hand and so he never knew the agony or the feeling of vulnerability that came when one of his arms was suddenly useless.

Rath sensed the fight was all but over and let Bell get to his feet, his left arm dangling, his hand already swelling.

"You found the bomb on the airplane." It was more statement than question.

"After I killed your suicidal sacrifice," Bell said over the sound of the idling lifeboat motor. He then went for the Browning behind his back. He moved as fast as he could, but the pain from his mangled hand slowed everything he did. The pistol came out and was coming around when Rath barreled into him again and yanked it free. He tossed the gun through the railing under the lifeboat's keel.

He smiled at Bell's helplessness. "How did you know about the *Admiral Lisboa* and our plans here?"

"You've been as subtle as a bull, Rath. Figuring out your plan took less deductive power than catching a toddler in a lie."

Rath rushed in and threw a right cross that grazed Bell's chin because it had been so telegraphed. Bell countered with a right to Rath's body that felt like he'd punched a truck tire. The motion sent fresh waves of pain radiating from his broken left hand. He closed his eyes in agony for less than a second. It was a moment of weakness that Rath saw and exploited. He landed two punches, a right-left combo that staggered Bell back into the underhull of the hanging lifeboat. He likely would have reeled all the way to the railing if not for the boat.

Bell moved forward and stepped to Rath's left. The one-eyed man immediately turned to protect his blind side.

"You left clues all over the place, Rath," Bell said, moving again to get the exact same response from Rath. The anarchist always moved to keep an opponent to his right, so he had a clear view with his mono vision. "And you told too much to Magdalena. I bet you didn't know that jilted girlfriends are a detective's best source of information."

"I will deal with her when I get back to Europe," Rath said dismissively. Then a wry, knowing smile spread across his face. "Besides, it doesn't matter. My men found your bomb in the magazine, Bell. They took it apart and tossed the remains into the water. You've failed."

With an enraged shout, Bell leapt at Rath like he'd lost all control. He threw a wild right that Rath blocked with one meaty arm. The man countered with a shot to the gut that Bell had anticipated and knew was worth the cost.

He had moved to Rath's blind side and had a momentary advantage. He took it, throwing a long and swinging left hook, a punch Rath never thought possible because of the condition of Bell's hand and a blow he never saw coming because of his missing eye. Bell had worked him to this exact position to use the only weapon he had to defeat the madman.

The punch landed at the hinge of Rath's jaw, perfectly placed and executed all the way to the follow-through. Even as Bell's mouth opened for a scream of unholy pain the likes he'd never felt before, Karl Rath's head snapped around. When his neck reached its maximum amount of twist, his torso started to torque as well. The momentum staggered him one step and then another. He had no control over the lengths of his strides nor the direction. It was all physics that Bell had mapped out in his head.

Reeling backward, Rath fell directly into the lifeboat's spinning propeller. The whirling brass blades chewed through the muscle, sinew, and bone of his right shoulder until they emerged out his back, so that only a few inches of skin kept the limb attached to his body.

Blood washed the deck in a crimson tidal wave and Rath's scream grew even more shrill than Bell's. He collapsed while Bell paced in a fast circle, clutching his hand as if that could somehow ease the pain of his doubly broken bones. Bell sucked air through his clenched teeth, mindful of nothing except his own agony.

The ship's main gun roared once again. Only a minute or two had elapsed since it had last fired. This snapped Bell from dwelling on his own misery as he realized the full bombardment of the city was underway. He had to go but he had to tell Rath something.

He dropped to his knees next to the killer. Rath's wound was ungodly gruesome and the man looked half crazed with pain. If a surgeon got to him in the next minute or so, his life might have been saved but that wasn't going to be Rath's fate.

"Rath, listen to me," Bell panted. "We planned for you to find that bomb because it would mean you'd stop looking for a second one we set. You can die knowing your plan failed at the eleventh hour."

Rath seemed unfazed. He grabbed Bell's arm. He spoke through his pain, his voice enfeebled by the blood loss leaching his life away. "There are others. Fulcrum will prevail in the end." And then he breathed his last.

"Sure thing," Bell said, dripping sarcasm. He ducked under the lifeboat and lurched to the rail. It was only a ten- or twelve-foot drop because the alcove was one deck below the main. He legged over the stanchion and was about to drop perilously into Long Island Sound when he saw his savior named *Alice N.* not forty feet away.

"There," he heard Joe Marchetti shout from the fishing boat's bow.

Captain Grimm spun the wheel to get closer. Bell leapt from the battleship, his left hand protected in his right. The impact still sent pain waves crashing through to the top of his skull, but an amazing thing happened by the time he'd resurfaced. The icy water numbed his hand so quickly the pain was temporarily tolerable.

Moments later and without fully stopping, Grey and Joe used a boat hook to help him over the motor sailer's transom. The instant his feet were out of the water, Grimm gunned his beloved old boat and they ran as hard as they could to get away from the warship.

Bell knew the chances were high that he and Joe would be spotted during their time on the *Saarland*. Rath and his men would know exactly what they were attempting and discover the bomb after they'd left. Bell's plan was then to intentionally give away their presence, let Rath find the device, and rely on a second, less obvious, bomb to destroy the warship. It increased the risk that more shells could be lobbed at New York, but it was the only way to guarantee Rath couldn't bombard the city for hours on end.

In the tight crawl space under the powder magazine elevator, Joe Marchetti had affixed a pressure sensor on one of the rails while Bell had been running around the battleship distracting its crew. The pressure switch became active when one of the lift's guide wheels reached the bottom of its rail. That was the point when crewmen returned to the magazine from up in the turret with their special trolley to fetch more high explosives.

The bomb he'd wired to the sensor would wait while hundreds of pounds of powder were loaded onto the cart and then wheeled back into the elevator. Only when the elevator rose would the sensor release and trigger the thirty pounds of explosives Bell had lugged aboard in his pack.

The *Alice N.* was a mile from the *Saarland* when the main gun fired a third salvo in relatively quick succession.

The men down in the magazine were hurrying to keep up. They were supposed to have fresh powder up to the guns by now and yet they were just now loading the last bags onto their cart. They didn't bother closing the powder room's armored door before wheeling the trolley down the corridor to the waiting elevator.

One of the men closed the accordion door and pressed the lift button. A fraction of a second after the elevator started to rise the bomb under their feet exploded. Joe had assembled his bomb so that much of its intensity was directed upward and so the blast front tore through the elevator car's floor and detonated the mountain of powder piled atop the cart. This was the second link in the chain reaction that set off the hundreds upon hundreds of tons of powder remaining in the ship's main magazine.

The battleship's belt armor kept much of the detonative force contained within the side hulls, but the blast ripped through her bottom and rebounded off the seafloor, lifting the front half of the ship out of the water. Her thick keel snapped like a piece of kindling and a rolling wave of fire and pressurized air exploded from where she tore in half. Steam from her boilers and sea water boiled by the heat added to the hellish tableau. The sound was dozens of times louder than the firing of one of her big guns, a sound that would carry to Albany and Baltimore and Providence, Rhode Island.

The detonation blew the forward turret clean off the ship and peeled back her decking. A visible blast wave moved through the air even faster than the sound of the explosion, followed soon after by surging walls of water that sloshed around in the tight confines of the upper East River. Moments after the main blast, the *Saarland* rolled onto her side and settled onto the seabed, air geysering from gaps in the exposed portion of her hull. The waters near the smoldering derelict were littered with the corpses of seabirds killed by the concussion and patches of burning bunker fuel.

Windows for miles around were shattered by the detonation and a few civilians were hurt by flying glass, but no fatalities would be reported. Because she'd been firing at the city, the very presence of the *Saarland* had run off any boaters from the area, so that the only vessel caught in the surging waves following the blast was the *Alice N*. She'd gone on the ride of her life, as she was too near the blast to avoid danger. The small boat was rocked by a torrential wave that sent her barreling north against her will. After surviving a second powerful tempest in as many weeks, she was left stranded fifteen feet up on a beach near the mouth of the Bronx River, her four crewmen battered, but safe.

EPILOGUE

⊰✦⊱

FEAR GRIPPED THE RESIDENTS OF NEW YORK CITY IN A PARA-lyzing stranglehold. Rumors ran like wildfire that German troops had landed on Long Island and were marching toward the city. Sidewalk whispers claimed an entire fleet of the Kaiser's battle-wagons were steaming toward New York Harbor to finish leveling Manhattan. Woodrow Wilson rushed to the city by private railcar the very next day, in order to both quell the rumors and to see for himself the damage done by the rogue dreadnought.

Seven eleven-inch naval shells had ultimately been fired at Man-hattan, six high explosive and one armor piercing. Despite the on-slaught, the city had been relatively lucky. The explosive shell aimed at Penn Station following the armor-piercing ranging shot had fallen short of the building and hit a streetcar on the north side of Thirty-Third Street. It had killed ten people, but would have killed far more had it struck the station. The later shells Rath had ordered Pesha Orsos to fire landed in Midtown. One destroyed a pair of brownstone row houses, while another flattened a merchant bank building.

Out of a city of over two million people, forty-eight lost their lives that fateful day, with several dozen more injured in some way. All knew it could have been much worse.

Repairs were already underway at Penn Station when President Wilson and his entourage took a quick walking tour of the building. Initial wreckage had been cleared away and the station was operating at a limited capacity. City road crews had repaired the blast holes left on the surrounding streets and sidewalks and there were plans being discussed to put up a memorial of some sort in nearby Bryant Park commemorating the victims of the attack.

Of course, there were no survivors of the explosion of the battleship *Admiral Joaquim Lisboa* nee *Saarland*. There weren't really any remains either. The Navy was already negotiating with a local salvage company to remove the ship's gutted carcass, once investigators had completed their examination of the remains that were above water, and hardhat divers had explored the sunken portion of the wreck.

After meeting with families of the victims and then speaking with reporters to allay fears about a further attack, the President entered the New York Yacht Club building in Midtown Manhattan. He was there for a private meeting with Bell arranged by Franklin Roosevelt, who was a member of the club. Bell was waiting at a corner table in the downstairs lounge when Wilson entered. The President waved off his assistants and approached alone.

"Mr. Bell," Wilson said as Bell stood and offered his right hand in greeting. "I've heard from Joe Van Dorn about what you did to save New York City, and what you've endured on my behalf the last few weeks. Had I known the toll it would take"—he pointed to Bell's left hand, wrapped in a bandage the size of a boxing glove—"I never would have asked you to be my eyes and ears on the battlefront."

Bell had known this meeting was coming and had taken as small a dose of painkiller as he could, but he still felt its effects and so spoke slowly and with great deliberation. "Mr. President, I assure you that my sacrifice and that of all the others who I have encountered was well worth my involvement."

"Our nation owes you a heartfelt thanks. And the City of New York an extra debt of gratitude. While I am eager to hear how you disabled the dreadnought, I am more interested in your visit to the front lines in Europe."

Bell relayed his overseas exploits, providing an unvarnished description of the horrors he witnessed at the front. He spoke of the unfailing bravery of the men he fought with, and of the higher vision that men like Winston Churchill saw of the critical nature of the war's outcome.

Wilson stared at him for a moment. "Are you saying this is a just war and we should do our part?"

"No, Mr. President. There is no such thing as a just war. But this is one we must fight if for no other reason than to bring it to a swift end. During our Civil War, the average soldier could fire his musket four times in a minute. In just three days at Gettysburg there were over fifty thousand casualties. Today that same average soldier can fire between twenty and thirty rounds a minute if you factor in all the machine guns. The Allies and Central Powers have already slaughtered millions of men with no end in sight. If they keep at each other, Europe's population will simply collapse and the remaining people will be driven back to the Dark Ages.

"And there's something more. Without our involvement in the fighting, we won't have a say in the peace accords that follow. The

Europeans need our leadership on this front if they are to break their generational cycle of war. By us fighting on the Allied side, we can ensure a lasting peace. You have an opportunity to make certain that this is the war that H. G. Wells said would finally end all war."

Wilson quietly repeated Bell's last words, then grew silent and reflective. "I have always been committed to peace," he said after a few moments. "Germany's unrestricted submarine warfare has placed our ships in harm's way. The news of this letter from Zimmerman to Mexico, seeking their aid to Germany in exchange for our southwestern states, is a further offense. Yet I still had hopes of a peaceful resolution." He gave a deep resigned sigh. "I can see from your report that we can no longer remain neutral."

"From what I saw, an Allied victory is essential for democracy and self-determination to survive. Not to mention a lasting peace. The impact, I believe, will go well beyond Europe."

"Then I suppose war it must be," Wilson replied with a heavy heart. He stood to leave.

"I have been made to understand that this attack on New York was not made by Germany, but by a group of independent anarchists."

"Yes. They wished to draw us into the war to help elevate their goal of chaos and destruction."

"A second enemy?"

Bell drew silent in thought. He recalled something Karl Rath had said just before his death that dovetailed with a comment Magdalena had made back in her father's tavern. Rath had claimed there were other men who would prevail. He'd mumbled something about fulcrum, a seemingly nonsensical comment, but now Bell was certain it meant more. He came to believe Rath was bragging about being part of a globe-spanning collective of anarchy cells that would outlast him, which he called Fulcrum.

"Yes," Bell replied to the President. "A second enemy that may very well still exist."

"If that's the case, Mr. Bell, I trust that I can rely on your help in defeating them, as well as the Germans."

Wilson turned and strode from the lounge before Bell could respond, already knowing the answer.

I T HAD BEEN A MONTH OF HEALING AND REFLECTION. THINGS were finally getting back to normal, with one notable difference. Upon hearing how her fiancé had put himself at risk following her boss on another of his harebrained adventures, Helen Mills demanded an immediate wedding. Joe Marchetti's long engagement came to an abrupt end three weeks after the incident.

The wedding had taken place at the nearby Holy Cross Church and now the wedding party was enjoying predinner drinks in the Knickerbocker Hotel's sumptuous main ballroom.

Isaac Bell's left hand was still in a cast. The Harvard doctor who'd set it had studied in Vienna under the famed surgeon Carl Nicoladoni. It had taken four excruciating hours of meticulous work to manipulate the broken bones into their proper alignment before he immobilized Bell's hand in plaster. The doctor was very optimistic, but it would be another month before the cast came off and Bell would know if he had two fully functioning hands. With one hand in a cast, the other was around a crystal flute of champagne.

With him were some of the principals from the office, Archie and James Dashwood, Grady Forrer, the head of the research department, as well as bulldog-faced Eddie Tobin. In the aftermath of the bombardment, Archie and James had needed stitches for their wounds and were prescribed a steady diet of liver and spinach to help replace lost blood, but otherwise they were fine. Hanzi Muntean had also made a full recovery and was currently awaiting trial in the city prison known as the Tombs. Hanna had come to accept her brother's fate when Bell had made her a promise that he would help get him a sentence in proportion to his crime rather than be scapegoated for the entire attack.

Joseph Van Dorn was also at the wedding reception, having come up from the Washington office. He was nursing his standard Bushmills Manhattan. This last-minute reception was his gift to the newlyweds.

The groom, looking sharp in his black dress uniform, and the bride's father, Army Brigadier General G. Tannenbaum Mills, rounded out the little group. Marion and Archie's wife, Lillian, along with James's date, Hanna Muntean, were in the ladies' room helping Helen with a dress emergency.

A band played softly in the background.

Bell had just finished telling his cohorts all about his escape from the German intelligence headquarters.

Archie added to the group, "For anyone keeping score, we can now add a tank to a locomotive and a whaling ship on the list of Isaac's stolen vehicles."

"And that's not including all the cars and trucks he's 'borrowed' over the years," James teased.

"I gave most of them back," Bell protested.

"Hard to believe it was all for nothing," Grady mused.

"What was all for nothing?" Lillian Abbott asked as she and the other ladies returned from the restroom.

"That Isaac's entire mission for President Wilson was a needless exercise," Archie replied. "The release of the telegram sent by German Foreign Secretary Zimmerman to entice Mexico into attacking us forced Wilson's hand to ask for a declaration of war."

Bell and Joseph exchanged a look. They were the only two who knew that Isaac had met secretly with President Wilson when he'd rushed to New York on the day after the attack. Only they were aware that it was Bell's report and opinion that had actually persuaded Wilson to declare war.

Bell smiled now as the newly crowned Helen Marchetti put her hands on her hips and said, "The heck you say. Issac and my Joe stopping the city from being reduced to rubble isn't what I would call a waste of time."

"Well said," Bell agreed.

"How do you feel about your mission to the front?" General Mills asked.

Bell paused, mulling his answer, before he said, "Though it may seem it, I don't have a death wish and so obviously I didn't enjoy nearly being blown up, shot down, or burned alive. On the other hand, I have a far better understanding of what our men are going to face. It will be far different than how the jingoistic press presents it as all glory and honor, as if those things actually have meaning on a modern battlefield.

"To show my esteem to them, and the sacrifices they are about to make, the answer is yes, it was worth it for no other reason than my personal solidarity with the men. It allows me to salute Helen, Lillian, Marion, and Hanna, and the other women who will all be making their own sacrifices in the months ahead."

"And our prospects for winning the war, Mr. Bell?"

"I firmly believe the twentieth century is going to be our century,

General, and the next thing we're going to do is crush the Kaiser's Second Reich so badly there will never be a Third."

"Here, here," Eddie Toban said. He raised a glass. "A toast—"

Bell cut him off, "No more talk of war or politics. A toast to the groom, the luckiest man to ever walk down the aisle, and the bride for being the most beautiful I've ever seen, Marion and myself excluded, of course. To the very best thing that resulted from this debacle, ladies and gentlemen, Mr. and Mrs. Joseph Marchetti."

As the champagne flutes tinkled, the band took up a dance tune. Bell hooked Marion around the waist with his clubbed hand and escorted her onto the dance floor.

"A swell wedding," she said. "Helen and Joe look very happy."

Bell gazed into his wife's eyes, instantly forgetting the fatigue of the last few weeks and the uneasy prospect of war on the horizon. "I'm happy, too," he said, giving her a desirous look and pulling her close.

"Isaac Bell, you are the most dangerous man in the world with two hands," she said, melting into his arms. "What on earth are you going to do with one?"

He whispered into her ear. "Try me."

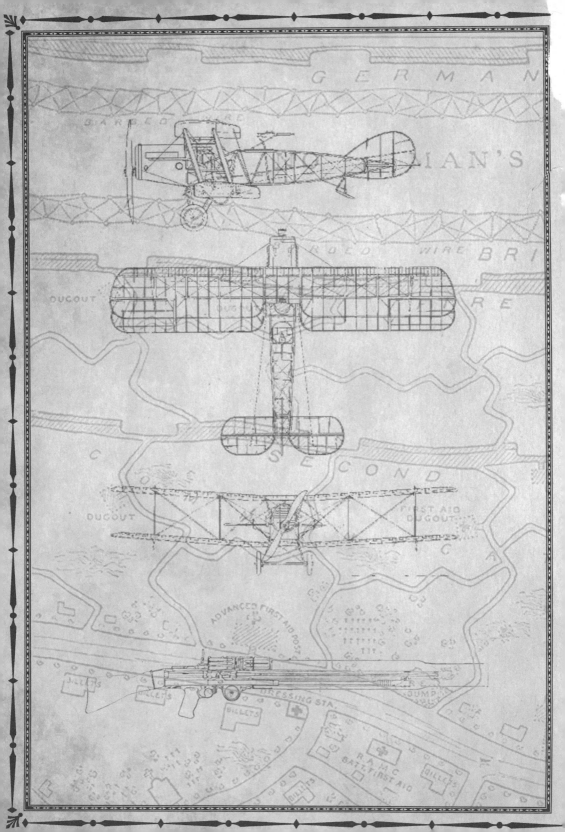